THE FIRST DEADLY SIN

"BREATHTAKINGLY EXCITING!"
—NEWSDAY

THE SECOND DEADLY SIN

"EASILY THE BEST OF THE YEAR!"
—BARKHAM REVIEWS

THE SIXTH COMMANDMENT

"THE WORK OF A MASTER!"
—NEW YORKER

THE TENTH COMMANDMENT

"OUTSTANDING!"
—NEW YORK TIMES

"HAD ME READING LATE INTO THE NIGHT!"
—WASHINGTON POST

W9-BZF-016

Jim Dingman

Lawrence Sanders

The Tenth Commandment

BERKLEY BOOKS, NEW YORK

This Berkley book contains the complete
text of the original hardcover edition.
It has been completely reset in a typeface
designed for easy reading and was printed
from new film.

THE TENTH COMMANDMENT

A Berkley Book / published by arrangement with
G. P. Putnam's Sons

PRINTING HISTORY
G. P. Putnam's Sons edition published 1980
Berkley edition / August 1981

All rights reserved.
Copyright © 1980 by Lawrence Sanders.
This book may not be reproduced in whole or in part,
by mimeograph or any other means, without permission.
For information address: G. P. Putnam's Sons,
200 Madison Avenue, New York, N.Y. 10016.

ISBN: 0-425-10431-1

A BERKLEY BOOK ® TM 757,375
Berkley Books are published by The Berkley Publishing Group,
200 Madison Avenue, New York, NY 10016.
The name "BERKLEY" and the "B" logo
are trademarks belonging to Berkley Publishing Corporation.

PRINTED IN THE UNITED STATES OF AMERICA

29   28   27   26   25   24   23   22   21

VIETNAM
PS
3569
.A 5125
T4
1981

"Blessed is he that readeth."
Rev. 1:3

Part I

1

I WAS AN only child—and so I became an only man.

My name is Joshua Bigg: a joke life played on me, as I am quite small. Five feet, three and three-eighths inches, to be precise. In a world of giants, those eighths are precious to the midget.

That was the first of fortune's tricks. There were others. For instance, I was orphaned at the age of three months when my parents were killed in the sudden collapse of a bridge over the Skunk River near Oskaloosa, Iowa. As their pickup truck toppled, I was thrown clear and was found later lying in a clump of laurel, gurgling happily and sucking my toe.

People said it was a miracle. But of course they weren't the orphan. Years later, when Roscoe Dollworth was teaching me to be an investigator, he had something to say on the subject. He had just learned that he had a small gastric ulcer, after months of worrying about stomach cancer. Just an ulcer. Everyone told him how lucky he was.

"Luck," Roscoe said, "is something that happens to other people."

I was raised by my mother's brother and his wife: Philo and

Velma Washabaugh. He had an Adam's apple and she smelled of muffins. But they were dear, sweet people and gave me compassion and love. I wish I could say the same for their three sons and two daughters, all older (and taller) than I. I suppose it was natural that I should be treated as an interloper; I was never allowed to forget my diminutive size and parentless status.

My uncle owned a hardware store in Ottuma, Iowa. Not a prosperous store, but there was always sufficient food, and if I was required to wear the outgrown clothing of my older and larger cousins, it seemed ungrateful to complain.

On the basis of my high school grades and financial need, I was able to obtain a scholarship to Grenfall. It was a very small scholarship to a very small liberal arts college. During term I held a variety of jobs: waiter, movie usher, gas station attendant, tutor of football players, etc. In the summers I worked in the hardware store.

It was my ambition to become a lawyer but by the time I was graduated, Bachelor of Arts, with honors, I had realized that a law degree was beyond my means.

A short man in tall America has a choice: he may become dark, embittered, malevolent, or clever, sunny, and manic. I chose the latter, determined that neither lack of bulk nor lack of funds would prevent me from making my way in a world in which I was forced to buy my clothes in Boys' Departments.

So, packing my one good blue suit, I stood on tiptoe to kiss uncle, aunt, and cousins farewell, and took the bus to New York City to seek my fortune. I was resolutely cheerful.

My first few years in the metropolis I lived in the YMCA on 23rd Street and worked at a succession of depressing jobs: dishwasher, drugstore clerk, demonstrator of potato peelers, etc. I lived a solitary, almost desolate life. I had no friends. I spent my free hours at museums (they didn't charge admittance then) or in the public library. I have always been an omnivorous reader. Balzac, Hugo, Dumas, and Theodore Dreiser are my favorite authors. I also enjoy reading history, biography, and novels in which the law plays an important part, as in Dickens.

Now I must tell you about my sex life. It won't take long.

It is true that in our society small men are at a decided disadvantage in wooing and winning desirable women. I have read the results of research studies proving that, in America, success is equated with physical size. Most corporation executives are large, imposing men. Most successful politicians are six-footers. Even the best-known attorneys and jurists, doctors and surgeons, seem to be men of heft. And then, of course, there are salesmen, policemen, professional football players, and bartenders. Size and poundage do count.

So I think it only natural that most women should link a man of impressive height and weight with determination, aggressiveness, energy, and eventual success. A small man, particularly a small, *penniless* man, is too frequently an object of amusement, pity, scorn, and automatic rejection.

However, during my four years at Grenfall College (co-educational), I had learned a valuable truth. And this was that if I wished to make myself attractive to women, I could not attempt to imitate the speech, manner, or forceful behavior of large or even normal-sized men. Rather, I could only succeed by exaggerating my minuteness, physical weakness, and meekness.

Despite what some advocates of the women's liberation movement may claim, I say there is a very strong "mother instinct" in most women, and they respond viscerally and warmly to helplessness, particularly in the male. So, during my college days, this was the string I plucked. And when they took me onto their laps, murmuring comforting words, I knew I was home free and might expect to see my fondest fantasy come true.

Six years before the story I am about to tell commences, I had been working as a temporary clerk in Macy's during the holiday season. After Christmas I was again unemployed, but I had money in my pocket and was able to take a week off without worries. I had a few good meals, wandered Manhattan, went to museums, read in libraries, saw the ballet, and called a young lady I had met while serving at the men's underwear counter. We went to a Chinese restaurant, saw a movie, and later I climbed onto her lap.

But then, since my funds were rapidly approaching the panic level once again, I bought the Sunday *Times* and spent the afternoon circling Help Wanted ads with a red crayon. I started out Monday morning, working my way up the eastern half of Manhattan. The fourth Help Wanted ad on my list was for a mailroom boy at a law firm. I was 26 and wasn't certain I qualified as a "boy." If necessary, I thought, I could lie about my age. But I didn't think it would be necessary. In addition to my shortness, I am small-boned and slender. My hair is almost flaxen, my eyes are softly brown, my features are regular. I shave only every other day. I felt my appearance was sufficiently juvenile to pass the initial inspection, and I headed right over.

TORT—the law firm of Tabatchnick, Orsini, Reilly, and Teitelbaum—was located on East 38th Street, in the Murray Hill section of Manhattan. It occupied a five-story converted townhouse, and when I arrived late in the morning, there was already a long line of men leading from the doorway, down the steps, along the sidewalk, halfway down the block. All ages, wearing overcoats, pea jackets, windbreakers, sweaters, whatever. Thin men, fat men, tall men, heavy men. I was, of course, the smallest.

"The mailroom job?" I asked the last man on line.

He nodded dolefully, and I took my place behind him. In a few moments, there were a half-dozen applicants behind *me*.

Then I noted a puzzling phenomenon: the line was moving forward swiftly, and men were exiting the building as fast as they entered. The flow was constant: the hopefuls in, the rejected out.

The man ahead of me grabbed the arm of one of the rejects. "What's going on in there?" he asked.

The rebuffed one shook his head bewilderedly.

"Beats me," he said. "No interviews. No applications. No questions even. This high-muck-a-muck takes a look at me and says, 'Sorry. You won't do.' Just like that. A nut!"

I was moving with the line up the block, along the sidewalk, up the stairs, through the door and finally into a large, imposing entrance hall with vaulted ceiling and walnut-paneled walls. The line stumbled up a wide carpeted staircase, so quickly that I scarcely had time to inspect the framed Currier and Ives lithographs on the walls.

I made it rapidly to the second-floor landing. The line now wavered down a long hallway and ended at a heavy closed door of carved oak. Placed alongside the door was a small desk, and seated behind the desk was a young woman, poised, expressionless. As each rejected applicant exited from the oak door, she called "Next!"

As the line moved forward, and I heard "Next! Next! Next!", I could not take my eyes from that comely guardian of the sacred portal. My initial reaction on seeing beautiful women is usually despair. They seem so unattainable to me, so distant, almost so *foreign*.

The line was moving forward quickly and I soon found myself the next specimen to be exhibited on the other side of that forbidding oak door.

It opened. The doleful one who'd been in front of me exited, head hanging. I heard "Next!" and I stepped into the chamber and closed the door softly behind me. I had a confused impression of an enormous, shadowed room, lined with law books in glass-enclosed cases. There were club chairs, a globe, a heavy dictionary on a pedestal.

But dominating the room was a gigantic mahogany desk, all carved flourishes and curlicues. The top was bare of papers, but set precisely with a student's lamp, blotter, pen-holder, letter opener, scissors—all leather-bound or leather-trimmed. There was a telephone-intercom with rows and rows of buttons and lights. Even the telephone handset had a leather-covered grip.

The man seated behind the desk appeared to have been bound in the same material: dark calfskin perhaps. He seemed ancient; the hands resting motionless on the desktop were empty gloves, and the face had the withered look of a deflated balloon.

But the blue eyes were bright enough, and when he said, "Come forward, please," his voice had vigor and resonance.

I moved to the desk. He was seated in a high-backed swivel chair. It was difficult to estimate his height, but I could see the narrow shoulders, a thin neck, slender arms.

"How tall are you?" he asked abruptly.

I lost all hope.

"Five feet, three and three-eighths inches, sir," I said.

He nodded. "How soon can you start?" he said.

I don't believe my jaw dropped. I don't believe I staggered, blinked, and swallowed. But I can't be sure.

"Immediately, sir," I said.

He nodded again. He leaned forward, lifted one of those dead hands, and with a forefinger that looked like it had been pickled in brine, depressed one of the buttons on the telephone intercom.

"Miss Apatoff," he said loudly, "the position has been filled. Thank the others and dismiss them."

Then he sat back in his swivel chair again and regarded me gravely.

"Name?" he said.

"Joshua Bigg, sir."

He didn't laugh, or even smile.

"From where?" he asked.

"Iowa, sir."

"Education?"

"BA degree, sir. With honors."

"Miss Apatoff, the lady in the hallway, will take you to our office manager, Hamish Hooter. He will complete the necessary paperwork and instruct you in your duties."

"Thank you, sir."

"Salary?" he said.

"Oh, well, yes, sir," I said confusedly. "What *is* the salary?"

"A hundred a week," he said, still staring at me. "Satisfactory?"

"Oh yes, sir."

He raised one finger from the desk blotter. I took this as a gesture of dismissal, and turned to go. I was at the door when he called...

"Mr. Bigg."

I turned.

He had risen. Now I could see his size.

"I," he said proudly, "am five feet, three and *seven*-eighths inches tall."

Only after I had left the office did it occur to me to ask the pulchritudinous receptionist to whom I had just been speaking. "Oh, that's Mr. Teitelbaum, senior partner, and I'm Yetta Apatoff," she added, bending forward enough so that I got a glimpse of cleavage I would never forget. "Welcome to TORT."

And that's how I came to work for Tabatchnick, Orsini, Reilly, and Teitelbaum.

I stayed in the mailroom about two years, during which my

salary was increased four times to a gratifying $150 a week, and my hopeless passion for Miss Yetta Apatoff, our nubile receptionist, grew in even larger increments.

And, finally, my opportunity for advancement came, as I knew it would.

One of the more than 50 employees of TORT was Mr. Roscoe Dollworth, who bore the title of Chief Investigator. This was a kindness since he was our *only* investigator. Dollworth was an ex-New York City policeman who had resigned from the Department for "medical reasons." He was an enormously fat drunk, but neither his girth nor his awesome intake of vodka (from a thermos kept in plain view on his desk) interfered with the efficient performance of his duties.

A salaried investigator for a large firm of attorneys is assigned the same tasks smaller legal associations might delegate to private investigators, as needed. Tracking down witnesses, verifying clients' alibis and those of the opposition, escorting recalcitrant witnesses to the courtroom, locating technical experts whose testimony might be advantageous, and so forth.

In addition, there had been several instances in which Roscoe Dollworth had conducted original investigations into the culpability of clients accused of crimes, although criminal defense was only a small part of TORT's activities. In all such cases, Dollworth's past association with the New York Police Department proved of great value. This was probably why his employment was continued despite that desktop jug of vodka. Also, the Chief Investigator was 61 years old at the time I joined Tabatchnick, Orsini, Reilly, and Teitelbaum, and he had made it clear that he intended to retire to Florida at the age of 65, to play shuffleboard and watch the pelicans.

I believe Roscoe Dollworth liked me. I know I liked him. He never made any slurring references to my size, and treated me more as a friend than as the lowest man on the TORT totem pole. So I was happy to run his errands: dash out to buy him a fresh quart of vodka or hurry back from my own lunch to bring him the hot pepperoni pizza he ate at his desk each day (the *whole* pizza, plus pickles, peppers, and a frightening wedge of pineapple cheesecake).

In return, he told me stories of cases in which he had been involved while he was a uniformed patrolman and later as a detective, third-grade. He also taught me the techniques and tricks of a professional investigator, all of which I found fascinating. I hadn't realized police methods were that complex, or how few of them could be found in books. They could only be learned through personal experience, or the experience of other cops.

Occasionally, when I had time, and always with the permission of one of the three senior partners of TORT (Sean Reilly had died seven years previously; he had choked to death on a piece of rare London broil), Roscoe Dollworth would send me out on an investigative task. These began as simple assignments: find the apartment number of so-and-so, check where this man parks his car, see if you can discover when this woman divorced her first husband.

Gradually, over a period of months, Dollworth's requests became more involved and more intriguing.

"Doing anything tonight, Josh? No? Good. Follow this guy. He says he goes to a chess club every Wednesday night. I ain't so sure. Don't let him spot you. This is a divorce action."

Or . . . "Find out who really owns this nightclub, will you? You'll have to start out down at the Hall, checking records. You'll learn how it's done."

Or . . . "See if this dame has any regular visitors. She lives alone—but who knows? You may have to slip the doorman a fin. But no more than that, or he won't respect you. This involves the probate of a will."

And so on . . .

I completed all my assignments successfully, and began to wonder if I didn't have a natural talent for investigation. Part of my success, I thought, might be due to my physical appearance. It was impossible for me to come on strong, and my shy, hesitant, almost helpless manner seemed to arouse the kind of sympathy which urged, "Let's help the boy out." And so I succeeded with the same methods that had aided me in my conquests of women: the whole world wanted to take me onto its lap.

I had been with TORT for almost two years when Roscoe Dollworth called me into his office, commanded me to shut the door and sit down.

This time, it wasn't about an assignment, exactly. It was about much more than that.

I said nothing, just watched Mr. Dollworth pour himself

a paper cup of vodka from his thermos. He sipped it slowly, staring at me thoughtfully across his desk.

He was a blobby man, with a belly that kept his swivel chair two feet from his desk. His scraggly, straw-colored hair was thinning; patches of freckled scalp showed through. Darkish eyebrows were so snarled that I had seen him comb them. His nose had evidently been broken several times; it just didn't know which way to turn. His lips were glutinous, teeth tobaccostained. But the eyes were hard and squinchy. Looking at those eyes made me happy I was his friend and not an enemy.

"Look, kid," he said finally in a deep, burpy voice, "let me tell you what's been happening. You know, I figure to retire in a couple of years, if this miserable ulcer don't kill me first. That means they got to replace me—right? So I went to old man Teitelbaum. He likes you—you know? He hired you because you're the only guy in the joint smaller than he is. You knew that, didn't you?"

"Yes," I said, "I knew."

"Well..." he said, sipping vodka, "you turned out real good. I mean, you work hard, don't steal stamps, and you're polite. Always ready with a smile. Everyone here likes you. Except maybe Hamish Hooter, that prick. But he don't like *anyone*. Except maybe Yetta Apatoff. Hooter would *like* to like her—about six inches' worth."

I nodded dumbly.

"So I says to Teitelbaum, how about promoting Josh Bigg to investigator? Let him work with me my last two years, I says, and I guarantee to teach him the ropes. By the time I step down, you'll have a spry young man ready to fill my shoes, a guy who knows his way around. I told Teitelbaum how good you done on those little jobs I gave you. This kid, I says, has got a good nut on his shoulders. Give him a chance, and you'll have an A-Number One Investigator in your organization."

I was excited. I slid forward to the edge of my chair. I leaned eagerly toward Dollworth.

"And what did he say?"

"He said no," the Chief Investigator said regretfully. "He said you were too young. He said you didn't have the experience. He said he wanted another ex-cop to take my place."

I collapsed.

"Wait a minute," Dollworth said, holding up a hand like a smoked ham. "I never take a turndown without I put up a fight. I said you might *look* young, but by the time I retire, you'll be thirty—right?—and your brain is older than that. Also, I says, as far as experience goes, I can teach you most of what you'll have to know, and the rest you'll pick up as you go along. And as for hiring an ex-cop, I says, if he wants another rumdum like me, that's his business. But an investigator gets out a lot, meets the public, and he should make a good impression as a representative of the firm. And you dress neat, wear a jacket and pants that match, and a tie and all. Then I throw in the clincher. Also, I tell Teitelbaum, you hire an ex-cop to take my place, you'll be lucky to get away paying him twenty G's a year. You could get Bigg to do the same work for half of that."

"What did he say to that?" I asked breathlessly.

"They're having a meeting this afternoon," Roscoe Dollworth said. "The three senior partners. I'll let you know how it comes out. Meanwhile, my jug is getting low. How's about you rushing the growler for me?"

Late that afternoon I was informed that the senior partners of Tabatchnick, Orsini, Reilly, and Teitelbaum, in solemn conclave assembled, had decreed that I was to be replaced in the mailroom and, for a period of two years, be apprenticed to Chief Investigator Dollworth. At the end of that period, the senior partners would accept Dollworth's judgment on whether I was or was not qualified to assume his office upon his retirement. During my apprenticeship, I would continue to earn $150 a week.

"Don't worry about a thing," Roscoe Dollworth assured me, winking. "It's in the bag. I'm going to run your ass ragged. You'll learn."

He did, and I did. For the next two years I worked harder than I thought possible, sometimes putting in an eighteen-hour day in my determination to master my new craft.

There were so many things Dollworth taught me that it would be impossible to list them all. They included a basic education in such matters as criminal and civil law, the right of privacy, and the rules of evidence, and instruction on such practical matters as how to pick a lock, the best methods of shadowing on a crowded street, and what equipment to take along on an extended stakeout. (The first item was an empty milk carton in which one might relieve oneself.)

In addition to Dollworth's lectures and the actual investigations assigned to me with increasing frequency, I also did a great deal of studying at home. My books were manuals of the New York Police Academy, which Dollworth obtained for me, plus heavy volumes on the law, legal procedures, and criminology which I purchased or borrowed from the public library.

At the end of my two-year apprenticeship, I felt, with my indefatigable optimism, that I had mastered the arcane mysteries of my new profession, and was well qualified to become Chief Investigator of TORT. I must have conveyed some of this conceit to my mentor, for a few days prior to his retirement, he called me into his office, slammed the door, and delivered himself of the following:

"You think you know it all, do you? You make me sick, you do! You know nothing. *Nothing!* A wise wrongo could have you running around in circles, chasing your tail. Wait'll you come up against a liar, a *good* liar. You won't know if you're coming or going. You're just on the ground floor, kiddo. You got a helluva lot to learn. I seen the way you look at that Yetta Apatoff. If she said jump out the window, out you'd go. But what if a twist exactly like her was a suspect, and you had to get the goods on her? Shit, all you'd see would be B&B, boobs and behind, and she'd take a walk. Bye-bye, birdie. Josh, you've got to learn to doubt *everyone*. Suspect *everyone*. It's a hard, cruel world out there, filled with bad guys and millions of others who would be bad if they weren't scared of being caught. Never, *never* believe what people tell you until you check it out. Never, *never* let your personal feelings interfere with your job. And most of all, never believe that because a woman is beautiful or a man is handsome, successful, and contributes to his church, that they can't be the slimiest crooks in the world. Most of the people you meet will be out to con you. So you just smile and say, 'Uh-huh,' and start checking them out. Josh, you've got a lot going for you. You got a brain on you, you can get people to open up, and you got a good imagination. Maybe too good. But what worries me most about you is that you're so innocent, so fucking *innocent!*"

But my shortcomings had not deterred Roscoe Dollworth from recommending me as his successor. A week later he was off to Florida with a set of matching luggage from the employees of TORT, a $5,000 retirement bonus, and a pair of fine German binoculars I gave him.

"To watch the pelicans," I told him.

"Sure, kid," he said, hitting my arm. "Very nice. I'll send you my address. Keep in touch. If I can ever help you out with the Department, let me know."

"Thank you, Mr. Dollworth," I said. "For everything."

During the next twenty-six months I was made mournfully aware of the difference between on-the-job training under the tutelage of an experienced investigator and having full responsibility, without supervision, for all investigative activities of Tabatchnick, Orsini, Reilly, and Teitelbaum.

First of all, requests for investigations flowed into my office from the three senior partners, seven junior partners (including Tabatchnick II and Orsini II and III), twelve associates, law clerks, paralegal assistants, and the despicable office manager, Hamish Hooter. It took me awhile to get a system of priorities organized and to learn to deal with all these strong-willed and redoubtable individuals. (The legal profession seems to have the effect of first enlarging egos and then setting them permanently in concrete.)

Everyone wanted his request for information dealt with *instanter*, and initially I was overwhelmed; but, after observing the snail's speed unraveling of most of the litigation handled by TORT, I came to realize that there are two kinds of time. One has sixty minutes to an hour, twenty-four hours to a day, moving along at a brisk clip. And then there is legal time, oozing so sluggishly that movement can scarcely be noted.

When a business executive says, "I'll get that letter off to you tomorrow," he usually means tomorrow, or in a few days, or a week at the most. When a lawyer says, "I'll get that letter off to you tomorrow," he usually means in six weeks, next November, or never. Always, in the practice of law, is the unspoken admonition: "What's the rush?" Shakespeare wrote of "the law's delay," everyone is aware of the lethargy of the courts, and even the youngest, brightest, most vigorous attorney, fresh from law school, soon adjusts to tardiness as a way of life. The law, sir, is a glacier. Attempting to hurry it usually proves counterproductive.

Once I had recognized that central truth, I was able to relax, realize that very few requests involved a crisis, and devote all my energy and wit to mastering the techniques of my new profession. In all modesty, I do not believe I functioned too badly. At least, my salary rose to $12,500 at the end of my first year as Chief Investigator, and to $15,000 at the completion of my second. Surely this was proof that TORT was well satisfied with my performance. The increase enabled me to move from the YMCA into my own apartment, replenish my wardrobe, and invite Miss Yetta Apatoff to a dinner that included a small bottle of French wine. She did not, however, invite me onto her lap in return.

Not everything was cotton candy. I made mistakes, of course. Not mistakes, perhaps, so much as failures to foresee a possible course of events. For instance, I was assigned to pick up a supposedly friendly witness in a personal liability case and insure his presence in the courtroom at the required time. When I showed up at his Bronx apartment, he simply refused to accompany me.

He was a loutish, overbearing individual, wearing a stained undershirt and chomping a soggy cigar.

"But you've got to come," I said.

"*Got* to?" he said, snorting. "I got to do nuttin."

"But you promised," I pleaded desperately.

"I changed my mind," he said casually.

"I insist you come with me," I said. I'm afraid my voice became slightly shrill.

"You *insist?*" he said. He laughed heartily. "What are you going to do—drag me down there, you little shit?"

I had to report my failure to the TORT attorney handling the case. Fortunately, he accepted my inefficiency philosophically, the witness's testimony was not crucial, a subpoena was not warranted, and he soon forgot the incident. But I did not; it rankled.

The next time I did my homework and learned all I could about the potential witness, even to the extent of following him for a few days and making notes of his activities.

As I anticipated, he also said he had changed his mind and refused to testify.

"Please change it back," I said. "I don't wish to inform your wife where you spent three hours yesterday afternoon."

He put on his coat.

He, too, said, "You little shit!"

So I learned to cope with those rare instances in which lack of physical bulk made my job more difficult. I was not a licensed private investigator, of course, and I had no desire to attempt to obtain a permit to carry a firearm. I felt I could handle all the demands of my job without resorting to violence.

But generally, those first two years as Chief Investigator of Tabatchnick, Orsini, Reilly, and Teitelbaum went swimmingly. I learned the truth of many of those things Roscoe Dollworth had shouted at me just before his retirement. People *did* lie, frequently for no reason other than they felt the truth was valuable and should not be revealed to a stranger without recompense. People *did* try to con me, and I soon learned to recognize the signs: a frank, open, unblinking stare and a glib, too-rapid way of speaking.

I also learned not to get personally involved with the people with whom I dealt, while maintaining a polite, sympathetic, low-key manner. I also learned an investigator's job requires infinite patience, an almost finicky attention to detail, tenacity, and the ability to endure long periods of boredom.

If I had one regret it was that circumstances never arose requiring an original investigation to uncover the truth in a case of some importance. I felt I had proved my ability to handle routine assignments that were, for the most part, matters requiring only a few phone calls, correspondence, or simple inquiries that needed no particular deductive talent. Now I craved more daring challenges.

My chance to prove my mettle came in February of my seventh year at TORT.

2

EACH MORNING I arrived at my office at about 8:30 A.M., carrying a container of black coffee and a buttered, toasted bagel. I liked to arrive early to organize my work for the day before my phone started ringing. On Tuesday morning, February 6th, I found on my desk blotter a memo from Leopold Tabatchnick: "I will see you in my office at 10:00 A.M. this morning, Feb. 6. L.T."

I postponed an outside inquiry I had planned to make that morning, and at 9:50 went into the men's room to make certain my hair was properly combed, the knot in my tie centered, and my fingernails clean. I also buffed my shoes with a paper towel.

The private offices of the senior partners occupied the largest (rear) suites on the second, third, and fourth floors, one over the other. Teitelbaum was on two, Orsini on three, Tabatchnick on four. Mr. Tabatchnick's secretary was seated at her desk in the hallway. She was Thelma Potts, a spinster of about sixty years, with a young face and whipped-cream hair. She wore high-necked blouses with a cameo brooch at the collar. She dispensed advice, made small loans, and never forgot birthdays

or anniversaries. The bottom drawer of her desk was full of
headache remedies, stomach powders, tranquilizers, Band-
Aids, cough syrups, cold capsules, etc., available to anyone
when needed. She kept a small paper cup among the drugs,
and you were supposed to drop in a few coins now and then
to help keep the pharmacy going.

"Good morning, Miss Potts," I said.

"Good morning, Mr. Bigg," she said. She glanced at the
watch pinned to her bodice. "You're three minutes early."

"I know," I said. "I wanted to spend them with you."

"Oh, *you!*" she said.

"I thought you were going to find me a wife, Miss Potts,"
I said sorrowfully.

"When did I ever say that?" she demanded, blushing. "I am
sure you are quite capable of finding a nice girl yourself."

"No luck so far," I said. "May I go in now?"

She consulted her watch again.

"Thirty seconds," she said firmly.

I sighed. We waited in silence, Miss Potts staring at her
watch.

"Now!" she said, like a track official starting a runner.

I knocked once on the heavy door, opened it, stepped inside,
closed it behind me.

Instead of law books here, the room was lined with aquaria
of tropical fish. There were tanks of all sizes and shapes,
lighted from behind. Bubbles rose constantly from aerators.
The atmosphere of the room was oppressively warm and humid.
There were guppies, sea horses, angels, zebras, pink damsels,
clowns, ghost eels, fire fish, purple queens, swordtails and a
piranha.

They all made a glittering display in the clear, back-lighted
tanks, darting about, blowing bubbles, kissing the glass, coming to the surface to spit.

The first time I'd met Mr. Tabatchnick, he'd asked me if
I was interested in tropical fish. I'd confessed I was not.

"Hmph," he'd said. "Then you have no conception of the
comfort to be derived from the silent companionship of our
finny friends."

This was followed by a half-hour, tank-by-tank tour of the
room, with Mr. Tabatchnick expounding on the Latin names,
lifestyles, dispositions, feeding habits, sexual tendencies, and

depravities of his finny friends. Most, apparently, ate their young. The lecture, I discovered later, had to be tolerated by every new employee. Thankfully, it was a one-shot, never repeated.

The man seated in the leather swivel chair behind the trestle table appeared to be in his middle seventies. He had a ponderous head set on a large, square, neckless frame, held so rigidly that you wondered if he had left a wooden coathanger in the shoulders of his jacket.

His hands were wide, with spatulate fingers, the skin discolored with keratosis. His arms seemed disproportionately long, and since he tended to lumber as he walked, with hunched shoulders, heavy head thrust forward, and a fierce scowl on his fleshy features, he was referred to by the law clerks and paralegal assistants as "King Kong." In very small voices, of course.

But there was nothing simian about his face. If anything, his were the features of a weary bloodhound, all folds and wrinkles, wattles and jowls, with protruding, rubbery lips (always moist), and eyes so lachrymose that he always seemed on the point of sobbing. His normal expression was one of mournful distress, and it was said that he used it with great effect during his days as a trial lawyer to elicit the sympathy of the jury.

"Good morning, Mr. Tabatchnick," I said brightly.

He bestowed upon me the nod of sovereign to serf, and gestured to a club chair at the side of the table.

"Sol Kipper," he said. His voice was stentorian, rumbling. An organ of a voice. I wished I had been in the courtroom to hear his summations.

"I beg your pardon, sir?" I said.

"Sol Kipper," he repeated. "Solomon Kipper, to be precise. The name means nothing to you?"

I thought desperately. It was not a name you would easily forget. Then it came to me...

"I remember," I said. "Solomon Kipper. A suicide about two weeks ago. From the top floor of his East Side townhouse. A small story in the *Times*."

"Yes," he said, the folds of skin wagging sadly, "a small story in the *Times*. I wish you to know, young man, that Sol Kipper was a personal friend of mine for fifty-five years and an esteemed client of this law firm for forty."

There didn't seem any fitting reply to that.

"We shall be handling the probate," Mr. Tabatchnick continued. "Sol Kipper was a wealthy man. Not *very* wealthy, but wealthy. Cut and dried. I anticipated no problems."

He paused, leaned forward, punched a button on the intercom on the table.

"Miss Potts," he said, "will you come in, please? Bring your notes on the conversation I had late yesterday afternoon with that stranger."

He settled back. We waited. Thelma Potts entered softly, carrying a spiral-bound steno pad. Mr. Tabatchnick did not ask her to sit down.

"Occasionally," he said in a magisterial tone, "I deem it appropriate, during certain telephone communications, to ask Miss Potts to listen in on her extension and make notes. Very well, Miss Potts, you may begin . . ."

Thelma flipped over a few pages and began to translate her shorthand, peering through rimless spectacles and speaking rapidly in a flat, precisely enunciated voice:

"At 4:46 P.M., on the afternoon of Monday, February 5th, this year, a call was received at the main switchboard downstairs. A male voice asked to speak to the lawyer handling the Kipper estate. The call was switched to me. The man repeated his request. I asked him exactly what it was he wanted, but he said he would reveal that only to the attorney of record. As is usual in such cases, I suggested he write a letter requesting an interview and detailing his interest in the matter. This he said he would not do, and he stated that if the lawyer refused to talk to him, he would be sorry for it later. Those were his exact words: 'He will be sorry for it later.' I then asked if he would hold. He agreed. I put him on hold, and called Mr. Tabatchnick on the intercom, explaining what was happening. He agreed to speak to the caller, but requested that I stay on the extension and take notes."

I interrupted.

"The male voice on the phone, Miss Potts," I said. "Young? Old?"

She stared at me for a few seconds.

"Middle," she said, then continued reading her notes.

"Mr. Tabatchnick asked the purpose of the call. The man

asked if he was handling the Kipper estate. Mr. Tabatchnick said he was. The man asked his name. Mr. Tabatchnick stated it. The man then said he had valuable information in his possession that would affect the Kipper estate. Mr. Tabatchnick asked the nature of the information. The caller refused to reveal it. Mr. Tabatchnick said he assumed then that the information would be available at a price. The caller said that was correct. His exact words were: 'Right on the button, baby!' Mr. Tabatchnick then suggested the caller come to his office for a private discussion. This the man refused to do, indicating he had no desire to have his conversation secretly recorded. But he said he would meet with Mr. Tabatchnick or his representative in a place of his, the caller's, choosing. Mr. Tabatchnick asked his name. The caller said 'Marty' would be sufficient. Mr. Tabatchnick asked his address, which Marty would not reveal. Mr. Tabatchnick then said he would have to give the matter some thought but would contact Marty if he or his representative wished to meet with him. Marty gave a number but the call had to be made within twenty-four hours. If Marty did not hear from Mr. Tabatchnick by five o'clock, Tuesday afternoon, February 6th, he would assume Mr. Tabatchnick was not interested in his, quote, valuable information regarding the Kipper estate, unquote, and he would feel free to contact other potential buyers. The conversation was then terminated."

Miss Potts closed her steno pad with a snap, and looked up.

"Will that be all, Mr. Tabatchnick?" she asked.

He raised his heavy head. "Yes, thank you."

She drifted from the room, closing the door quietly behind her.

He stared somberly at me.

"Well?" he demanded. "What do you think?"

I shrugged. "Impossible to say, sir. Not enough to go on. Could be attempted blackmail, or attempted extortion, or just a cheap chiseler trying to make a couple of bucks on a fast con."

"You think I should communicate with this man and arrange to meet him?"

"No, sir," I said. "I think *I* should. He said you or your representative."

"I don't like it," Leopold Tabatchnick said fretfully.

"I don't like it either, sir," I said. "But I think it wise to meet with him and try to find out what this 'valuable information' is he thinks he has."

"Mmm . . . yes . . . well . . ." Tabatchnick said, drumming his thick fingers on the tabletop.

Then he was silent a long moment, and I had the oddest impression that he knew something or guessed something he hadn't told me, and was debating with himself whether or not to reveal it. He finally decided not to.

"All right," he said finally, bobbing that weighty head slowly, "you call him and arrange to meet. Try to find out exactly what it is he's selling. Refuse to buy a pig in a poke. And don't commit the firm for any amount, large or small."

"Of course not, sir."

"Inform him you will deliver his terms to me."

"Yes, sir."

"Inform him that only I can authorize payment under these circumstances."

"I understand, sir."

"And endeavor to ascertain his full name and address."

"Yes, sir," I said, suppressing a sigh. Sometimes they still treated me like a mailroom boy.

3

WHEN I CAME out of Mr. Tabatchnick's fish-lined sanctuary, I stopped at Thelma Potts' desk to get the telephone number of the mysterious Marty, then proceeded down the main staircase.

Mr. Romeo Orsini was holding court on the third-floor landing, surrounded by aides, most of them women. He was in his middle sixties, tall, erect, with thick, marvelously coiffed snow-white hair. He carried himself with the vigor and grace of a man one-third his age, and his pink complexion, dark, glittering eyes, hearty good health, meticulous grooming, and self-satisfaction produced the image of the perfect movie or TV lawyer.

Romeo Orsini specialized in divorce actions, and was enormously successful in obtaining alimony and child support payments far in excess of his clients' most exaggerated hopes. It was also said that he was frequently the first to console the new divorcée.

I was hoping to slip around his group on the landing without being noticed, but his hand shot out from the circle and clamped on my arm.

"Josh!" he cried gaily. "Just the man I wanted to see!"

He drew me close and, not for the first time, I became aware of his cologne.

"Heard a joke I think you'll appreciate," he said slyly, grinning at me.

My heart sank. All the jokes he told me involved small men.

"There was this midget," he began, looking around his circle of aides. They were preparing their faces to break into instant laughter, several of them smiling already.

"And he married the tallest woman in the circus," Orsini continued. He paused for effect. I knew what was coming.

"His friends put him up to it!" he concluded, followed by guffaws, giggles, roars, and thigh-slapping by his assistants. To my shame, I laughed as loudly as any, and finally broke free to continue my descent, cursing myself.

On the ground floor, I was confronted with the bristling presence of Hamish Hooter, the office manager.

"See here, Bigg," he said.

That's the way Hooter began all his conversations: "See here." It made me want to reach up and punch him in the snoot.

"What is it, Hooter?" I said resignedly.

"What's this business about a private secretary?" he demanded, waving a sheet of paper in my face. I recognized it as a memo I had forwarded the previous week.

"It's all spelled out in there," I said. "I've been typing all my own correspondence up to now, but the workload is getting too much. I can't ask the secretaries and typists to help me out; they all have their own jobs."

"Dollworth didn't need a secretary," he sneered.

"Dollworth was a notoriously poor record-keeper," I said. "He admitted it himself. As a result, we have incomplete histories of investigations he conducted, no copies of letters he may have written, no memos of phone calls and conversations. Such records could be vital if cases are overturned on appeal or reopened for any reason. I really have to set up a complete file and keep it current."

"I can't believe you're so busy that you can't handle it yourself," he said. Then he added nastily, "You seem to have plenty of time to gossip with Yetta Apatoff."

I stared at him. He really was a miserable character. What's more, he *looked* like a miserable character.

He was of average height, but with such poor posture (rounded shoulders, bent back, protruding potbelly) that he appeared shorter. He had an extremely pale complexion, with small, watery eyes set too far apart. His lips were prim, and his nose looked like a wedge of cheddar. He had jet-black, somewhat greasy hair, and he was, I was happy to note, going bald in back. He combed his slick locks sideways in an attempt to conceal the tonsure.

His voice was high-pitched and reedy, somewhere between a whine and a yawp. He also had the habit of sucking his teeth after every sentence, as if he had a little fiber of celery in there and couldn't get it out. Let's see, what else . . . Oh yes, he had eyes for Yetta Apatoff (hot, beady eyes), and that alone was enough to condemn him as far as I was concerned. I knew they lunched together occasionally, and I could only conclude that she accompanied him out of pure kindness, as one might toss a peanut to a particularly disgusting, purple-assed orangutan in the zoo.

"So I gather I'm not getting a secretary," I said.

"You gather correctly," he said, sucking his incisors noisily.

I looked at him with loathing. But if I couldn't outwit that beast, I'd turn in my Machiavelli badge. I spun away from him, marched down to my office, slammed the door.

The first thing I did was call Marty's number. I let it ring ten times, but there was no answer. So I gathered up my notebook, stopwatch, and coat, and started out on a routine investigation.

Yetta Apatoff was at her desk, but she was busy with an elderly couple who were trying to explain something to her in heavily German-accented English. Yetta waggled her delicious fingers at me as I went by. I waggled back.

I spent the morning establishing that a young client could not have robbed a camera store in the Port Authority Bus Terminal, on Eighth Avenue at 40th Street at 12:06 P.M. and travel nineteen blocks in time to be positively identified at an electronics trade show at the Coliseum on Columbus Circle at Eighth Avenue and 59th Street at 12:14.

Three times I traveled from the Bus Terminal to the Coliseum by taxi, three times by subway, three times by bus (making the return trips by cab in all cases). I used the stopwatch and timed each northbound run to the split second, keeping very careful notes.

I completed the time trials at about 2:30 in the afternoon. I had a hamburger and dialed Marty's number from a pay phone. Still no answer. I was getting a little antsy. Marty had said the deadline was 5:00 P.M.

Yetta Apatoff was on the phone when I entered the TORT building at approximately 3:20. She smiled up at me (a glory, that smile!) and, still speaking on the phone, handed me a small sheet of paper. Another memo. This one was from Mr. Teitelbaum's secretary. I was to call her as soon as I returned.

I went into my office, took off my coat, dialed Marty's number. Still no answer. I then called Ada Mondora, Teitelbaum's secretary. She said he wanted to see me as soon as possible, but was busy with a client at the moment; she'd buzz me as soon as he was free.

Then I took off my jacket, sat down at the typewriter, and began to bang out a report on the time trials.

My office, on the first floor, was not quite as small as a broom closet. There was room for one L-shaped desk, with the typewriter on the short wing. One steel swivel chair. One steel armchair for visitors. One steel file cabinet. A wastebasket, a coat tree, a small steel bookcase. And that was it. When Roscoe Dollworth, with his explosive girth, had occupied the premises, this cubbyhole seemed filled to overflowing. I provided a little more space, but the room was still cramped and depressing. No windows. If I succeeded in obtaining a secretary, my next project would be larger quarters to accommodate the secretary. My ambition knew no limits.

I had almost finished typing my report when Ada Mondora called and said I could come up now. I put on my jacket, went into the men's room to make myself presentable, then climbed the stairs to the second floor.

"Hi, Josh," Ada said in her bass rumble. She was pushing fifty and sounded as if she had smoked Coronas all her life. "He's been trying to reach you all day. You can go right in."

"Thank you, Ada."

I went through the approved drill: knocked once, opened the door, stepped in, closed the door gently behind me.

Ignatz Teitelbaum was six years older than the day he hired

me, but you'd never know it. Apparently he had reached a plateau, a certain number of years (seventy? seventy-five?), and then just didn't age anymore. He would go to his grave looking exactly as he did at that moment, the skin leathery, the blue eyes bright, the voice vigorous.

"Sit down, young man," he said to me.

I chose the club chair closest to the desk. The light from the student's lamp fell on me, but his face was in shadow.

"A client," he said abruptly. "Yale Stonehouse. Professor Yale Stonehouse. A very litigious man. You are familiar with the term?"

I murmured wisely.

"Well," he said. "Professor Stonehouse would sue, at any time, for any reason—or none at all. He sued plumbers and electricians who did repair work in his apartment. He sued his landlord. He sued department stores. He sued cabdrivers and the companies that employed them. He sued newspapers, magazines, manufacturers, hotels, the bus company, the telephone company, Consolidated Edison, the City of New York, the Boy Scouts of America, the makers of Tootsie Rolls, and a poor fellow who had the misfortune to jostle him accidentally on the street. On one occasion, Professor Stonehouse sued the United States of America."

"Did he ever win, sir?" I asked.

"Rarely," Mr. Teitelbaum said with a wintry smile. "And when he did, the damages granted were never sufficient to cover the cost of bringing the suit. In one case I recall, the bench awarded him one cent. But Professor Stonehouse didn't care—or said he didn't. He insisted the principle involved was all that counted." Mr. Teitelbaum paused to sigh heavily. "I am not certain Professor Stonehouse was completely sane. He was eccentric, certainly."

"*Was?*" I repeated. "Is the gentleman no longer our client? Or is he deceased?"

Mr. Teitelbaum ignored my questions and continued:

"As I said, we attempted to dissuade him from this unwarranted litigation, but he insisted. His suits, ah, provided good experience for some of the younger, newer members of the firm. In addition to the suits, we also handled the legal end of several investments Professor Stonehouse made in real estate and certain other properties. He was, I would say, well-to-do.

Exactly how prosperous he was I had no way of knowing, since this firm did not prepare his will nor play any part in his general investments and estate planning. On the one occasion when I asked him if he had executed a will, he replied in hostile tones that it had been taken care of. His reaction to my question was such that I never cared to pursue the matter further. I merely assumed he had a will prepared by another attorney, a not uncommon practice."

Then he was silent. And I was silent, wondering where all this was leading.

Ignatz Teitelbaum laced his crinkled little fingers on the desktop. He looked down at them, and wiggled one at a time. He seemed surprised that they could still move. Staring at his hands, he continued his story in a quiet, dreamy voice...

"Yesterday, Professor Stonehouse's wife came to see me. She informed me that her husband had, after dinner one evening, simply walked out of their apartment without saying where he was going and never returned. Not to this date, he hasn't."

"Did he leave a note, sir? Did he take any clothes with him? Had he withdrawn any large amounts from his bank accounts? Did he give any hint of his intention to leave?"

Mr. Teitelbaum raised his head slowly to stare at me.

"I asked Mrs. Stonehouse those same questions. Her answers to all were negative."

"Mrs. Stonehouse went to the police, I presume?"

"Of course. They checked hospitals and the morgue, accident reports, things of that nature. They spoke to the Professor's associates at New York University. Stonehouse was retired, but was sometimes invited as a guest lecturer. His specialty was British maritime history of the seventeenth century. No one at the University had seen him or heard from him for months. The New York Police Department has listed Professor Yale Stonehouse as a Missing Person. I have some, ah, contacts in the Department and was able to speak to the investigating officer. It is his opinion that the Professor disappeared of his own free will and will reappear eventually for reasons of his own."

"Does the investigating officer have any evidence for that belief, sir?"

"Not that I was able to determine. Apparently the officer

was basing his judgment on his experience and percentages in the analysis of the behavior of missing persons."

"Do you know, sir, if the investigating officer checked airport, bus terminals, and railroad stations?"

"He did, yes. No record of reservations in the Professor's name. But that is hardly conclusive. Reservations could have been made under another name, and tickets can frequently be purchased for cash without any reservations at all, as I am sure you are well aware."

"Yes, sir."

"But the investigating officer also showed a photograph of Professor Stonehouse to employees at airports, bus terminals, and railroad stations. No results."

"Did the Professor own a car, sir?"

"He did. It was still garaged the day after his disappearance."

I took a deep breath. "Well, sir, that seems to cover it. Can Mrs. Stonehouse offer any reason at all for her husband's absence?"

Mr. Teitelbaum made a vague gesture.

"She believes the Professor went for a walk and perhaps stumbled and fell or met with an accident that resulted in amnesia, and that he is now wandering the city with no knowledge of his identity."

"Ummm," I said. "Possible, sir, but not likely."

"No," he said, "not likely."

"How old was—how old *is* Professor Stonehouse?"

"Seventy-two."

"And Mrs. Stonehouse?"

"I would estimate in her late fifties. Perhaps sixty. Their children, a young daughter and young son, are thirty-one and twenty-eight respectively. The Stonehouses were married relatively late in life."

"Are the children married, sir?"

"No, they are not."

Then we sat in silence again. I mulled over what I had just heard. I had no ideas about it at all. The Professor's disappearance was simply inexplicable.

"May I ask a question, sir?" I said finally.

Ignatz Teitelbaum nodded gravely.

"What is our interest in the Professor's disappearance, sir?"

"Mrs. Ula Stonehouse wishes to retain us as legal counsel," he said tonelessly. "Her problem is threefold. First, she would like us to employ a private investigator to look further into her husband's disappearance. I believe I persuaded her that this would be a useless expenditure. I cannot imagine what a private investigator could possibly accomplish that officers of the Missing Persons Bureau have not already done. Do you agree?"

"Yes, sir. Sounds to me like the police have done a thorough job."

"Precisely. However, I was not able to convince Mrs. Stonehouse completely of that, so I assured her that the disappearance of her husband would be examined fully by our own investigation department."

Four years ago I was a mailroom boy and now I was a department. Success!

Mr. Teitelbaum continued: "Mrs. Stonehouse's second problem is financial in nature. All her husband's assets, including his checking and savings accounts, are in his name alone. So Mrs. Stonehouse, with no assets of her own, is, ah, feeling the pinch."

"I should think so, sir—if he's been gone a month."

"Yes. I am having the whole matter of the status of the assets of a missing person researched at the present moment. I believe I will be able to petition the court to grant the family an allowance for living expenses prior to the time her missing husband is declared legally dead—if indeed he is ever so declared."

"If he is, sir," I said, "I mean, declared legally dead at some future time, who gets the money? How is the estate divided?"

"The third problem," Mr. Teitelbaum said somberly. "Mrs. Stonehouse cannot find her husband's will. It seems to be missing."

4

THE MOMENT I returned to my office, I called Marty again. Still no answer. It was then 4:25 P.M. I finished my report on the time trials, read it over, put the original in my Out basket, and the carbon in my file cabinet. I then started two new folders, labeling them KIPPER and STONEHOUSE. At the moment, I had nothing to put in the latter, and only Marty's phone number to file in the former.

I relaxed for a few moments, put my feet up on the desk, and reviewed my recent interview with Teitelbaum.

All Teitelbaum wanted me to do was to meet and interview the Stonehouse family and servants, to ask them any questions I thought might be germane to the disappearance of the Professor, and generally to nose about and try to make some educated guesses as to what had actually happened.

"You are a clever young man," Mr. Teitelbaum had said. "Perhaps you will think of an approach or an angle that the police have neglected."

When he or the assigned TORT attorney went into court to beg that an allowance be granted to the Stonehouse family from the missing man's assets, Teitelbaum wanted to be able to assure the bench that every possible effort had been made to locate the Professor.

"We can already present the unsuccessful efforts of the New York Police Department," he'd suggested. "In addition, I want to show that Mrs. Stonehouse made a personal effort, working through us, her legal representative, to find her husband. I want you to keep a careful record of the number of hours you spend on this inquiry. The more, the better—without neglecting your other responsibilities, of course. In addition to that, I plan to place advertisements in the local papers offering a reward for information on the fate and present whereabouts of Professor Stonehouse. We may even have fliers printed up and distributed in their neighborhood, making the same offer of reward. Personally, I do not feel anything will come of these efforts, but the purpose is to prove to the court that we have made a bona fide effort to locate the missing man prior to petitioning for the right to draw on his assets without his permission."

That made sense to me. It was no great blow to my self-esteem to know that my investigation was to be merely part of a legal ploy and that no great results were expected.

Back in my office at four minutes to five, I dialed Marty's number once again. This time it was picked up after the third ring. A man's voice answered:

"Yeah?"

"Marty?"

"Yeah. Who's this?"

"I'm calling for Mr. Leopold Tabatchnick."

"About time. You got in just under the wire."

"I've been calling all day."

"Yeah?" he said. "Well, I been in and out."

It was a thick, clotty voice with an uneducated New York accent. He was silent, waiting for me to speak.

"Mr. Tabatchnick wants me to meet with you," I said politely. "At your convenience. To discuss matters relevant to the estate of Solomon Kipper."

"That's what I'm here for," he said cheerily. "I'm selling, and you're buying—right?"

"Uhh, that's to be determined," I said hastily. "When and where can we meet?"

He paused a moment, then:

"There's a gin mill on West 46th Street between Eighth and Ninth. Closer to Ninth. Called the Purple Cow. Meet me there at 11:30 tomorrow morning. Got that?"

I had been scribbling quick notes.

"I have it," I said. "How will I know you?"

"I'll be sitting in the last booth on the left," he said. Then his voice turned guttural. "You coming alone?"

"Of course," I said.

"Good," he said. "No foolishness."

He clicked off.

I hung up slowly, staring down at my notes. I tried to analyze how he had sounded. Not menacing, I finally concluded, but very sure of himself.

I sighed, added that note to the Kipper file, and stored it away in my steel cabinet. Then I put on my coat and started home, exchanging "Good nights" with other departing employees. Yetta Apatoff's desk was bare; apparently she had already left.

It had been a gray day, raw, the light coarse and the air smelling damply of snow. But the temperature had moderated somewhat; the wind still nibbled, but it had freshened, and the evening sky showed patches of pale blue. Rather than try to jam my way aboard crowded buses, I decided to walk home to the West 20s.

I lived on a street in Chelsea that had once been lined with private homes. Most of the houses had cast-iron railings in front, sandstone steps leading up to ornate front doors. Those that hadn't been gutted still had marble fireplaces and high ceilings with plaster embellishments.

My building had adequate heat and hot water because the owner lived there. On the first floor was a firm of architects, Armentrout & Pook; and Hooshang Aboudi, Inc., importers of general merchandise.

The owner and her daughter, Hermione and Cleo Hufnagel, lived on the second floor in separate apartments. I shared the third floor with Bramwell Shank, an elderly ex-ferryboat captain who was confined to a wheelchair. On the top floor, the fourth, were the apartments of Madama Zora Kadinsky, who said she had once sung at the Met and still practiced scales during the day. The other fourth-floor apartment was occupied by Adolph Finkel, a retail shoe salesman.

The apartments were dark but the ceilings were high and the fireplaces worked. I paid $350 a month plus utilities.

On this particular evening Bramwell Shank was waiting for me in the third-floor hallway. His bottle of muscatel was in his lap, with a clean glass ready for me and a half-empty one he was sipping. He wheeled himself into my apartment as soon as I unlocked the door and launched into a recital of the day's TV activities before I could get my coat off.

In his prime he must have been a stalwart bruiser, with solid shoulders, corded arms, and fists that looked like geological specimens. Now, imprisoned in a wheelchair, puddled by drink, he still had a thrusting, assertive brawler's presence. His voice rattled the windows and all his gestures were outsize and violent.

Because he was bald, he wore a captain's cap all day; below the peak of the cap was a pulpy face that ranged from pink to deep purple. He wore black turtleneck sweaters and a brass-buttoned blue officer's jacket.

I let him thunder on about the shows he had seen and when he paused to fill our glasses again, I asked him if he'd care to eat with me.

"I was planning to scramble some eggs with salami," I said. "Maybe a salad. And a piece of pie. You're welcome to share, Captain."

"Nah," he said. "I already made my own slop and et it. Where'd you get the pie—Powerful Katrinka give it to you?"

That was what he called our landlady, Mrs. Hufnagel. It was an apt nickname; she stood five eleven and was at least a welterweight.

"Yes, she did," I said. "It's Dutch apple, and very good. Homemade."

"Uh-huh," he said, looking at me and grinning. "She's real friendly to you, ain't she?"

"Isn't she friendly to *you?*"

"She don't bake me no pies. You going to the party?"

"What party?"

"Saturday night. Katrinka invited all the tenants."

"I haven't been invited."

"You will be."

"What's the occasion?"

"Valentine's Day—she says. But I got my own ideas about that."

"You're talking in riddles tonight, Captain."

He watched me assemble paper and kindling in the fireplace.

"You ain't doing that right!" he roared. "Pile up your kindling crisscross."

"I do it like this. It always works."

The fire caught this time, too. We were watching it, wineglasses in hand, when there came a rapid knocking on the door.

"'allo, 'allo!" caroled Mme Kadinsky. "Joshy? You are een there?"

"Don't let her in," growled the Captain.

"Madame Kadinsky," I said, smiling at her. "Nice to see you. Do come in."

She tapped my cheek. "You promised to call me Zora, you naughty boy." Then she was inside the room, moving with quick little steps. "But you already have company. The Captain Shink."

"Shank," he growled.

"I am interrupting somesing?" She laughed gaily.

"Not at all," I told her. "We're just having a glass of wine. Let me get you a glass."

"Joshy," she said, "you are going to the party Saturday night?"

"I haven't been invited."

Like Bramwell Shank, she said, "You will be." They both smiled.

"What's going on with you two?"

Zora put a hand to her cheek, rolled her eyes.

"He don't know," Shank said.

"Tell me!" I burst out.

"Powerful Katrinka has her eye on you for Cleo," the Captain said.

They departed soon after, and I went into the kitchen to make my omelette. I suppose I felt a kind of smirky pride; I am as vain as the next man. The whole thing was ridiculous, of course. Cleo Hufnagel seemed a pleasant, soft-spoken young woman. We smiled and exchanged greetings. But more was impossible. Cleo was at least five ten, and taller in heels.

But my thoughts kept returning to the Great Hufnagel Plot.

When the knock came I knew at once who it was. It was Mrs. Hufnagel bearing a plate covered with a paper napkin.

"Mrs. Hufnagel! What a surprise! Won't you come in?"

"Well . . . just for a minute. I don't want to disturb you."

"Not at all," I said. "Would you like a cup of coffee?"

"No, nothing, thanks," she said. "We just finished dinner. My, that was a fine meal Cleo cooked. Swiss steak with mashed potatoes, fresh stringbeans, and the best gravy ever. Have you had your coffee yet?"

I said truthfully that I hadn't.

"Well, Cleo baked these chocolate chip cookies and we thought you might enjoy some with your coffee."

"Mrs. Hufnagel, you're too generous."

"Try one," she commanded.

Obediently I bit into a cookie.

"Delicious," I said.

"Yes," she said, sighing. "That Cleo—so talented in the kitchen. She'll make some man a wonderful wife."

"I'm sure she will," I murmured. "Would you like the plate back now? I can put the cookies in a tin."

"No rush," she said. "You can return it whenever you like. Actually, Mr. Bigg, the cookies were just one of the reasons I came up. I *also* wanted to invite you to a party Cleo and I are having Saturday night."

5

THE PURPLE COW smelled of spilled beer and cheap cigars, even at 11:30 A.M. The men at the bar hunched glowering over their drinks, awaiting the end of the world. I found Marty in the last booth on the left. He sat facing the door, fingers laced around a stein of beer. In the dim light he appeared to be about forty-five, skinny, with a pitted complexion and a pale, small mustache.

He watched me approach without interest. I stopped alongside his booth.

"Marty?" I said.

"Yeah?"

"I'm from Mr. Leopold Tabatchnick."

He showed his teeth. "Who are you, the office boy?"

I slid into the booth opposite him.

"I am Mr. Tabatchnick's executive assistant, acting on his behalf."

"That's sweet," he said.

"Could you tell me what this is all about?" I asked. "You claim you—"

"Want a drink?" he interrupted.

"No," I said. "Thank you."

"For what?" he said. "I wasn't going to pay for it."

"You claim you have information affecting the estate of the late Solomon Kipper. Is that correct?"

"I don't claim it. I got it."

"Could you tell me the nature of this information?"

"You kidding? That's what I'm selling."

I sighed and sat back.

"Then I'm afraid we've reached an impasse," I said. "Surely you don't expect us to make an offer for something we know nothing about."

He leaned toward me across the table. He had very sour breath. His eyes seemed almost colorless, and I noticed the lobe of his left ear was missing. He was dressed in a tweed cap, green anorak, maroon shirt, and flowered pink tie. The parka was stained, there was a stubble of whitish beard, and his nails were rimmed with black. His voice was even more gluey than it had sounded on the phone.

"Listen, sonny," he said, "I ain't asking you to make an offer; I'm going to tell you how much I want. Second of all, I ain't telling you what I got because then I got nothing to sell. That makes sense, don't it? I'll tell you this much: what I got is going to upset the applecart. With what I got, the Kipper will ain't worth the paper it's printed on."

"And how much are you asking for this information?"

"Fifty thousand," he said promptly. "Take it or leave it."

I think I succeeded in hiding my shock.

"That's a great deal of money," I said slowly.

"Nah," he said, "it's peanuts. How much is that estate— four mil? Five mil? It's worth fifty grand to make sure it goes to the right people, ain't it?"

"Well . . ." I said, "I'll certainly bring this to Mr. Tabatchnick's attention the moment I get back to the office."

"Don't jerk me around, sonny," he said. "I got another hot customer for this property. I'm meeting with them later today. First come, first served."

"I'll contact you as soon as Mr. Tabatchnick comes to a decision," I said. "Would you mind giving me your full name? You can't expect us to make a payment of that size to someone we know only as Marty."

He thought that over, squinching his eyes and wrinkling his nose.

"I guess it won't do no harm," he said. "It's Reape. R-e-a-p-e. Marty Reape. As in 'Rook before you Reape'—right? You can reach me at that number I gave you. I'll be in late this afternoon."

I nodded and slid out of the booth. "Nice meeting you, Mr. Reape."

"Yeah." He showed no intention of leaving with me. That this was a ploy to avoid being followed was obvious, but he underrated my professionalism.

Outside I turned west, crossed Ninth, and immediately chose a doorway for the stakeout. Then I settled down to wait, hands in my pockets. I stamped my feet occasionally to keep them from becoming lumps. Now and then I took my hands from my pockets to hold my ears. He came out finally and stood at the curb, zipping up his parka and looking around. Then he turned and started walking east toward Times Square.

He was on the south side of West 46th Street. I stayed on the north side, well back of him. The sidewalk was filling up with people rushing to get a lunch table at one of the restaurants that lined the street, so Marty Reape moved slowly. Even in the crowd the cap and anorak were easy to spot. If he suspected he might be followed, he certainly gave no indication of it; never once looked over his shoulder or glanced in a store window to catch a reflection. I tailed him to a few doors east of Eighth on 49th, where he turned into a building next to a porn movie house that was showing "Teenage Honey Pot." When he'd had time to clear the lobby I trotted across the street and ducked in. There was a directory on the greasy marble wall.

MARTIN REAPE: PRIVATE INVESTIGATIONS.

I practically ran back to the office to give Mr. Tabatchnick my report, but Thelma Potts said he was at lunch and that she would buzz me when he returned.

I had a cheeseburger and a container of milk sent in and ate at my desk while I typed a report of my meeting with Martin Reape. I put it away in the Kipper file and then I called Mr. Teitelbaum's office. *He* never went out to lunch; he had a cup of tea and two graham crackers at his desk. I told him I'd like to meet and question the Stonehouse family and I thought it would go a lot easier if he called first and set up the appointment for a time when all the family and the servants would be present.

"Yes, yes," he said testily. "I'll call you back." He hung up abruptly.

Maybe his graham crackers had been stale.

I had no sooner hung up than Thelma Potts called. I took the elevator to the fourth floor with two clerks carrying stacks of law books up to their eyebrows.

"Twice in two days," Thelma Potts said. "My, what would this company do without you?"

"Stick with me, kid," I said, "and you'll be wearing diamonds."

I knocked once and went in. He was feeding his fish, crumbling some white stuff into the tanks and making little sounds with his tongue and teeth. It sounded like, "nk, nk, nk."

"Mr. Tabatchnick," I said, "I had a meeting with Marty about the Kipper estate."

He went on feeding fish. "Sit down and tell me," he said.

When I mentioned the $50,000, Mr. Tabatchnick's hand jerked and one of his finny friends got an unexpected banquet. I finished describing the meeting and he came back to his swivel chair behind the trestle table, dusting his hands.

"I like it less and less," he said. "If he had asked for five hundred, or a thousand, or even five thousand, I would have assumed he was merely a cheap chiseler. But he obviously believes his information is of considerable value. And if he is a private investigator, he may indeed have discovered something of consequence. Repeat exactly what he said regarding the nature of his information."

"He said, quote, What I got is going to upset the applecart. With what I got, the Kipper will ain't worth the paper it's printed on. Unquote."

"And he said he has another potential customer?"

"Yes, sir. He said he was meeting with them later today. That's his word: 'them.'"

We sat in silence for a long time. Finally he stirred and said, "I dislike this intensely. As an officer of the court I cannot become involved in shenanigans. At the same time, I have a responsibility to our deceased client and to the proper distribution of his estate as set forth in his last will and testament."

He stared at me without expression. I didn't catch on for a moment. Then I knew what he wanted.

"Sir," I said, "is there anything odd about that will?"

"No, no," he said. "It's a relatively short and simple document. But I have not been entirely forthcoming with you, Mr. Bigg. On the morning of the day he committed suicide, Sol Kipper called this office and said he wished to execute a new will."

"I see," I said softly.

"Do you?" he said. "I don't. Now we have this 'Marty' claiming to have information that may invalidate the existing will."

"Yes, sir," I said. "You want to pay him, Mr. Tabatchnick?"

"I told you," he thundered, "I cannot let myself become involved!"

"Of course not, sir. But I'm not an officer of the court; I have latitude to act in this matter."

That was what he wanted to hear. Mr. Tabatchnick settled back, entwined his fingers across his solid stomach, regarded me gravely.

"What do you propose, Mr. Bigg?"

"The funds can't come from this firm, sir. There can be no connection, nothing on our books. The money must be made available from an outside source."

He thought a moment. "That can be arranged," he said finally.

"And I must be the only contact Reape knows. No one else in the firm can speak to him or meet with him."

"I agree."

"The first thing for me to do is to call Reape and tell him we agree to his terms. Before he makes a deal with his other customers. I will then arrange a date for the transfer, postponing it as long as possible. Then I hand over the money and he hands over his information or delivers it orally."

"Why do you wish to postpone the transfer as long as possible?"

"To give me time to devise some plan for getting the information without paying."

"Splendid, young man!" he said. "If you can. But your primary objective must be acquiring the information. I hope you understand that."

"I do, sir."

"Good. Keep me informed. I'll need a day or two to provide the funds."

"Mr. Tabatchnick, it would help if you could tell me something about the existing Kipper will. Specifically, who stands to inherit the most? And if the will is for some reason declared invalid, who would stand to profit the most?"

He looked down at his big hands, now clasped on the tabletop.

"For the moment," he said in a low voice, "I would prefer to keep that information confidential. Should the time come when it is vital to the successful conclusion of your, ah, investigation, I will then make available to you a copy of the will."

It was time for me to go.

"Mr. Bigg," he said.

I turned back from the door.

"This conversation never took place," he said sternly.

"What conversation, sir?" I asked.

He almost smiled.

6

I CALLED MARTY REAPE when I returned to my office. No answer. I wondered if he was meeting with his other customers.

I took off my jacket and started hacking away at inquiries that had been submitted by junior partners and associates. Most of these could be handled with a single phone call or a letter, or a look into Roscoe Dollworth's small library of dictionaries, atlases, almanacs, census reports, etc.

What was the Hispanic population of the Bronx in 1964?

How long does it take to repaint a car?

In what year was penicillin discovered?

Who was the last man to be electrocuted in New York State?

What are the ingredients of a Molotov cocktail?

I tried twice to call Marty Reape. Ada Mondora called to say I had an appointment with the Stonehouse family. I was to be at their apartment on Central Park West and 70th Street at 8:00 P.M.

It was then about 4:30. I decided that instead of going home I would do better to have my dinner midtown, then go to West 70th Street. I checked my wallet, then I called Yetta Apatoff.

"Oh, Josh," she said. "I wish you'd called sooner. I would

43

have loved to, but just a half-hour ago Hammy asked me to have dinner with him."

"Hammy?"

"Hamish. Hamish Hooter."

She called him Hammy.

"Yes, well, I'm sorry you can't make it, Yetta. I'll try another time."

"Promise?" she breathed.

"Promise."

So I worked in the office until 6:30. I called Marty Reape twice more. No reply. I tried him again before I left the restaurant, where I ate alone. Again there was no answer. I began to fear that he had concluded a deal with his other customers.

I had time to spare, so I walked to 42nd Street, boarded a Broadway bus, and rode up to West 70th Street. Then I walked over to Central Park West. The sky was murky; a light drizzle was beginning to fall. Wind blew in sighing gusts and smelled vaguely of ash. A fitting night to investigate a disappearance.

The Stonehouses' apartment house was an enormous, pyramidal pile of brick. Very old, very staid, very expensive. The lobby was all marble and mirrors. I waited while the uniformed deskman called to learn if I would be received.

"Mr. Bigg to see Mrs. Stonehouse," he announced. Then he hung up and turned to me. "Apartment 17-B."

The elevator had been converted to self-service, but the walls and ceiling were polished walnut with beveled oval mirrors; the Oriental carpet had been woven to fit.

Seventeen-B was on the Central Park side. I rang the bell and waited for a long time. Finally the door was opened by a striking young woman. She smiled.

"Mr. Bigg?" she said. "Good evening, I'm Glynis Stonehouse."

She hung my coat in a foyer closet. Then she led me down a long, dimly lighted corridor lined with antique maps and scenes of naval battles. I saw why it had taken so long to answer the door. It was a hike to the living room. The apartment was huge.

She preceded me into a living room larger than my apartment. I had a quick impression of a blaze in a tiled fireplace, chairs and sofas of crushed velvet, and floor-to-ceiling windows overlooking the park. Then Glynis Stonehouse was leading me toward a smallish lady curled in the corner of an overstuffed couch, holding a half-filled wineglass. There was a bottle of sherry on the glass-topped table before her.

"My mother," Glynis said. Her voice was low-pitched, husky, and almost toneless.

"Mrs. Stonehouse," I said, making a little bow. "I'm Joshua Bigg from Mr. Teitelbaum's office. I'm happy to meet you."

"My husband's dead, isn't he?" she said. "I know he's dead."

I was startled by her words, but even more shocked by her voice. It was trilly and flutelike.

"Mother," Glynis said, "there's absolutely no evidence of that."

"I know what I know," Mrs. Stonehouse said. "Do sit down, Mr. Bigg. Over there, where I can look at you."

"Thank you." I took the chair she had indicated. I was thankful that my feet touched the floor, though only just.

"Have you dined?" she asked.

"Yes, ma'am, I have."

"So have we," she said brightly, "and now I'm having a glass of sherry. Glynis isn't drinking. Glynis never drinks. Do you, dear?"

"No, Mother," the daughter said patiently. "Would you care for something, Mr. Bigg?"

"A glass of sherry would be welcome," I said. "Thank you."

Glynis got a glass from a bar cart and filled it from her mother's bottle. She handed it to me, then seated herself at the opposite end of the couch. She was graceful and controlled.

"Mr. Teitelbaum told Mother you will be investigating my father's disappearance."

"Yes," I said. "We believe the police have done everything they possibly can, but surely it will do no harm to go over it again."

"He's dead," Mrs. Ula Stonehouse said.

"Ma'am," I said, "according to Mr. Teitelbaum, you believed your husband had met with an accident and was suffering from amnesia."

"I did think that," she said, "but I don't anymore. He's dead. I had a vision."

Glynis Stonehouse was inspecting her fingernails. I took out a notebook and pen. "I hate to go over events which I'm sure are painful to you," I said. "But it would help if you could tell me exactly what happened the evening the Professor disappeared."

Mrs. Stonehouse did most of the talking, her daughter correcting her now and then or adding something in a quiet voice. I took notes as Mrs. Stonehouse spoke, but it was really for effect, to impress them how seriously Tabatchnick, Orsini, Reilly, and Teitelbaum regarded their plight.

I glanced up frequently from my scribbling to stare at Mrs. Stonehouse.

As she talked, sipping her sherry steadily and leaning forward twice to refill her glass, her eyes, as pale as milk glass, flickered like candle flames. She had a mop of frizzy blonde curls, a skin of chamois, and a habit, or nervous tic, of touching the tip of her retroussé nose with her left forefinger. Not pushing it, but just touching it as if to make certain it was still there.

She had fluttery gestures, and was given to quick expressions—frowns, smiles, pouts, moues—that followed one another so swiftly that her face seemed in constant motion. She was dressed girlishly in chiffon. In her tucked-up position she was showing a good deal of leg.

She spoke rapidly, as if anxious to get it all out and over with. That warbling voice rippled on and on, and after a while it took on a singsong quality like a child's part rehearsed for a school play.

On the 10th of January the Stonehouse family had dinner at 7:00 P.M. Present were Professor Yale Stonehouse, wife Ula, daughter Glynis, and son Powell. The meal was served by the live-in cook-housekeeper, Mrs. Effie Dark. The maid, Olga Eklund, was away on her day off.

Glynis Stonehouse left the dinner table early, at about 8:00, to get to a performance of *Man and Superman* at the Circle in the Square. After dinner the family moved into the living room. At about 8:30, Professor Stonehouse went into his study. He came back to the living room a few minutes later and announced he was going out. He walked down the long corridor to the foyer. Later it was determined he had taken his hat, scarf, and overcoat. Mrs. Stonehouse and her son heard the outer door slam. The deskman in the lobby remembered that the Professor left the building at approximately 8:45.

He was never seen again.

This recital finished, mother and daughter looked at me expectantly, as if waiting for an instant solution.

"Has Professor Stonehouse attempted to communicate with you since his disappearance?"

"No," Glynis said. "Nothing."

"Was this a common occurrence—the Professor going out at that hour? For a walk, say?"

"No," Mrs. Stonehouse said. "He never went out at night."

"Rarely," Glynis corrected her. "Once or twice a year he went to a professional meeting. But it usually included a dinner, and he left earlier."

"He didn't say where he was going when he left on the evening of January 10th?"

"No," Mrs. Stonehouse said.

"You didn't ask, ma'am?"

The mother looked to her daughter for help.

"My father was—" she began, then said, "My father is a difficult man. He didn't like to be questioned. He went his own way. He was secretive."

"Would you say there was anything unusual in his behavior at dinner that night?"

This time daughter looked to mother.

"Nooo," Mrs. Stonehouse said slowly. "He didn't say much at the table, but then he never said much."

"So you'd say this behavior that evening was entirely normal? For Professor Stonehouse," I added hastily.

They both nodded.

"All right," I said. "There are a few things I'd like to come back to, but first I'd like to hear what happened after the Professor left."

At my request Mrs. Stonehouse took up her story again.

She and her son, Powell, stayed in the living room, watched a Beckett play on Channel 13, had a few drinks. Mrs. Dark came in at about 10:30 to say goodnight and went to her room at the far end of the apartment.

They did not begin to become concerned about the Professor's whereabouts until 11:00 P.M. They called the deskman in the lobby, who could only report that Stonehouse had left the building at 8:45 and hadn't returned. They awoke Mrs. Dark to ask if the Professor had mentioned anything to her about where he was going. She said he hadn't, but she shared their concern and joined them in the living room, wearing a robe over her nightgown. They then called some of the Professor's professional associates, apologizing for the lateness of the hour. No one had seen him or heard from him. He had no friends other than professional associates.

By 11:30 they all were worried and uncertain what they should do. They were hesitant about calling the police. If they called and he walked in a few minutes later, he'd be furious.

"He had a violent temper," Glynis said.

Glynis returned from the theatre a little after midnight and was told of her father's absence. She suggested they call the garage to see if Stonehouse had taken out his car. Powell called and was informed that the car was still parked there.

The four of them waited until 2:00 A.M. and then called the local precinct. The officer they spoke to told them that it would not be a matter for the Missing Persons Bureau until the Professor was absent for 24 hours, but meanwhile he would check accident reports and hospital emergency rooms. He said he'd call them back.

They waited, awake and drinking coffee, until 3:20 when the police officer called and told them there were no reports of accidents involving Professor Stonehouse or anyone answering his description.

There seemed to be nothing more they could do. The next day they made more phone calls, and Powell rang the bells of neighbors and even walked around neighborhood streets, asking at newsstands and all-night restaurants. No one had seen his father or anyone like him.

After twenty-four hours had passed, they reported the Professor as a missing person to the New York Police Department, and that was that.

I took a deep breath.

"I don't like to take so much of your time on this first meeting," I said. "I hope you'll allow me to come back again, or call as questions occur to me."

"Of course," Glynis Stonehouse said. "And take as much time as you like. We're anxious to do anything we can to help."

"Just a few questions then," I said, looking at her. "Did

your father have any enemies? Anyone who might harbor sufficient ill-will to..."

I let that trail off, but she didn't flinch. Then again, she didn't look like the flinching type.

Glynis Stonehouse was taller than her mother. A compact body, curved with brio. Tawny hair hung sleekly to her shoulders. She had a triangular face with dark eyes of denim blue. Wide, sculpted lips with a minimum of rouge. She was wearing a simple shift, thin stuff that touched breast, hip, thigh. No jewelry.

I had the impression of a lot of passion there, kept under disciplined control. The dark eyes gave nothing away, and she rarely smiled or frowned. She had the habit of pausing, very briefly, before answering a question. Just a half-beat, but enough to convince me she was giving her replies extra thought.

"No, Mr. Bigg," she said evenly. "I don't believe my father had enemies who hated him enough to do him harm."

"But he did have enemies?" I persisted.

"There are a lot of people who disliked him. He was not an easy man to like."

"Oh, Glynis," her mother said sorrowfully.

"Mr. Bigg might as well know the truth, Mother; it may help his investigation. My father was—*is* a tyrant, Mr. Bigg. Opinionated, stubborn, dictatorial, with a very low boiling point. Constantly suing people for the most ridiculous reasons. Of course he had enemies, at the University and everywhere else he went. But I know of no one who disliked him enough to—to do him injury."

I nodded and looked at my notes.

"Mrs. Stonehouse, you said that just before leaving the apartment, Professor Stonehouse went into his study?"

"Yes, that's right."

"Do you know what he did in there?"

"No. The study is his private room."

"Off-limits to all," Glynis said. "He rarely let us in."

"He let *you* in, Glynis," her mother said.

"He even cleaned the room himself," Glynis went on. "He was working on a book and didn't want his papers disturbed."

"A book? What kind of a book?"

"A history of the *Prince Royal*, a famous British battleship of the seventeenth century."

"Has your father published anything before?"

"A few monographs and articles in scholarly journals. He's also an habitual writer of letters to the newspapers. Would you care for more sherry, Mr. Bigg?"

"No, thank you. That was delicious. Mrs. Stonehouse, your son is not here tonight?"

"No," she said. "He's . . ."

She didn't finish that, but leaned forward to fill her glass.

"My brother doesn't live here," Glynis said evenly. "Powell has his own place in the Village. He stayed over the night Father disappeared because we were all so upset."

"Your brother and father didn't get along?" I asked.

"Well enough," she said. "Powell comes to dinner two or three times a week. In any event, the relations between my father and brother have nothing to do with your investigation."

"Powell tried so hard," her mother mourned.

Glynis leaned far across the couch to put a hand on her mother's arm. Her body was stretched out, almost reclining. I saw the bold rhythm of thigh, hip, waist, bosom, shoulder . . .

"We all tried hard, Mother," she said softly.

I closed my notebook, put it away. "I think I've asked you ladies enough questions for one evening. But before I leave, if I may, I'd like to see Professor Stonehouse's study, and I'd like to talk to your housekeeper for a few minutes."

"Of course," Glynis said, rising. I followed her over to a door on the far side of the room. It opened into a dining room, cold and austere, lit dimly.

There were two doors in the opposite wall, one the swinging type used in kitchens.

"That one to the kitchen?" I asked.

"Yes."

"And the other one to your father's study?"

"That's correct."

"Your mother told me that your father went into his study before he went out. But they couldn't have seen where he went. He might have gone into the kitchen."

"You're very sharp, Mr. Bigg," she said. "Mrs. Dark was still cleaning up in here after dinner, and she saw him go into his study."

Glynis opened the study door, reached in to turn on the

light, then stood aside. I stepped forward to look in. For a moment I was close to her. I was conscious of her scent. It wasn't cologne or perfume; it was *her*. Warm, womanly, stirring. I walked forward into the study.

"I won't disturb anything," I said.

"I'm afraid we already have," she said. "Looking for Father's will."

"You didn't find it?" I said.

She shook her head, shiny hair swinging. "We found his passbook and checkbook, but no will."

"Did your father have a safe deposit box?"

"Not at either of the banks where he has his savings and checking accounts."

"Miss Stonehouse, are you sure a will exists?"

"Oh, it exists," she said. "Or did. I saw it. I don't mean I read it. I just saw it on his desk one night. It was four or five pages and had a light blue backing. When Daddy saw me looking at it, he folded it up and put it in a long envelope. 'My will,' he said. So I know it did exist."

"Does your mother know what's in it?"

"No. Father never discussed money matters with her. He just gave her an allowance and that was that."

"Did your father give you an allowance, Miss Stonehouse?"

She looked at me levelly.

"Yes," she said, "he did."

"And your brother?"

"No," she said. "Not since he moved out." Then she added irritably, "What has all this to do with my father's disappearance?"

"I don't know," I said truthfully, and turned back to the study.

It was a squarish chamber with a high-beamed ceiling. There was another tiled fireplace, built-in bookcases, large cabinets for oversized books, magazines, journals, rolled-up maps.

There was a club chair upholstered in maroon leather, with a hassock to match. Alongside it was a drum table with a leather top chased with gold leaf. A silver tray was on the drum table bearing a new bottle of Rémy Martin cognac, sealed, and two brandy snifters. A green-shaded floor lamp stood in back of the chair.

In the center of the study was a big desk with leather top

and brass fittings, littered with papers, charts, maps, books, pencils and pens in several colors. Also, a magnifying glass, a pair of dividers, and a device that looked like an antique compass.

But it was the far wall that caught my eye. It was covered, from chair rail to ceiling, with model hull forms. I don't know whether you've ever seen hull models. They're made of hardwood, the hull sliced longitudinally. The flat side is fixed to the plaque. Each plaque bore a brass plate with the ship's name and date of construction. I stepped closer to examine them. I had never seen so many in one place, and never any as lovely.

Glynis had noted my interest. "Father had them made by a man in Mystic, Connecticut. When he dies, there won't be anyone left in the country who can carve hull models from the plans of naval architects."

"They're handsome," I said.

"And expensive."

But if that room had something to tell me, I couldn't hear it. I turned toward the door.

"Your father didn't have a safe?" I asked.

"No," she said. "And the drawers of his desk were unlocked."

"Did he usually leave them unlocked?"

"I really don't know. Mrs. Dark might."

I was wondering if she'd want to be present while I questioned Mrs. Dark, but I needn't have worried. She led me into the brightly lighted kitchen and said to the woman there: "Effie, this is Mr. Bigg. He's looking into Father's disappearance for the lawyers. Please answer his questions and tell him whatever he wants to know. Mr. Bigg, this is Mrs. Effie Dark. When you're finished here, I'm sure you can find your way back to the living room." Then she turned and left.

Mrs. Dark was a tub of a woman with three chins and a bosom that encircled her like a pneumatic tube. She had sausage arms, and ankles that lopped over nurse's shoes. Stuck in that roly-poly face were bright little eyes, shiny as blueberries in a pie. Her hips were so wide, I knew she had to go through doors sideways.

"Mrs. Dark," I said, "I hope I'm not disturbing you?"

"Why no," she said. "I'm just waiting for the water to boil, and then I'm going to have a nice cup of tea. Would you like one?"

"I'd love a cup of tea," I lied.

She heaved herself to her feet and went to the counter. While the tea was steeping, she set out cups, saucers, and spoons for us. I held my saucer up to the light and admired its translucence.

"Beautiful," I said.

"Nothing but the best," she said. "When it came to his own comfort, he didn't stint."

"How long have you been with the Stonehouse family, Mrs. Dark?"

"Since the Year One," she said. "I was the Professor's cook and housekeeper whilst I was married and before he was. Then my mister got took, and the Professor got married, so I moved in with him and his family."

I watched her pour us cups of russet-colored tea. She held her cup in both hands and savored the aroma before she took a sip. I did the same.

"Mrs. Stonehouse and Glynis told me what happened the night the Professor disappeared," I started. "They said they noted nothing unusual in his behavior that night. Did you?"

She thought a moment.

"Nooo," she said, drawling it out. "He was about the same as usual. He was a devil." She tasted the word on her plump lips, seemed to like it, and repeated it forcefully: "A devil! But I wouldn't take any guff from him, and he knew it. He liked my cooking, and I kept the place nice for him. He knew his wife couldn't run this menagerie, and his daughter wasn't interested. That's why he was as nice as pie as far as I was concerned. And he paid a good dollar, I'll say that."

"All this on a professor's salary?"

"Oh no. No no no. He comes from old money. His grandfather and father were in shipping. He inherited a pile."

"What was he so sore about?" I asked her. "He seems to have hated the world."

She shrugged her thick shoulders.

"Who can tell a thing like that? I know he had some disappointments in his life, but who hasn't? I know he got passed over for promotion at the University—that's why he resigned—

and once, when he was younger, he got jilted. But nothing important enough that I know of that would turn him into the kind of man he was. To tell you the truth, I think he just enjoyed being mean. More tea?"

"Please."

I watched her pour and dilute with hot water. "They've been looking for the Professor's will," I said. "It's missing. Did you know that?"

"Did I? They tore my kitchen apart looking for it. Even the flour bin. Took me hours to get it tidy again."

"Glynis told me her father cleaned his study himself. Wouldn't let anyone in there. Is that right?"

"Recently," she said. "In the month before he disappeared. Before that, he let me in to dust and straighten up. We have a cleaning crew that comes in once a week to give the place a good going-over, vacuum the rugs and wash down the bathrooms—things like that. He'd let them in his study if I was there. Then, about a month before he vanished, he wouldn't let anyone in. Said he'd clean the place himself."

"Did he give any reason for this change?"

"Said he was working on this book, had valuable papers in there and didn't want them disturbed."

"Uh-huh," I said. "Mrs. Stonehouse and her daughter told me that just before he walked out on the evening of January 10th, he went into his study for a few minutes. Did you see him?"

"I did. I was in the dining room. It was Olga's night off, so I was cleaning up after dinner. He came in from the living room, went into the study, and came out a few minutes later. That was the last time I saw him."

"Did he close the study door after he went in?"

"Yes."

"Did you hear anything in there?"

"Like what?" she asked.

"Anything. Anything that might give me an idea of what he was doing. Thumping around? Moving furniture?"

She was silent, trying to remember. I waited patiently.

"I don't know . . ." she said. "It was a month ago. Maybe I heard him slam a desk drawer. But I couldn't swear to it."

"That's another thing," I said. "The desk drawers. Did he keep them locked?"

"Yes," she said definitely. "He did keep them locked when he wasn't there. I remember because once he lost his keys and we had to have a locksmith come in and open the desk."

"No one else had a key to his desk?"

"Not that I know of."

"Effie, what happened between the Professor and his son?"

"The poor lamb," she mourned. "Powell got kicked out of the house."

"Why?"

"He wouldn't get a job, and he wouldn't go back to the University to get his degree, and he was running with a wild bunch in Greenwich Village. Then the Professor caught Powell smoking pot in his bedroom, and that did it."

"Does Powell have a job now?"

"Not that I know of."

"How does he live?"

"I think he has a little money of his own that his grandmother left him. Also, I think Mrs. Stonehouse and Glynis help him out now and then, unbeknownst to the Professor."

"When did this happen?"

"Powell getting kicked out? More than a year ago."

"But he still comes here for dinner?"

"Only in the last two or three months. Mrs. Stonehouse cried and carried on so and said Powell was starving, and Glynis worked on her father, too, and eventually he said it would be all right for Powell to have dinner here if he wanted to, but he couldn't move back in."

"All right," I said. "Now what about Glynis? Does she work?"

"Not anymore. She did for a year or two, but she quit."

"Where did she work?"

"I think she was a secretary in a medical laboratory. Something like that."

"But now she does nothing?"

"She's a volunteer three days a week in a clinic downtown. But no regular job."

"Have many friends?"

"Seems to. She goes out a lot. The theatre and ballet and so forth. Some weeks she's out every night."

"One particular boyfriend?"

"Not that I know of."

"Does she ever have her friends here? Does she entertain?"

"No," Mrs. Effie Dark said sadly. "I never see any of her friends. And there hasn't been much in the way of entertaining in this house. Not for years."

She waved a plump hand around, gesturing toward overhead racks, the utensils, the bins and spice racks, stove, in-the-wall oven, refrigerator, freezer.

"See all this? I don't use half this stuff for months on end. But when the kids were growing up, things were different. The Professor was at the University most of the day, and this place was filled with the kids' friends. There were parties and dances right here. Even Mrs. Stonehouse had teas and bridge games and get-togethers for her friends. My, I was busy. But we had another maid then, a live-in, and I didn't mind. There was noise and everyone laughed. A real ruckus. Then the Professor resigned, and he was home all day. He put a stop to the parties and dances. Gradually, people stopped coming, he was such a meany. Then we began living like hermits, tiptoeing around so as not to disturb him. Not like the old days."

I nodded and stood up.

"Effie," I said, "I thank you for the refreshments and for the talk."

"I like to talk," she said, grinning, "as you have probably noticed. A body could climb the walls here for the want of someone to chat with."

"Well, I enjoyed it," I said, "and I learned a lot. I hope you'll let me come back and chat with you again."

"Anytime," she said. "I have my own telephone. Would you like the number?"

As she dictated, I wrote it down in my notebook.

"Effie," I said in closing, "what do you think happened to Professor Stonehouse?"

"I don't know," she said, troubled. "Do you?"

"No," I said, "I don't."

When I went back into the living room Mrs. Stonehouse was alone, still curled into a corner of the couch. The sherry bottle was empty.

"Hi there," she fluted. She tried to touch her nose and missed.

"Hi," I said.

"Glynis went beddy-bye," she giggled.

I glanced at my watch. It was a few minutes to ten. Early for beddy-bye.

I caught the subway on CPW, got off at 23rd Street, and walked the three blocks to my home. I kept to the curb and I didn't dawdle. When I was inside the building, I felt that sense of grim satisfaction that all New Yorkers feel on arriving home safely. Now, if a masked intruder was not awaiting me in my living room, drinking my brandy, all would be well.

It was not a would-be thief awaiting me, but Captain Bramwell Shank, and he was drinking his own muscatel. His door was open, and he wheeled himself out into the hallway when he heard me climb the stairs.

"Where the hell have you been?" he said querulously. "Come on in and have a glass of wine and watch the eleven o'clock news with me."

"I think I better take a raincheck, Captain," I said. "I've had a hard day and I want to get to bed early." But I went in anyway, moved laundry off a chair, and sat watching the 24-inch color set.

"You get your invite to the party?" Captain Shank demanded, pouring himself another glass of wine.

"Yes," I said, "I got it."

"Knew you would," he said, almost cackling. "Happened just like I said, didn't it?"

I took a sip of wine, put my head back, closed my eyes.

The local news came on, and we heard more dire predictions of New York's financial fate. We saw a tenement fire in the Bronx that killed three. We watched the Mayor hand a key to the city to a champion pizza twirler.

I was contemplating how soon I could decently leave when the news came on. The anchorman read a few small items of local interest to which I drifted off. Then he said:

"Service was halted for an hour on the Lexington Avenue IRT this evening while the body of a man was removed from the express tracks at the 14th Street station. He apparently fell or jumped to his death at the south end of the station just as the train was coming in. The victim has tentatively been identified as Martin Reape of Manhattan. No additional details are available at this time. And now, a message to all denture wearers . . ."

"What?" I said, waking up. "What did he say?"

7

I READ THE story in the *Times* on the 23rd Street crosstown bus in the morning. It was only a paragraph in "The City" column:

"Police are seeking witnesses to the death of Martin Reape of Manhattan who fell or jumped at the 14th Street station of the Lexington Avenue IRT subway. The accident occurred during the evening rush hour and resulted in delays of more than an hour. The motorman of the train involved told police he had just entered the station and had applied his brakes when 'the body came flying out of nowhere.'"

Rook before you Reape.

I made it to the office a few minutes before 9:00, called Thelma Potts, and told her I had to see Mr. Tabatchnick as soon as possible.

"You're getting to be a regular visitor," she said.

"Just an excuse to see you," I said.

"Oh *you!*" she said.

I spent an hour typing up a report of my conversations with the Stonehouses and Mrs. Dark. I tried to leave nothing out, because at that time I had no conception of what was important and what was just sludge. After reading over the report, I could detect no pattern, not even a vague clue to the Professor's disappearance. Just then Thelma Potts called to say Mr. Tabatchnick would see me. When I entered his office, he was standing behind the trestle table, drinking from a mug that had "Grandpa" painted on it. He was in a testy mood.

"What is so urgent that it couldn't wait until I had a chance to inspect my fish?"

I laid the *Times* column on his desk. I had boxed the Reape item with a red grease pencil.

Mr. Tabatchnick removed a heavy pair of black horn-rimmed glasses from his breast pocket. He took out a clean, neatly pressed handkerchief and slowly polished the glasses, breathing on them first. He donned the spectacles and, still standing, began to read. He read it once, looked up and stared at me, then read it again. His expression didn't change, but he lowered himself slowly into his swivel chair.

"Sit down, Mr. Bigg," he said. The voice wasn't irritable anymore. In fact, it sounded a little shaky. "What do you think happened?"

"I think he was murdered, sir. Pushed onto the tracks by that other customer or customers he was going to see."

"You have a vivid imagination, Mr. Bigg."

"It fits, sir."

"Then wouldn't he have had the money on him if he had sold the information? The paper mentions nothing of that. Or if he hadn't made the deal, wouldn't he have had the information on his person?"

"Not necessarily, sir. First of all, we don't know that his information was physical evidence. It may have been just something he knew. And it's possible he went to see his other customers just to discuss the details of the deal, and no exchange took place prior to his death. But after talking to him, his customers feared the payment would be only the first of a series of demands, and so they decided his death was the only solution."

He exhaled heavily.

"Very fanciful," he said. "And totally without proof."

"Yes, sir," I said, "I admit that. But during my meeting with Reape, I said something to the effect that fifty thousand was a lot of money, and he said, quote, It's worth fifty grand to make sure it goes to the right people, ain't it? Unquote. He was speaking of the estate, sir. So perhaps his other customers were the wrong people. You follow, Mr. Tabatchnick?"

"Of course I follow," he said furiously. "You're saying that with Reape out of the picture, the wrong people will profit. That means that the beneficiaries named in the existing will may include the wrong people."

He didn't like that at all. He leaned forward to read the Reape story for the third time. Then he angrily shoved the paper away.

"I wish," he said, "that I could be certain that this Reape person actually did possess what he claimed. He may merely have read the news story of Sol Kipper's suicide and devised this scheme to profit from the poor man's death. It might have been just a confidence game, a swindle."

"Mr. Tabatchnick, did the news story of Sol Kipper's suicide mention the value of his estate?"

"Of course not!"

"During my meeting with Reape, he said, quote, How much is that estate—four mil? Five mil? Unquote. Was that a close estimate of the estate, Mr. Tabatchnick?"

"Close enough," he said in a low voice. "It's about four million six."

"Well, how would Reape have known that if he hadn't been intimately involved with the Kipper family in some way? Surely his knowledge of the size of the estate is a fairly solid indication that he had the information he claimed."

Leopold Tabatchnick sighed deeply. Then he sat brooding, head lowered. He pulled at his lower lip. I was tempted to slap his hand and tell him his lips protruded enough.

I don't know how long we sat there in silence. Finally, Tabatchnick sighed again and straightened up. He put his thick hands on the tabletop, palms down.

"All right," he said, "I realize what you are implying. You feel that if Martin Reape told the truth and had evidence to upset the will of Sol Kipper, then an investigation into Kipper's suicide would be justified."

"The alleged suicide," I said. "Yes, sir, that's the way I feel."

"Very well," he said. "You may conduct a discreet inquiry. I repeat, a *discreet* inquiry. To avoid prejudicing your investigation. I will not disclose to you at this time the principal beneficiaries of Sol Kipper's estate."

"As you wish, sir," I said. "But it would help a great deal if you would give me some background on the man and his family. You mentioned that he had been a personal friend of yours for fifty-five years."

"Yes," he said. "We were classmates at CCNY together. I went on to law school and Sol went into his father's textile business. But we kept in touch and saw each other frequently. He was best man at my wedding, and I at his. Our wives were good friends. That was Sol's first wife. She died six years ago and Sol remarried."

Did I detect a note of disapproval in his voice?

"Sol was an enormously successful businessman. After his father's death, he became president of Kipmar Textiles, and expanded to include knitting mills in New England, South Carolina, Spain, and Israel. They went public ten years ago, and Sol became a wealthy man. He had three sons and one daughter by his first wife. All his children are grown now, of course, and married. Sol had eleven grandchildren. Shortly after his second marriage, he semiretired and turned over the day-to-day operations of Kipmar Textiles to two of his sons. The third son is a doctor in Los Angeles. His daughter lives in Boca Raton, Florida. What else would you care to know?"

"The second wife, sir—what can you tell me about her?"

"She is younger than Sol was—considerably younger. I believe she was on the stage. Briefly. Her name is Tippi."

Now I was certain I heard that note of disapproval in his voice.

"Yes, sir. And now the man himself. What was he like?"

"Sol Kipper was one of the dearest, sweetest men it has ever been my good fortune to know. He was generous to a fault. A fine, loving husband and an understanding father and grandfather. His children worshiped him. They took his death very hard."

"Why did he commit suicide, sir—if he did? Was there any reason for it?"

Tabatchnick wagged his big head sadly. "Sol was the worst hypochondriac I've ever known or heard about. He was continually running to doctors with imaginary physical ailments. It was a joke to his family and friends, but we could never convince him that he was in excellent health, even when doctor after doctor told him the same thing. He had only to read a medical article on some obscure illness and he was certain he had the symptoms. He dosed himself with all kinds of nostrums and, to my personal knowledge, swallowed more than fifty vitamin pills and mineral capsules a day. He was like that when he was young, and it worsened as he grew older, sometimes resulting in extreme depression. I assume he committed suicide while in that condition."

"After making an appointment with you to execute a new will?"

"That's the way it happened," Mr. Tabatchnick said crossly.

"I think that's about all, sir," I said, standing. "I'll report to you if there is anything you should know."

"By all means," he said. "If there is anything I can do to help, please let me know. You may call me at home, should that become necessary. I am in the book. I am depending on you, Mr. Bigg, to conduct your investigation quietly and diplomatically."

"Yes, sir, I understand. I'd like to start by talking to that officer who investigated Mr. Kipper's death. Do you happen to recall his name?"

"Not offhand, but Miss Potts has his name and phone number. I'll instruct her to give them to you."

"Mr. Tabatchnick, the detective will probably want to know the reason for our interest. May I tell him about Martin Reape?"

He pondered that for a while.

"No," he said finally, "I'd prefer you didn't. If nothing comes of this, the role of Reape will be of no significance, and I don't wish anyone else to know of our willingness to deal with him. If the detective asks the reason for our interest, tell him merely that it concerns the estate and insurance. I am sure that will satisfy him. You might take him to lunch or dinner. I suspect he may be more forthcoming over a few drinks and a good meal. I will approve any expense vouchers. Any *reasonable* expense vouchers."

Detective second-grade Percy Stilton was the cop on the Kipper case. I got his number from Thelma Potts. I called him the moment I returned to my office, but the man who answered said Detective Stilton would not come on duty until 4:00 P.M. I said I'd call him then.

I started typing notes of my conversation with Mr. Tabatchnick, leaving out all mention of Marty Reape. When I had done that I phoned the Stonehouse apartment; a very throaty voice answered. I assumed that it was the maid, Olga Eklund. Mrs. Stonehouse came on in that trilly voice. I asked her questions about her husband's health. He had been well at the time of his disappearance but had recently been ill.

"It started late in the summer," she said. "But it got progressively worse. October and November were very bad. But then he just snapped out of it. He was a Scorpio, you know."

"October and November?" I repeated. Then he must have recovered about a month prior to his disappearance.

"What was the nature of his illness, Mrs. Stonehouse?"

"Oh, I don't really know," she said blithely. "My husband was so tight-lipped about things like that. The flu, I suppose, or a virus that just hung on. He simply refused to go to a doctor, but then he got so weak and miserable he finally had to go. Went several times, as a matter of fact, and the doctor did all kinds of tests. He must have discovered what it was, because Yale recovered very quickly."

"Could you tell me the doctor's name, Mrs. Stonehouse?"

"His name?" she said. "Now what *is* his name? Morton, I think, or something like that."

I heard her call, "Olga!" and there was confused talking in the distance. Then Mrs. Stonehouse came back on the phone. "Stolowitz," she said. "Dr. Morris Stolowitz."

I looked up the phone number of Dr. Morris Stolowitz. He was on West 74th Street, within easy walking distance of the Stonehouse apartment. I called, and a woman's voice answered: "Doctor's office." Doctor was busy with a patient. I left my name and number and asked that he get back to me.

I had my doubts that Dr. Stolowitz would ever return my call. I was debating the wisdom of asking Mrs. Stonehouse to intercede for me, when Hamish Hooter came barging into my office and threw my pay envelope onto the desk.

"See here," he said.

"What is it now, Hooter?"

"I've been trying to tell you in a nice way," he said, sucking his teeth noisily. "But apparently you're not catching on. Yetta Apatoff and I are an item. I want you to stop bothering her."

"If I am *bothering* her," I said, "which I sincerely doubt, let the lady tell me herself."

He muttered something threatening and rushed from my office, banging the door.

So, of course, I had to call Yetta immediately.

"Hi, it's Josh," I said, wondering why my speech became so throaty and—well, *intimate*, when I spoke to her.

"Hi, Josh," she said in her breathy, little girl's voice. "Long time no see."

Now did that sound like a woman I was bothering?

"How about lunch today?" I suggested. "Just to celebrate payday?"

"Ooh, marvy!" she said. "Let's go to the Chink place on Third."

When I went out to her reception desk at noon, she was waiting for me, her coat on her arm, a fluffy powder-blue beret perched enchantingly on her blonde ringlets. She was wearing a tightly fitted knitted suit of a slightly darker blue, and when I saw that divine topography, I felt the familiar constriction of my breathing and my knee joints seemed excessively oiled.

While we walked over to Third Avenue, she took my arm, chatting innocently, apparently unaware of what her soft grip was doing to my heartbeat and respiration. As always when I was with her, I was blind and deaf to our surroundings. All my senses were zeroed in on her, and once, when she shivered with cold, said, "Brrr!" and hugged my arm to her yielding breast, I almost sobbed with joy.

In the restaurant all I wanted was to look at her, watch those perfect white teeth bite into a dumpling, note how the soft column of her throat moved when she swallowed, and how she patted her mouth delicately with a paper napkin when a small burp rose to her lips.

"Oh, Josh," she said, between bites and swallows, "did I tell you about this absolutely marvy sweater I saw in this store on Madison? I'd love to get it, but it's *soo* expensive, and also it's cut *way* down. I mean it really is a plunging neckline, and I suppose I'd have to wear a scarf with it, something that would cover me a little if I wore it to work, or maybe a blouse under it, but that would spoil the lines because it's *sooo* clinging, and it's like a forest green. Do you like green, Josh?"

"Love green," I said hoarsely.

"It costs *sooo* much, but maybe just this once I'll spend more than I should because I believe that if you really want something, you should get it no matter what it costs. I have this saying, 'I don't want anything but the best,' and that's really the way I feel, and I suppose you think I'm just terrible."

"Of course not. You deserve the—"

"Oh well," she said, giggling, "maybe I'll buy it as a birthday present to me from myself."

"It's your birthday?" I cried.

"Oh not yet, Josh. Not until next week. But I certainly hope you don't think I'm, you know, telling you that for any, you know, ulterior motive like I was angling for a present or anything, because I'm certainly not that kind of a girl."

"I know that, Yetta."

She reached across the table to put a hand briefly on mine.

We got fortune cookies with our ice cream. Yetta's fortune was A NEW LIFE AWAITS YOU. Mine read: A NEW LIFE AWAITS YOU.

Yetta stared at me, suddenly solemn.

"Josh," she said, "isn't that the strangest thing that ever happened to you? I mean, we're *both* going to have a new life. I certainly think that's strange. You don't suppose—?"

She broke off, glanced at her watch.

"Goodness," she said, "look at the time! I've really got to get back. Duty calls!"

We strolled back to the office together. Just before we got there I said, "Yetta, that store where you saw the sweater you liked..."

"Between 36th and 37th," she said. "On the west side. It's in the window."

I resolutely stayed in my office all afternoon and worked hard on routine inquiries from the junior partners and associates. A few minutes after four o'clock, I called the officer who had investigated Sol Kipper's suicide. He answered the phone formally.

"Detective Percy Stilton."

"Sir," I said, "my name is Joshua Bigg. I work for the legal firm of Tabatchnick, Orsini, Reilly, and Teitelbaum. Mr. Tabatchnick gave me your name and address. He said you investigated the suicide of Solomon Kipper."

"Kipper?" he said. "Oh yes, that's right. I caught that one."

"I was hoping I could talk to you about it," I said. "This concerns a matter of estate and insurance claims."

"I can't show you the file," he said.

"Oh no," I said hastily. "Nothing like that. I mean, this isn't official. Very informal. You won't be asked to testify. I just wanted to ask a few questions."

"You say this concerns insurance?"

"Yes, sir."

"Uh-huh," he said. He was silent a moment. Then: "Well, I guess it wouldn't do any harm. You want to come over here?"

"I was wondering if we might meet somewhere. Dinner perhaps?"

"Dinner?" he said. "You on an expense account?"

"Yes, sir," I said.

"Great," he said. "I'm getting tired of pizza. Want to make it tonight?"

"That would be fine."

"I have to do some work later at Midtown Precinct North. That's on West 54th Street. I should be finished about eight o'clock, and be able to break loose for a while. I'll meet you at eight or thereabouts at the Cheshire Cheese on West 51st Street between Eighth and Ninth. It's veddy British."

I was tidying up my desk, getting ready to leave, when my phone rang. That was a welcome change.

"Joshua Bigg," I answered.

"Just a moment, Mr. Bigg," a woman's voice said. "Dr. Morris Stolowitz calling." When he came on he was loud and irascible. "What's this about Professor Stonehouse?" he demanded.

I told him who I was and whom I worked for, and explained that I wanted to talk to him. He wanted to know where I got his name and snarled that the doctor-patient relationship was confidential. In the end he said he could see me for five minutes the next day. He slammed down the phone and I decided to call it a day.

Since my route home took me to Madison Avenue, I found the store Yetta Apatoff had mentioned. The green sweater was in the window, displayed on a mannequin. Yetta hadn't exaggerated; that neckline didn't plunge, it submerged. About as far down as my spirits when I saw the price: $59.95. Maybe she'd like a nice handkerchief instead. I decided to think about it for a while; after all, her birthday wasn't until next week. I continued down Madison to 23rd Street, took a crosstown bus to Ninth Avenue, then walked home from there. Captain Shank wasn't on the third-floor landing to greet me, but I could hear his TV set blaring behind his closed door. I sneaked into my own apartment and shut my door ever so softly. I liked the old man, I really did, but I was not partial to muscatel.

At 7:30 I took the Eighth Avenue bus uptown and arrived at 51st Street ahead of time. I found the Cheshire Cheese, a few steps down from the sidewalk. It was, as Stilton had said, an English-style restaurant with a long bar on the left as you entered, and small tables for two along the right wall. In the rear, I could see a larger dining room with tables for four.

It was a pleasantly dim place, redolent with appetizing cooking odors and decorated with horse brasses and coats of arms. The theatre crowd had already departed, and there were few diners: two men together, two couples, and a foursome. No Detective Stilton.

I waited near the entrance until a slender man wearing a long white apron came from behind the bar and approached me. He was polishing a wine goblet with a cloth.

"Sir?" he said.

"I'm meeting a gentleman," I said. "Perhaps I'll take a table and have a drink while I'm waiting."

"Very good," he said, looking around. "How about the corner?"

So that's where I was seated after I had hung up my coat. My back was to the wall, and I could watch the entrance. A waiter came over and I ordered a Scotch and water.

I had taken only one sip when a tall black man came into the Cheshire Cheese and looked around. He took off his coat and hat, stowed them on the open rack, and came walking directly toward me with a light, bouncy stride. I struggled out of my chair to shake his hand.

"Mr. Bigg?" he said. "I'm Stilton." As he shifted the free chair from my right to sit opposite me, the waiter scurried over to move the pewter serving platter, napkin, utensils, and water goblet in front of the detective.

"Waiting long?" Stilton asked.

"Just got here," I told him. "I'm having a drink. Something for you?"

He ordered a dry martini straight up, no twist or olive. It arrived with lightning speed.

"All right?" I asked him.

"Just right," he said. "How long have you been a Chief Investigator?"

He smiled at my shock. I managed to regain composure.

"Two years. But I was an assistant for two years before that. To a man named Roscoe Dollworth. He was with the Department. Did you know him?"

"Dolly? Oh hell yes. He was some kind of a cop before the sauce got to him. He still alive?"

"He's retired and living in Florida."

"I think we better order," he said. "We can talk while we're eating. I've got maybe an hour before the loot starts getting antsy. I know exactly what I want. Roast beef on the bone, very rare. Yorkshire pudding. Whatever vegetable they're pushing. And a salad. And a mug of ale."

I had a steak-and-kidney pie, salad, and ale.

"About this Kipper thing," Stilton said abruptly. "You say your interest is in the insurance?"

"The claim," I said, nodding. "We have to justify the claim with the company that insured him."

"What company is that?"

"Uh, Metropolitan Life," I said.

"That's odd," he said. "About a week after Kipper died, I got a visit from a claim adjuster from Prudential. He said they had insured Kipper."

He looked at me steadily. I think I was blushing. I know I couldn't meet his stare. I may have hung my head.

"You don't mind if I call you Josh, do you?" Stilton asked gently.

"No, I don't mind."

"You can call me Perce," he offered. "You see, Josh, two years in this business, or even four years, aren't enough to learn how to be a really good liar. The first rule is only lie when you have to. And when you do lie, keep it as close to the truth as you can and keep it simple. Don't try to scam it up. If you do, you're sure to get in trouble. When I asked you if your interest was the insurance, you should have said yes and let it go at that. I probably would have swallowed it. It's logical that lawyers handling the estate would be interested in a dead man's insurance. But then you started fumbling around with justifying the claim, and I knew you were jiving me."

"And I didn't even know the name of the company," I said sadly.

He put his head back and laughed, so loudly that the other diners turned to look.

"Oh, Josh," he said. "I don't know what company insured Kipper either. No claim adjuster ever visited me. I just said Prudential to catch your reaction. When you collapsed, I knew you were running a game on me."

Our food was served, and we didn't speak until the waiter left the table.

"Then you won't tell me about the Kipper case?" I said.

"Why the hell not?" he said, astonished. "I'm willing to cooperate. It's all a matter of public record. That boss of yours, the guy with the fish, could probably even get a look at the file if he pushed hard enough. How's the steak-and-kidney pie?"

"Delicious," I said. "I'm really enjoying it. Is your roast beef rare enough?"

"If it was any rarer, it would still be breathing. All right, now let me tell you about the Kipper thing. I went over the file before I left the office, just to refresh my memory. Here's what happened . . ."

As he spoke, and ate steadily, I glanced up frequently from my own plate to look at him.

I guessed him to be in his early fifties. He was about six feet tall, with narrow shoulders and hips. Very willowy. He was dressed with great care and polish, in a double-breasted blue pinstripe that closed at the lower button with a graceful sweep of a wide lapel. His shirt was a snowy white broadcloth with a short, button-down collar. He wore a polka-dot bowtie with butterfly wings. He had a gold watch on one wrist and a gold chain identification bracelet on the other. If he was wearing a gun—and I presumed he was—it certainly didn't show.

His color was hard to distinguish in the dim light, but I judged it to be a dark brown with a reddish tinge, not quite

cordovan but almost. His hair was jet black and lay flat on his
skull in closely cropped waves. His hands were long, fingernails manicured.

His eyes were set deep and wide apart. His nose was somewhat splayed, and his thick lips turned outward. High cheekbones, like an Indian. He had a massive jaw, almost square,
and a surprisingly thick, corded neck. Small ears were flat to
his head.

I would not call him a handsome man, but his features were
pleasant enough. He looked amused, assured, and competent.
When he was pondering, or trying to find the right word or
phrase, he had the habit of putting his tongue inside his cheek,
bulging it.

I think I was most impressed by the cool elegance of the
man, totally unlike what I envisioned a New York police detective would be. He really looked like a business executive
or a confident salesman. I thought this might be an image he
projected deliberately, as an aid in his work.

"Let's start with the time sequence," he began. "This happened on January 24, a Wednesday. The first call went to 911,
and was logged in at 3:06. That's P.M., the afternoon. A squad
car was dispatched from the One-Nine Precinct and arrived at
the premises at 3:14. Not bad, huh? Two cops in the squad.
They took a look at what had happened and called their precinct. This was at 3:21. Everyone was doing their jobs. We
don't fuck up *all* the time, you know. The squeal came to the
Homicide Zone where I work at 3:29. It didn't sound like a
homicide, but these things have to be checked out. I arrived
at the scene at 3:43. I was with my partner, Detective Lou
Emandola. We no sooner got in the place when the loot called
and pulled Lou away. Some nut was holding hostages in a
supermarket over on First Avenue, and they were calling out
the troops.

"So Lou took off and I was left alone. I mean I was the
only homicide guy there. There were plenty of cops, the am-
bulance guys, the Medical Examiner, the lab truck technicians,
a photographer, and so forth. A real mob scene. I questioned
the witnesses then, but they were so spooked I didn't get much
out of them, so I left. I went back again that evening, and I
went twice more. Also, I talked to neighbors, the ME who did
the PM, your Mr. Tabatchnick, Kipper's doctor, and Kipper's

sons. After all this, it looked like an open-and-shut suicide, and that's how we closed it out. Any questions so far?"

"Who made the first call to 911?" I asked.

"I'm getting to that," Stilton said. "I've hardly started yet." He paused, drained his tankard of ale, and looked at me. I called the waiter and ordered two more. The detective continued:

"Here's the story . . . First of all, you've got to understand the scene of the crime, although there was no crime, unless you want to call suicide a crime. Anyway, that townhouse is a palace. Huge? You wouldn't believe. You could sleep half of East Harlem in there. It's six floors high and it's got a double-basement, plus an elevator. I never did get around to counting all the rooms. Thirty at least, I'd guess, and most of them empty. I mean they were furnished, but no one lived in them. A terrible waste of space. The top floor, the sixth, is one big room fronting on the street. It runs halfway back the depth of the building. The rear half is an open terrace. The room up front is used for parties. It has a big-screen TV, bar, hi-fi equipment, movie projector, and so forth. The rear terrace has plants, and trees, and outdoor furniture. Sol Kipper took his dive from that terrace. It has a wall around it thirty-eight inches high—I measured it—but that wouldn't be hard to climb over, even for an old guy like Kipper."

He paused again to take a swallow of his new ale. I used the interruption to dig into my dinner. I had been so engrossed in his story, not wanting to miss anything, that I had neglected to eat. He had finished most of his beef and was now whittling scraps off the rib, handling his knife with the dexterity of a surgeon.

"The nearer the bone," he said, "the sweeter the meat. All right, here's what I found out: At 2:30 P.M. on that Wednesday, there were five people in the townhouse. Sol Kipper, his wife, Tippi—she's a looker, that one—and the three servants. Sol and Tippi were in their bedroom, the master bedroom on the fifth floor. The servants were on the ground floor, in and around the kitchen. Tippi was expecting a guest, a Protestant minister named Knurr. He was a frequent visitor, and he was usually served a drink or two and some little sandwiches. The servants were setting up for him.

"Mrs. Kipper came downstairs about ten minutes to three to make sure everything was ready for the Reverend Knurr. Now we got four people downstairs, and only Sol Kipper upstairs—right? In the back of the townhouse there's a patio. Most of it is paved with tiles, and there's aluminum furniture out there: a cocktail table, chairs, an umbrella table—stuff like that. Farther in the rear is a small garden: a tree, shrubs, flowers in the summer, and so on. But most of the patio is paved with tiles. There are two ways of getting out there: one door through the kitchen, and French doors from the dining room.

"A few minutes after three, the four people hear a tremendous crash and a big, heavy thump on the patio. They all hear it. They rush to the kitchen door and look out, and there's Sol Kipper. He was squashed on the tiles. That was the thump they heard. And one of his legs had hit the umbrella table, dented it, and overturned it. That was the crash they heard. They ran out, took one look, and knew Sol Kipper was as dead as a mackerel—no joke intended."

Stilton finished his dinner. He pushed back his chair, crossed his knees, and adjusted his trouser crease. He lighted a cigarette and sipped at what remained of his ale.

"Instant hysteria," he went on. "Mrs. Kipper fainted, the cook started bawling, and right about then the front doorbell rang."

"The guest?" I said.

"Right. Reverend Knurr. The butler went to the front door, let him in, and screamed out what had just happened. I gather this Knurr more or less took charge then. He's a put-together guy. He called 911, and he got Tippi Kipper revived, and the others quieted down. By the time I got there, they had found the suicide note. How about some coffee?"

"Sure," I said. "Dessert? A brandy?"

"A brandy would be fine," he said. "May I suggest Rémy Martin?"

So I ordered two of those and a pot of coffee.

"I've got a lot of questions," I said tentatively.

"Thought you might have," he said. "Shoot."

"Are you sure there were only four people in the house besides Sol Kipper?"

"Absolutely. We searched every room when we got there.

No one. And the witnesses swear no one left."

"The time sequence you gave me of what happened—did you get that from Mrs. Kipper?"

"And the servants. And Reverend Knurr. All their stories matched within a minute or so. None of them sounded rehearsed. And if you're figuring maybe they were all in on it together, forget it. Why should they all gang up on the old guy? According to the servants, he treated them just right. A fast man with a buck. The wife says the marriage was happy. None of them showed any signs of a struggle. No scratches or bruises—nothing like that. And if one of them, or all of them wanted to get rid of Sol, it would have been a lot easier to slip something into one of his pill bottles. You should have seen his medicine chest. He had a drugstore up there. And, of course, there was the suicide note. In his writing."

"Do you remember what it said?" I asked. "Exactly?"

"It was addressed to his wife. It said: 'Dear Tippi. Please forgive me. I am sorry for all the trouble I've caused.' It was signed 'Sol.'"

I sighed. Our coffee and cognac arrived, and we sat a moment in silence, then sipped the Rémy Martin. Very different from the California brand I drank at home.

"Did you check the wall on the terrace?"

Stilton looked at me without expression.

"You're all right," he said. "Dolly did a good job on you. Yes, we checked the terrace wall. It's a roughly finished cement painted pink. There were scrape marks on the top where Kipper went over. And there were crumbs of pink cement on the toes of his shoes, stuck in the welt. Any more questions?"

"No," I said, depressed. "Maybe I'll think of some later, but I can't think of any now. So it was closed out as a suicide?"

"Did we have any choice?" Detective Percy Stilton said almost angrily. "We have a zillion unsolved homicides to work on. I mean, out-and-out, definite homicides. How much time can we spend on a case that looks like a suicide no matter how you slice it? So we closed the Kipper file."

I took a swallow of brandy, larger than I should have, and choked on it. Stilton looked at me amusedly.

"Go down the wrong way?" he said.

I nodded. "And this suicide," I said, still gasping, "it sticks in my throat, too. Perce, how do you feel about it? I mean personally? Are you absolutely satisfied in your own mind that Sol Kipper committed suicide?"

He stared at me, bulging his cheek with his tongue, as if trying to make up his mind. Then he poured himself more coffee.

"It's trade-off time," he said softly.

"What?" I said. "I don't understand."

"A trade-off," he said. "Between you and me. You tell me what your interest is in how Sol Kipper died and I'll tell you what I personally think."

I took a deep breath and wished I had never asked Mr. Tabatchnick if I could tell the detective about Marty Reape. Tabatchnick had definitely said no. If I hadn't asked, I could have traded with Stilton without a qualm. I pondered where my loyalty lay. I decided.

"It means my job," I said, "if any of this gets out."

"No one will hear it from me," Stilton said.

"All right," I said. "I trust you. I've got to trust you. Here it is . . ."

And I told him all about Marty Reape. Everything, beginning with his telephone call to Mr. Tabatchnick, then my call to him, my meeting with him, what he said and what I said, the decision to meet his price, and how he died Wednesday evening under the wheels of a subway train.

Stilton listened closely to this recital, not changing expression. But he never took his eyes off me, and I noticed he chain-smoked while I was speaking. He was about to light another when I finished. He broke the cigarette in two and threw it down.

"I smoke too damned much," he said disgustedly.

"What do you think?" I said, leaning forward eagerly, "about Marty Reape?"

"Your boss could be right," he said slowly. "Reape could have been a cheap chiseler trying to pull a con."

"But he was killed!" I said vehemently.

"Was he?" Stilton said. "You don't know that. And even if he was, that doesn't prove he had the information he claimed. Maybe he tried to pull his little scam on some other people who aren't as civilized as you and your boss, and they stepped on him."

"But he knew the size of the Kipper estate," I argued.

"Doesn't that prove he knew the family or had some dealings with them?"

"Maybe," he said. "And maybe Sol Kipper told someone what's in his will, and maybe that someone told Marty Reape. Or maybe Reape just made a lucky guess about the size of the estate."

It was very important to me to convince this professional detective that my suspicions about the death of Sol Kipper had merit and justified further investigation. So, having come this far in betraying Mr. Tabatchnick's trust, I felt I might as well go all the way.

"There's another thing," I said. "On the morning of the day Sol Kipper died, he called Tabatchnick and set up an appointment. He said he wanted to change his will."

Stilton had been turning his cigarette lighter over and over in his long fingers, looking down at it. Now he stopped his fiddling and raised his eyes slowly until he was staring at me.

"Jesus," he breathed, "the plot thickens."

"All right," I said, sitting back. "That's my trade. Now let's have yours. Do you really think Sol Kipper committed suicide?"

He didn't hesitate.

"That's the official verdict," he said, "and the file is closed. But there were things about it that bugged me from the start. Little things. Not enough to justify calling it homicide, but things, three, to be exact, that just didn't set right with me. First of all, committing suicide by jumping from the sixth floor is far from a sure thing. You can jump from a higher place than that and still survive.

"That's why most leapers go higher up than six stories. They want to kill themselves, but they don't want to take the chance of being crippled for life. This Kipper owned a textile company. He was semiretired, his sons run the business, but Kipper went there for a few hours three or four days a week. The office is on the thirty-fourth floor of a building in the garment center. He could have gone out a window there and they'd have had to pick him up with a blotter."

"Perce, what actually killed him when he went off the sixth-floor terrace?"

"He landed on his head. Crushed his skull. All right, it could happen from six floors. He could also break both arms and legs, have internal injuries, and still live. That could happen, too. It couldn't happen from thirty-four floors. That's the first thing that bothered me: a suicide from the sixth floor. It's like trying to blow your brains out with a BB gun.

"The second thing was this: When jumpers go out, from a window, ledge, balcony, whatever, they usually drop straight down. I mean, they just take one giant step out into space. They don't really leap. Practically all the jumpers I've seen have landed within six feet of the side of the building. They usually squash on the sidewalk. When they go from a really high place, maybe their bodies start to windmill. But even then they hit the sidewalk or, at the most, crush in the top of a parked car. But I've never seen any who were more than, say, six or seven feet out from the side of the building. Kipper's body was almost ten feet away."

I puzzled that out.

"Perce, you mean someone threw him over?"

"Who? There were four other people in that house—remember? Kipper weighed about one-sixty. None of the women could have lifted him over that terrace wall and thrown him so he landed ten feet from the side of the building. And the only man, the butler, is so fat it's all he can do to stand up. Maybe Kipper just took a flying leap."

"An old man like that?"

"It's possible," he said stubbornly. "The third thing is even flimsier than the first two. It's that suicide note. It said: 'I am sorry for all the trouble I've caused.' Get it? '*Caused.*' Please forgive me for something I've done. That note sounds to me like he's referring to something he did in the past, not something he was planning to do in a few minutes. Also, the note is perfectly legible, written in straight lines with a steady hand. Not the kind of handwriting you'd expect from a guy so mixed up in his skull that a few minutes later he was going to take a high dive from his terrace. But again, it's possible. I told you it's flimsy. All the things that bug me are flimsy."

"I don't think they are," I said hotly. "I think they're important."

He gave me a half-smile, looked at his watch, and began to stow away his cigarette case and lighter.

"Listen," I said desperately, "where do we go from here?"

"Beats me," he said.

"Can't you—" I began.

"Reopen the case?" he said. "No way can I do that on the evidence we've got. If I even suggested it, my loot would have me committed. You're the Chief Investigator—so investigate."

"But I don't know where to start," I burst out. "I know I should talk to the Kipper family and servants, but I don't know what excuse I can give them for asking questions."

"Tell them what you told me," he advised. "Say you're collecting information to justify the insurance claim. They'll buy it."

"You didn't," I pointed out.

"They're not as cynical as I am," he said, grinning. "They'll believe what you tell them. Just remember what I said about lying. Keep it simple; don't try to gussy it up. While you're nosing around, I'll see what I can find out about how Marty Reape died. From what you told me, it's probably been closed as an accident—but you never know. Keep in touch. If anything turns up, you can always reach me at that number you've got or leave a message and I'll call back. Can I call you at Tabatchnick and whatever?"

I thought about that.

"Better not, Perce," I said. "I'd rather keep our, uh, relationship confidential."

"Sure," he said. "I understand."

"I'll give you my home phone number. I'm in almost every night."

"That'll do fine."

He copied my number in a little notebook he carried. It was black pinseal with gold corners. Like all his possessions, it looked smart and expensive.

I paid the bill, left a tip, and we walked toward the door.

"I still don't think it was a suicide," I said.

"You may be right," he said mildly. "But thinking something and proving it are entirely different. As any cop can tell you."

We put on our coats and moved out onto the sidewalk. He was wearing a navy blue chesterfield and a black homburg. A dandy.

"Thanks for the dinner, Josh," he said. "Real good."

"My pleasure," I said.

"Which way you going?" he asked.

"Ninth Avenue. I'll catch a downtown bus. I live in Chelsea."

"I'll walk you over," he said, and we headed westward.

"Don't give up on this one, Josh," he said, suddenly earnest. "I can't do it; my plate is full. But I've got the feeling someone is jerking us around, and I don't like it."

"I'm not going to give up," I said.

"Good," he said. "And thanks for meeting with me and filling me in.

"Listen," he added hesitantly, "if what you think turns out to be right, and someone snuffed Sol Kipper and pushed Marty Reape under a train, then they're not nice people—you know? So be careful."

"Oh sure. I will be."

"You carry a piece?" he asked suddenly.

It was a few seconds before I understood what he meant.

"Oh no," I said. "I don't believe in violence."

He sighed deeply.

"And a little child shall lead them," he said. "Good night, Josh."

8

I AWOKE THE next morning bright-eyed and bushy-tailed. Although Detective Stilton had insisted that all we had were unsubstantiated suspicions, what he had told me confirmed my belief that the death of Sol Kipper was not a suicide. And I was convinced that Stilton, despite his cautious disclaimers, felt the same way.

It had snowed slightly overnight; there was a light, powdery dusting on sidewalks and cars. But it was melting rapidly as the new sun warmed. The sky was azure; the air sparkled. It suited my mood perfectly, and as I set out for my appointment with the missing Yale Stonehouse's doctor, I took the weather as an augury of a successful day.

Dr. Stolowitz had his offices on the street floor of a yellow brick apartment house that towered over neighboring brownstones. I arrived at 8:15. His receptionist was tall, lanky, with a mobcap of frizzy red curls. Her thin features seemed set in a permanent expression of discontent. I noticed her extremely long, carmined fingernails and a bracelet of a dozen charms on her bony wrist that jangled when she moved. She greeted me with something less than warmth.

"Joshua Bigg to see Dr. Stolowitz," I said, smiling hopefully.

"You're early," she snapped. "Sit down and wait."

So I sat down and waited, coat and hat on my lap.

At precisely 8:25, another nurse came out—a little one this time—and beckoned to me.

"Doctor will see you now," she said.

The man standing behind the littered desk was of medium height, stocky, with a heavy belly bulging in front of his short white jacket. He was wearing rimless spectacles with thick lenses that gave him a popeyed look. He was smoking a black cigar; the air was rancid with fumes.

"Good morning, Doctor," I said.

"Five minutes," he snapped. "No more."

"I understand that, sir."

"Just what is your connection with Yale Stonehouse?" he demanded.

"As I explained to you on the phone," I said patiently, "I'm investigating the Professor's disappearance."

"Are you a private detective?" he said suspiciously.

"No, sir," I said. "I am employed by the Professor's attorneys. You may check with Mrs. Stonehouse if you wish."

He growled.

He hadn't asked me to be seated.

"All right," he said. "Ask your questions. I may answer and I may not."

"Could you tell me when Professor Stonehouse consulted you, sir?"

He picked up a file from his desk and flipped through it rapidly, the cigar still clenched between his teeth.

"Seven times during October and November of last year. Do you want the exact dates of those visits?"

"No, sir, that won't be necessary. But Mrs. Stonehouse told me his illness started late last summer."

"So?"

"But he did not consult you until October?"

"I just told you that," he said peevishly.

"Could you tell me if Professor Stonehouse consulted any other physician prior to coming to you?"

"Now how the hell would I know that?"

"He mentioned no prior treatment?"

"He did not."

"Doctor," I said, "I don't expect you to tell me the nature of the Professor's illness, but—"

"Damned right I won't," he interrupted.

"But could you tell me if the Professor's illness, if untreated, would have proved fatal?"

His eyes flickered. Then he ducked his head, looked down, began to grind out his cigar butt in an enormous crystal ashtray. When he spoke, his voice was surprisingly mild.

"An ingrown toenail can be fatal if untreated."

"But when Professor Stonehouse stopped coming to see you, was he cured?"

"He was recovering," he said, the ill-tempered note coming back into his voice.

"Was his illness contagious?"

"What's this?" he said angrily, "a game of Twenty Questions?"

"I am not asking you to tell me the specific illness, Doctor," I said. "Just whether or not it was contagious."

He looked at me shrewdly.

"No, it was not a venereal disease," he said. "That's what you're really asking, isn't it?"

"Yes, sir. What would you say was the Professor's general mental attitude?"

"A difficult, cantankerous patient." (Talk about the pot calling the kettle black!) "But if you mean did he exhibit any symptoms of mental disability not connected with his illness, the answer is no, he did not."

He didn't realize what he had just revealed: that there were symptoms of mental disorder connected to the Professor's ailment.

"Did he ever, in any way, give you a hint of indication that he intended to desert his wife and family?"

"He did not."

"Would you characterize your patient's illness as a disease, Doctor?"

He looked at the clock on the wall.

"Your five minutes are up," he said. "Goodbye, Mr. Bigg."

I put on my coat in the outer office. Three or four people were waiting to see the doctor.

"Thank you very much," I said to the receptionist, giving

her my best little-boy smile. It doesn't always work, but this time it did; she thawed.

"He's a bear, isn't he?" she whispered.

"Worse," I whispered back. "Is he always like that?"

She rolled her eyes. "Always," she said. "Listen, may I ask you a personal question?"

"Five feet, three and three-eighths inches," I said, and waved goodbye.

I stopped at the first phone booth I came to and called the office. I left a message for Thelma Potts telling her that I was engaged in outside work and would call later to let her know when I'd be in.

I took the Broadway bus down to 49th Street and walked over to the decrepit building where Marty Reape had his office. His name was still listed on the lobby directory, but when I got to the ninth floor, the door to Room 910 was open and a bearded man in stained painter's overalls was busy scraping with a razor blade at the outside of the frosted glass panel. Half of the legend, MARTIN REAPE: PRIVATE INVESTIGATIONS, was already gone.

I stood behind the painter and peeked through the open door. The room was totally bare. No desk, chair, file cabinet, or anything else. Just stained walls, dust-encrusted window, cracked linoleum on the floor.

"Want something?" the painter demanded.

"Do you know what happened to the furniture in this office?"

"Ask the manager," he said.

"Is this office for rent?"

"Ask the manager."

"And where will I find the manager?"

"Downstairs."

"Could you tell me his name?"

He didn't answer.

In the rear of the lobby was a steel door with a square of cardboard taped to it: MANAGER'S OFFICE. I opened the door with some effort. A flight of steel steps led steeply downward. I descended cautiously, hanging on to the gritty banister. A gloomy, cement-lined corridor stretched away to the back of the building. The ceiling was a maze of pipes and ducts. At the end of this tunnel was a scarred wooden door. I pushed in.

It was like going into a prisoner's cell. The only thing
lacking was bars. Cement ceiling, walls, floor. No windows.
The furniture looked like tenants' discards. There were two
people in that cubbyhole. A very attractive Oriental girl clattered away at an ancient Underwood, pausing occasionally to
brush her long black hair away from her face. A small brown
man sat behind the larger desk, talking rapidly on the telephone
in a language I could not identify. There was a neat brass plate
on his desk: CLARENCE NG, MANAGER.

Neither of the occupants had looked at me when I entered.
I waited patiently. Mr. Ng rattled on in his incomprehensible
language, then suddenly switched to English.

"The same to you, shmuck!" he screamed, and banged down
the phone. Then he looked at me.

"Ah, may I be of service, sir?" he asked softly.

"Perhaps you can help me," I said. "I'm looking for Martin
Reape, Room 910. But his office is completely empty."

"Ah," he said. "Mr. Reape is no longer with us."

"Oh?" I said. "Well, could you tell me where he moved?"

"Ah," Mr. Ng said. "Mr. Reape did not move. Mr. Reape
is dead."

"Dead?" I cried. "Good heavens! When did this happen?"

"Two days ago. Mr. Reape fell under a subway train. You
were, ah, a friend of his?"

"A client," I said. "This is terrible. He had some very
important papers belonging to me. Do you know what happened
to his files?"

"His, ah, widow," Mr. Ng said. "She arrived yesterday and
removed everything."

"And you let her?" I exclaimed.

The manager turned his palms upward and shrugged. "A
man's widow is entitled to his possessions."

"But are you certain it *was* the widow?"

"Ah, Mr. Reape owed two months' back rent," Mr. Ng said
smoothly. "The woman paid."

"That doesn't prove she was actually his widow," I said
angrily.

The Oriental girl stopped typing, but didn't turn to look at
me.

"It was her all right," she said. "I saw them together in the
lobby once, and he introduced us."

"You see?" Mr. Ng said triumphantly. "The widow."

"Do you happen to have her phone number?"

"Ah, regrettably no."

"The home address then?"

"Also, no."

"Surely it was on his lease?" I said.

"No lease," Mr. Ng said. "We rent by the month."

"Well, I'll look it up in the phone book then," I said.

Mr. Ng paused for just a second. "Ah, no," he said sadly. "Mr. Reape had an unlisted number."

I thanked Mr. Ng and left. I walked through that dank tunnel and was almost at the stairway when I heard a shouted "Hey, you!" I turned. The Oriental girl was running toward me.

"Ten bucks," she said.

"What?" I said.

"Ten bucks," she repeated. "For the Reapes' address."

She plucked the bill from my fingers and was already flying back down the tunnel.

"It's in the phone book," she called.

I had little doubt but that Mr. Ng would get his share of the money.

I had to walk two blocks before I could find a Manhattan telephone directory. I opened it with some trepidation, fearing that I had been twice gulled. But it was there: the 49th Street office and another on 93rd Street.

I took an uptown bus on Eighth Avenue, still smarting at the ease with which I and my money had been parted.

The Reapes lived on Sorry Street, between Somber and Gaunt. The tallest building on the block appeared to be a welfare hotel; most of the brownstones had been converted to rooming houses, with drawn shades at the windows instead of curtains; and the basement stores all had front windows tangled with dusty ivy, drooping ferns, and scrawny philodendrons. Graffiti was everywhere, much of it in Spanish. I wondered what *puta* meant.

The Reapes' house was one of the better buildings, a three-story structure of gray stone, now greasy and chipped. There were few remnants of its former elegance: a fancily carved lintel, beveled glass in the door panels, an ornate brass escutcheon around the knob.

I pushed the bell alongside M. REAPE and waited. Nothing.

I tried again. Still no answer. I tried once more, with no result. When I went back down to the sidewalk, an elderly lady with blue hair was just starting up the steps. She was laden down with two heavy bags of groceries.

"May I help you, ma'am?" I asked.

She looked at me, frightened and suspicious.

"Just up to the front door," I said. "Then I'll go away."

"Thank you, young man," she said faintly.

I carried her bags up and left them beside the inner door. When I came out again, she had negotiated only three steps, pausing on each to catch her breath.

"Asthma," she said, clutching her chest. "It's bad today."

"Yes, ma'am," I said sympathetically. "I wonder if you——"

"Sometime it's like a knife," she said, wheezing. "Cuts right through me."

"I'm sure it's painful," I said. "I'm looking for——"

"Didn't get a wink of sleep last night," she said. "Cough, cough, cough."

"Mrs. Reape," I said desperately. "Mrs. Martin Reape. She lives here. I'm trying to find her."

The suspicion returned.

"What do you want with her?" she demanded. "You're too sawed off to be a cop."

"I'm not a cop," I assured her. "It's about her husband's insurance."

That hooked her.

"Did he leave much?" she whispered.

"I'm sorry, but I can't tell you that. I'm sure you understand. But I think Mrs. Reape will be happy to see me."

"Well . . ." the old lady said, sniffing, "she ain't exactly hurting from what I hear. Unless I miss my guess, young man, you'll find her at The Dirty Shame. That's a saloon on the next block toward Broadway."

The Dirty Shame was one long, reasonably clean room, with a few tables and booths in the rear. But most of the action was at the bar. When I entered there was no doubt that a party was in progress. There must have been at least forty men and women in attendance.

The air was clotted with smoke and the din was continuous—shouts, laughter, snatches of song—competing with a juke box playing a loud Irish jig. Two bartenders were hustling and the bartop was awash. A beefy, red-faced celebrant clamped an arm about my shoulders.

"Friend of Marty's?" he bawled.

"Well, actually, I'm—"

"Step right up," he shouted, thrusting me toward the bar. "Blanche is picking up the tab."

A glass of beer was handed to me over the heads of the mob. My new friend slapped me heartily on the back; half my beer splashed out. Then he turned away to welcome another newcomer.

It was a raffish crew that filled The Dirty Shame. They all seemed to know each other. I moved slowly through the throng, looking for the widow.

I finally found her, surrounded by a circle of mourners who were trying to remember the words of "When Irish Eyes are Smiling." She was a suety woman with a mass of carroty hair, heavily made up. She wore a white mustache of beer foam. Her widow's weeds were of some thin, shiny material, straining at the seams and cut low enough in front to reveal the exuberant swell of a freckled bosom which had been heavily powdered.

"Mrs. Reape," I said, when she paused for breath, "I'd like to express my—"

"What?" she yelled, leaning down to me from her stool. "I can't hear you with all this fucking noise."

"I want to tell you how sorry I—"

"Sure, sure," she said, patting my shoulder. "Very nice. Hey, your glass is empty! Tim, let's have a biggie over here! You a friend of Marty's?"

"Well, actually," I said, "I was a client."

Perhaps I imagined it, but I thought her smile froze and became a grimace, wet lips stretched to reveal teeth too perfect to be her own.

"A client?" she repeated. "Well, he didn't have many of those."

She started to turn away, and I went on with a rush, fearing to lose her.

"Mrs. Reape," I said hurriedly, "I went up to your husband's office, but everything's been—"

"Yeah," she said casually, "I cleaned the place out. He had a bunch of junk there, but I got a couple of bucks from the ragpicker."

"What about his records?" I asked. "The files? He had some important paper of mine."

"No kidding?" she said, her eyes widening. "Jeez, I'm real sorry about that. I threw all that stuff out in the gobbidge last night."

"Then it might be in the garbage cans in front of your house?" I said helpfully.

"Nah," she said, not looking at me. "They collected early this morning. All that paper's in the city insinuator by now."

"Do you remember if—"

But then I was shouldered out of the way.

I left my stein on a table and slipped away from The Dirty Shame as inconspicuosly as I could.

I put in a call to the office. Yetta Apatoff said no one had been looking for me.

"Josh, did you see that sweater I happened to mention to you?" she inquired.

I told her I had seen it and thought it lovely.

"It's so revealing," she said, giggling. "I mean, it doesn't leave *anything* to the imagination."

"Oh, I wouldn't say that," I said. "Exactly. Listen. Yetta, I won't be in until after lunch in case anyone wants me. Okay?"

"Sure, Josh," she said. "And green's really my color—don't you think?"

I finally got off the phone.

I arrived on West 74th Street with time to spare. I took up my station across the street from the office of Dr. Morris Stolowitz and down the block toward Columbus Avenue. The redheaded receptionist came out a few minutes after noon. I scurried across the street and walked directly toward her.

I lifted my head with a start of surprise. Then I stopped. I tipped my hat.

"We meet again," I said, smiling.

She stopped, too, and looked down at me.

"Why, it's Mr. Bigg," she said. "Listen, I hope you weren't insulted this morning. You know, when I asked you a personal question?"

"I wasn't insulted," I assured her. "People are always commenting on my size. In a way, it's an advantage; they never forget my name."

"Mine neither," she said. "Not that my name is so great.

People are always making jokes about it."

"What is your name?"

"Peacock, Ardis Peacock."

"Ardis Peacock? Why, that's a lovely name. The peacock is a beautiful bird."

"Yeah," she said, "with a big tail. You live around here?"

"No, just taking care of business. I'm getting hungry and thought I'd grab something to eat. Any good places in the neighborhood?"

"Lots of them," she said. "There's a McDonald's on 71st Street and Amsterdam, and a Bagel Nosh on the east side of Broadway. But I usually go around the corner to Columbus Avenue. There's all kinds of restaurants there—Mexican, Indian, Chinese, whatever."

"Sounds good," I said. "Mind if I walk along with you?"

"Be my guest," she said.

We started back toward Columbus.

"Ever think of getting elevator shoes?" she asked me.

"Oh, I've thought of it, but they'd only give me another inch or so. Not enough to make a real difference. What I need is stilts."

"Yeah," she said, "it's a shame. I mean, here I am a long drink of water, and I think it's a drag. You should be taller and I should be shorter. But what the hell."

"You carry it well," I told her. "You've got good posture, and you're slender. Like a model."

"Yeah?" she said, pleased. "No kidding?"

We ate at the Cherry Restaurant on Columbus Avenue between 75th and 76th streets. Ardis ordered shrimp with lobster sauce. I had ham and scrambled eggs with home fries.

"That boss of yours gave me a hard time this morning," I said casually.

"Don't let it get you down," she advised. "He gives everyone a hard time. Me, especially. Sometimes I think he's got the hots for me."

"Shows he's got more sense than I thought," I said.

"Hey, *hey!*" she said. She turned and pushed me playfully. Almost off the stool.

"What was it all about?" she asked. "That Stonehouse guy you mentioned on the phone?"

"That's the one," I said. "He was seeing Dr. Stolowitz in

October and November of last year. Remember him?"

"Do I ever!" she said. "What a crab. Always complaining about something. He had to wait, or the office was too cold, or the Doc's cigars were stinking up the place. He was a real pain in the you know where."

"Stolowitz should be happy he wasn't sued," I said. "This Stonehouse is always suing someone."

"Is he suing you?"

"Not me personally," I said, "but maybe the outfit I work for." Then I launched into the scenario I had contrived. "I'm an investigator with the claims division of a health insurance company. Isley Insurance. Ever hear of us?"

"No," she said, "can't say that I have."

"It's a small outfit," I admitted. "We specialize in health coverage for the faculties of educational institutions. You know: schools, colleges, universities—like that. Group policies. Well, this Stonehouse used to teach at New York University. He's retired now, but he's still covered because he pays the premiums personally. You follow?"

"Oh sure," she said. "I make out all the Medicare forms for Stolowitz. It's a pain in the you know what."

"I agree," I said. "Well, you know when you fill out those forms, you have to state the nature of the illness—right?"

"Of course," she said. "Always."

"Well, this Stonehouse refuses to state what was wrong with him. He says it's his own business, and asking him to reveal it is an invasion of his privacy."

"He's whacko!" she burst out.

"Absolutely," I said. "No doubt about it. He refused to tell Medicare and they rejected his claim. Now he's suing them."

"Suing Medicare?" she said, aghast. "That's the U.S. Government!"

"Correct," I said. "And that's who he's suing. Can you believe it?"

"Unreal," she said.

"Anyway, he also made a claim against my company, Isley Insurance. But he won't tell us what his illness was either. So naturally his claim was rejected, and now he's suing us. We'll fight it, of course, but it'll drag out and cost a lot of money. For lawyers and all. So we'd rather settle with him. How about some dessert?"

"Chocolate sundae," she said promptly.

I had another cup of coffee, and after she demolished her sundae, I lighted her cigarette. I always carry matches for other people's cigarettes.

"So I went to Stolowitz," I continued, "figuring maybe he'd tell me what Stonehouse was suffering from. But no soap."

"That's right," she said. "It's confidential between him and the patients. Me and the nurses, we got very strict orders not to talk about the patients' records. As if anyone *wanted* to. That place gives me the creeps. It's no fun working around sick people all the time, I can tell you."

The waiter dropped separate checks in front of us. I grabbed up both.

"Here," Ardis Peacock said halfheartedly, "let's go Dutch."

"No way," I said indignantly. "I asked you to lunch."

We walked slowly back toward her office.

"This Stonehouse thing has me stumped," I said, shaking my head. "All we need is the nature of the illness he had. Then we can process his claim. Now I guess we'll have to defend ourselves against his lawsuit."

I glanced sideways at her, but she hadn't picked up on it.

"I wish there was some way of getting a look at his file," I said fretfully. "That's all it would take. We don't need the file; just a look to see what his ailment was."

That did it. She took hold of my arm.

"It would save your company a lot of money?" she said in a low voice. "Just to find out why Stonehouse was sick?"

"That's right," I said. "That's all we need."

"Would it be like, you know, confidential?"

"I'd be the only one who would know where it came from," I said. "My company doesn't care where or how I get the information, just as long as I get it."

We walked a few more steps in silence.

"Would you pay for it?" she asked hesitantly. "I mean, I'm into those files all the time. It's part of my job."

She wanted $500. I told her my company just wouldn't go above $100, ignoring inflation and how people must live somehow.

"All you want to know is what his sickness was—right?"

"Right," I said.

"Okay," she said. "A hundred. Now?"

"Fifty now and fifty when you get me the information."

"All right," she smiled, as I discreetly slipped her the first payment. "You'll be hearing from me." With a cheery wave, Ardis strode off to work, and I hailed a cab for the East Side.

9

I STOOD ON the sidewalk in front of the Kipper townhouse on East 82nd Street, between Fifth and Madison. To the west I could see the Metropolitan Museum. To the east the street stretched away in an imposing façade of townhouses, embassies, consulates, and prestigious foundations. No garbage collection problems on this block. No litter. No graffiti.

The Kipper home was an impressive structure of gray stone with an entrance framed in wrought iron. There were large bow windows on the third and fourth floors, the glass curved. I wondered what it cost to replace a pane. Above the sixth floor was a heavily ornamented cornice, and above that was a mansard roof of tarnished copper.

A narrow alleyway separated the Kipper building from the next building east. It had an iron gate and bore a small polished brass sign: DELIVERIES. I wondered if I would be sent around to the tradespeople's entrance.

Despite Detective Stilton's advice, I had decided not to attempt to claim that my visit was concerned with Sol Kipper's insurance. That would surely be handled by investigators from the insurance company involved, and I had neither the documentation nor expertise to carry off the impersonation successfully.

I rang the bell outside the iron grille door. The man who opened the carved oaken inner door almost filled the frame. He was immense, one of the fattest men I have ever seen. He was neither white nor black, but a shade of beige. He looked like the Michelin tire man, or one of those inflated rubber dolls which, when pushed over, bobs upright again. But I didn't think he'd bob upright from a knockdown. It would require a derrick.

"Yes, sah?" he inquired. His voice was soft, liquid, with the lilt of the West Indies.

"My name is Joshua Bigg," I said. "I am employed by Tabatchnick, Orsini, Reilly, and Teitelbaum, who are Mrs. Kipper's attorneys. I would appreciate a few minutes of Mrs. Kipper's time, if she is at home."

He stared at me with metallic eyes that bulged like the bowls of demitasse spoons. Apparently he decided I was not a potential assassin or terrorist, for . . .

"Please to wait, sah," he said. "A moment . . ."

He closed the door and I waited outside in the cold. True to his word, he was back in a moment and stepped down the short stairway to unlatch the iron door. He had unexpectedly dainty hands and feet, and moved in a slow, fastidious way as if he found physical action vulgar.

He led me into a tiled entrance hall that rose two floors and was large enough to accommodate a circus troupe. A wide floating staircase curved up to the left. There were double doors on both sides and a corridor that led to the rear of the house. The hall was decorated with live trees in pots and an oversized marble Cupid, his arrow aimed at me.

The butler took my hat and coat; I hung on to my briefcase. He then led me to the left, knocked once, opened the doors, and ushered me in.

This was obviously not the formal living room; more like a family room or sitting room. It was impossible to make a chamber of that size cozy or intimate, but the decorator had tried by placing chairs and tables in groups. He only succeeded in making the place look like the cardroom of a popular club. But it was cheerful enough, with bright colors, flower prints on the walls, and what to my untrained eye appeared to be an original Cézanne over the mantel.

There were two people in this cavern. As I walked toward them, the man rose to his feet, the woman remained seated, fitting a cigarette into a gold holder.

I repeated my name and those of my employers. The man shook my hand, a firm, dry grip.

"Mr. Bigg," he said. "A pleasure. I am Godfrey Knurr. This lady is Mrs. Kipper."

I set the briefcase I had been lugging all day on the floor and moved forward to light her cigarette.

"Ma'am," I murmured, "I'm happy to meet you."

"Thank you," she said, holding out a slender white hand. "Won't you sit down, Mr. Bigg? No, not there. That's Godfrey's chair."

"Oh, Tippi," he said in a bright, laughing voice. "Any chair will do. I think there are enough of them."

But I didn't take his chair. I selected one closer to the small fire in the grate and so positioned that I could look at both of them without turning.

"What a beautiful home you have, Mrs. Kipper," I said. "Breathtaking."

"More like Grand Central Station," Knurr said in his ironic way. Then he said exactly what Perce Stilton had said: "A terrible waste of space."

Mrs. Kipper made a sound, a short laugh that was almost a bark.

"You see, Mr. Bigg," she said, "Mr. Knurr is a minister, the Reverend Godfrey Knurr. He does a great deal of work with the poor, and he's hinted several times that it would be an act of Christian charity if I allowed a mob of his ragamuffins to live in my lovely home."

"Beginning with me," Knurr said solemnly, and they both laughed. I smiled politely.

"Ma'am," I said, "I hope you'll pardon me for not phoning in advance, but I was in the neighborhood on other company business and took the chance of calling on you. If you wish to confirm that I am who I claim to be, I suggest you phone Mr. Tabatchnick."

"Oh, I don't think that will be necessary," she said lazily. "How is dear Leonard?"

"Leopold, ma'am. In good health. Busy as ever."

"With that odd hobby of his? What is it—postage stamps or breeding Yorkies or something?"

"Tropical fish, ma'am," I said, passing her tests.

"Of course," she said. "Tropical fish. What a strange hobby for an attorney. You'd think he would prefer more energetic pets."

"Some of them are quite aggressive, Mrs. Kipper. Belligerent, in fact."

I was conscious of the Reverend Knurr regarding me narrowly, as if he were wondering if my words implied more than they meant. I hadn't intended them to, of course. I am not that devious.

"Well," Mrs. Kipper said, "I'm sure you didn't call to discuss Mr. Tabatchnick's fish. Just why *are* you here, Mr. Bigg?"

"It concerns your late husband's estate, ma'am," I said, and glanced toward Godfrey Knurr.

"Tippi, would you prefer I not be present?" he asked. "If it's something confidential—family matters—I can adjourn to the kitchen and gossip with Chester and Perdita for a while."

"Nonsense," she said. "I'm sure it's nothing you shouldn't hear. Mr. Bigg, Godfrey has been a close friend for many years, and has been a great help since my husband's death. You may speak freely in front of him."

"Yes, ma'am," I said submissively. "There is nothing confidential about it. At present, your attorneys are engaged in striking a tentative total value for your late husband's estate. This includes stocks, bonds, miscellaneous investments, personal property, and so forth. The purpose of this is for filing with the proper Federal and State authorities for computation of the estate tax."

"Godfrey?" she asked, looking to him.

"Yes," he said, "that's correct. Render unto Caesar what is Caesar's. In this case, Tippi, I'm afraid you're going to be unpleasantly surprised by what Caesar demands."

"Well, we'd like our computation of assets to be as accurate as possible," I continued. "It sometimes happens that the IRS and State Tax Bureau make estimates of the value of an estate that are, uh, in variance with those of the attorneys submitting the will to probate."

"You mean they're higher," Pastor Knurr said with his rueful laugh.

"Frequently," I agreed. "Naturally, as the attorneys of record, we hope to keep estate taxes to their legal minimum. I have been assigned the task of determining the value of this home, its furnishings, and your late husband's personal possessions."

Knurr settled back in his armchair. He took a pipe and tobacco pouch from the side pocket of his jacket. He began to pack the pipe bowl, poking the tobacco down with a blunt forefinger.

"This is interesting," he said. "How do you determine the value of a house like this, Mr. Bigg?"

That one was easy.

"Current market value," I said promptly. "How much you could expect to receive if it was put up for sale. Other factors would be the current property tax assessment and comparison with the value of other houses in the neighborhood. When it comes to furnishings, things get a little more complicated. We would like to base our evaluation on the original purchase cost minus depreciation—to keep the total value as low as possible, you understand—but the IRS usually insists on replacement value. And that, in these inflationary times, can sometimes be much more than the original cost."

"I should think so," Mrs. Kipper said sharply. "Why, some of my beautiful things couldn't be bought for double what I paid for them. And some simply can't be replaced at any price."

"Tippi," Knurr said, lighting his pipe with deep drags, "don't tell the tax people *that!*"

I paused, looking at him, while he got his pipe evenly lighted to his satisfaction. He used three matches in the process. His tobacco smoke smelled of fruit and wine.

The Reverend Godfrey Knurr was a few inches short of six feet. He was a stalwart man, bulging the shoulders and sleeves of his hairy tweed jacket. He wore gray flannel slacks and oxblood moccasins. A checked gingham shirt was worn without a tie, but buttoned all the way up. Still, it revealed a strong, corded neck. He had square hands with short fingers.

His hair and beard were slate-colored. The beard was not full; it was mustache and chin covering, cut straight across at the bottom. It was trimmed carefully around full, almost rosy lips. He had steady, brown, no-nonsense eyes, and a nose that was slightly bent. It was not a conventionally handsome face, but attractive in a craggy, masculine way. A lived-in face. His age, I estimated, was in the early forties, which would make him about ten years younger than Mrs. Kipper. He moved well, almost athletically, and had an erect carriage and forceful gestures.

I turned my attention back to the widow.

"My assignment," I said, "will necessitate my taking a complete inventory of the furnishings, I'm afraid. I don't expect to do that today, of course. It may take several days. I'll do my best not to inconvenience you, ma'am, and I'll try to be as unobtrusive as possible while I'm here. Today. I hope merely to make a preliminary survey, count the number of rooms, and plan how best to proceed with the inventory. Is that acceptable to you, Mrs. Kipper?"

"Damn!" she said fretfully. "I wish this was all over with."

She took another cigarette from a porcelain box on the table beside her. I sprang to my feet and rushed to light it.

"Thank you," she said, looking at me amusedly. "You're very polite. You don't smoke?"

"No, ma'am."

"Drink?"

"Occasionally," I said. "Wine mostly."

"For thy stomach's sake," Knurr rumbled.

"Would you care for a glass of wine now, Mr. Bigg?"

"Oh no, thank you, Mrs. Kipper. I'd really like to get started on my preliminary inspection."

"In a minute or two," she said. "How long have you been with Mr. Tabatchnick?"

"About six years."

"Married?"

"No, ma'am."

"No?" she said, widening her eyes theatrically. "Well, we'll have to do something about that!"

"Now, Tippi," Godfrey Knurr said, groaning, "don't start playing matchmaker again."

"What's so wrong with that?" she flashed out at him. "Sol and I were so happy together, I want everyone to be that happy."

Godfrey Knurr winked at me.

"Watch out for us, Mr. Bigg," he said with his brisk laugh. "Tippi brings them together and I marry them. It's a partnership."

"Oh, Godfrey," she murmured, "you make it all sound so—so coldblooded."

"Cold blood—hot marriage," he said. "An ancient Greek proverb."

"Which you just made up," she said.

"That's right," he allowed equably, and now they both laughed.

"I wonder if I might—" I started.

"Well, if you won't have a drink, Mr. Bigg," the widow said, "I think the Reverend and I shall. The usual, Godfrey?"

"Please," he said.

I looked at him and I thought he shrugged a bit in resignation.

I did not believe Mrs. Kipper was being deliberately obstructive. She would let me inspect her home—in her own good time. She wanted to make it perfectly clear to me that she was mistress of this house, and her wish was law, no matter how foolish or whimsical others might think her. So I waited patiently while drinks were served.

Mrs. Kipper pushed a button at the end of a long extension cord. We waited in silence for a moment before the obese butler came stepping quietly into the room.

"Mom?" he asked.

"Drinks, Chester," she said. "The usual for the Reverend and me. Mr. Bigg isn't indulging."

"Yes, mom," he said gravely and moved out silently. For his size, he was remarkably light on his feet. His movements were almost delicate.

While he was gone, Mrs. Kipper began talking about the preview of an art exhibit at a Madison Avenue gallery she had attended the previous evening. Although she looked at me occasionally, ostensibly including me in the conversation, most of her remarks were directed to Knurr. In other words, she did not ignore me, but made little effort to treat me as other than a paid employee to whom one could be polite without being cordial. That was all right; it gave me a chance to observe the lady.

She was silver blonde, pretty in a flashy way, with her hair up and meticulously coiffed. Not a loose end or straggle. She had a really excellent, youthful figure: slender arms and smashing legs, artfully displayed by her short, sleeveless shift of buttery brown velvet. She had a small, perfect nose, and cat's eyes with a greenish tinge. Her thin lips had been cleverly made up with two shades of rouge to appear fuller.

It was a crisp face, unlined, with tight skin over prominent cheekbones. I wondered if that seamless face and perfect nose owed anything to a plastic surgeon's skill. She kept her sharp chin slightly elevated, and even when laughing she seemed to take care lest something shatter.

I thought she would make a brutal and vindictive enemy.

Chester came in with the drinks. They appeared to be a Scotch and soda for Knurr and a dry martini straight up for Mrs. Kipper. She spoke before the butler left the room.

"Chester," she said, "Mr. Bigg wishes to inspect the house, top to bottom. Will you escort him about, please? Show him anything he wishes to see?"

"Yes, mom," the butler said.

I rose hastily to my feet, gripping my briefcase.

"Mrs. Kipper," I said, "thank you for your kindness and hospitality. I appreciate your cooperation. Mr. Knurr, it's been a pleasure meeting you."

He stood up to shake my hand.

"Hope to see you again, Mr. Bigg," he said. "Good luck on your inventory."

"Thank you, sir."

I followed the mountainous bulk of Chester out of the room. He closed the doors behind us, but not before I heard the laughter, quickly hushed, of Mrs. Tippi Kipper and the Reverend Godfrey Knurr.

The butler paused in the entrance hall and turned to face me.

"You wish to see all the rooms, sah?"

"Please. I'm going to be taking an inventory of the furnishings. Not today, but during several visits. So you'll be seeing a lot of me. I'll try not to be too much of a nuisance."

He looked at me, puzzled.

"To figure the value of the estate," I explained. "For taxes."

"Ah, yes," the big man said, nodding. "Many beautiful,

expensive things. You shall see. This way, sah."

He led the way along the corridor at the rear of the hall. He stopped before a conventional door and swung it open. Within was a sliding steel gate, and beyond that a small elevator. Chester opened the gate, allowed me to enter, then followed me in. He slid the gate closed; the outer door closed automatically, and I immediately became conscious of his sweet cologne. The butler pressed a button, a light came on in the elevator, and we began to ascend, slowly.

"How long have you been with the Kippers?" I asked curiously.

"Seventeen years, sah."

"Then you knew the first Mrs. Kipper?"

"I did indeed, sah. A lovely lady. Things have—"

But then he stopped and said nothing more, staring straight ahead at the steel gate.

The elevator halted abruptly. Chester pushed the gate aside and opened the outer door. He stepped out and held the door open for me.

"The sixth floor, sah."

I looked around.

"The main staircase doesn't come up this high?"

"It does not, sah. The main staircase stops on the fifth floor. But there is a back staircase, smaller, that comes all the way up. Also the elevator, of course."

I opened my briefcase, took out my notebook, and prepared to make what I hoped would appear to be official jottings.

This was the party room Detective Stilton had described to me, a single chamber that occupied the front half of the building. I noted bistro tables and chairs, a giant TV set, hi-fi equipment, a clear central area obviously used for dancing, a movie projector, etc.

"This room is used for entertaining?" I asked.

"Quite so, sah."

"And those two doors?"

"That one to the rear staircase, and that one to a lavatory," he said, pronouncing it la*vora*tree.

"Mrs. Kipper does a lot of entertaining?"

"Not since Mr. Kipper's passing, sah. But she has said she will now begin again. A buffet dinner is planned for next week."

I wondered if I detected a note of disapproval in his voice, but when I glanced at him, he was staring into space with those opaque eyes, expressionless as a blind man's.

I walked toward the rear of the room. Two sets of French doors opened onto the terrace. I could see the potted plants, trees, and outdoor furniture Stilton had mentioned. I tried the knob of one of the doors. It was locked.

"Mrs. Kipper has ordered these doors to be kept locked, sah," Chester said in sepulchral tones. "Since the accident."

"Could I take a quick look outside, please? Just for a moment?"

He hesitated, then said, "As you wish, sah."

He had a heavy ring of keys attached to a thin chain fastened to his belt. He selected a brass key with no fumbling about and unlocked the door. He followed me out onto the terrace. I wandered around, making quick notes: *4 otdr tbls, 8 mtl chrs, cktl tbl, 2 chse lngs, 2 endtbls, plnts, trees, etc.*

I walked to the rear of the terrace. The cement wall had recently been repainted.

"This is where the accident happened?" I asked.

He nodded dumbly. I thought he had paled, but it may have been the hard outdoor sunlight on his face.

I leaned over cautiously and looked down. I didn't care what Perce had said, it seemed to me I was a long way up, and no one could survive a fall from that height.

Directly below was the ground floor patio, with more outdoor furniture, and in the rear a small garden now browned and desolate. The patio was paved with tiles, as described. I could see where Sol Kipper had landed, because bright new tiles had replaced those broken when he hit.

I think that was the first time I really comprehended what I was doing. I was not merely trying to solve an abstract puzzle; I was trying to determine how a human being had met his death. That withered garden, those smashed tiles, the drop through empty space—now it all seemed real to me: the dark figure pinwheeling down, arms and legs outspread, wind whipping his clothing, ground rushing up, sickening impact...

"Did he cry out?" I asked in a low voice.

"No, sah," Chester said in a voice as quiet as mine. "We heard nothing until the poor mon hit."

I shivered.

"Cold out here," I said. "Let's go in."

Apparently Chester didn't enjoy using stairs, up or down, for we rode the elevator to the fifth floor.

"On this floor," Chester said, "we have the master bedroom, with two bathrooms, and Mrs. Kipper's dressing room. Also, the maid has her apartment on this floor, the better to be able to assist Mrs. Kipper. In addition, Mr. Kipper had a small private office on this floor. As you can see, sah, the main staircase stops here."

We went through all the rooms, or at least looked in at them, with me busily making notes. I was particularly interested in the master bedroom, an enormous chamber with furniture in cream-colored French provincial decorated with painted vines and flowers. Two bathrooms were connected to the bedroom, and another door led to Mrs. Kipper's dressing room.

This was a squarish area with a full-length, three-way mirror; a chaise longue covered in pink satin; a littered dresser, the mirror surrounded by electric bulbs; an antique phone on an ormolu-mounted table; and a brass serving cart with a small selection of bottles, glasses, and bar accessories. Two walls of the room were louvered folding doors.

"Mrs. Kipper's wardrobe, sah," Chester said. "Do you wish to see?"

"Oh no," I said hastily. "That won't be necessary."

"A hundred pairs of shoes," he remarked drily.

There were two unused rooms on the fifth floor. One, Chester explained, had originally been the nursery, and the other had been the children's playroom.

"Before your time, I imagine," I said.

"Yes, sah," Chester said gravely. "My father was in service with the Kipper family at that time."

I looked at him with new interest.

"What is your last name, Chester?" I asked.

"Heavens," he said.

I thought at first that was an exclamation of surprise, but then he said, "Chester Heavens, sah," and I knew that we had something else in common.

"The maid is Perdita Schug," he continued, "and Mrs. Bertha Neckin is our cook and housekeeper. That is our permanent staff, sah. We three have our apartments here. In addition, the house is serviced by a twice-a-week cleaning crew and a janitor who comes in for a few hours each morning for garbage removal, maintenance chores, and jobs of that nature. Temporary staff are employed as needed for special occasions: large dinners, parties, dances, and so forth."

"Thank you, Chester," I said. Then, to convince him I was not interested in information or gossip extraneous to my assignment, I said, "The furnishings in the apartments of the permanent staff—are they owned by Mrs. Kipper?"

"Oh yes, sah. The furniture is, yes. We have a few personal possessions. Pictures, radios, bric-a-brac—things of that sort."

"I understand," I said, making quick notes.

We descended via elevator to the fourth floor. This level, Chester told me, was totally uninhabited. But all the rooms were furnished, all the doors unlocked. There were four bedrooms (each with its own bathroom) that had been used by the Kipper children. In addition, there were two large guest bedrooms, also with baths. There was also a sewing room, a completely equipped darkroom that had been used by one of the Kipper sons with an interest in photography, and one room that seemed designed and furnished with no particular activity in mind.

"What is this room?" I asked.

"Just a room, sah," Chester said casually, and I found myself repeating silently what Detective Stilton and Godfrey Knurr had already said: "A terrible waste of space."

The third floor appeared to be a little more lived-in. It included a comfortable, wood-paneled library-den which, Chester said, had frequently been used by the late Sol Kipper to entertain old friends at pinochle or gin rummy games, or just to have a brandy and cigar after dinner.

Also on this floor was the apartment of the cook-housekeeper, Mrs. Bertha Neckin. It was a snug suite with bright Indian rugs on polished parquet floors and a lot of chintz. Framed photographs were everywhere, mostly of children.

There were two more guest bedrooms on the third floor and one long chamber across the front of the house illuminated by two bow windows. This was called the "summer room" and was furnished with white wicker, circus and travel posters on the walls and, at one end, a little stage for the production of puppet shows, an enthusiasm, Chester told me, of all the Kipper children when they were young. I liked that room.

The second floor consisted of a large, mirrored ballroom, with a raised platform at one end for a band or entertainment. Straight chairs lined the walls, and there were connecting bathrooms and a small dressing room for the ladies.

Chester Heavens had his apartment on this floor. It consisted of a bedroom, small study, and bathroom. The furnishings revealed no more than the man himself. Everything was clean, neat, squared away. Almost precise. No photographs. Few books. A radio and a small, portable TV set. The paintings on the walls were empty landscapes.

"Very nice," I said politely.

Then I asked the butler if the house was ever filled, if all those bedrooms were ever used. He said they had been, when the first Mrs. Kipper was alive, during the holiday season. Then all the Kipper children and *their* children and sometimes cousins, aunts, and uncles came to spend a week or longer. There were big dinners, dances, parties. There was confusion, noise, and laughter.

"But not after Mr. Kipper remarried?" I asked.

"No, sah," he said, his face expressionless. "The family no longer gathers."

On the ground floor, in addition to the entrance hall and sitting room which I had already seen, were the formal living room, dining room, kitchen and pantry. I took a quick look through the French doors of the dining room at the patio. It looked even more forlorn that it had from six floors up.

Then Chester Heavens led me back along the corridor to the kitchen and pantry area. I had thought the kitchen in the Stonehouse apartment was large; this one was tremendous, with a floor area that must have measured 15×25 feet. It looked like a hotel or restaurant kitchen, with stainless steel fixtures and appliances, and utensils of copper and cast iron hanging from overhead racks.

There were four doors leading from the kitchen. One was the entrance from the corridor which we used. A swinging door led to the dining room. A rear door, glass paneled, allowed access to the patio. The fourth door was heavily bolted and chained, and had a peephole. Chester told me it opened onto the alleyway and was used for deliveries.

"Mrs. Neckin is off today," the butler said in his soft voice, "but perhaps you would care to meet the other member of our staff."

He led the way into the pantry. It was large enough to accommodate a square oak table and four high-backed oak chairs. Seated in one of the chairs, leafing idly through the afternoon *Post*, was a vibrant young lady who looked up pertly as we entered.

"Mr. Bigg," Chester said formally, "may I present our maid, Miss Perdita Schug. Perdita, this gentleman is Mr. Joshua Bigg. Stand up, girl, when you're meeting a guest of this house."

She rose lazily to her feet, smiling at me.

"How do you do, Miss Schug," I said.

"I do all right," she said saucily. "And you can call me Perdita. Everyone else does. Except Chester here, and I won't tell you what *he* calls me!"

He looked at her with the first emotion I had seen him exhibit—disgust.

"Watch your tongue, girl," he said wrathfully, and in reply she stuck out her tongue at him.

He turned away. I nodded at Perdita, smiling, and started to follow the butler. Then a buzzer sounded and I heard a sharp click. Chester looked up at the monitor mounted on the wall. It had two rows of indicators in a glass case. When a servant was summoned from anywhere in the house, the monitor buzzed and an indicator clicked up to show a white square. A label was pasted on the glass above each square showing in which room the button had been pushed. I counted the labels. Thirty-two.

"They'll want their tea now, I expect," Chester said. "Excuse me a moment, Mr. Bigg. Get the tray ready, Perdita."

I was standing in the pantry entrance. There was plenty of room, but Perdita brushed closely by.

"Pardon me," she said blithely, "but duty calls."

She took a plate from the refrigerator and whisked away the damp cloth covering it. The sandwiches were crustless and about the size of postage stamps. She put the plate on a doily on a large silver serving tray, then added a silver teapot, china cups and saucers, spoons, silver creamer and sugar bowl. She turned the light up under a teakettle on the range and, while the water was coming to a boil, dumped four teaspoons of tea into the pot, making no effort to measure it exactly. All her movements were deft and sure.

Chester returned and examined the tray.

"Napkins," he snapped.

Perdita opened the cupboard and added two small, pink linen napkins to the tray.

"Mr. Bigg," the butler said to me, "Mrs. Kipper asked if you were still in the house, and when I said you were, she requested that I inquire if you would care for a cup of tea or coffee."

"That's very kind of her," I said. "Coffee would be fine. If it isn't too much trouble."

"No trouble, sah," he assured me. "Perdita, make enough for all of us. I'll be back as soon as I've served."

The copper kettle was steaming now, and the butler filled the teapot. Then he lifted the tray up before him with both hands. He had to carry it extended at some distance; his stomach intruded. He moved down the corridor at a stately pace.

Perdita was no more than an inch or two taller than I. A dark, flashing button of a woman. Shiny black hair cut as short and impudently as a flapper's. Sparkling eyes. Her long tongue kept darting between small white teeth and wet lips. I watched her as she assembled our belowstairs treat.

She was formed like a miniature Venus. Almost as plump as that marble Cupid in the entrance hall. Creamy skin. In a steamy fantasy, I saw her wearing an abbreviated satin skirt, tiny lace apron and cap, pumps, a shocking décolletage—the classic French maid from the pages of *La Vie Parisiènne*. She frightened me with her animal energy, but I was attracted to her.

She came into the pantry bringing a plate of macaroons. She fell into the chair across the table from me. She put an elbow on the tabletop, cupped her chin in a palm. She stared at me, eyes glittering.

"You're cute," she said.

"Thank you, Perdita," I said, trying to laugh. "You're very kind."

"I am not kind," she protested. "I'm just telling you the truth. I always say what I feel—straight out. Don't you?"

"Well . . . not always," I said judiciously. "Sometimes that's difficult to do without hurting people."

"What do you think of me—straight out?"

I was rescued by the return of Chester Heavens. He sat down heavily at the oak table. He ate three macaroons swiftly: one, two, three.

"The coffee is ready," he said. "Perdita, will you do the honors?"

She rose, passed behind his chair. She stroked the back of his sleekly combed hair. He reached up to knock her hand away, but she was already in the kitchen.

"Please excuse the girl, sah," he said to me. "She has a certain wildness of spirit."

Perdita returned with the percolator and we sat having our coffee and macaroons. I wondered how to bring them around to a discussion of Sol Kipper's plunge.

"Sad times, sah," Chester said, wagging his big head dolefully. "Mr. Kipper was the best of marsters."

"A doll," Perdita said.

"It was a tragedy," I said. "I don't know the details, but it must have been very distressing to all of you."

Then they started reliving those horror-filled moments beginning when they heard the crash and thump on the patio. What they told I had already learned from Percy Stilton. Like him, I was convinced they were telling as much of the truth as they knew.

"And there were only the four of you in the house when it happened?" I asked.

"Five, sah," Chester said. "Counting poor Mr. Kipper."

"The janitor wasn't here then?"

"Oh no, sah. It was in the afternoon. He comes only in the morning."

"Terrible," I said. "What an awful experience. And Mrs. Kipper fainted, you say?"

"Just fell away," Perdita said, nodding. "Just crumpled right up. And Mrs. Neckin started screeching."

"Weeping, girl," the butler said reprovingly.

"Whatever," the maid said. "She was making enough noise."

"You all must have been terribly upset," I said, "when you heard the noise, rushed out, and saw him."

The butler sighed.

"A bad few moments, sah," he said. "Girl, are there more

macaroons? If not, there is a pecan ring. Bring that. Yes, sah, it was a bad few moments. The marster was dead, Mrs. Kipper had fainted, Mrs. Neckin was wailing—it was a trouble to know what to do."

"But then the Reverend Knurr rang the bell?" I prompted.

"Exactly, sah. That gentleman waiting outside was our salvation. He took charge, Mr. Bigg. Called the police department, revived Mrs. Kipper, moved us all into the sitting room and served us brandy. I don't know what we would have done without him."

"He seems very capable," I said, my attention wandering because Perdita had brought the pecan ring to the table. She was standing next to me, cutting it into wedges. Her soft hip was pressed against my arm.

"He is that, sah," Chester said, selecting the wedge with the most pecans on top and shoving it into his mouth. "A fine gentleman."

"Oh fine," Perdita said, giggling. "Just fine!"

"Watch your tongue, girl," he said warningly again, and again she stuck out her tongue at him. It seemed to be a ritual.

"I gather the Reverend is a frequent visitor," I said musingly, pouring myself another half-cup of coffee. "Where is his church?"

"He does not have a regular parish, sah," the butler said. "He provides personal counseling and works with the poor young in Greenwich Village. Street gangs and such."

"But he *is* a frequent visitor?" I repeated.

"Oh yes. For several years." Here the butler leaned close to me and whispered, "I do believe Mrs. Kipper is now taking religious instruction, sah. From Reverend Knurr. Since the death of her husband."

"The shock," I said.

"The shock," he agreed, nodding. "For then it was brought home to her the shortness of life on this earth, and the eternity of life everlasting. And only those who seek the love of the Great God Jehovah shall earn the blessing thereof. Yea, it is written that only from suffering and turmoil of the spirit shall we earn true redemption and forgiveness for our sins."

Then I knew what *his* passion was.

The monitor buzzer sounded again and I welcomed it. I stood up.

"I really must be going," I said. "Chester, I appreciate your invaluable assistance. As I told you, I shall be back again. I will call first. If it is inconvenient for you or Mrs. Kipper, please tell me and I'll schedule another time."

Perdita preceded me along the corridor to the entrance hall. I watched her move. She helped me on with my coat.

"Bundle up," she said, pulling my collar tight. "Keep warm."

"Yes," I said. "Thank you."

"Thursday is my day off," she said.

"Oh?"

"We all have our private phones," she said. "I'm in the book. Schug. S-c-h-u-g."

Back home that evening in my favorite chair, eating a spaghetti Mug-o-Lunch, I scribbled notes to add to the Kipper file and jotted a rough report of my conversations with Dr. Stolowitz and Ardis Peacock.

I was interrupted in my work by a phone call. I was delighted to hear the voice of Detective Percy Stilton. His calling proved he was sincere in his promise to cooperate. I was almost effusive in my greetings.

"Whoa," he said. "Slow down. I got nothing great to tell you. I checked on Marty Reape. Like I figured, they closed it out as an accident. No witnesses came forward to say otherwise. What did they expect? In this town, no one wants to get involved. One interesting thing though: he had a sheet. Nothing heavy or they would have pulled his PI license. But he was charged at various and sundry times. Simple assault; charges dropped. Attempted extortion; charges dropped. Trespassing; no record of disposal. That tell you anything?"

"No," I said.

"Well, I asked around," Perce said. "This Reape apparently was a cruddy character. But they didn't find any great sums of money on the corpse. And they didn't find anything that looked like legal evidence of any kind. And that's about it. You got anything?"

I told him how I had gone to Reape's office looking for the evidence, left out how I had been conned by Mr. Ng; I described the mourners at The Dirty Shame. He laughed.

I told him I thought that someone had got to Blanche Reape

before me, because she had money to pay the office rent and
pick up the bill for the funeral party.

"Well . . . yes," Stilton said cautiously. "That listens. I can
buy that. If the case was still open, I'd go over and lean on
the lady and see if I could find out where those greenies came
from. But I can't, Josh. She sounds like a wise bimbo, and
if I throw my weight around, she might squeal. Then it gets
back to the brass, and my loot wants to know what I'm doing
working on a closed case. Then my ass is out on a branch, just
hanging there. You understand?"

"Of course I understand," I said, and told him I didn't think
there was anything we could do about Mrs. Reape other than
rifling her apartment in hopes that she still had the evidence
that got her husband killed. And burglary was out of the question.

Then I told Stilton all about my afternoon visit to the Kipper
townhouse. He listened carefully, never interrupting until I
mentioned that I had asked Chester Heavens if Sol Kipper had
cried out while he was falling, and the butler said they hadn't
heard a thing until the awful sounds of the body thumping to
earth.

"Son of a bitch," Percy said again.

"What's wrong?" I asked.

"Nothing," he said, "except that I should have asked that
question and didn't. You're okay, Josh."

I was pleased. I finished my report and we agreed I had
discovered nothing that shed any additional light.

"Except that religious angle," Perce said. "Knurr being a
minister and that fat butler sounding like a religious fanatic."

"What does that mean?" I asked.

"Haven't the slightest," he admitted cheerfully. "But it's
interesting. You're going to keep on with it, Josh?"

"Oh sure," I said. "I'm going back there as often as I can.
I want to talk to the cook-housekeeper, and I'd like to look
around a little more. How do you like my cover story?"

"Fantastic," he said. "You're becoming a hell of a liar."

"Thank you," I said faintly.

10

I SLEPT LATE on Saturday morning and woke to find it was snowing: big fat flakes that were piling up rapidly. But the radio reported it would taper off by noon, and temperatures were expected to rise to the upper 30s.

I had a large breakfast and spent the day in the apartment, housecleaning and thinking about the cases.

In the early evening I showered and, in honor of the occasion, shaved. I dressed in a white oxford cloth shirt with a maroon rep tie, a navy blue blazer, gray flannel slacks, and polished black moccasins. Now I looked like a prep school student—but I was used to that.

I was tucking a white handkerchief into my breast pocket when someone knocked on my front door.

"Who is it?" I called before unlocking.

"Finkel," came the reply.

I opened the door, smiling, and motioned Adolph Finkel inside. He was the fourth-floor tenant who lived across the hall from Madame Zora Kadinsky.

"Uh, good evening, Bigg," he said. "I guess we're supposed to help Shank get downstairs."

I glanced at my watch.

"We have a few minutes," I said. "How about a drink to give us strength?"

"Well . . . don't go to any bother." But he let me press some Scotch on him.

"Happy days," I said.

"You're all dressed up," he said sadly. "I worked today and didn't have time to change."

"You look fine," I assured him.

He looked down at himself.

"The manager told me I shouldn't wear brown shoes with a blue suit," he said. "The manager said it doesn't look right for a shoe salesman to wear brown shoes with a blue suit. Of course, it's a ladies' shoestore where I work . . . but still. What do you think, Bigg?"

"Maybe black shoes would look better."

"I could go up and change," he said earnestly. "I have a pair of black shoes."

"Oh, don't bother," I said. "I doubt if anyone will notice."

He was tall, six-one at least, and exceedingly thin, with rounded shoulders, bent neck, head pecked forward like a hungry bird. He had a wild mass of kinky, mouse-colored hair hanging over a low brow. His complexion was palely blotched, washed-out. He had hurt eyes.

Apology was in his voice and in his manner. There is an ancient story of two men condemned to be shot to death. One spits in the face of his executioner. His companion reproves him, saying, "Don't make trouble." That was Adolph Finkel.

"Uh, do you think the party will be in Mrs. Hufnagel's apartment," he asked me, "or in Cleo's?"

"I really don't know. Probably Mrs. Hufnagel's."

"Uh, I suppose you go out with a lot of women?"

I laughed. "What gave you that idea, Finkel? No, I don't go out with a lot of women." Madame Kadinsky had been right. He was trying to discover if I had any interest in Cleo Hufnagel. "There is one," I said. "A girl at my office. She's lovely."

He beamed—or tried to. It was a mistake; it revealed his teeth.

Finkel and I took Captain Shank downstairs in his wheelchair. It wasn't as difficult as I feared it would be; we just tilted the chair back onto its big wheels and let it roll down, a step at a time. Finkel gripped the handles in back and I went ahead, trying to lift the footrest sufficiently to cushion the jars as the chair bumped down. It would have been a lot easier without Shank's roared commands. He carried wine I had bought.

When we arrived at the second-floor hallway, the three women, having heard our pounding descent, were waiting for us. I had been in error; the door to Cleo Hufnagel's apartment was open, and it was obvious the party would be held there.

"You said—" Finkel started to whisper.

"Forget it," I said, determined to stay as far away from him as I could.

I handed the wine to Mrs. Hufnagel and told her the bottles were contributions from Shank and myself.

"Isn't that nice!" she said. "Just look at this, Cleo. Look at what Mr. Bigg brought!"

"And the Captain," I reminded her.

"'allo, 'allo, Joshy and Captain Shink!" Madame Zora Kadinsky caroled.

"Shank," he said.

Cleo's apartment, obviously furnished to her mother's taste, was dull, overstuffed, suffocating. The great Hufnagel Plot was being forwarded.

The party was a punch-and-cookies affair. I was glad I'd had a ham sandwich late in the afternoon. The punch tasted like fruit juice.

"What the hell is this?" asked Captain Shank. "No kick. Dump about half the muscatel into it."

I did so, and in a while I stole upstairs and got vodka and brandy to add to it. The guests had been stiffish, and forcing themselves to try to match the abundant party styles of Mrs. Hufnagel and Mme Kadinsky. But less than an hour after our arrival things were brightening up.

Mme Kadinsky sang "Ah, Sweet Mystery of Life" and other suboperatic selections. The Captain bellowed and pounded the arm of his wheelchair. Urged by Madame Kadinsky and her mother, Cleo and I sedately danced to "Stardust" rendered on an upright piano by Madame K. Finkel showed signs of cutting in, but Mrs. Hufnagel grappled him away to dance with her.

In time things progressed to a jig by Mrs. Hufnagel, skirts

held high to reveal thick support hose, and a final maudlin rendering of "Auld Lang Syne." A very morose Finkel and I had great trouble getting Bramwell Shank back upstairs.

I was too keyed up to attempt to sleep immediately, so I sat in the darkness of the living room, dressed for bed, staring into the cold fireplace. It was, perhaps, almost 1:30 A.M., and I was dozing happily, trying to summon the strength to rise and go to bed, when I heard a light knocking at my door, a timid tapping.

"Who is it?" I whispered hoarsely.

A moment of silence, then: "Cleo. Cleo Hufnagel."

I unlocked and unchained the door. She was still wearing her party clothes.

"I was just going to bed," I said in a voice that sounded to me unnecessarily shrill.

"I just wanted to talk to you for a minute," she said.

"Uh, sure," I said, and ushered her in. She sat in my favorite armchair. I sat opposite her. I sat primly upright, my pajamaed knees together, my robe drawn tightly.

"First of all," she said in a low voice, "I want to thank you for what you did. The party was my mother's idea. I thought it would be horrible. And it was, until you helped. Then it turned out to be fun."

I made a gesture.

"Don't thank me," I said. "It was the punch."

She smiled wanly. "Whatever," she said, "I really enjoyed it."

"I did, too," I said. "It *was* fun. I'm glad you invited me."

"It was Mother's idea," she repeated, then drew a deep breath. "You see, I'm almost thirty years old, and she's afraid that I . . ."

Her voice faded away.

"Yes," I said gently, "I understand."

She looked up at me hopefully.

"Do you?" she said. Then: "Of course you do. You're intelligent. You know what she's doing. Trying to do. I wanted you to know that it was none of my doing. I'm sure it must be very embarrassing to you and I wanted to apologize. For my mother."

"Oh, Cleo," I said. "Listen, is it all right if I call you Cleo and you call me Josh?"

She nodded silently.

"Well, Cleo . . . sure, I know what your mother's doing. Trying to do. But is it so awful? I don't blame you and I don't blame her."

"It's just so—so vulgar!" she burst out. "And I wanted you to know that it wasn't my idea, that I'd never do anything like that."

"I know," I said consolingly. "It must be very distressing for you. But don't condemn your mother, Cleo. She only wants what she thinks is best for you."

"I know that."

"She loves you and wants you to be happy."

"I know that, too."

"So, would it be so terrible if we just let her do her thing? I mean, now that you and I know, it wouldn't be so awful to let her think she's helping you—would it?"

"I guess not."

We sat in silence awhile, not looking at each other.

"What about Adolph Finkel?" I asked finally.

"Oh no," she said instantly. "No. Did you see that he was wearing one brown shoe and one black shoe tonight?"

"No," I said, "I didn't notice."

"But it's not only that," she said. "It's everything."

"Is there anyone else you're interested in?" I asked. "I don't mean to pry, but we're being so frank . . ."

"No," she said. "No one else."

This was said in tones so empty, so devoid of hope, that my breath caught. I looked at her. She really was a tall, slender beauty, almost Spanish in her reserve and mystery. It was criminal that she should be unwanted.

"Listen, Cleo," I said desperately, "this doesn't mean that we can't be friends. Does it?"

She raised luminous eyes to look at me steadily. I couldn't see any implication there. Just deep, deep eyes, unfathomable.

"I'd like that," she said, smiling at last. "To be friends."

The whole thing lightened.

"We can learn some new dance steps. The Peabody."

"The Maxixe," she said and laughed a little.

Just before she slipped out into the hallway, she bent down to kiss my cheek. A little peck.

"Thank you," she said softly.

By the time I had rechained and relocked the door, I was wiped out, tottering. I didn't want to think, or even feel. I just wanted sleep, to repair my punished body and dull a surfeit of impressions, memories, conjectures.

I fell into bed. I was halfway into a deep, dreamless slumber when my phone rang.

"Lo?"

"Josh?"

"Yes. Who is this?"

"Ardis. Ardis Peacock. Remember?"

I came suddenly awake.

"Of course I remember," I said heartily. "How are you, Ardis?"

"Where have you been?" she demanded. "I been calling all night."

"Uh, I had a late date."

"You scamp, you!" she said. "Listen, I got what you wanted on Stonehouse."

"Wonderful!" I said. "What was his illness?"

"Do I get the other fifty bucks?"

"Of course you do. What was it?"

"You'll never guess," she said.

"What *was* it?" I implored.

"Arsenic poisoning," she said.

Part II

1

I WAS WAITING to see Mr. Ignatz Teitelbaum on Monday morning, loitering outside his office and gossiping with Ada Mondora. She stared at me calculatingly.

"I don't know what to do," she said.

"About what?" I asked innocently.

"About you," she said. "And Yetta Apatoff. And Hamish Hooter."

"Oh," I said. "That." With a shamed, sinking feeling to learn that my intimate affairs were a matter of public knowledge.

"There's an office pool," she said. "Didn't you know?"

I shook my head.

"You put up a dollar," she explained, "on who marries Yetta—you or Hooter. Right now the betting is about evenly divided, so all you can win is another dollar."

"Who are you betting on?" I asked her.

She looked at me narrowly.

"I don't know," she said. "I haven't made up my mind. Are you serious about her, Josh?"

"Sure," I said.

"Uh-huh," she said. "We shall see what we shall see."

The door of Mr. Teitelbaum's office opened and Hamish Hooter exited, carrying a heavy ledger.

He looked at me, then looked at Ada Mondora, then strode away. Wordless.

"Mr. Personality," Ada said. "You can go in now, Josh."

He looked smaller than ever. He looked like a deflated football, the leather grained and wrinkled. He sat motionless behind that big desk, sharp eyes following me as I entered and approached. He jerked his chin toward an armchair. I sat down.

"Report?" he said, half-question and half-command.

"Mr. Teitelbaum," I started, "about this Stonehouse business...I hope you'll approve an expenditure of a hundred dollars. For confidential information."

"What information?"

"For a period of about six months, ending a month prior to his disappearance, Professor Stonehouse was suffering from arsenic poisoning."

If I was expecting a reaction, I was disappointed; there was none.

"Sir, the information was obtained in such a manner that the firm's name will not be connected with it. I believe it is valid. The Professor was a victim of arsenic poisoning beginning in late summer of last year. Finally the symptoms became so extreme that he consulted a physician. After a series of tests, the correct diagnosis was made."

"You know all this?" he asked. "For a fact?"

"I'm extrapolating," I admitted. "From information received from several sources. After the Professor became aware of what was going on, he apparently took steps to end the poisoning. In any event, he recovered. He was in reasonably good health at the time of his disappearance."

He began to swing slowly back and forth in his swivel chair, turning his head slightly each time he swung to keep me in view.

"You think he was being deliberately poisoned, Mr. Bigg?"

"Yes, sir."

"By a member of his family?"

"Or his household, sir. There are two servants. I don't see how else it could have been done. It's my impression that he rarely dined out. If he was ingesting arsenic, he had to get it in his own home."

"No one else in the household became ill?"

"No, sir, not to my knowledge. It's something I'll have to check out."

He thought about this a long time.

"Ugly," he said finally. There was no disgust in his voice, no note of disappointment in the conduct of the human race. It was just a judicial opinion: "Ugly."

"Yes, sir."

"What would be the motive?" he asked. "Presuming what you believe is true, why would anyone in the Stonehouse family wish to poison him?"

"That I don't know, sir. Perhaps it had something to do with the will. The missing will. Mr. Teitelbaum, can a person draw up his own will?"

He stared at me.

"A holographic will?" he said. "In the handwriting of the testator? Properly drawn and properly witnessed? Yes, it would be valid. With several caveats. A husband, for instance, could not totally disinherit his wife. A testator could not make bequests contrary to public policy. To finance the assassination of a president, for example. And so forth. There are other requirements best left to the expertise of an attorney. But a simple will composed by the testator could be legal."

"With what you know about Professor Stonehouse, sir, do you think he was capable of drawing up such a document?"

He didn't hesitate.

"Yes," he said. "He would be capable. In fact, it would be likely, considering the kind of man he was. You think that's what he did?"

"I just don't know," I admitted. "It's certainly possible. Did you ask Mrs. Stonehouse if her husband had dealings with any other attorneys?"

"I asked," he said, nodding. "She said she knew of none. That doesn't necessarily mean he didn't, of course. He was a very secretive man. Mr. Bigg, I find this whole matter increasingly disturbing. I told you I feared Professor Stonehouse was dead. I had nothing to base that belief on other than a feeling, instinct, a lifetime of dealing with the weaknesses of

very fallible human beings. Your news that Professor Stonehouse was the victim of poisoning only confirms that belief."
He paused. "We have both used the term 'victim.' You do not
suppose, do you, that the poisoning could have been acci-
dental?"

"I don't think so, sir." We sat awhile in silence. "Mr.
Teitelbaum," I said, "do you want me to continue the investigation?"

"Yes," he said, in such a low voice that it came out a faint
"Ssss."

"You don't feel the matter of the arsenic poisoning should
be reported to the police?"

He roused, a little, and sat up straighter in his chair.

"No, not as yet. Continue with your inquiries."

I walked down to the main floor, hoping to have a moment
to chat with Yetta Apatoff. But Mr. Orsini was just coming
through the main entrance, the door held ajar for him by a
worshipful aide, and two more bobbing along in his wake.

"Josh," he cried, grabbing my arm. "I've got a new one
you'll love!"

He pulled me close. His aides clustered around, twittering
with eagerness.

"This very short man is sitting in a bar," Orsini said, "and
down at the other end he sees this great big gorgeous blonde
by herself. Get the picture?"

When it was over I stumbled back to my office, called
Ardis, and asked her to meet me on 74th and Amsterdam in
twenty minutes, about 1:45. Next I rang up the Stonehouse
residence and asked if I could come by at 2:00 P.M., to talk
to the maid, Olga Eklund, and to pick up a photograph of
Professor Stonehouse to be used on reward posters. This was
a ruse to get into the house again. I spoke to Glynis Stonehouse;
she told me that she and her mother would be happy to see
me.

I grabbed a gyro and a Coke on my way to meet Ardis. She
was on the northwest corner, waiting for me.

"Thank God! You're on time! I had one of the nurses cover
for me, but if Stolowitz calls in and I'm not at my desk, he'll
go crazy."

"Thank you, Ardis," I said in a low voice, handing her an
envelope. "A big help."

"Any time," she said, whisking the envelope out of sight. "You're in the neighborhood, give me a call. We'll have lunch—or whatever."

"I'll do that," I said.

I walked south on Central Park West to the Stonehouse apartment house and went through the business of identifying myself to the man behind the desk.

The door to 17-B was opened by a Valkyrie. She lacked only a horned helmet. This was undoubtedly Olga Eklund. She was almost a foot taller than I, broad in the shoulders and hips, with long, sinewy arms and legs. Her head seemed no wider than her strong neck, and beneath her black uniform I imagined a hard torso, muscle on muscle, and tight skin flushed with health.

I had fantasized flaxen tresses. They existed, but had been woven into a single braid, thick as a hawser, and this plait had been wound around and around atop her head, giving her a gleaming crown that added another six inches to her impressive height. The eyes, as I had fancied, were a deep-sea blue, the whites as chalky as milk. She wore no makeup, but the full lips were blooming, the complexion a porcelainized cream.

She gave such an impression of bursting good health, of strength and vitality, that it made me shrink just to look at her. She seemed of a different species, someone visiting from Planet 4X-5-6-Gb, to demonstrate to us earthlings our sad insufficiencies.

"Mr. Bigg," she asked in the sultry, throbbing voice that had conjured up all those exciting images when I had heard it on the phone.

"Yes," I said. "You must be Miss Eklund."

"Yah," she said. "Hat? Coat?"

She hung my things away in the hall closet. I followed her down the long corridor. She moved with a powerful, measured tramp. Beneath the skirt, rounded calves bunched and smoothed. She had the musculature of a trapeze artist, marble under suede. I was happy she hadn't offered to shake hands.

Mrs. Ula Stonehouse and Glynis were waiting for me in the living room. There was a tea service on one of the small cocktail tables, and at their urging I accepted a cup of tea from the efficient Olga Eklund.

"I'm sorry I have no news to report," I told mother and

daughter. "I have discovered nothing new bearing on the Professor's disappearance."

"Mother said you asked about Father's health," Glynis said. "His illness last year. Did you speak to his doctor?"

She was curled into one corner of the long couch, her splendid legs tucked up under her.

"Yes, I spoke to Dr. Stolowitz," I said, addressing both of them. "He wouldn't reveal the exact nature of the illness, but I gathered it was some kind of flu or virus. Tell me, was anyone else in the family ill at the same time the Professor was sick?"

"Let me think," Mrs. Stonehouse said, cocking her head. "That was last year. Oh yes. I had a cold that lasted and lasted. And poor Effie was sniffling for a least a week. Glynis, were you sick?"

"Probably," the daughter said in her husky voice. "I don't really remember, but I usually get at least one cold when winter comes. Does this have anything to do with my father's disappearance, Mr. Bigg?"

"Oh no," I said hastily. "I just wanted to make certain he was in good health on January 10th. And from what you and Dr. Stolowitz have told me, he apparently was."

Glynis Stonehouse looked at me a moment. I thought she was puzzled, but then her face cleared.

"You're trying to determine if he might have had amnesia?" she asked. "Or be suffering some kind of temporary mental breakdown?"

"Yes," I said, "something like that. But obviously we can rule that out. Mrs. Stonehouse, I wonder if you'd mind if I talked to your maid for a few moments. Just to see if she might recall something that could help."

"Not at all," Glynis Stonehouse said before her mother could answer. "She's probably in the kitchen or dining room. You know the way; go right ahead. I've already instructed Olga to tell you whatever you want to know."

"Thank you," I said, rising. "You're very kind. It shouldn't take long. And then there are a few more things I'd like to discuss with you ladies, if I may."

I found the maid in the dining room, seated at one end of the long table. She was reading *Prevention*.

"Hi," I said brightly. "Miss Stonehouse said it was all right if I talked to you in private. May I call you Olga?"

"Yah," she said.

She sat erect, her straight spine not touching the back of the chair; seated, she still towered over me.

"Olga," I said, "I work for the family's attorneys and I'm investigating the disappearance of Professor Stonehouse. I was hoping you might be able to help me."

She focused those turquoise eyes on mine. It was like a dentist's drill going into my pupils. I mean I was *pierced*.

"How?" she said.

"Do you have any idea what happened to him?"

"No."

"I realize you weren't here the night he disappeared, but had you noticed anything strange about him? I mean, had he been acting differently?"

"No."

"At the time he disappeared, he was in good health?"

She shrugged.

"But he had been sick last year? Right? Last year he was very ill?"

"Yah."

"But then he got better."

"Yah."

I sighed. I was doing just great. Yah, no, and one shrug.

"Olga," I said, "you work here from one o'clock to nine, six days a week—correct?"

"Yah."

"You serve the afternoon lunch and dinner?"

"Yah."

"Did he eat anything special no one else ate?"

"No."

I gave up. The Silent Swede. Garbo was a chatterbox compared to this one.

"All right, Olga," I said, beginning to rise. "You've been very kind, and I want to—"

Her hand shot out and clamped on my arm, instantly cutting off the circulation. She drew me to her. I instinctively resisted the force. Like trying to resist a Moran tugboat. She pulled me right up to her. Then her lips were at my ear. I mean I could *feel* her lips on my ear, she clutched me so tightly.

"He was being poisoned," she whispered.

The warm breath went tickling into my ear, but I was too
stunned to react. Was this the breakthrough I needed?

"By whom?" I asked.

"I could have saved him," she said.

I stared.

For answer to my unspoken question she solemnly raised
the health and diet magazine and pointed to it.

She meant Stonehouse was sick of commercial-food processing, like everyone else.

In the living room Glynis and her mother were as I left
them. Mrs. Stonehouse was licking the rim of a filled glass.

"Nothing," I said, sighing. "It's very frustrating. Well...I'll
keep trying. The only member of the family I haven't spoken
to, Mrs. Stonehouse, is your son. He was here the night his
father disappeared. Perhaps he can recall something..."

They gave me his address and unlisted phone number. Then
I asked to see any family photos they might have, and presently
I was sitting nervously on the couch between the two women,
and we went through the stack of photos slowly. It was an odd
experience. I felt sure I was looking at pictures of a dead man.
Yale Stonehouse was, or had been, a thin-faced, sour man,
with sucked-in cheeks and lips like edges of cardboard. The
eyes accused and the nose was a knife. In the full-length photos,
he appeared to be a skeleton in tweed, all sharp angles and
gangling. He was tall, with stooped shoulders, carrying his
head thrust forward aggressively.

"Height?" I asked.

"Six feet one," Mrs. Stonehouse said.

"A little shorter than that, Mother," Glynis said quietly.
"Not quite six feet."

"Color of hair?"

"Brownish," Ula said.

"Mostly gray," Glynis said.

We finally selected a glossy 8 × 10 publicity photo. I
thanked Ula and Glynis Stonehouse and assured them I'd keep
them informed of the progress of my investigation.

Downstairs, I asked the man behind the desk if he had been
on duty the night Yale Stonehouse had walked out the apartment house, never to be seen again. He said No, that would
be Bert Lord, who was on duty from 4:00 P.M. to midnight.

Bert usually showed up around 3:30 to change into his uniform in the basement, and if I came back in fifteen or twenty minutes, I'd probably be able to talk to him.

So I walked around the neighborhood for a while, trying to determine Professor Stonehouse's possible routes after he left his apartment house.

There was an IND subway station on Central Park West and 72nd Street. He could have gone uptown or downtown.

He could have taken a crosstown bus on 72nd Street that would have carried him down to 57th Street, across to Madison Avenue, then uptown to East 72nd Street.

He could have walked over to Columbus Avenue and taken a downtown bus.

He could have taken an uptown bus on Amsterdam.

A Broadway bus would have taken him down to 42nd Street and eastward.

A Fifth Avenue bus, boarded at Broadway and 72nd Street, would have taken him downtown via Fifth to Greenwich Village.

The Seventh Avenue IRT could have carried him to the Bronx or Brooklyn.

Or a car could have been waiting to take him anywhere.

When I returned to the apartment house precisely seventeen minutes later, there was a different uniformed attendant behind the desk.

"Mr. Lord?" I asked.

"That's me," he said.

I explained who I was and that I was investigating the disappearance of Professor Stonehouse on behalf of the family's attorneys.

"I already told the cops," he said. "Everything I know."

"I realize that," I said. "He left the building about 8:45 on the night of January 10th—right?"

"That's right," he said.

"Wearing hat, overcoat, scarf?"

"Yup."

"Didn't say anything to you?"

"Not a word."

"But that wasn't unusual," I said. "Was it? I mean, he wasn't exactly what you'd call a sociable man, was he?"

"You can say that again."

I didn't. I said, "Mr. Lord, do you remember what the weather was like that night?"

He looked at me. He had big, blue, innocent eyes.

"I can't recall," he said. "It was a month ago."

I took a five-dollar bill from my wallet, slid it across the marble-topped desk. A chapped paw appeared and flicked it away.

"Now I remember," Mr. Bert Lord said. "A bitch of a night. Cold. A freezing rain turning to sleet. I remember thinking he was some kind of an idiot to go out on a night like that."

"Cold," I repeated. "A freezing rain. But he didn't ask you to call a cab?"

"Him?" he said. He laughed scornfully. "No way. He was afraid I'd expect tow bits for turning on the light over the canopy."

"So he just walked out?"

"Yup."

"You didn't see which way he headed?"

"Nope. I couldn't care less."

"Thank you, Mr. Lord."

"My pleasure."

I went directly home, arrived a little after 5:00 P.M., changed into chino slacks and an old sports jacket, and headed out to eat. And there was Captain Bramwell Shank in his wheelchair in the hallway, facing the staircase. He whirled his chair expertly when he heard my door open.

"What the hell?" he said. "I been waiting for you to come home, and you been inside all the time!"

"I got home early," I explained. "Not so long ago."

"I been waiting," he repeated.

"Captain," I said, "I'm hungry and I'm going out for something to eat. Can I knock on your door when I come back? In an hour or so?"

"After seven," he said. "There's a rerun of *Ironsides* I've got to watch. After seven o'clock is okay. Nothing good on till nine."

Woody's on West 23rd was owned and managed by Louella Nitch, a widowed lady whose late husband had left her the restaurant and not much else. She was childless, and I think she sometimes thought of her clientele as her family. Most of the customers were from the neighborhood and knew each other. It was almost a club. Everyone called her Nitchy.

When I arrived on the blowy Monday night, there were only a dozen drinkers in the front room and six diners in back. But the place was warm, the little lamps on the tables gleamed redly, the juke box was playing an old and rare Bing Crosby record ("Just a Gigolo"), and the place seemed a welcoming haven to me.

Louella Nitch was about forty and the skinniest woman I had ever seen. She was olive-skinned and she wore her hair cut short, hugging her scalp like a black helmet. Her makeup was liberally applied, with dark eyeshadow and precisely painted lips. She wore hoop earrings, Victorian rings, necklaces of baroque medallions and amulets.

She was seated at the front of the bar when I entered, peering at a sheaf of bills through half-glasses that made her small face seem even smaller: a child's face.

"Josh!" she said. "Where have you been? You know, I dreamed about you the other night."

"Thank you," I said.

I took the stool next to her and ordered a beer. She told me about her dream: she was attending a wedding and I stood waiting for the bride to come down the aisle; I was the groom.

"What about the bride?" I asked. "Did you get a look at her?"

She shook her head regretfully. "I woke up before she came in. But I distinctly saw you, Josh. You're not thinking of getting married, are you?"

"Not likely," I said. "Who'd have a runt like me?"

She put a hand on my arm. "You think too much about that, Josh. You're a good-looking man; you've got a steady job. Lots of girls would jump at the chance."

"Name one," I said.

"Are you serious?" she said, looking at me closely. "If you are, I could fix you up right now. I don't mean a one-night stand. I mean a nice, healthy, goodhearted neighborhood girl who wants to settle down and have kids. How about it? Should I make a call?"

"Well, uh, not right now, Nitchy," I said. "I'm just not ready yet."

"How old are you—twenty-eight?"

"Thirty-two," I confessed.

"My God," she said, "you've only got two years to go. Statistics prove that if a man isn't married by the time he's thirty-four, chances are he'll never get hitched. You want to turn into one of those old, crotchety bachelors I see mumbling in their beer?"

"Oh, I suppose I'll get married one of these days."

I think she sensed my discomfort, because she abruptly changed the subject.

"You here for a drink, Josh, or do you want to eat? I'm not pushing, but the chef made a nice beef stew, and if you're going to eat, I'll have some put aside for you before the mob comes in and finishes it."

"Beef stew sounds great," I said. "I'll have it right now. Can I have it here at the bar?"

"Why not?" she said. "I'll have Hettie set you up. There's a girl for you, Josh—Hettie."

"Except she outweights me by fifty pounds."

"That's right," she said, laughing raucously. "They'd be peeling you off the ceiling!"

The stew was great.

I was putting on my parka when Louella Nitch came hurrying over.

"So soon?" she asked.

"Work to do," I lied, smiling.

"Listen, Josh," she said, "I wasn't just talking; if you want to meet a nice girl, let me know. I mean it."

"I know you mean it, Nitchy," I said. "You're very kind. But I'll find my own."

"I hope so," she said sadly. Then she brightened. "Sure you will. Remember my dream? Every time you've come in here you've been alone. But one of these days you're going to waltz through that door with a princess on your arm. A princess!"

"That's right," I said.

2

MR. TABATCHNICK, DUSTING fish feed from his fin~~~ ~
at me as if he expected th~   ~~ ~~gers, looked
    "And ~   ~~ ~~e worst.
    ~~~~ exactly how, Mr. Bigg," he asked in that trumpeting
voice, "were you able to gain entrance to the Kipper household?"

I wished he hadn't asked that question. But I couldn't lie
to him, in case Mrs. Tippi Kipper called t~ ~' ~ ~
story. So I ad~~~~~ ~   ~~~~~ to cneck on my cover
    ~~~~ admitted I had claimed to be engaged in making
an inventory of the Kipper estate. I had feared he would be
angered to learn of my subterfuge. Instead, he seemed diverted.
At least all those folds and jowls of his bloodhound face seemed
to lift slightly in a grimace that might have been amu~~~~
                                                     ~~~sement.
    But when he spoke, his voice wa~ ~*~
    "Mr. Bigg," he ~~~'   ~~~~~~   ~~ stern.
~~~~~ ~   ~~ said, "when a complete inventory of the
~~~~~ is submitted to competent authorities, it must be signed
by the attorney of record and, in this case, by the co-executor.
Who just happens to be me. Failure to disclose assets, either
deliberately or by inadvertence, may constitute a felony. Are
you aware of that?"

    "I am now, sir," I said miserably. "But I didn't intend to

135

make the final, *legal* inventory. All I wanted to do was—"

"I am quite aware of what you wanted to do," he said impatiently. "Get inside the house. It wasn't a bad ploy. But I suggest that if Mrs. Kipper or anyone else questions your activities in the future, you state that you are engaged in a preliminary inventory. The final statement, to which I must sign my name, will be compiled by attorneys and appraisers experienced in this kind of work. Is that clear?"

"Yes, sir," I said. "Just one thing, sir. In addition to this Kipper matter, I am also looking into something for Mr. Teitelbaum. The disappearance of a client. Professor Yale Stonehouse."

"I am aware of that," he said magisterially.

"In addition to my regular duties," I reminded him. "So far, I have been able to keep up with my routine assignments. But the Kipper and Stonehouse cases are taking more and more of my time. It would help a great deal if I had the services of a secretary. Someone to handle the typing and filing."

He stared at me.

"Not necessarily full time," I added hastily. "Perhaps a temporary or part-time assistant who could come in a few days a week or a few hours each day. Not a permanent employee. Nothing like that, sir."

He sighed heavily. "Mr. Bigg," he said, "you would be astounded at the inevitability with which part-time or temporary assistants become permanent employees. However, I think your request has some merit. I shall discuss the matter with the other senior partners."

I was about to ask for a larger office as well, but then thought better of it. I would build my empire slowly.

"Thank you, Mr. Tabatchnick," I said, gathering up my file. "One final question. I'd like your permission to speak to the two Kipper sons, the ones who are managing the textile company."

"Why not?" he said.

"And what story do you suggest I give them, sir? As an excuse for talking to them about the death of their father?"

"Oh . . ." he said, almost dreamily, "I'll leave that to you, Mr. Bigg. You seem to be doing quite well—so far."

I called Powell Stonehouse. It was the second time I had tried to reach him that morning. A woman had answered the first call and told me that he was meditating and could not be disturbed. This time I got through to him. I identified myself, explained my interest in the disappearance of his father, and asked when I could see him.

"I don't know what good that would do," he said in a stony voice. "I've already told the cops everything I know."

"Yes, Mr. Stonehouse," I said, "I'm aware of that. But there's some background information only you can supply. It won't take long."

"Can't we do it on the phone?" he asked.

"I'd rather not," I said. "It concerns some, uh, rather confidential matters."

"Like what?" he said suspiciously.

He wasn't making it easy for me.

"Well . . . family relationships that might have a bearing on your father's disappearance. I'd really appreciate talking to you in person, Mr. Stonehouse."

"Oh . . . all right," he said grudgingly. "But I don't want to spend too much time on this."

The bereaved son.

"It won't take long," I assured him again. "Any time at your convenience."

"Tonight," he said abruptly. "I meditate from eight to nine. I'll see you for an hour after nine. Don't arrive before that; it would have a destructive effect."

"I'll be there after nine," I promised. "I have your address. Thank you, Mr. Stonehouse."

"Peace," he said.

That caught me by surprise. Peace. I thought that had disappeared with the Flower Children of the 1960s.

My next call was to butler Chester Heavens at the Kipper townhouse. I told him I'd like to come by at 2:00 P.M. to continue my inventory, if that was satisfactory. He said he was certain it would be, that "mom" had left orders that I was to be admitted whenever I asked.

I went out to lunch at 1:00 P.M., had a hotdog and a mug of root beer at a fast-food joint on Third Avenue. Then I walked back to Madison and took another look in the window of that dress shop. The green sweater was still there.

I arrived at the Kipper home ahead of time and walked around the block until it was 2:00 P.M. Then I rang the bell at the iron gate. I was carrying my briefcase, with pens, notebook, and rough plans I had drawn from memory of the six townhouse floors.

Chester Heavens let me in, looking like an extremely well-fed mortician. He informed me that Mrs. Kipper was in the sitting room with the Reverend Godfrey Knurr and a few other close friends. Mrs. Bertha Neckin and Perdita Schug were in the kitchen, preparing tea for this small party.

"You are most welcome to join us there, sah, if you desire a cup of coffee or tea," the butler said.

I thanked him but said I'd prefer to get my inventory work finished first. Then I'd be happy to join the staff in the kitchen. He bowed gravely and told me to go right ahead. If I needed any assistance, I could ring him from almost any room in the house.

I had something on my mind. On the afternoon Sol Kipper had plunged to his death, his wife said she had been with him in the fifth-floor master bedroom. Then she had descended to the ground floor. The servants testified to that. Minutes later, Kipper's body had thudded onto the tiled patio.

What I was interested in was how Mrs. Kipper had gone downstairs. By elevator, I presumed. She was not the type of woman who would walk down five long flights of stairs.

If she descended by elevator, then it should have been on the ground floor at the time of her husband's death. Unless, of course, Kipper rang the bell, waited for the lift to come up from the ground level, then used it to go up to the sixth-floor terrace.

But that didn't seem likely. I stood inside the master bedroom. I glanced at my watch. I then walked at a steady pace out into the hallway, east to the rear staircase, up the stairs to the sixth floor, into the party room, over to the locked French doors leading to the terrace. I glanced at my watch again. Not quite a minute. That didn't necessarily mean a man determined to kill himself *wouldn't* wait for a slow elevator. It just proved it was a short walk from the master bedroom, where the suicide note had been found, to the death leap.

I spent the next hour walking about the upper stories of the townhouse, refining my floor plans and making notes on furniture, rugs, paintings, etc., but mostly trying to familiarize myself with the layout of the building.

I examined the elevator door on each floor. This was not just morbid curiosity on my part; I really felt the operation of the elevator played an important part in the events of that fatal afternoon.

The elevator doors were identical: conventional portals of heavy oak with inset panels. All the panels were solid except for one of glass at eye-level that allowed one to see when the elevator arrived. Each door was locked. It could only be opened when the elevator was stopped at that level. You then opened the door, swung aside the steel gate, and stepped into the cage.

Fixed to the jamb on the outside of each elevator door was a dial not much bigger than a large wristwatch. The dials were under small domes of glass, and they revolved forward or backward as the elevator ascended or descended. In other words, by consulting the dial on any floor, you could determine the exact location of the elevator and tell whether or not it was in motion.

I didn't know at the time what significance that might have, but I decided to note it for possible future reference.

As I was coming down to the ground floor, I heard the sounds of conversation and laughter coming from the open doors of the sitting room. Perdita Schug rushed by, carrying a tray of those tiny sandwiches. She hardly had time to wink at me. Chester Heavens followed her at a more stately pace, with a small salver holding a single glass of what appeared to be brandy.

I walked toward the kitchen and pantry. I turned at the kitchen door and looked back. From that point I could see the length of the corridor, the elevator door, the doors to the sitting room, and a small section of the entrance hall. I could not see the front door.

I went into the disordered kitchen, then back to the pantry. A lank, angular woman was seated in one of the high-backed chairs, sipping a cup of tea. She was wearing a denim apron over a black uniform with white collar and cuffs.

"Mrs. Neckin?" I asked.

She looked up at me with an expression of some distaste.

"Yus?" she said, her voice a piece of chalk held at the wrong angle on a blackboard.

"I'm Joshua Bigg," I said with my most ingratiating smile. I explained who I was, and what I was doing in the Kipper home. I told her Chester Heavens had invited me to stop in the kitchen before I left.

"He's busy," she snapped.

"For a cup of tea," I continued pointedly, staring at her. "For a nice, friendly cup of tea."

I could almost see her debating how far she could push her peevishness.

"Sit down then," she said finally. "There's a cup, there's the pot."

"Thank you," I said. "You're very kind."

Irony had no effect. She was too twisted by ill-temper.

"A busy afternoon for you?" I asked pleasantly, sitting down and pouring myself a cup.

"Them!" she said with great disgust.

"It's probably good for Mrs. Kipper to entertain again," I remarked. "After the tragedy."

"Oh yus," she said bitterly. "Him not cold, and her having parties. And I don't care who you tell I said it."

"I have no intention of telling anyone," I assured her. "I am not a gossip."

"Oh yus?" she said, looking at me suspiciously.

"You've been with the Kippers a long time, Mrs. Neckin?" I asked, sipping my tea. It was good, but not as good as Mrs. Dark's at the Stonehouses'.

"I was with Mr. Sol all my working days," she said angrily. "Long before *she* came along." The housekeeper accompanied this last with a jerk of a thumb over her shoulder, in the general direction of the sitting room.

"I understand she was formerly in the theatre," I mentioned casually.

"The theatre!" she said, pronouncing it thee-*ay*-ter. "A cootch dancer was what she was!"

Then, as if she were grateful to me for giving her an opportunity to vent her malice, she rose, went into the kitchen, and brought back a small plate of petit-fours. And she replenished my cup of tea without my asking.

Mrs. Neckin was a rawboned farm woman, all hard lines and sharp angles. The flat-chested figure under the apron and uniform moved in sudden jerks, pulls, twists, and pushes. When she poured the tea, I had the uneasy feeling that she'd much rather be wringing the neck of a chicken.

"He was a saint," she said, seating herself again. In a chair closer to mine, I noted. "A better man never lived. He's in Heaven now, I vow."

I made a sympathetic noise.

"I'm getting out," she said in a harsh whisper. "I won't work for that woman with Mr. Sol gone."

"It's hard to believe," I said, "that a man like that would take his own life."

"Oh yus!" she said scornfully. "Take his own life! That's what *they* say."

I looked at her in bewilderment.

"But he jumped from the terrace," I said. "Didn't he?"

"He may have jumped," she said, pushing herself back from the table. "I ain't saying he didn't. But what drove him to it? Answer me that: what drove him to it?"

"Her?" I said in a low voice. "Mrs. Kipper?"

"Her?" she said disgustedly. "Nah. She's got milk in her veins. She's too nicey-nice. It was *him*."

"Him?"

"Chester Heavens," she said, nodding.

"*He* drove Mr. Kipper to suicide?" I said. I heard my own voice falter.

"Sure he did," Mrs. Bertha Neckin said with great satisfaction. "Put the juju on him. That church of his. They drink human blood there, you know. I figure Chester called up a spell. That's what made Mr. Sol jump. He was drove to it."

I gulped the remainder of my tea. It scalded.

"Why would Chester do a thing like that?" I asked.

She leaned closer, so near that I could smell her anise-scented breath.

"That's easy to see," she said. "I know what's going on. I live here. I see." She made a circle of her left forefinger and thumb, then moved her right forefinger in and out of the ring in a gesture so obscene it sickened me. "That's what he wants. He's a nig, you know. I don't care how light he is, he's still a nig. And she's a white lady, dirt-cheap though she may be. That's why he put the juju on Mr. Sol. Oh yus."

I pushed back my chair.

"Mrs. Neckin," I said, "I thank you very much for the

refreshment. You've been very kind. And I assure you I won't repeat what you've told me to a living soul."

In the corridor I stood aside as Perdita Schug came toward the kitchen with a tray of empty highball and wineglasses. She paused, smiling at me.

"Thursday," she said. "I'm off on Thursday. I'm in the book. I told you."

"Yes," I said, "so you did."

"Try it," she said. "You'll like it."

I was still stammering when she moved on to the kitchen.

I had advanced to the entrance hall when Chester Heavens came from the sitting room. He preceded Mrs. Tippi Kipper and the Reverend Godfrey Knurr. Through the open doors I could see several ladies sitting in a circle, chattering as they drank tea and nibbled on little things.

"Well, Mr. Bigg," Mrs. Kipper said in her cool, amused voice, "finished for the day?"

"I think so, ma'am," I said. "There's still a great deal to be done, but I believe I'm making progress."

"Did Chester offer you anything?" she asked.

"He did indeed, ma'am. I had a nice cup of tea, for which I am grateful."

"I wish that was all I had," Godfrey Knurr said, patting his stomach. "Tippi, you keep serving those pastries and I'll have to stop coming here."

"You must keep up your strength," she murmured, and he laughed.

They were standing side by side as the butler took Knurr's hat and coat, and mine, from the closet. He held a soiled trenchcoat for Knurr, then handed him an Irish tweed hat, one of those bashed models with the brim turned down all the way around.

"Can I give you a lift, Mr. Bigg?" Knurr said. "I've got my car outside."

His car was an old Volkswagen bug. It had been painted many times.

"Busted heater," he said as we got in. "Sorry about that. But it's not too cold, is it? Maybe we'll go down Fifth and then cut over on 38th. All right?"

"Fine," I said. Then I was silent awhile as he worked his

way into traffic and got over to Fifth Avenue. "Mrs. Kipper seems to be handling it well," I remarked. "The death of her husband, I mean."

"She's making a good recovery," he said, beating the light and making a left onto Fifth. "The first few days were hard. Very hard. I thought for a while she might have to be hospitalized. Good Lord, she was practically an eyewitness. She heard him hit, you know."

"It was fortunate you were there," I said.

"Well. I wasn't *there*. I showed up a few minutes later. What a scene that was! Screaming, shouting, everyone running around. It was a mess. I did what I could. Called the police and so forth."

"Did you know him, Pastor?"

"Sol Kipper? Knew him well. A beautiful man. Generous. So generous. So interested in the work I'm doing."

"Uh, do you mind if I ask about that? The work you're doing, I mean. I'm curious."

"Do I mind?" he said, with that brisk laugh of his. "I'm delighted to talk about it. Well...Listen, may I call you Joshua?"

"Josh," I said, "if you like."

"I prefer Joshua," he said. "It has a nice Old Testament ring. Well, Joshua, about my work...Did you ever hear of the term 'tentmakers'?"

"Tentmakers? Like Omar?"

"Not exactly. More like St. Paul. Anyway, the problem is basically a financial one. There are thousands and thousands of Protestant clergymen and not enough churches to go around. So more and more churchmen are turning to secular activities. There's an honorable precedent for it. St. Paul supported his preaching by making tents. That's why we call ourselves tentmakers. You'll find the clergy in business, the arts, working as fund-raisers, writing books, even getting into politics. I'm a tentmaker. I don't have a regular church, although I sometimes fill in for full-time pastors who are on vacation, sick, hung over, or on retreat. Whatever. But mostly I support myself by begging." He glanced sideways at me, briefly. "Does that shock you?"

"No," I said. "Not really. I seem to recall there's an honorable precedent for that also."

"Right," he said approvingly. "There is. Oh hell, I don't mean I walk the streets like a mendicant, cup in hand. But it amounts to the same thing. You saw me at work today. I meet a lot of wealthy people, usually women, and some not so wealthy. I put the bite on them. In return I offer counseling or just a sympathetic ear. In nine cases out of ten, all they want is a listener. If they ask for advice, I give it. Sometimes it's spiritual. More often than not it's practical. Just good common sense. People with problems are usually too upset to think clearly."

"That's true, I think."

"So that's part of my tentmaking activities; spiritual adviser to the wealthy. I assure you they're just as much in need of it as the poor."

"I believe you," I said.

"But when they offer a contribution, I accept. Oh boy, do I accept! Not only to keep me in beans, but to finance the other half of my work. It's not a strorefront church exactly. Nothing half so fancy as Chester Heavens' Society of the Holy Lamb up in Harlem. It's not a social club either. A combination of both, I guess. It's in Greenwich Village, on Carmine Street. I live in the back. I work with boys from eight to eighteen. The ones in trouble, the ones who have been in trouble, the ones who are going to get in trouble. I give them personal counseling, or a kind of group therapy, and plenty of hard physical exercise in a little gym I've set up in the front of the place. To work off some of their excess energy and violence."

By this time we were down at 59th Street where the traffic was truly horrendous. Knurr swung the Bug in and out, cutting off other drivers, jamming his way through gaps so narrow that I closed my eyes.

"Where are you from, Joshua?" The sudden question startled me.

"Uh—Iowa," I said. "Originally."

"Really? I was born right next door in Illinois. Peoria. But I spent most of my life in Indiana, near Chicago, before I came to New York. It's a great city, isn't it?"

"Chicago?" I said.

"New York," he said. "It's the only place to be. The center. You make it here or you never really make it. The contrasts!

The wealth and the poverty. The ugliness and the beauty. Don't you feel that?"

"Oh yes," I said, "I do."

"The opportunity," he said. "I think that's what impresses me most about New York: the opportunity. A man can go to the stars here."

"Or to the pits," I said.

"Oh yes," he said. "That, too. Listen, there's something I'd like you to do. Say no, and I'll understand. But I wish you'd visit my place down in Greenwich Village. Look around, see what I'm doing. Trying to do. Would you do that?"

"Of course," I said instantly. "I'd like to. Thank you very much."

"I suspect I'm looking for approval," he said, glancing at me quickly again with a grin. "But I'd like you to see what's going on. And, to be absolutely truthful, there are a few little legal problems I hope you might be able to help me with. My lease is for a residential property and I'm running this church or club there, whatever you want to call it. Some good neighbors have filed a complaint."

I was horrified.

"Mr. Knurr," I said, "I'm not a lawyer."

"You're not?" he said, puzzled. "I thought you worked for Mrs. Kipper's attorneys?"

"I do," I said. "In a paralegal job. But I'm not an attorney myself. I don't have a law degree."

"But you're taking the estate inventory?"

"A preliminary inventory," I said. "It will have to be verified and authenticated by the attorney of record before the final inventory of assets is submitted."

"Oh," he said. "Sure. Well, the invitation still stands. I'll tell you my problems and maybe you can ask one of the attorneys in your firm and get me some free legal advice."

"That I'd be glad to do," I said. "When's the best time to come?"

"Anytime," he said. "No, wait, you better give me a call first. I'm in the book. Mornings would be best. Afternoons I usually spend with my rich friends uptown. Listening to their troubles and drinking their booze."

Then he pulled up outside the TORT offices. He leaned over to examine the building through the car window.

"Beautiful," he said. "Converted townhouse. It's hard to believe places like that were once private homes. The wealth! Unreal."

"But it still exists," I said. "The wealth, I mean. Like the Kipper place."

"Oh yes," he said, "it still exists." He slapped my knee. "I don't object to it," he said genially. "I just want to get in on it."

"Yes," I said mournfully. "Me, too."

"Listen, Joshua, I was serious about that invitation. The hell with the free legal advice. I like you, I'd like to see more of you. Give me a call and come down and visit me."

Acknowledging his invitation with a vague promise to contact him, I took my leave and headed to my office.

I was adding somewhat fretfully to my files of reports, wondering if I was getting anywhere, when my phone rang. It was Percy Stilton; he sounded terse, almost angry.

He asked me if I had come up with anything new, and I told him of my most recent visit to the Kipper townhouse. He laughed grimly when I related what Mrs. Neckin had said about Chester Heavens putting a curse on Sol Kipper.

"I should have warned you about her," Stilton said. "A whacko. We get a lot of those. They make sense up to a point, and then they're off into the wild blue yonder. What was your take on Godfrey Knurr?"

"I like him," I said promptly. "For a clergyman, he swears like a trooper, but he's very frank and open. He invited me down to Greenwich Village to see what he's doing with juvenile delinquents. He certainly doesn't impress me as a man with anything to hide."

"That's the feeling I got," Perce said. "And that's it? Nothing else?"

"A silly thing," I said. "About the elevator."

"What about the elevator?"

I explained that if Mrs. Kipper had come downstairs on that elevator, it should have been on the ground floor at the time her husband plunged to his death. Unless he had brought the elevator up again to take it from the master bedroom on the fifth floor to the sixth-floor terrace.

"He could have," Stilton said.

"Sure," I agreed. "But I timed the trip from bedroom to

terrace. Walking along the hall and up the rear staircase. Less than a minute."

I didn't have to spell it out for him.

"I get it," he said. "You want me to talk to the first cops on the scene and see if any of them remember where the elevator was when they arrived?"

"Right," I said gracefully.

"And if it was on the ground floor, that shows that Mrs. Kipper brought it down, which proves absolutely nothing. And if it was on the sixth floor, it only indicates that *maybe* Sol Kipper took it up to his big jump from the terrace. Which proves absolutely nothing. Zero plus zero equals zero."

I sighed.

"You're right, Perce. I'm just grabbing at little things. Anything."

"I'll ask the cops," he said. "It's interesting."

"I suppose so."

"Josh, you sound down."

"Not down, exactly, but bewildered."

"Beginning to think Sol Kipper really was a suicide?"

"I don't know . . ." I said slowly. "Beginning to have some doubts about my fine theories, I guess."

"Don't," he said.

"What?"

"Don't have any doubts. I told you I thought someone was jerking us around. Remember? Now I'm sure of it. Early this morning the harbor cops pulled a floater out of the North River. Around 34th Street. A female Caucasian, about fifty years old or so. She hadn't been in the water long. Twelve hours at most."

"Perce," I said, "not . . . ?"

"Oh yeah," he said tonelessly. "Mrs. Blanche Reape. Positive ID from her prints. She had a sheet. Boosting and an old prostitution rap. No doubt about it. Marty's widow."

I was silent, remembering the brash, earthy woman in The Dirty Shame saloon, buying drinks for everyone.

"Josh?" Detective Stilton demanded. "You there?"

"I'm here."

"Official verdict is death by drowning. But a very high alcoholic content in the blood. Fell in the river while drunk. That's how it's going on the books. You believe it?"

"No," I said.

"I don't either," he said. "Sol Kipper falls from a sixth-floor terrace. Marty Reape falls in front of a subway train. His widow falls in the river. This sucks."

"Yes," I said faintly.

"What?" he said. "I can't hear you."

"Yes," I said, louder, "I agree."

"You bet your damp white fanetta!" he said furiously. Then suddenly he was shouting, almost gargling on his bile. "I don't like to be messed with," he yelled. "Some sharp, bright son of a bitch is messing me up. I don't like that. No way do I like that!"

"Perce," I said, "please. Calm down."

"Yeah," he said. "Yes, I mean. Yes. I'm calm now. All cool."

"You think the three of them . . . ?"

"Oh yes," he said. "Why not? Kipper was the first. Then Marty, because he had the proof. Then the widow lady. It fits. Someone paid her for the files. The evidence Marty had on the Kipper estate. Then she got greedy and put the bite on for more. Goodbye, Blanche."

"Someone would do that? Kill three people?"

"Sure," he said. "It's easy. The first goes down so slick, and so smooth, and so nice. Then they can do no wrong. They own the world. Why I'm telling you all this, Josh, is to let you know you're not wasting your time on this Kipper thing. I can't open it up again with what we've got; you'll have to carry the ball. I just wanted you to know I'm here, and ready, willing, and able."

"Thank you, Perce."

"Keep in touch, old buddy," he said. "I'll check on that elevator thing for you. That cocksucker!" he cried vindictively. "We'll fry his ass!"

Powell Stonehouse lived on Jones Street, just off Bleecker. It was not a prepossessing building: a three-story loft structure of worn red brick with a crumbling cornice and a bent and rusted iron railing around the areaway. I arrived a few minutes after 9:00 P.M., rang a bell marked Chard-Stonehouse, and was buzzed in almost immediately. I climbed to the top floor.

I was greeted at the door of the loft by a young woman, very dark, slender, of medium height. I stated my name. She introduced herself as Wanda Chard, in a whisper so low that I wasn't certain I had heard right, and asked her to repeat it.

She ushered me into the one enormous room that was apparently the entire apartment, save for a small bathroom and smaller kitchenette. There was a platform bed: a slab of foam rubber on a wide plywood door raised from the floor on cinder blocks. There were pillows scattered everywhere: cushions of all sizes, shapes, and colors. But no chairs, couches, tables. I assumed the residents ate off the floor and, I supposed, reclined on cushions or the bed to relax.

The room was open, spare, and empty. A choice had obviously been made to abjure things. No radio. No TV set. No books. One dim lamp. There were no decorations or bric-a-brac. There was one chest of drawers, painted white, and one doorless closet hung with a few garments, male and female. There was almost nothing to look at other than Ms. Chard.

She took my coat and hat, laid them on the bed, then gestured toward a clutch of pillows. Obediently I folded my legs and sank into a semireclining position. Wanda Chard crossed her legs and sat on the bare floor, facing me.

"Powell will be out in a minute," she said.

"Thank you," I said.

"He's in the bathroom," she said.

There seemed nothing to reply to that, so I remained silent. I watched as she fitted a long crimson cigarette to a yellowed ivory holder. I began to struggle to my feet, fumbling for a match, but she waved me back.

"I'm not going to smoke it," she said. "Not right now. Would you like one?"

"Thank you, no."

She stared at me.

"Does it bother you that you're very small?" she asked in a deep, husky voice that seemed all murmur.

Perhaps I should have bridled at the impertinence of the question; after all, we had just met. But I had the feeling that she was genuinely interested.

"Yes, it bothers me," I said. "Frequently."

She nodded.

"I'm hard of hearing, you know," she said. "Practically deaf. I'm reading your lips."

I looked at her in astonishment.

"You're not!" I said.

"Oh yes. Say a sentence without making a sound. Just mouth the words."

I made my mouth say, "How are you tonight?" without actually speaking; just moving my lips.

"How are you tonight?" she said.

"But that's marvelous!" I said. "How long did it take you to learn?"

"All my life," she said. "It's easy when people face me directly, as you are. When they face away, or even to the side, I am lost. In a crowded, noisy restaurant, I can understand conversations taking place across the room."

"That must be amusing."

"Sometimes," she said. "Sometimes it is terrible. Frightening. The things people say when they think no one can overhear. Most people I meet aren't even aware that I'm deaf. The reason I'm telling you is because I thought you might be bothered by your size."

"Yes," I said, "I understand. Thank you."

"We are all one," she said somberly, "in our weakness."

Her hair was jet black, glossy, and fell to her waist in back. It was parted in the middle and draped about her face in curved wings that formed a dark Gothic arch. The waves almost obscured her pale features. From the shadows, two luminous eyes glowed forth. I had an impression of no makeup, pointy chin, and thin, bloodless lips.

She was wearing a kimono of garishly printed silk, all poppies and parrots. When she folded down onto the bare floor, I had noted her feline movements, the softness. I did not know if she was naked beneath the robe, but I was conscious of something lubricious in the way her body turned. There was a faint whisper there: silk on flesh. Her feet were bare, toenails painted a frosted silver. She wore a slave bracelet about her left ankle: a chain of surprisingly heavy links. There was a tattoo on her right instep: a small blue butterfly.

"What do you do, Miss Chard?" I asked her.

"Do?"

"I mean, do you work?"

"Yes," she said. "In a medical laboratory. I'm a research assistant."

"That's very interesting," I said, wondering what on earth

Powell Stonehouse could be doing in the bathroom for such a long time.

As if I had asked the question aloud, the bathroom door opened and he came toward us in a rapid, shambling walk. Once again I tried to struggle to my feet from my cocoon of pillows, but he held a palm out, waving me down. It was almost like a benediction.

"Would you like an orange?" he asked me.

"An orange? Oh no. Thank you."

"Wanda?"

She shook her head, long hair swinging across her face. But she held up the crimson cigarette in the ivory holder. He found a packet of matches on the dresser, bent over, lighted her cigarette. I smelled the odor: more incense than smoke. Then he went to the kitchenette and came back with a small Mandarin orange. He sat on the bare floor next to her, facing me. He folded down with no apparrent physical effort. He began to peel his orange, looking at me, blinking.

"What's all this about?" he said.

Once again I explained that I had been assigned by his family's attorneys to investigate the disappearance of his father. I realized, I said, that I was going over ground already covered by police officers, but I hoped he would be patient and tell me in his own words exactly what had happened the night of January 10th.

I thought then that he glanced swiftly at Wanda Chard. If a signal passed between them, I didn't catch it. But he began relating the events of the evening his father had disappeared, pausing only to pop a segment of orange into his mouth, chomp it to a pulp, and swallow it down.

His account differed in no significant detail from what I had already learned from his mother and sister. I made a pretense of jotting notes, but there was really nothing to jot.

"Mr. Stonehouse," I said, when he had finished, "do you think your father's mood and conduct that night were normal?"

"Normal for him."

"Nothing in what he did or said that gave you any hint he might be worried or under unusual pressure? That he might be contemplating deserting his family of his own free will?"

"No. Nothing like that."

"Do you know of anyone who might have, uh, harbored

resentment against your father? Disliked him? Even hated him?"

Again I caught that rapid shifting of his eyes sideways to Wanda Chard, as if consulting her.

"I can think of a dozen people," he said. "A hundred people. Who resented him or disliked him or hated him." Then, with a small laugh that was half-cough, he added, "Including me."

"What exactly was your relationship with your father, Mr. Stonehouse?"

"Now look here," he said, bristling. "You said on the phone that you wanted to discuss 'family relationships.' What has that got to do with his disappearance?"

I leaned forward from the waist, as far as I was able in my semirecumbent position. I think I appeared earnest, sincere, concerned.

"Mr. Stonehouse," I said, "I never knew your father. I have seen photographs of him and I have a physical description from your mother and sister. But I am trying to understand the man himself. Who and what he was. His feelings for those closest to him. In hopes that by learning the man, knowing him better, I may be able to get some lead on what happened to him. I have absolutely no suspicions about anyone, let alone accusing anyone of anything. I'm just trying to learn. Anything you can tell me may be of value."

This time the consultation with Wanda Chard was obvious, with no attempt at concealment. He turned to look at her. Their eyes locked. She nodded once.

"Tell him," she said.

He began to speak. I didn't take notes. I knew I would not forget what he said.

He tried very hard to keep his voice controlled. Unsuccessfully. He alternated between blatant hostility and a shy diffidence, punctuated with those small, half-cough laughs. Sometimes his voice broke into a squeak of fury. His gestures were jerky. He glanced frequently sideways at his companion, then glared fiercely at me again. He was not wild, exactly, but there was an incoherence in him. He didn't come together.

He had his father's thin face and angular frame, the harsh angles softened by youth. It was more a face of clean slants, with a wispy blond mustache and a hopeful beard scant enough so that a mild chin showed. He was totally bald, completely,

the skull shaved. Perhaps that was what he had been doing in
the bathroom. In any event, that smooth pate caught the dim
light and gave it back palely. Big ears, floppy as slices of veal,
hung from his naked skull.

He had tortoise-shell eyes, a hawkish nose, a girl's tender
lips. A vulnerable look. Everything in his face seemed a-trem-
ble, as if expecting a hurt. As he spoke, his grimy fingers were
everywhere: smoothing the mustache, tugging the poor beard,
pulling at his meaty ears, caressing his nude dome frantically.
He was wearing a belted robe of unbleached muslin. The belt
was a rope. And there was a cowl hanging down his back. A
monk's robe. His feet were bare and soiled. Those busy fingers
plucked at his toes, and after a while I couldn't watch his eyes
but could only follow those fluttering hands, thinking they
might be enchained birds that would eventually free themselves
from his wrists and go whirling off.

The story he told was not an original, but no less affecting
for that . . .

He had never been able to satisfy his father. Never. All he
remembered of his boyhood was mean and sour criticism. His
mother and sister tried to act as buffers, but he took most of
his father's spleen. His school marks were unacceptable; he
was not active enough in sports; his table manners were slov-
enly.

"Even the way I stood!" Powell Stonehouse shouted at me.
"He didn't even like the way I walked!"

It never diminished, this constant litany of complaint. In
fact, as Powell grew older, it increased. His father simply hated
him. There was no other explanation for his spite; his father
hated him and wished him gone. He was convinced of that.

At this point in his recital, I feared he might be close to
tears, and I was relieved to see Wanda Chard reach out to
imprison one of those wildly fluttering hands and grasp it
tightly.

His sister, Glynis, had always been his father's favorite,
Powell continued. He understood that in most normal families
the father dotes on the daughter, the mother on the son. But
the Stonehouses were no normal family. The father's ill-temper
drove friends from their house, made a half-mad alcoholic of
his wife, forced his daughter to a solitary life away from home.

"I would have gone nuts," Powell Stonehouse said furiously. "I was *going* nuts. Until I found Wanda."

"And Zen," she murmured.

"Yes," he said, "and Zen. Now, slowly, through instinct and meditation, I am becoming one. Mr. Bigg, I must speak the truth: what I feel. I don't care if you never find my father. I think I'm better off without him. And my sister is, too. And my mother. And the world. You must see, you must understand, that I have this enormous hate. I'm trying to rid myself of it."

"Hate is a poison," Wanda Chard said.

"Yes," he said, nodding violently, "hate is a poison and I'm trying hard to flush it from my mind and from my soul. But all those years, those cold, brutal scenes, those screaming arguments . . . it's going to take time. I know that: it's going to take a long, long time. But I'm better now. Better than I was."

"Oh, forgive him," Wanda Chard said softly.

"No, no, no," he said, still fuming. "Never. I can never forgive him for what he did to me. But maybe, someday, with luck, I can forget him. That's all I want."

I was silent, giving his venom a chance to cool. And also giving me a chance to ponder what I had just heard. He had made no effort to conceal his hostility toward his father. Was that an honest expression of the way he felt—or was it calculated? That is, did he think to throw me off by indignation openly displayed?

"Doubt *everyone*," Roscoe Dollworth had said. "Suspect *everyone*."

He had also told me something else. He said the only thing harder than getting the truth was asking the right questions. "No one's going to volunteer *nothing!*" Dollworth said that sometimes the investigator had to flounder all over the place, striking out in all directions, asking all kinds of extraneous questions in hopes that one of them might uncover an angle never before considered. "Catching flies," he called it.

I felt it was time to "catch flies."

"Your sister was your father's favorite?" I asked.

He nodded.

"How did he feel toward your mother?"

"Tolerated her."

"How often did you dine at your father's home? I mean after you moved out?"

"Twice a week maybe, on an average."

"Do you know what your father's illness was? Last year when he was sick?"

"The flu, Mother said. Or a virus."

"Do you know any of your sister's friends?"

"Not really. Not recently. She goes her own way."

"But she goes out a lot?"

"Yes. Frequently."

"Where?"

"To the theatre, I guess. Movies. Ballet. Ask her."

"She's a beautiful woman. Why hasn't she married?"

"No one was ever good enough for Father."

"She's of age. She can do as she likes."

"Yes," Wanda Chard said, "I've wondered about that."

"She wouldn't leave my mother," Powell said. "She's devoted to my mother."

"But not to your father?"

He shrugged.

"Anything you can tell me about the servants?"

"What about them?"

"You trust them?"

"Of course."

"What did you and your father quarrel about? The final quarrel?"

"He caught me smoking a joint. We both said things we shouldn't have. So I moved out."

"You have an independent income?"

"Enough," Wanda Chard said quickly.

"Your sister doesn't have one particular friend? A man, I mean. Someone she sees a lot of?"

"I don't know. Ask her."

"Was your father on a special diet?"

"What?"

"Did he eat any special foods or drink anything no one else in the house ate or drank?"

"Not that I know of. Why?"

"In the last month or two before your father disappeared, did you notice any gradual change in his behavior?"

He thought about that for a few seconds.

"Maybe he became more withdrawn."

"Withdrawn?"

"Surlier. Meaner. He talked even less than usual. He ate his dinner, then went into his study."

"His will is missing. Did you know that?"

"Glynis told me. I don't care. I don't want a cent from him. Not a cent! If he left me anything, I'd give it away."

"Why did your mother stay with such a man as you describe?"

"What could she do? Where could she go? She has no family of her own. She couldn't function alone."

"Your mother and sister could have left together. Just as you left."

"Why should they? It's their home, too."

"You never saw your father's will?"

"No."

"Did you see the book he was working on? A history of the *Prince Royal*, a British battleship?"

"No, I never saw that. I never went into his study."

"Did your father drink? I mean alcohol?"

"Maybe a highball before dinner. Some wine. A brandy before he went to bed. Nothing heavy."

"Are you on any drugs now?"

"A joint now and then. That's all. No hard stuff."

"Your mother or sister?"

"My mother's on sherry. You probably noticed."

"Your sister?"

"Nothing as far as I know."

"Your father?"

"You've got to be kidding."

"Either of the servants?"

"Ridiculous."

"Do you love your mother?"

"I have a very deep affection for her. And pity. He ruined her life."

"Do you love your sister?"

"Very much. She's an angel."

Wanda Chard made a sound.

"Miss Chard," I said, "did you say something? I didn't catch it."

"Nothing," she said.

That's what I had—nothing. I continued "catching flies."

"Did your father ever come down here?" I asked. "To this apartment?"

"Once," he said. "I wasn't here. But Wanda met him."

"What did you think of him, Miss Chard?"

"So unhappy," she murmured. "So bitter. Eating himself up."

"When did he come here? I mean, how long was it before he disappeared?"

They looked at each other.

"Perhaps two weeks," she said. "Maybe less."

"He just showed up? Without calling first?"

"Yes."

"Did he give any reason for his visit?"

"He said he wanted to talk to Powell. But Powell was in Brooklyn, studying with his master. So Professor Stonehouse left."

"How long did he stay?"

"Not long. Ten minutes perhaps."

"He didn't say what he wanted to talk to Powell about?"

"No."

"And he never came back?"

"No," Powell Stonehouse said, "he never came back."

"And when you saw him later, in his home, did he ever mention the visit or say what he wanted to talk to you about?"

"No, he never mentioned it. And I didn't either."

I thought a moment.

"It couldn't have been a reconciliation, could it?" I suggested. "He came down here to ask your forgiveness?"

He stared at me. His face slowly congealed. The blow he had been expecting had landed.

"I don't know," he said in a low voice.

"Maybe," Wanda Chard murmured.

3

OLGA EKLUND AGREED to meet me in a health-food cafeteria on Irving Place. The salad, full of sprouted seeds, was really pretty good. I washed it down with some completely natural juice.

I listened to her lecture on health and diet as patiently as I could. When she paused I said, "So when you told me Professor Stonehouse was being poisoned, you were referring to the daily food served in his house?"

"Yah. Bad foods. I tell them all the time. They don't listen. That Mrs. Dark, the cook—everything with her is butter and cream. Too much oil. Too rich."

"But everyone in the house eats the same thing?"

"Not me. I eat raw carrots, green salads with maybe a little lemon juice. Fresh fruit. I don't poison myself."

"Olga," I said, "you serve the evening meal every night?"

"Except my day off."

"Can you recall Professor Stonehouse eating or drinking anything the others didn't eat or drink?"

She thought a moment.

"No," she said. Then: "Except at night maybe. After I left."

"Oh? What was that?"

"Every night he worked in his study. Late, he would have a cup of cocoa and a brandy before he went to bed."

I was alive again.

"Where did the cocoa come from?"

"Come from?" she asked, puzzled. "From Holland."

"I mean, who made the cocoa every night for Professor Stonehouse?"

"Oh. Mrs. Dark made it before she went to bed and before I went home. Then, when the Professor wanted it late, Glynis would heat it up, skim it, and bring it to his study."

"Every night?"

"I think so."

"No one else in the house drank the cocoa?"

"I don't know."

It was sounding better and better.

"Let me get this sequence right," I said. "Every night Mrs. Dark made a pot of cocoa. This was before you went home and before she went to bed. Then, later, when the Professor wanted it, Glynis would heat it up and bring it to him in his study. Correct?"

"Yah," she said placidly, not at all interested in why I was so concerned about the cocoa.

"Thank you, Olga," I said. "You've been very helpful."

"Yah?" she said, surprised.

"Does Glynis go out very often? In the evening, I mean."

"Oh, yah."

"Does she have a boyfriend?"

She pondered that.

"I think so," she said, nodding. "Before, she was very sad, quiet. Now she smiles. Sometimes she laughs. She dresses different. Yah, I think she has a man who makes her happy."

"How long has this been going on? I mean, when did she start to be happy?"

"Maybe a year ago. Maybe more. Also, one night she said she was going to the theatre. But I saw her that night in a restaurant on 21st Street. She did not see me and I said nothing to her."

"Was she with anyone?"

"No. But I thought she was waiting for someone."

"What time of night was this?"

"Perhaps nine, nine-thirty. If she had gone to the theatre, as she said, she would not be in the restaurant at that time."

"Did you ever mention that incident to her?"

"No," she said, shrugging. "Is no business of mine."

"What do you think of Powell Stonehouse, Olga?"

"He poisons himself with marijuana cigarettes." (She pronounced it "mary-jew-anna.") "Too bad. I feel sorry for him. His father was very mean to him."

I drained the remainder of all that natural goodness in my glass and rose to my feet.

"Thank you again, Olga," I said, "for your time and trouble. The food here is delicious. You may have made a convert of me."

What a liar I was getting to be.

When I got back to TORT I was confronted by Hamish Hooter, that tooth-sucking villain. "See here," Hooter said indignantly, glaring at me from sticky eyes, "what's this about a secretary?"

"I need one," I said. "I spoke of it to Mr. Tabatchnick."

"*I* am the office manager," he said hotly. "Why didn't you speak to *me?*"

"Because you would have turned me down again," I said in what I thought was a reasonable tone. "All I want is a temporary assistant. Someone to help with typing and filing until I complete a number of important and complex investigations."

I had always thought the description "He gnashed his teeth" was a literary exaggeration. But Hamish Hooter *did* gnash his teeth. It was a fascinating and awful thing to witness.

"We'll see about that," he grated, and whirled away from me.

As soon as I reached my desk I phoned Yetta Apatoff and made a lunch date for Friday, then got back to business.

Headquarters for Kipmar Textiles were located in a building on Seventh Avenue and 35th Street. When I phoned, a dulcet voice answered, "Thank you for calling Kipmar Textiles," and I wondered what the reaction would be if I screamed that I was suing Kipmar for six zillion dollars. After being shunted to two more extensions, I finally got through to a lady who stated she was Miss Gregg, secretary to Mr. Herschel Kipper.

I forbore commenting on the aptness of her name and occupation, but merely identified myself and my employer and asked if it might be possible for me to see Mr. Herschel Kipper and/or Mr. Bernard Kipper at some hour that afternoon, at their convenience. She asked me the purpose of my request, and I replied that it concerned an inventory of their late father's estate that had to be made for tax purposes.

She put me on hold—for almost five minutes. But I was not bored; they had one of those attachments that switches a held caller to a local radio station, so I heard the tag end of the news, a weather report, and the beginning of a country singer's rendition of "I Want to Destroy You, Baby," before Miss Gregg came on the line again. She informed me that the Kipper brothers could see me "for a very brief period" at 3:00 P.M. I was to come directly to the executive offices on the 34th floor and ask for her. I thanked her for her kindness. She thanked me, again, for calling Kipmar Textiles. It was a very civilized encounter.

I walked over from the TORT building, starting out at 2:30, heading due west on 38th. I strolled down Fifth Avenue to 35th, where I made a right into the garment district and continued over to Seventh. The garment center in Manhattan is quintessentially New York. From early in the morning till late at night it is thronged, jammed, packed. The rhythm is frantic. Handtrucks and pedestrians share the sidewalks. Handtrucks, pedestrians, taxis, buses, private cars, and semitrailers share the streets. There is a cacophony that numbs the mind: shouts, curses, the bleat of horns, squeal of brakes, sirens, bells, whistles, the blast of punk rock from the open doors of music shops, the demanding cries of street vendors and beggars.

I suppose there were streets in ancient Rome similar to these, and maybe in Medieval European towns on market day. It is a hurly-burly, a wild tumult that simply sweeps you up and carries you along, so you find yourself trotting, dashing through traffic against the lights, shouldering your way through the press, rushing, rushing. Senseless and invigorating.

Kipmar's executive offices were decorated in neutral tones of oyster white and dove gray, the better to accent the spindles of gaily colored yarns and bolts of fabrics displayed in lighted wall niches. There were spools of cotton, synthetics, wools, silks, rayon, and folds of woven solids, plaids, stripes, checks, herringbones, satins, metallics, and one incredible bolt of a gossamer fine as a spider's web and studded with tiny rhine-stones. This fabric was labeled with a chaste card that read: STAR WONDER. Special Order. See Mr. Snodgrass.

At the end of the lobby a young lady was seated behind a desk that bore a small sign: RECEPTIONIST. She was on the phone, giggling, as I approached, and I heard her say, "Oh, Herbie, you're just *awful!*" She covered the mouthpiece as I halted in front of her desk.

"Yes, sir?" she said brightly. "How may I help you?"

"Joshua Bigg," I said, "to see Mr. Kipper. I was told to ask for Miss Gregg."

"Which Mr. Kipper, sir?"

"Both Mr. Kippers."

"Just a moment, sir," she said. Then, *sotto voce,* "Don't go away, Herbie." She pushed some buttons and said primly, "Mr. Joshua Bigg to see Mr. Kipper. Both Mr. Kippers." She listened a moment, then turned to me with a divine smile. "Please take a seat, sir. Miss Gregg will be with you in a moment."

I sat in one of the low leather sling chairs. True to her word, Miss Gregg came to claim me in a moment. She was tall, scrawny, and efficient. I knew she was efficient because the bows of her eyeglasses were attached to a black ribbon that went around her neck.

"Mr. Bigg?" she said with a glassy smile. "Follow me, please."

She preceded me through a labyrinth of corridors to a door that bore a small brass plate: H. KIPPER, PRES.

"Thank you," I said to her.

"Thank *you*, sir," she said, ushered me in, then closed the door gently behind me.

It was a corner office. Two walls were picture windows affording a marvelous view of upper Manhattan. The floor was carpeted deeply, almost indecently. The desk was a slab of black marble on a chrome base—more table than desk. Two men stood behind the desk.

I had an initial impression that I was seeing double or seeing identical twins. They were in fact merely brothers, but Herschel and Bernard Kipper looked alike, dressed alike, shared the same speech patterns, mannerisms, and gestures; during the interview that followed I was continually confused, and finally looked between them when I asked my questions and let him answer who would.

Both were men of medium height, and portly. Both had long strands of thinning hair combed sideways over pink scalp. Their long cigars were identical.

Both were clad in high garment district fashion in steel-gray, raw silk suits. Only their ties were not identical. When they spoke their voices were harsh, phlegmy, with a smokers' rasp, their speech rapid, assertive. They asked me to be seated, although they remained standing, firmly planted, smoking their cigars and staring at me with hard, wary eyes.

Once again I explained that I was engaged in a preliminary inventory of their father's estate, and had come to ascertain if he had left any personal belongings in the offices.

"I understand he maintained a private office here," I added softly. "Even after his retirement."

"Well . . . sure," one of them said. "Pop had an office here."

"But no personal belongings," the other said. "I mean, Pop's desk and chairs and all, the furnishings, they belong to the company."

"No personal possessions?" I persisted. "Jewelry? A set of cufflinks he might have kept in his desk? Photographs? Silver frames?"

"Sure," one of them said. "Pop had photographs."

"We took them," the other one said. "They were of our mother, and Pop's mother and father."

"And all us kids," the other said. "And his grandchildren. In plain frames. No silver or anything like that. And one photograph of *her*. She can have it."

"The bitch!" the other Kipper son said wrathfully.

I had pondered how I might introduce the subjects of Tippi and the will without seeming to pry. I needn't have fretted.

"I assume you're referring to the widow?" I said.

"I said bitch," one of them said, "and I mean bitch!"

"Listen," the other said, "we're not complaining."

"We're not hurting," his brother agreed. "But that gold-digger getting a piece of the company is what hurts."

"Who knows what that birdbrain might do?"

"She might dump her shares."

"Upset the market."

"Or waltz in here and start poking around."

"She knows zilch about the business."

"She could make plenty of trouble, that fake."

"I understand," I said carefully, "that she was formerly in the theatre?"

"The theatre!" one of them cried.

"That's a laugh!" the other cried.

"She was a nightclub dancer."

"A chorus girl."

"All she did was shake her ass."

"And she wasn't very good at that."

"Probably hustling on the side."

"What else? Strictly a horizontal·talent."

"She played him like a fish."

"She knew a good thing when she saw one, and she landed him."

"And made his life miserable."

"Once the contract was signed, no more nice-nice."

"Unless she got what she wanted."

"The house, which they didn't need, and clothes, cars, cruises, jewelry—the works. She took him good."

"It hurt us to see what was going on."

"But he wouldn't listen. He just wouldn't listen."

"Uh," I said, "I understand she also persuaded your father to make contributions to charity. A certain Reverend Godfrey Knurr . . . ?"

"Him!"

"That gonniff!"

"Hundreds!"

"Thousands!"

"To his cockamamie club for street bums."

"Pop wasn't thinking straight."

"Couldn't see how they were taking him."

"Even after he's dead and gone."

"But you probably know that."

I didn't know it. Didn't know to what he was referring. But I didn't want to reveal my ignorance by asking questions.

"Well . . ." I said judiciously, "it's not the first time it's happened. An elderly widower. A younger woman. Does she have family?"

"Who the hell knows?" one of them said.

"She came out of nowhere," the other said. "A drifter. Chicago, I think. Somewhere near there."

"She doesn't talk about it."

"He met her in Vegas."

"Went out there on one of those gambling junkets and came back with a bride. Some bride! Some junket!"

"He lost!"

"We all lost."

"A chippie."

"A whore."

"Everyone could see it but him. Pussy-whipped."

"An old man like that. Our father. Pussy-whipped."

"It hurt."

They glowered at me accusingly. I ducked my head and made meaningless jottings in my notebook, pretending their anger was worth recording. Though I had learned more than I had hoped, there were questions I wanted desperately to ask, but I didn't dare arouse their suspicions.

"Well," I said, "I think that covers the matter of your father's personal belongings. There is one additional thing you may be able to help me with. A claim for a thousand dollars has been filed against the estate by an individual named Martin Reape. We have been unable to contact Mr. Reape, and we wondered if either of you is acquainted with him or knows the reason for the claim."

Again they looked at each other. Then shook their heads.

"Martin Reape?"

"Never heard of him."

"We thought it might possibly be a business expense. Is there any way . . . ?"

"Sure. It can be checked out."

"We got everything on film."

"We can tell you if he was a supplier, a customer, or whatever. Heshie, give Al Baum a call."

Heshie picked up a silver-colored phone.

"Get me Al Baum," he snapped. Then, in a moment, "Al? Herschel. I'm sending you down a lawyer. He wants to check into a certain individual. To see if he's on our books. You understand? Right. Al, you give him every possible cooperation."

He hung up.

"That's Al Baum, our comptroller," he said to me. "He's on the 31st floor. If we've got this guy—what's his name?"

"Martin Reape."

"If we've got this Martin Reape on our books Al will put him on the screen and see if we owe him. Okay?"

I stood up.

"Gentlemen," I said, "you've been very kind, and I appreciate it."

"You filed for probate yet?"

"Well, uh, I think you better talk to Mr. Tabatchnick about that. He's handling it personally."

"Sure . . . what else? Uncle Leo and Pop were old friends. They go way back together."

"Give Uncle Leo our best."

"I'll do that," I said. "Thank you again for your time and trouble."

I got out of there. They were still standing shoulder to shoulder behind the desk, still furious. Their cigars were much shorter now. The marble top was littered with white ash.

The 31st floor was different from the executive enclave on the 34th. Wood floors were carpeted with worn runners, walls were tenement green, chipped and peeling. There was no receptionist; directly in front of the elevators began a maze of flimsy metal cubicles. There was constant noise here; banging and clattering, shouted questions and screamed answers, and a great scurrying to and fro. Large office machines, some with keyboards, some with hidden keys clacking, some quiescent, burping forth a sheet or two of paper at odd moments.

I approached a desk where a young black man was shuffling through an enormous pile of computer printout. He wore wire-rimmed glasses, and a steel comb pushed into his Afro.

"I beg your pardon," I said timidly.

He continued his rapid riffling of the folded stack of paper before him.

"I beg your pardon," I said, louder.

He looked up.

"Say what?" he said.

"I'm looking for Mr. Baum. I wonder if—"

"Al!" he bawled at me. "Oh you, Al! Someone here!"

I drew back, startled. Before I knew what was happening,

my elbow was gripped. A little butterball of a man had me imprisoned.

"Yes, yes, yes?" he spluttered. "Al Baum. What, what, what?"

"Joshua Bigg, Mr. Baum," I said. "I'm the—"

"Who, who, who?" he said. "From Lupowitz?"

"No, no, no," I said. It was catching. "From Tabatchnick, Orsini, Reilly, and Teitelbaum. Mr. Herschel Kipper just called and asked—"

"Right, right, right," he said. "Follow me. This way. Just follow me. Don't trip over the cables."

He darted away and I went darting after him. We rushed into an enormous room where tall gray modules were lined up against the walls, all with tape reels whirling or starting and stopping.

"Computers," I said foolishly.

"No, no, no," Baum said rapidly. "Data processing and retrieval. Payrolls, taxes, et cetera, but mostly inventory. Hundreds of yarns, hundreds of fabrics: all coded. What's this gink's name?"

"Reape," I said. "Martin Reape. R-e-a-p-e."

I scurried after him into a cramped corner office where a young lady sat before a keyboard and what appeared to be a large television screen.

"Josie," Baum said, "look up a Martin Reape. R-e-a-p-e." He turned to me. "What is he?" he asked. "A supplier? Buyer? What, what, what?"

"I don't know," I said, feeling like an idiot. "You may have paid him for something. A supplier. Call him a supplier."

Josie's fingers sped over the keyboard. Mr. Baum and I leaned over her shoulder, watching the screen. Suddenly printing began to appear, letter by letter, word by word, left to right, then down to the next line, with a loud chatter. Finally the machine stopped. The screen showed seven payments of five hundred dollars each. The payee was Martin Reape, the address was his 49th Street office. The first payment was made in August of the previous year. The last payment was made one week prior to the death of Sol Kipper.

"There he is," Al Baum said. "That what you wanted?"

"Yes," I said, feeling a fierce exaltation. "Would it be possible to see the canceled checks?"

"Why not?" he said. "We got everything on film. Josie?"

She pushed more buttons. The screen cleared, then was filled with a picture of the Kipmar Textile checks made out to Martin Reape. I leaned closer to peer. All the checks had been signed by Albert Baum, Comptroller.

I turned to him.

"You signed the checks?" I said.

I must have sounded accusing. He looked at me pityingly.

"Sure I signed. So, so, so?"

"Do you remember what it was for? I mean, why was Martin Reape paid that money?"

He shrugged. "I sign a thousand checks a week. At least. Who can remember? Josie, let's see the bills."

She pushed more buttons. Now the bills appeared on the screen. They had no printed heading, just the typewritten name and address of Martin Reape. Each was for $500. Each merely said: "For services rendered."

"See, see, see?" Al Baum demanded. "Down there in the corner of every bill? 'OK/SK.' That's Sol Kipper's initials and handwriting. He OK'd the bills, so I paid."

"You have no idea of the services Martin Reape rendered?"

"Nope, nope, nope."

"Is there any way I can get a copy of the bills and canceled checks?"

"Why not?" he said. "Mr. Heshie said to give you full cooperation. Right, right, right? Josie, run a printout on everything—totals, bills, checks: the works."

"Thank you," I said. "You've been very—"

"Happy, happy, happy," he rattled, and then he was gone.

I waited while Josie pushed more buttons, and printout came stuttering out of an auxiliary machine. I watched, fascinated, as it printed black-and-white reproductions of the bills from Martin Reape, the checks paid by Kipmar Textiles, and a neat summation of dates billed, dates paid, and totals. Josie tore off the sheet of paper and handed it to me. I folded it carefully and tucked it into my inside jacket pocket.

"Thank you very much," I said.

"Sure, bubi," she chirped.

I found a phone booth in the street-floor lobby, and looked up a number in my book. She answered on the first ring.

"Yes?" she said.

"Perdita?" I asked, "Perdita Schug?"

"Yes. Who's this?"

"Joshua Bigg. You probably don't—"

"Josh!" she said. "How cute! I was hoping you'd call."

"Yes . . . well . . . how are you?"

"Bored, bored, bored," she said. I wondered if she knew Al Baum. "What I need is a little excitement. A new love."

"Uh . . . yes. Well, why I called . . . I remembered you said Thursday was your day off. Am I correct?"

"Right on," she said. "I get off at noon tomorrow and I don't have to be back until Friday noon. Isn't that cute?"

"It certainly is," I said bravely. "What do you usually do on your day off?"

"Oh," she said, "This and that. I should go out to visit my dear old mother in Weehawken. You got any cuter ideas?"

"Well, I was wondering if you might care to have dinner with me tomorrow night?"

"I accept," she said promptly.

"We can make it early," I suggested, "so you'll have plenty of time to get over to New Jersey."

She laughed merrily.

"You're so funny, Josh," she said. "You're really a scream."

"Thank you," I said. "Is there any place you'd like to go? For dinner, I mean. Some place where we can meet?"

"Mother Tucker's," she said. "Second Avenue near Sixty-ninth Street. You'll like it. I hang out there all the time. Seven or eight o'clock, like that, OK?"

As I walked homeward west on my street, I saw Cleo Hufnagel coming east, arms laden with shopping. I hurried to help her.

"Thank you, Josh," she said. "I had no idea they'd be so heavy."

She was wearing a red plaid coat with a stocking hat pulled down to her eyes. The wind and fast walking had rosied her cheeks. Her eyes sparkled. She looked very fetching and I told her so. She smiled shyly.

"Home from work so soon?" I asked as we climbed the steps.

"I had the day off," she said, "but I'll have to work Saturday. You're home early."

"Playing hooky," I said. I took the other bag of groceries

while she hunted for her keys. She unlocked the doors and held them open for me.

"Can I carry these into your kitchen for you?" I asked.

"Oh no," she said hastily. "Thank you, but most of these things are for Mother."

So I set the bag down in the hallway outside Mrs. Hufnagel's apartment after huffing my way up to the second floor.

"Thank you so much, Josh," Cleo said. "You were very kind."

I waved my hand. "No tip necessary," I said, and we both laughed. Then we just stood there, looking at each other. It didn't bother me that I had to look up to meet her eyes. I blurted out, "Cleo, would you like to come up to my place for a glass of wine after dinner?"

"Thank you," she said in a low voice. "I'd like that. What time?"

"About eight. Is that all right?"

"Eight is fine. See you then."

I trudged up to my apartment, meditating on what I had done.

Checking my wine cellar, I found I was in short supply, so after I showered and got into my Chelsea clothes I headed out on a run to the liquor store. Bramwell Shank was there on the landing, waiting for me with the wine in his lap.

"Goddamn!" he shouted. "I've been waiting here for you and all the time you've been in there!"

This was obviously my fault. I explained how I had come home early, and explained why, and offered to pick up anything he needed from the stores, and got away with a promise to have a drink with him when I came back in. This seemed a good idea or he might barge in later on my tête-à-tête with Cleo.

She arrived promptly at 8:00 P.M., knocking softly on my door. I leaped to my feet and upset what was left in a glass of wine on my chair arm. Fortunately, the glass fell to the rug without breaking, and none of the wine splashed on me.

"Coming!" I shouted. Hastily, I retrieved the glass and moved the armchair to cover the stain on the rug. Then I had to move the endtable to bring it alongside, and when I did that, the lamp tipped over. I caught it before it could crash, set it upright again, then rushed to the door.

"Come in, come in!" I said heartily and ushered her to the armchair. "Sit here," I said. "It's the most comfortable."

"Well..." Cleo Hufnagel said doubtfully, "isn't it a little close to the fire? Could you move it back a bit?"

I stared at her, then started laughing. I told her what had happened just before she entered. She laughed, too, and assured me a stained rug wouldn't offend her. So we moved everything back in place.

"Much better," she said, seating herself. "I do that all the time. Spilling things, I mean. You shouldn't have bothered covering it."

We settled down with drinks. Happily I asked her if she had noticed signs of rapprochement between Captain Shank and Madame Kadinsky. There had been signs of romance. That did it. In a moment she had kicked off her shoes and we were gossiping like mad.

Presently I heard myself saying, "But if they married, they might tear each other to tatters. Argue, fight. You know."

"Even that's better than what they had before, isn't it?"

The conversation was making me uneasy. I went into the kitchen to fetch fresh drinks.

"Cleo," I said when I came back, "I really know very little about what you do. I know you work in a library. Correct?"

"Yes," she said, lifting her chin. "I'm a librarian."

I spent five minutes assuring her that I admired librarians, that some of the happiest hours of my life had been spent in libraries, that they were a poor man's theatre, a portal to a world of wonder, and she was in a noble and honored profession, etc., etc. I really laid it on, but the strange thing was that I believed every word of it.

"You're very kind," she said doubtfully. "But what it comes down to is some bored housewife looking for the new Jackie Onassis book or a Gothic. You're with a legal firm, Josh?"

"Yes," I said, "but I'm not a lawyer. I'm just an investigator."

I explained to her what I did. I found myself talking and talking. She seemed genuinely interested, and asked very cogent questions. She wanted to know my research sources and how I handled abstruse inquiries. I told her some stories that amused her: how I had spent one Sunday morning trying to buy beer in stores on Second Avenue (illegal), how I manipulated recalcitrant witnesses, how people lied to me and how, to my shame, I was becoming an accomplished liar.

"But you've got to," she said. "To do your job."

"I know that," I said, "but I'm afraid I'll find myself lying in my personal life. I wouldn't like that."

"I wouldn't either," she said. "Could I have another drink?"

I came back from the kitchen with fresh drinks. She reached up with a languid hand to take her glass. She was practically reclining in the armchair, stretched out, her head far back, her stockinged feet toward the dying fire.

She was wearing a snug, caramel-colored wool skirt, cinched with a narrow belt, and a tight black sweater that left her neck bare. All so different from the loose, flowing costumes she usually wore. The last flickering flames cast rosy highlights on throat, chin, brow. She had lifted her long, chestnut hair free. It hung down in back of the chair. I wanted to stroke it.

I was shocked at how beautiful she looked, that willowy figure stretched out in the dim light. Her features seemed softened. The hazel eyes were closed, the lips slightly parted. She seemed utterly relaxed.

"Cleo," I said softly.

Her eyes opened.

"I just thought of something. I have a favor to ask."

"Of course," she said, straightening up in her chair.

I explained that one of my investigations involved a man who had been a victim of arsenic poisoning. I needed to know more about arsenic: what it was, how it affected the human body, how it could be obtained, how administered, and so forth. Could Cleo find out the titles of books or suggest other places where I might obtain that information?

"I can do that," she said eagerly. "I'm not all that busy. When do you need it?"

"Well...as soon as possible. I just don't know where to start. I thought if you could give me the sources, I'd take it from there."

"I'll be happy to," she said. "Did he die?"

"No, but he's disappeared. I think the poisoning had something to do with it."

"You mean whoever was poisoning him decided to, uh, take more direct measures?"

I looked at her admiringly. "You're very perceptive."

"I have a good brain, I know," she said. It was not bragging; she was just stating a fact. "Too bad I never get a chance to use it."

"Were you born in New York, Cleo?" I asked her.

"No," she said, "Rhode Island." She told me the story of her family. Her father had disappeared from Newport one day and Mrs. Hufnagel had brought tiny Cleo to Chelsea to live in the house, which had been bought with their last money as an investment.

I told her my little history—little in at least two ways. I told her how I was raised by my uncle and aunt and what I had to endure from my cousins.

"But I'm not complaining," I said. "They were good people."

"Of course they were, to take you in. But still . . ."

"Yes," I said. "Still . . ."

We sat awhile in silence, a close, glowing silence.

"Another drink?" I asked finally.

"I don't think so," she said. "Well, maybe a very small one. Just a sip."

"A nightcap?" I said.

"Right," she said approvingly.

"I'm going to have a little brandy."

"That sounds good," she said. "I'll have a little brandy, too."

So we each had a little brandy. I thought about her father, a shy man who flew kites before he vanished. It seemed to go with the quiet and winking embers of the fire.

"I've never flown a kite," I confessed. "Not even as a kid."

"I think you'd like it."

"I think I would, too. Listen, Cleo, if I bought a kite, could we go up to Central Park some day, a Sunday, and fly it? Would you show me how?"

"Of course—I'd love to. But we don't have to go up to Central Park. We can go over to those old wharves on the river and fly it from there."

"What kind of a kite should I buy?"

"The cheapest one you can get. Just a plain diamond shape. And you'll need a ball of string. I'll tear up some rags for a tail."

"What color would you like?" I said, laughing.

"Red," she said at once. "It's easier to see against the sky, and it's prettier."

A green sweater for Yetta and a red kite for Cleo.

We sat in silence, sipping our brandies. After a while her free hand floated up and grasped my free hand. Hers was warm and soft. We remained like that, holding hands. It was perfect.

4

I AWOKE TO a smutty day, a thick sky filled with whirling gusts of sleet and rain. A taut wind from the west whipped the pedestrians hunched as they scurried, heads down. The TORT building didn't exhibit its usual morning hustle-bustle. Many of the employees lived in the suburbs, and roads were flooded or blocked by toppled trees, and commuter trains were running late.

I had brought in a container of black coffee and an apple strudel. I made phone calls over my second breakfast. The Reverend Godfrey Knurr agreed to show me his club that day, and Glynis Stonehouse said she would see me. She said her mother was indisposed, in bed with a virus. (A sherry virus, I thought—but didn't say it.)

Despite the wretched weather I got up to the West 70s in half an hour. Glynis Stonehouse answered the door. We went down that long corridor again, into the living room. I noticed that several of the framed maps and naval battle scenes had disappeared from the walls, to be replaced by bright posters and cheery graphics. Someone did not expect Professor Stonehouse to return.

We sat at opposite ends of the lengthy couch, half-turned so we could look at each other. Glynis said Mrs. Stonehouse was resting comfortably. I declined a cup of coffee. I took out my notebook.

"Miss Stonehouse," I started, "I spoke to your brother at some length."

"I hope he was—cooperative?"

"Oh yes. Completely. I gather there had been a great deal of, uh, enmity between Powell and his father?"

"He made my brother's life miserable," she said. "Powell is such a *good* boy. Father destroyed him!"

I was surprised by the virulence in her husky voice, and looked at her sharply.

The triangular face with cat's eyes of denim blue was expressionless, the sculpted lips firmly pressed. Her tawny hair was drawn sleekly back. A remarkably beautiful woman, with her own secrets. She made me feel like a blundering amateur; I despaired of ever penetrating that self-possession and discovering—what?

"Miss Stonehouse, can you tell me anything about Powell's ah, companion? Wanda Chard?"

"I don't know her very well. I met her only once."

"What is your impression?"

"A very quiet woman. Deep. Withdrawn. Powell says she is very religious. Zen."

"Your father met her two weeks before he disappeared."

That moved her. She was astonished.

"Father did?" she said. "Met Wanda Chard?"

"So she says. He went down to your brother's apartment. Powell wasn't at home. He stayed about ten minutes talking to Miss Chard. Your father never mentioned the visit?"

"No. Never."

"You have no idea why he might have visited your brother— or tried to?"

"None whatsoever. It's so out of character for my father."

"It couldn't have been an attempted reconciliation with your brother, could it?"

She pondered a moment.

"I'd like to think so," she said slowly.

"Miss Stonehouse," I said, "I'd like to ask a question that

I hope won't offend you. Do you believe your brother is capable of physical violence against your father?"

Those blue eyes turned to mine. It was more than a half-beat before she answered. But she never blinked.

"He might have been," she said, no timbre in her voice. "Before he left home. But since he's had his own place, my brother has made a marvelous adjustment. Would he have been capable of physical violence the night my father disappeared? No. Besides, he was here when my father walked out."

"Yes," I said. "Do you think Wanda Chard could have been capable of physical violence?"

"I don't know," she said. "I just don't know. It's possible, I suppose. Perfectly normal, average people are capable of the most incredible acts."

"Under pressure," I agreed. "Or passion. Or hate. Or any strong emotion that results in loss of self-control. Love, for instance."

"Perhaps," she said.

Noncommittal.

"Miss Stonehouse," I said, sighing, "is Mrs. Dark at home?"

"Why, yes. She's in the kitchen."

A definite answer. What a relief.

"May I speak to her for a moment?"

"Of course. You know the way, don't you?"

When I entered the kitchen, Effie was seated at the center table, smoking a cigarette and leafing through the morning *Daily News*. She looked up as I came in, and her bright little eyes crinkled up with pleasure.

"Why, Mr. Bigg," she said, her loose dentures clacking away. "This *is* nice."

"Good to see you again, Effie. How have you been?"

"Oh, I've got no complaints," she said cheerily. "What are you doing out on such a nasty morning? Here . . . sit down."

"Thank you," I said. "Well, Effie, I wanted to ask you a few more questions. Silly things that probably have nothing to do with the Professor's disappearance. But I've got to ask them just to satisfy my own curiosity."

"Sure," she said, shrugging her fat shoulders, "I can understand that. I'm as curious as the next one. Curiouser."

"Effie, what time of night do you usually go to bed?"

"Well, I usually go to my room about nine-thirty, ten. Around then. After I've cleaned up here. Then I read a little, maybe watch a little television. Write a letter or two. I'm usually in bed by eleven."

I laughed. "Lucky woman. Do you leave anything here in the kitchen for the family? In case they want a late snack?"

"Oh, they can help themselves," she said casually. "They know where everything is." Then, when I was wondering how to lead into it, she added: "Of course, when the Professor was here, I always left him a saucepan of cocoa."

"Cocoa?" I said. "I didn't think people drank cocoa anymore."

"Of course they do. It's delicious."

"And you served the Professor a cup of cocoa before you went to bed?"

"Oh no. I just made it. Then I left it to cool. Around midnight, Miss Glynis would come in and just heat it up. Even if she was out at the theatre or wherever, she'd come home, heat up the cocoa, and bring a cup to her father in his study."

"So I understand. Glynis brought the Professor his cup of cocoa every night?"

"That's right."

"And no one else in the house drank it?"

"No one," she said, and my heart leaped—until she said, "except me. I finished it in the morning."

"Finished it?"

"What was left in the pan. I like a cup of hot cocoa before I start breakfast."

That seemed to demolish the Great Cocoa Plot. But did it?

"Effie, who washed out the Professor's cocoa cup in the morning?"

"I did. He always left it on the kitchen sink."

"Why on earth did he drink cocoa so late at night?"

"He claimed it helped him sleep better." She snickered. "Just between you, me, and the lamppost, I suspect it was the brandy he had along with it."

"Uh-huh," I said. "Well, Effie, I think that covers it. There's just one other favor I'd like to ask. I want to take another look in the Professor's study."

"Help yourself," she said. "The door's unlocked."

"I don't want to go in alone."

"Oh?" She looked at me shrewdly. "So you'll have a witness that you didn't take anything?"

"Right," I said gratefully.

The study looked exactly as it had before. I stood near the center of the room, my eyes half-closed. I turned slowly, inspecting.

The drum table. Brandy bottle and two small balloon glasses on an Edwardian silver tray. The Rémy Martin bottle was new, sealed.

Where did he hide the will? Not up the chimney. Not in the littered desk. Not behind a secret panel. Ula and Glynis would have probed up the chimney, searched the desk, tapped the walls, combed every book and map.

But I thought I knew where the will was hidden.

Glynis seemed not to have moved since I left. Still reclined easily in a corner of the couch. She was not fussing with her scarf, stroking her sleeked-back hair, inspecting her nails. She had the gift of complete repose.

"Miss Stonehouse," I said, "could you spare me a few more minutes?"

"Of course."

"I have some very distressing information," I told her. "Something I think you should be aware of. I hoped to inform your mother, but since she is indisposed—temporarily, I trust—I must tell you."

She cocked her head to one side, looking puzzled.

"When your father was ill last year, for a period of months, he was suffering from arsenic poisoning."

Something happened to her face. It shrank. The flesh seemed to become less and the skin tightened onto bone, whitened and taut. Genuine surprise or the shock of being discovered?

"What?" she said.

"Your father. He was being poisoned. By arsenic. Finally, in time, he consulted a physician. He recovered. That means he must have discovered how he was being fed the arsenic. And by whom."

"Impossible," she said. Her voice was so husky it was almost a rasp.

"I'm afraid it's true," I said. "No doubt about it. And since your father rarely dined out, he must have been ingesting arsenic here, in his own home, in some food or drink that no one else in the house ate or drank, because no one else suffered the same effects. I have an apology to make to you, Miss Stonehouse. For a brief period, I thought the arsenic might have been given to him in that nightly cup of cocoa which you served him. Something I thought no one else in the household drank. But Mrs. Dark has just told me that she finished the cocoa every morning and was none the worse for it. So I apologize to you for my suspicions. And now I must try to find some other way that your father was being poisoned."

That jolted her. The repose was gone; she began to unbutton and button her black gabardine jacket. She was wearing a brassiere, but I caught quick glimpses of the smooth, tender skin of her midriff.

"You thought that I . . ." she faltered.

"Please," I said, "I do apologize. I know now it wasn't the cocoa. I'm telling you this because I want you to think very carefully and try to remember if your father ate or drank anything that no one else in the household ate or drank."

"You're quite sure he was being poisoned?" she said faintly.

"Oh yes. No doubt about it."

"And you think that had something to do with his disappearance?"

"It seems logical, doesn't it?"

Her face began to fill out again. Her color returned to normal. She looked at me squarely. She stopped fussing with her buttons and settled back into her original position. She took a deep breath.

"Yes," she said softly, "I think you're right. If someone was trying to kill him . . ."

"Someone obviously was."

"But why?"

"Miss Stonehouse," I said, "I just don't know. My investigation hasn't progressed that far. As yet."

"But you are making progress?"

It was my turn to be noncommittal.

"I have discovered several things," I said, "that may or may not be significant. But to get back to my original question, can you think of any way your father may have been poisoned? Other than the cocoa?"

She stared at me a long moment, but she wasn't seeing me.

"No," she said, "I can't. We all ate the same things, drank the same things. Father bought bottled water, but everyone drank that."

"He wasn't on a special diet of any kind?"

"No."

"Well..." I said, "if you recall anything, please let me know."

"Mr. Bigg," she said slowly, "you said you suspected me of poisoning my father's cocoa."

"Not exactly," I said. "For a time I did think the cocoa you served him might have been poisoned. But anyone in the household could have done that. But I realized I was mistaken after Mrs. Dark told me she finished the leftover cocoa every morning."

"She *told* you," Glynis Stonehouse said steadily. "I've never seen Mrs. Dark have a cup of cocoa in the morning, and I don't believe anyone else has either."

Again our eyes locked, but this time she was really looking at me, her gaze challenging, unblinking.

The sleet had lessened, but the sky was still drooling. I ducked into a curbside phone kiosk on Columbus Avenue and called the office, and chatted with Yetta Apatoff. I reminded her of our lunch date on Friday. She hadn't forgotten. Yetta said the office manager had left me a message. He had hired a temporary assistant for me. She would appear at my office at three o'clock, which still gave me time to run downtown to visit the good Reverend Knurr.

I took the Seventh Avenue IRT local down to Houston Street and walked up to Carmine Street. I stopped at a bodega along the way and brought a six-pack. I had the address, but was a few minutes early, so I walked by across the street, inspecting the premises. It was no smaller or larger than any of the other storefronts on the street. But the glass window and door had been painted a dark green. An amateur sign across the front read: TENTMAKERS CLUB. I crossed the street and went in. The door rang a bell as it opened.

"Halloo?" Knurr's voice shouted from the rear.

"Joshua Bigg," I yelled back.

"Be with you in a minute, Joshua. Make yourself at home."

There was a small open space as one entered. Apparently

it was used as an office, for there was a battered wooden desk, an old, dented file cabinet, three chairs (none of which matched), a coat tree, and several cartons stacked on the floor. They all seemed to be filled with used and tattered paperback novels.

Beyond the makeshift office was a doorway curtained with a few yards of sleazy calico nailed to the top of the frame. I pushed my way through and found myself in a large bare chamber with fluorescent lights overhead. On the discolored walls were charts showing positions and blows in judo, jiu-jitsu, and karate. There were also a few posters advertising unarmed combat tournaments.

In one corner was a tangle of martial arts jackets, kendo staves and masks, dumbbells. There was a rolled-up wrestling mat against one wall.

I was inspecting an illustrated directory of kung fu positions and moves taped to the wall when the Reverend Godfrey Knurr entered from a curtained rear doorway.

"Joshua," he said, "good to see you. Thanks for coming."

"Here," I said, thrusting the damp brown bag at him. "I brought along a cold six-pack. For lunch."

He peeked into the bag.

"Wonderful," he said. "Come on back. I'll put the beer in the fridge and you can hang your things away."

There was a short corridor that debouched into kitchen and bedroom.

The kitchen was just large enough to contain a wooden table and four chairs, refrigerator, sink, cabinets, and a tiny stove. The walls were pebbled with umpteen coats of paint. There was a small rear window looking out onto a sad little courtyard, squalid in the rain. The same view was available from the window in the bedroom. This was a monk's cell: bed, closet, chest of drawers, straight-back chair, bedside table with lamp and telephone, a bookcase.

"Not *quite* the Kipper townhouse, is it?" Knurr said. He was putting the beer in the refrigerator when we heard the jangle of the front door bell.

"They'll be coming in now," he said. "Let's go up front."

I followed him to the gym. He was wearing a gray sweatsuit, out at elbow and knee. His sneakers were stained and torn; the laces broken and knotted.

Three boys were taking off wet things in the office. They tossed their outer apparel onto the desk, then came back to the larger room where they divested themselves of shoes, sweaters, shirts, and trousers, kicking these into a corner.

Knurr introduced me casually: "Joshua, these brutes are Rafe, Tony, Walt. This is Josh."

We all nodded. They appeared to me to be about 13 to 15, bodies skinny and white, all joints. Their faces and necks were pitted with acne.

The bell jangled again; more boys entered. Finally Knurr had a dozen boys milling around the gym in their drawers and socks.

"Cut the shit!" the Reverend yelled. "Line up and let's get started."

They arranged themselves in two files, facing him. At his command they began to go through a series of what I presumed were warmup exercises, following Knurr. He stood with left foot advanced, left arm extended, hand clenched, knuckles down. The right foot was back, right arm cocked, right fist clenched. Then, at a shouted "Hah!" everyone took a step forward onto the right foot, striking an imaginary opponent with the right fist while bending the left arm and retracting the left fist to the shoulder. At the second "Hah!" they all took a step backward to their original position.

I revised my guess at their age group upward to 12 to 17. Some of them were quite large, including a six-foot black. There were four blacks, one Oriental, and two I thought were Hispanic. All were remarkably thin, some painfully so, and most had the poor skin tone of slum kids. There were scars and bruises in abundance, and one shambling youth had a black patch over one eye.

Knurr led them through a series of increasingly violent exercises, culminating with a series of high front and back kicks.

After the exercise period was finished, Godfrey Knurr assigned partners and the boys paired off. They went through what appeared to me to be mock combat. No actual blows were struck, no kicks landed, but it was obvious that all the youths were in dead earnest, punching and counterpunching, kicking out and turning swiftly to avoid their opponents' kicks. As they fought, Knurr moved from pair to pair, watched them closely, stopped them to demonstrate a punch or correct the position of their feet. He had a few words to say to each boy in the room.

"All right," he shouted finally. "That's enough. Unroll the mat. We'll finish with a throw."

The wrestling mat was spread in the center of the bare wood floor. They gathered around and I moved closer. Knurr strode out onto the mat and beckoned one of the lads.

"Come on, Lou," he said. "Be my first victim."

There was laughter, some calls and rude comments as the six-foot black stepped forward on the mat to face Knurr.

"All right," Knurr said, "lead at me with a hard right. And don't tighten up. Stay loose. Ready?"

Lou fell into the classic karate stance, then punched at Knurr's throat with his right knuckles. The pastor executed a movement so fast and flowing that I could scarcely follow it. He plucked the black's wrist out of the air, lifted it as he turned, bent, put a shoulder into the boy's armpit, pulled down on the arm, levered up, and Lou's feet went flying high in the air, cartwheeling over Knurr's head. He would have crashed onto the mat if Knurr hadn't caught him about the waist and let him down gently.

There was more laughter, shouts, exclamations of delighted surprise. The Reverend helped Lou to his feet and then they went through the throw very slowly, Knurr pausing frequently to explain exactly what he was doing, calling his students' attention to the position of his feet, how his weight shifted, how he used the attacker's momentum to help disable him.

"Okay," he said, "that was just a demonstration. Tomorrow you're all going to work on that throw. And you'll work on it and work on it until everyone can do it right. Then I'll show you the defense against it. Now . . . who's going to show up for the bullshit session tonight?" He looked around the room. But heads were hanging; no one volunteered. "Come on, come on," Knurr said impatiently, "you've got to pay for your fun. Who's coming for the talk?"

A few hands went up hesitantly, then a few more. Finally about half the boys had hands in the air.

"How about you, Willie?" Knurr demanded, addressing the shambling youth with the black eyepatch. "You haven't been around for weeks. You must have a wagonload of sins to confess. I especially want you."

This was greeted with laughter and shouts from the others.
"Right on!"

"Get him, Faddeh!"

"Make him spill everything!"

"He's been a *baaaad* boy!"

"Aw right," Willie said with a tinny grin, "I'll be here."

"Good," Knurr said. "Now dry off, all of you, then get the
hell out of here. The gym will be open from five to eight
tonight if any of you want to work out. See you all tomorrow."

They began to pick up their garments from the floor, with
the noise and horseplay you'd expect. Knurr rolled up the mat
and flung it against the wall. His sweatshirt was soaked dark
under the arms, across the back and chest. While he showered
I sat at the kitchen table, sipping beer from the can, listening
to shouts and laughter of departing boys. I looked up through
the window. In the apartment house across the courtyard an
old woman fed a parakeet seeds from her lips, bird perched
on finger.

Godfrey Knurr came into the kitchen wearing a terrycloth
robe, toweling head and beard. He put the towel around his
neck, took a beer from the refrigerator. He sat across from me.

"Well?" he demanded. "What do you think?"

"Very impressive," I said. "You speak to them in their own
language. They seem to respect you. They obey you. The only
thing that bothers me is—"

"I know what bothers you," he interrupted. "You're wondering if I'm not teaching those monsters how to be expert
muggers."

"Yes," I said. "Something like that."

"It's a risk," he admitted. "I know it exists. I keep pounding
at them that they're learning the martial arts only for self-
defense. And God knows they need it, considering what their
lives are like. And they do need physical exercise."

"Does it have to be karate?" I asked. "Couldn't it be basketball?"

"Or tiddledywinks?" he said sourly. "Or I could read them
Pindar's odes. Look, Joshua, most of those kids have records.
Violence attracts them. All I'm trying to do is capitalize on
that. Listen, every time they punch the air and shout 'Hah!'
they're punching out the Establishment. I'm trying to turn that
revolt to a more peaceable and constructive channel."

"You can kill with karate, can't you?" I asked him.

"I don't teach them killing blows," he said shortly. "Also, what you just saw is only half of my program. The other half is group therapy and personal counseling. I try to become a father figure. Most of their natural fathers are drunks, on drugs, or have disappeared. Vamoosed. So I'm really the only father they've got, and I do my damndest to straighten out their tiny brains. Some of those brutes are so screwed up—you wouldn't believe! *Mens sana in corpore sano.* That's really what I'm hoping for these kids. What I'm working toward. Let's eat."

He had made a salad of cut-up iceberg lettuce topped with gobs of mayonnaise. The roast beef sandwiches had obviously been purchased in a deli; they were rounded with the meat filling, also slathered with mayonnaise. He opened two more beers for us and we ate and drank. And he talked.

He was a very intelligent, articulate man, and he talked well. What impressed me most about him was his animal energy. He attacked his sandwich wolfishly, forked the salad into his mouth in great, gulping mouthfuls, swilled the beer in throat-wrenching swallows.

"But it all costs money," he was saying. "Money, money, money: the name of the game. There's no church available for me—for any of the tentmakers. So we have to make our own way. Earn enough to do the work we want to do."

"Maybe that's an advantage," I said.

He looked at me, startled. "You're very perceptive, Joshua," he said. "If you mean what I think you mean, and I think you do. Yes, it's an advantage in that it keeps us in closer touch with the secular life, gives us a better understanding of the everyday problems and frustrations of the ordinary working stiff—and stiffess! A pastor who's in the same church for years and years grows moss. Sees the same people day in and day out until he's bored out of his skull. There's a great big, cruel, wonderful, striving world out there, but the average preacher is stuck in his little backwater with weekly sermons, organ music, and the terrible problem of how to pay for a new altar cloth. No wonder so many of them crawl in a bottle or run off with the soprano in the choir."

"How did you meet Tippi Kipper?" I asked.

Something fleeting through his eyes. He became a little less voluble.

"A friend of a friend of a friend," he said. "Joshua, the rich of New York are a city within a city. They all know each other. Go to the same parties. I was lucky enough to break into the magic circle. They pass me along, one to another. A friend of a friend of a friend. That's how I met Tippi."

"Was she in the theatre?" I asked.

He grinned. "That's what she says. But no matter. If she wants to play Lady Bountiful, I'm the bucko who'll show her how. Don't get me wrong, Joshua. I'm grateful to Tippi Kipper and I'll be eternally grateful to her kind, generous husband and remember him in my prayers for the rest of my life. But I'm a realist, Joshua. It was an ego thing with the Kippers, I suppose. As it is for all my patrons. And patronesses."

"Sol Kipper contributed to your, uh, activities?" I asked.

"Oh sure. Regularly. What the hell—he took it off his taxes. I'm registered in the State of New York. Strictly nonprofit. Not by choice!" he added with a harsh bark of laughter.

"When you counsel your patrons," I said slowly, trying to frame the question, "the rich patrons, like Tippi Kipper, what are their problems mostly? I mean, it seems unreal to me that people of such wealth should have problems."

"Very real problems," he said soberly. "First of all, guilt for their wealth when they see poverty and suffering all around them. And then they have the same problems we all have: loneliness, the need for love, a sense of our own worthlessness."

He was staring at me steadily, openly. It was very difficult to meet those hard, challenging eyes.

"He left a suicide note," I said. "Did you know that?"

"Yes. Tippi told me."

"In the note, he apologized to her. For something he had done. I wonder what it was?"

"Oh, who the hell knows? I never asked Tippi and she never volunteered the information. It could have been anything. It could have been something ridiculous. I know they had been having, ah, sexual problems. It could have been that, it could have been a dozen other things. Sol was the worst hypochondriac I've ever met. I'm sure others have told you that."

"When did you see him last?" I asked casually.

"The day before he died," he said promptly. "On a Tuesday. We had a grand talk in his office and he gave me a very generous check. Then he had to go somewhere for a meeting."

We sat a few moments in silence. We finished our second beers. Then I glanced at my watch.

"Good heavens!" I said. "I had no idea it was so late. I've got to get back to my office while I still have a job. Pastor, thank you for a very delightful and instructive lunch. I've enjoyed every minute of it."

"Come again," he said. "And often. You're a good listener; did anyone ever tell you that? And bring your friends. And tell them to bring their checkbooks!"

I returned to the TORT building at about 2:50, scurrying out of a drizzly rain that threatened to turn to snow. Yetta Apatoff greeted me with a giggle.

"She's waiting for you," she whispered.

"Who?"

She indicated with a nod of her head, then covered her mouth with her palm. There was a woman waiting in the corridor outside my office.

She was at least 78 inches tall, and wearing a fake monkey fur coat that made her look like an erect gorilla. As I approached her, I thought this was Hamish Hooter's particularly tasteless joke, and wondered how many applicants he had interviewed before he found this one.

But as I drew closer, I saw she was no gorgon. She was, in fact, quite pleasant looking, with a quiet smile and that resigned placidity I recognized. All very short, very tall, and very fat people have it.

"Hello," I said. "I'm Joshua Bigg. Waiting for me?"

"Yes, Mr. Bigg," she said, not even blinking at my diminutive size. Perhaps she had been forewarned. She handed me an employment slip from Hooter's office. "My name is Gertrude Kletz."

"Come in," I said. "Let me take your coat."

I sat behind the desk and she sat in my visitor's chair. We chatted for almost half an hour, and as we talked, my enthusiasm for her grew. Hooter had seen only her huge size, but I found her sensible, calm, apparently qualified, and with a wry sense of humor.

She was married to a sanitation worker and, since their three children were grown and able to take care of themselves, she had decided to become a temporary clerk-typist-secretary: work she had done before her marriage. If possible, she didn't want to work later than 3:00 P.M., so she could be back in Brooklyn in time to cook dinner. We agreed on four hours a day, 11:00 A.M. to 3:00 P.M., with no lunch period, on Monday, Wednesday, and Friday.

She was a ruddy woman with horsey features and a maiden's innocent eyes. Her hair was iron-gray and wispy. For a woman her size, her voice was surprisingly light. She was dressed awkwardly, although I could not conceive how a woman of her heft could possibly be garbed elegantly. She wore a full gray flannel skirt that would have provided enough material for a suit for me. With vest. A no-nonsense white blouse was closed at the neck with a narrow black ribbon, and she wore a tweed jacket in a hellish plaid that would have looked better on Man-o-War. Opaque hose and sensible brogues completed her ensemble. She wore only a thin gold wedding band on her capable hands.

I explained to her as best I could the nature of my work at Tabatchnick, Orsini, Reilly, and Teitelbaum. Then I told her what I expected from her: filing, typing finished letters from my rough drafts, answering my phone, taking messages, doing simple, basic research from sources that I would provide.

"Think you can handle that, Mrs. Kletz?" I asked.

"Oh yes," she said confidently. "You must expect me to make mistakes, but I won't make the same mistake twice."

She sounded better and better.

"There is one other thing," I said. "Much of my work—and thus your work, too—will involve matters in litigation. It is all strictly confidential. You cannot take the job home with you. You cannot discuss what you learn here with anyone else, including husband, family, friends. I must be able to depend upon your discretion."

"You can depend on it," she said almost grimly. "I don't blab."

"Good," I said, rising. "Would you like to start tomorrow or would you prefer to begin on Monday?"

"Tomorrow will be fine," she said, heaving herself upright. "Will you be here then?"

"Probably," I said, thinking about my Friday schedule. "If not, I'll leave instructions for you on my desk. Will that be satisfactory?"

"Sure," she said equably.

I stood on tiptoe to help her on with that ridiculous coat. Then we shook hands, smiling, and she was gone. I thought her a very serene, reassuring woman, and I was grateful to Hamish Hooter. I'd never tell him that, of course.

The moment Mrs. Kletz had departed, I called Hooter's office. Fortunately he was out, but I explained to his assistant what was needed: a desk, chair, typewriter, wastebasket, stationery and supplies, phone, etc., all to be installed in the corridor directly outside my office door. By eleven o'clock the following morning.

"Mr. Bigg!" the assistant gasped in horror. I knew her: a frightened, rabbity woman, thoroughly tyrannized by her boss. "We cannot possibly provide all that by tomorrow morning."

"As soon as possible, then," I said crisply. "My assistant was hired with the approval of the senior partners. Obviously she needs a place to work."

"Yes, Mr. Bigg," she said submissively.

I hung up, satisfied. Today, a temporary assistant. Soon, a full-time secretary. A larger office. Then the *vvorrld!*

I spent the remainder of the afternoon at my desk. Outside, the snow had thickened; TORT employees with radios in their offices reported that three to five inches of snow were predicted before the storm slackened around midnight. Word came down from upstairs that because of the snowfall anyone who wished to leave early could do so. Gradually the building emptied until, by 5:00 P.M., it was practically deserted, the noise stilled, corridors vacant. I stayed on. It seemed foolish to go home to Chelsea and then journey uptown to meet Perdita Schug at Mother Tucker's at 7:00. So I decided to remain in the office until it was time for my dinner date.

I got up and looked out into the main hallway. The lights had already been dimmed and the night security guard was seated at Yetta Apatoff's desk. Beyond him, through the glass entrance doors, I saw a curtain of snow, torn occasionally by heavy gusts.

I went back into my office, wishing that Roscoe Dollworth had left a bottle of vodka hidden in desk or file cabinet. A hopeless wish, I knew. Besides, on a night like that, a nip of brandy would be more to my liking. Now if only I had—

I sank slowly into my chair, suddenly realizing what it was

that had puzzled me about Professor Yale Stonehouse's study: the bottle of Rémy Martin on the silver salver was new, uncorked, still sealed. That meant, apparently, that it had been there since the night he disappeared.

There was a perfectly innocent explanation, of course: he had finished his previous bottle the night before and had set out a fresh bottle, intending to return when he left the Stonehouse apartment on the night of January 10th.

There was another explanation, not so innocent. And that was that Professor Stonehouse had been poisoned not by doctored cocoa, but by arsenic added to his brandy. He had both cocoa and brandy every night before retiring. The lethal doses could have been added in either. And if he had discovered the source, it might account for the sealed bottle in his study.

I glanced at my watch. It was a few minutes past 5:30—a bad time to call. But I had to know. I dialed the Stonehouse apartment.

"Yah?" Olga Eklund said.

"Hi, Olga," I said. "This is Joshua Bigg."

"Yah."

"How are you?"

"Is not nice," she said. "The weather."

"No, it looks like a bad storm. Olga, I wonder if I could talk to Mrs. Dark for a moment—if it isn't too much trouble."

"I get her," she said stolidly.

I waited impatiently for almost three minutes before Mrs. Dark came on the line.

"Hello, dearie," she said brightly.

"Effie," I said, "I'm sorry to bother you at this hour. I know you must be busy with the evening meal."

"No bother. Everything's cooking. Now it's just a matter of waiting."

"I have a few more little questions. I know you'll think they're crazy, but they really are important, and you could be a big help in discovering what happened to the Professor."

"Really?" she said, pleasantly surprised. "Well, I'll do what I can."

"Effie, who buys the liquor for the family—the whiskey, wine, beer, and so forth?"

"I do. I call down to the liquor store on Columbus Avenue and they deliver it."

"And after they deliver it, where is it kept?"

"Well, I always make certain the bar in the living room is kept stocked with everything that might be needed. Plenty of sherry for you-know-who. The reserve I keep right here in the kitchen. In the bottom cupboard."

"And the Professor's brandy? That he drank every night?"

"I always kept an extra bottle or two on hand. God forbid we should ever run out when he wanted it!"

"How long did a bottle last him, Effie? The bottle in his study, I mean?"

"Oh, maybe ten days."

"So he finished about three bottles of cognac a month?"

"About."

"And those bottles were kept in the kitchen cupboard?"

"That's right."

"Who put a fresh bottle in the Professor's study?"

"He'd come in here and fetch it himself. Or I'd take it to him if he had a dead soldier. Or like as not, Glynis would bring him a new bottle."

"And there was usually a bottle of Rémy Martin in the living room bar as well?"

"Oh no," she said, laughing. "The brandy in there is Eye-talian. The Professor kept the good stuff for himself."

He would, I thought, gleeful at what I had learned.

"One more question, Effie," I said. "Very important. Please think carefully and try to recall before you answer. In the month or so before the Professor disappeared, do you remember bringing a fresh bottle of brandy to his study?"

She was silent.

"No," she said finally, "I didn't bring him any. Maybe Glynis did, or maybe he came into the kitchen and got it himself. Wait a minute. I'm on the kitchen extension; it'll just take me a minute to check."

She was gone a short while.

"That's odd," she said. "I was checking the cupboard. I remember having two bottles in there. There's one there now and one unopened bottle in the Professor's study."

"Do you recall buying any new bottles of Rémy Martin in the month or six weeks before the Professor disappeared?"

Silence again for a moment.

"That's odd," she repeated. "I don't remember buying any,

but I should have, him going through three bottles a month.
But I can't recall ordering a single bottle. I'll have to go through
my bills to make sure."

"Could you do that, Effie?"

"Be glad to," she said briskly. "Now I've got to ring off;
something's beginning to scorch."

"You've been very kind," I said hurriedly. "A big help."

"Really?" she said. "That's nice."

We hung up.

If I had been Professor Stonehouse, learning I was a victim
of arsenic poisoning, I would have set out to discover how it
was being done and who was doing it. And, I was certain, he
had discovered who had been doing the fiddling.

It was then getting on to 6:00 P.M. I had no idea how long
it would take me to get uptown in the storm, so I donned
rubbers, turned up the collar of my overcoat, pulled my hat
down snugly, and started out. I said goodnight to the security
guard and stepped outside.

I was almost blown away. This was not one of your soft,
gentle snowfalls with big flakes drifting down slowly in silence
and sparkling in the light of streetlamps and neon signs. This
was a maelstrom, the whole world in turmoil. Snow came
whirling straight down, was blown sideways, even rose up in
gusty puffs from drifts beginning to pile up on street corners.

There were at least twenty people waiting for the Third
Avenue bus. After a wait that seemed endless but was probably
no more than a quarter-hour, not one but four buses appeared
out of the swirling white. I wedged myself aboard the last one.
The ride seemed to take an eternity. At 69th, five other passengers alighted and I was popped out along with them. I
fought my way eastward against the wind, bent almost double
to keep snow out of my face.

And there, right around the corner on Second Avenue, was
a neon sign glowing redly through the snow: MOTHER TUCKER'S.

"Bless you, Mother," I said aloud.

Perdita was there, in the front corner of the bar, perched
on a stool, wearing a black dress cut precariously low. Her
head was back, gleaming throat exposed, and she was laughing
heartily at something the man standing next to her had just
said. The place was jammed in spite of the weather, but Perdita
was easy to find.

She saw me almost the instant I saw her. She slid off the barstool with a very provocative movement and rushed to embrace me with a squeal of pleasure, burying me in her *embonpoint*.

"Josh!" she cried, and then made that deep, growling sound in her throat to signify pleasure. "I never, never, never thought you'd show up. I just can't believe you came out in all this shit to see little me." Her button eyes sparkled, her tongue darted in and out between wet lips. "You poor dear, we must get you thawed out. Col, see if you can get a round from Harry."

"What's your pleasure, sir?" her companion asked politely.

"Scotch please, with water."

We introduced ourselves. He was Clyde Manila—Colonel Clyde Manila. Perdita called him Col, which could have meant in his case either Colonel or Colonial.

A bearded bartender, working frantically, heard the call, paused, and cupped his ear toward Colonel Manila.

"More of the same, Harry, plus Scotch and water."

Harry nodded and in a few moments set the drinks before us. I reached for my wallet but Harry swiftly extracted the required amount from the pile of bills and change on the bar in front of the Colonel.

"Thank you, sir," I said. "The next one's on me."

"Forget it," Perdita advised. "The Col's loaded. Aren't you, sweetheart?"

"I mean to be," he said, swallowing half his drink in one enormous gulp. "No use trying to get home on a night like this—what?" His tiny eyes closed in glee.

He was genially messy in effect—white walrus mustache, swollen boozy nose, hairy tweed hacking jacket, all crowned with an ill-fitting ginger toupee.

"I'm awfully hungry," I said. "Perdita, do you think there's any chance of our getting a table?"

"Sure," she said. "Col, talk to Max."

Obediently he moved away, pushing his way through the mob.

"A pleasant place," I said to Perdita, who was winking at someone farther down the bar.

"This joint?" she said. "A home away from home. You can

always score here, Josh. Remember that: you can always score at Mother Tucker's. Here comes Col."

I turned to see Colonel Manila waving wildly at us.

"He's got a table," Perdita said. "Let's go."

"Is he going to eat with us?" I asked.

"Col? No way. He never eats."

I wanted to thank him for obtaining a table for us, but missed him in the crush.

At the table she said, "I want another drink, and then I want a Caesar salad, spaghetti with oil and garlic, scampi, and a parfait for dessert."

I cringed from fear that I might not have enough to pay for all that. I do not believe in credit cards.

"What are you drinking?" I asked.

"Who knows?" she said. "I've been here since one o'clock this afternoon."

A waitress appeared in a T-shirt that said "Flat is Beautiful." We settled on a drink for Perdita and the waitress left.

"Don't worry about the check," Perdita said breezily. "Colonel Manila will pay."

"Absolutely not," I said indignantly. "I invited you. He doesn't have to pay for our dinner."

"Don't be silly," she said. "He likes to buy me things. I told you—he's loaded. Light my cigarette."

Talking to her was no problem; it was only necessary to listen. She babbled through our second round of drinks, through her gargantuan meal and a bottle of Chianti. I tried, several times, to bring the conversation around to the Kipper household, saying such things as: "I imagine this is better food than Mrs. Neckin's." But Perdita picked up on none of these leads; her monologue would not be interrupted. I gave up and asked for a check, but the waitress assured me, "It's been taken care of."

"I told you," Perdita said, laughing. "The Colonel's always doing things like that for me. He thinks it buys him something."

"And does it?" I asked her.

"Sure," she said cheerfully. "What do you think? Let's go back to the bar."

This was not really necessary as she was quite drunk already. We rejoined the Colonel, and the idea of going to Hoboken for clams was raised. I said I wouldn't. Two young men came and whispered in Perdita's ear and she told them to bug off. They disappeared quickly. The noise was incredible.

Colonel Clyde Manila was seated, lopsided, on Perdita's barstool. The moment he saw us, he slid off and bowed to Perdita.

"Keeping it warm f'you, dear lady," he said, in a strangled voice.

"Colonel," I shouted, "I want to thank you for your kindness. The dinner was excellent."

Those pale little eyes seemed to have become glassy. "Good show," he said.

"May I buy you a drink, sir?" I asked.

"Good show," he said.

"Oh, don't be such a pooper, Josh," Perdita said. "Come dance with me."

She clasped me in her arms, closed her eyes, began to shuffle me about. "I just love Viennese waltzes," Perdita Schug said dreamily.

"I think that's 'Beautiful Ohio,'" I said.

"Nasty brutes," Colonel Manila said. He was at my shoulder, staggering after us around the minuscule dance floor. "They smell, y'know. Did you ever sheep a shear?" I had suspected that he was Australian.

"The last time I saw Paris," Perdita crooned in my ear. "Let's you and me make yum-yum."

"Perdita," I said, "I really—"

"Can we go to your place?" she whispered.

"Oh no. No, no, no. Really. I'm afraid that wouldn't—"

"Where is your place?"

"Miles from here. Way downtown. West side."

"Where is your place?" she said. "Yum-yum."

"Way downtown," I started again.

"Col!" she screamed. "We're going."

"Good show," he said.

We came out of Mother Tucker's and turned our backs to a vindictive wind that stung with driven snow. Manila motioned and we went plodding after him around the corner onto 69th Street. He halted at a car and began to fumble in his coat pockets for his keys. We all piled into the front, Perdita sitting in the middle.

"A joint," the Colonel said.

"Oh no, sir," I said. "I thought it was a very pleasant restaurant."

Perdita, already fishing in her purse, got out a fat, hand-rolled cigarette, both ends twisted.

She lighted it, took a deep drag, and held it out to the Col. He took a tremendous drag and half the cigarette seemed to disappear in a shower of sparks.

"Now then," the Colonel said. He handed the joint back to Perdita, then busied himself with switches and buttons. In a few moments he had the headlights on, engine purring, the heater going. The snow on the windows began to melt away.

"Whiskey," the Colonel said, like a drillmaster rapping out commands.

Perdita twisted around, got onto her knees on the front seat, and leaned far over into the rear compartment. Her rump jutted into the air. Colonel Manila slapped it lightly.

"There's a gel," he said affectionately.

She flopped back to her original position with a full decanter and three tumblers, all in cut crystal. She poured us all drinks, big drinks, then set the decanter on the floor between her feet.

I *knew* we would be stopped. I knew the police would arrest us. I could imagine the charges. Perhaps, I thought hopefully, I might get off with three years because of my youthful appearance and exemplary record.

Nothing of the sort happened. The Colonel drove expertly. Even after he turned on the radio to a rock-and-roll station and kept banging the steering wheel with one palm in time to the music, still he smoked, drank, stopped for traffic lights, negotiated turns skillfully, and pulled up right in front of my door, scrunching the limousine into a snowbank. I laughed shrilly.

"Well, this has certainly been a memorable evening," I said, listening to the quaver in my voice. "I do want to thank—"

"Out," Perdita Schug growled, nudging me. "Let's go."

I stumbled out hastily into the snow. She came scrambling after me. I looked back in at Colonel Clyde Manila. He waggled fingers at me. I waggled back. Perdita slammed the car door, then took my arm in a firm, proprietary grip.

"Up we go," she said gaily.

It was then around midnight. I think. Or it could have been

ten. Or it might have been two. Whatever it was, I hoped Mrs. Hermione Hufnagel, Cleo, Captain Bramwell Shank, Adolph Finkel, and Madame Zora Kadinsky were all behind locked doors and sleeping innocently in their warm beds.

"Shh," I said to Perdita Schug, leading her upstairs. I giggled nervously.

"What's with this *shh* shit?" she demanded.

I got her inside my apartment. She was moving now with deliberate and exaggerated caution.

I switched on the overhead light. I draped our coats and hats over a chairback. She looked around the living room. I awaited her reaction. There was none. She flopped into my armchair.

"Come sit on my lap," she said with a vulpine grin.

I began to stammer, but she grabbed my wrist, drew me to her with surprising strength, and plunked me down onto her soft thighs.

She kissed me. My toes curled. Inside shoes and the rubbers I had neglected to remove.

"Mmm," she said. "That's better. Much better."

She wriggled around, pulled me tighter onto her lap. She had a muscled arm around my neck. She pressed our cheeks together. "The last time I saw Paris," she sang.

"Perdita," I said, giving it one last try, "I can't understand how you can endure doing the work you do. I mean, you've got so much personality and, uh, talent and experience. Why do you stay on as a maid for Tippi Kipper?"

"It's a breeze," she said promptly. "The pay is good. And I get meals and my own apartment. My own telephone. What should I be doing—selling gloves in Macy's?"

"But still, it must be boring."

"Sometimes yes," she said. "Sometimes no. Like any other job."

"Is Mrs. Kipper, ah, you know, understanding?"

"Oh sure," she said, laughing. "I get away with murder. That Chester Heavens would like to bounce my ass right out of there, and Mrs. Neckin called me 'the spawn of the devil.' They'd both like me out of there, but Tippi will never can me. Never."

"Why not?"

"Give us another kissy," she said.

I gave her another kissy.

"You're learning," she said. "Listen, Tippi plays around as much as I do. And she knows I know it."

"Plays around now or before? I mean, when her husband was alive?"

"Oh shit, Josh, she's *always* played around. As long as I've been there. That'll be four years come April."

"How do you know?"

"How do I know? Oh, you poor, sweet, innocent lamb. You think I don't smell the grass on her and see her underwear and notice her hair is done a different way when she comes home from what she said was a bridge party? Listen, a woman *knows* these things. A maid especially. Scratches on her back. Fingerprints on her ass. Oh, she's making it; no doubt about *that*. Listen, Josh, I'm out of joints. You got any Scotch?"

"Well...uh, sure," I said. "But are you certain you want—"

"Get me a Scotch," she commanded.

I got her a drink.

"Where's yours?" she asked.

"We'll share this one," I said.

"A loving cup," she said. "And then the yum-yum. Where's the bed?"

"In the bedroom."

"Not yet," she said, shaking a reproving finger at me. "Don't be in such a rush, tiger."

"I'm really not," I assured her. "I mean, it's not what you—"

She grabbed my arm and pulled me down onto her lap again. I went to my fate willingly.

"So cute," she said drowsily. "You really are cute."

"Tippi isn't making it with Knurr, is she?"

"Ho-ho-ho," Perdita Schug said. "Is she ever. Two, three times a week, at least. He's very big in her life right now. Even in the house—can you beat that? I mean it. And while Sol was alive, too. The two of them in the elevator. How does that grab you? Did you ever make it in an elevator, Josh?"

"No, I never have."

"Me, neither," she said sorrowfully. "But once in a closet," she said brightening. "The funny thing is...." Her voice trailed away.

"What's the funny thing?" I asked.

"I could have him like that," she said, trying to snap her fingers. But they just slid over each other. "Knurr, I mean. He's warm for my form. Always coming on strong. Copping a feel when she isn't looking. The guy's a cocksman. A religious cocksman. Now I'm ready for yum-yum."

She found the bedroom. I didn't turn on the bedside lamp; there was enough illumination coming from the hallway. She looked around dazedly, put a hand against the wall to support herself. She turned her back to me.

"Unzip," she said.

Obediently, I drew the long zipper down to her waist. She shrugged the dress off her shoulders, let it fall to the floor, stepped out of it. She was wearing bra, panties, sheer black pantyhose. She shook her head suddenly, flinging her short flapper-cut about in a twirl.

"I'm zonked," she announced.

She plumped down suddenly on the bed, fell back, raised her legs high in the air.

"Peel me," she said.

There were a lot of other questions I wanted to ask her about Tippi Kipper and the Reverend Godfrey Knurr, but somehow this didn't seem the right time. I peeled off her pantyhose.

She rolled around and wiggled beneath the bedclothes, pulled sheet and blanket up to her chin. In a moment, a slim white arm popped out and she tossed brassiere and panties onto the floor.

"Okay, tiger," she said sleepily. "The time is now. The moment of truth."

I stooped to pick up her dress. I shook out the wrinkles and hung it away in the closet. I picked up her lingerie and draped it neatly over the dresser.

When I turned back to the bed, she was asleep, breathing steadily, her head turned sideways on the pillow.

I brought her shoes from the living room, set them neatly beside the bed.

I awoke the next morning with cricks in my neck, shoulders, hips, thighs, and ankles, from a rude bed I had made of two chairs. Sometimes small stature is advantageous. I staggered to my feet and, in my underwear, began to waggle, flapping my arms, shaking my legs, rotating my head on my neck, and so forth. Such is the resilience of youth that I was soon able to walk upright with just the merest hint of a limp.

Perdita still slept tranquilly, head sideways on the pillow, covers drawn up to her chin, knees bent, as I had left her. Only the slow rise and fall of the blanket proved she was not deceased.

I went into the bathroom as noisily as I could, slammed the door, sang in the shower. I brushed my teeth, decided it was unnecessary to shave, and came bouncing out, a towel wrapped demurely about my loins.

"Hello, hello, hello," I caroled, then peeked into the bedroom. She was still sleeping.

I dressed in fresh linen and clothing, trying to make as much noise as possible. Finally dressed, I went back into the kitchen and banged around, boiling water for instant coffee. I brought two filled cups into the bedroom and set them on the bedside table. It was almost 8:30.

I sat on the bed and shook her shoulder gently. Then with more vigor. Then, I am ashamed to say, violently. Her eyes suddenly opened. She stared at the opposite wall.

"Wha'?" she said.

"Perdita," I said gently, "it is I, Joshua Bigg, and you are in my apartment in Chelsea. Colonel Clyde Manila drove us here. Do you remember?"

"Sure," she said brightly. She sat up suddenly in bed, the covers falling to her waist, and reached to embace me. I hugged her gingerly.

"Feel all right?" I asked.

"Marvy," she said. "Just marvy."

"There's coffee here. Would you like a cup?"

"Why not?" she said. "Got any brandy?"

"I do," I said.

"Slug me," she said.

I went into the living room for the brandy bottle. By the time I returned, she was out of bed and in her lingerie. She drank off a little of her coffee and I topped it off with brandy. She stuck in a forefinger, stirred it around, then licked her finger.

She sat on the edge of the bed, sipping her coffee royal. I sat next to her. She turned to look at me.

"Josh," she said tenderly, "was I good for you?"

"You were wonderful for me."

"I didn't make too much noise, did I?"

"Not at all," I assured her. "It was perfect."

"For me, too," she said, sighing. "Perfect. I feel so loose and relaxed. We must get together again."

"Absolutely," I said.

"I'm always at Mother Tucker's on Thursday. Just drop by."

"I will."

"Promise?"

"I promise," I said, kissing the tip of her nose.

She finished her coffee, took her purse, and scampered into the bathroom for a short while. She came out looking radiant, eyes sparkling, lips wet. She dressed swiftly. We put on our coats and hats.

"Kissy," she said, turning her face up to me.

I unlocked my door, we went out into the hallway, and there was Adolph Finkel. He stared at us. He coughed once, a short, explosive blast.

"Good morning, Finkel," I said.

"Good morning, Bigg," he said.

He goggled at Perdita Schug.

"Hi," she said brightly.

"Uh, hi," he said. He nodded insanely, his head bobbing up and down on his thin neck. Then he turned and fled down the steps ahead of us.

"A neighbor," I explained.

"Unreal," Perdita murmured.

I had planned to get a cab, but when we came out onto the street, there was a chocolate-colored Rolls-Royce, and Colonel Clyde Manila behind the wheel, his furred collar turned up to his ears, his black leather cap set squarely atop his gingery toupee. He was sipping from a cut-glass tumbler of Scotch.

It hadn't registered with me that it was a Rolls. I turned to Perdita in disbelief.

"He's still here?" I said. "Waiting for you?"

"Sure," she said. "What do you think?"

5

YETTA APATOFF WAS on the phone, but gave me a warm smile and a flutter of fingers as I passed. I fluttered in return. Workmen were busy in the corridor outside my office, moving a desk, swivel chair, lamp, and other accessories into position. A telephone installer was on his knees at the baseboard, running a wire to connect with my office phone.

I sat at my desk and went over the latest additions to my file of pending requests for investigation. I divided the stack into two piles: those I felt could be answered by Mrs. Kletz, and those it would be necessary to handle myself. I then went through those I had delegated to my new assistant and scrawled in the margins the sources where she could obtain the information required.

I had started going through the Manhattan Yellow Pages, but was dismayed by the number of chemical laboratories listed and decided to entrust my new assistant with a sensitive assignment. I left a typed note, asking her to call each of the labs listed and say that she represented the attorneys handling the estate of the late Professor Yale Stonehouse. A question had arisen concerning a check the Professor had written to the lab without any accompanying voucher. She was to ask each laboratory to consult their files to establish the date of billing and the purpose for which the money was paid.

On my way out I stopped at Yetta Apatoff's desk to tell her that my assistant would be in at eleven. She giggled.

"Oh, Josh," she said, "she's so big and you're so small. It's so *funny* seeing the two of you together."

"Yes, yes," I said impatiently. "But I'm sure you and everyone else in the office will get used to it."

"So *funny!*" she repeated, squinching up her face in mirth. I wished she hadn't done that; it gave her the look of a convulsed porker.

I told her I'd return in plenty of time to take her to lunch at one o'clock. She nodded, still giggling as I left. It seemed to me she was exhibiting a notable lack of sensitivity.

I took a cab up to the Kipper townhouse, pondering what I might say to Tippi if I got the opportunity and how I might draw her out on matters not pertaining to my alleged inventory of her late husband's estate. I could devise no devilishly clever ploy, and decided my best approach was to appear the wide-eyed innocent.

Chester Heavens answered my ring at the outside iron gate. "Good morning, sah," he said, friendly enough.

"Good morning, Chester. I trust I am not causing any inconvenience by dropping by without calling first?"

"Not at all, sah," he said, ushering me into the looming entrance hall and holding out his hands for my hat and coat. "Mom is breakfasting in the dining room. If you'll just wait a moment, sah, perhaps I should inform her of your arrival."

I waited, standing, until he returned. "Mom asks if you would care to join her for a cup of coffee, sah?"

"I'd like that very much."

Mrs. Kipper was seated at the head of a long table. In the center was a silver bowl of camelias and lilies. She held a hand out to me as I entered.

"Good morning, Mr. Bigg," she said, smiling. "You're out early this morning."

"Yes, ma'am," I said moving forward quickly to take her hand. "I'm anxious to finish up. Almost as anxious, I imagine, as you are to see the last of me."

"Not at all," she murmured. "You've had breakfast?"

"Oh yes, ma'am."

"But surely you'll join me for a cup of coffee?"

"Thank you. I'd like that."

"Chester, will you clear these things away, please, and bring Mr. Bigg a cup. And more hot coffee."

"Yes, mom," he said.

"Now you sit next to me, Mr. Bigg," Tippi said, gesturing toward the chair on her right. "I've always enjoyed a late, leisurely breakfast. It's really the best meal of the day—is it not?" Her manner seemed patterned after Loretta Young or Greer Garson.

I must admit she made a handsome picture, sitting erect at the head of that long, polished table: Portrait of a Lady. In pastels. She was wearing a two-layer nightgown peignoir, gauzy and flowing, printed with pale gardenias.

She seemed born to that splendid setting. If the Kipper sons had been telling the truth, if she had the background they claimed, she had effected a marvelous transformation. The silver-blonde hair was up, and as artfully coiffed as ever. No wrinkles in that half-century-old face; its masklike crispness hinted of a plastic surgeon's "tucks." The brown eyes with greenish flecks showed clear whites, the nose was perfectly patrician, the tight chin carried high.

I felt a shameful desire to dent that assured exterior by risking her ire.

"Mrs. Kipper," I said, "a small matter has come up concerning your late husband's estate, and we hoped you might be able to help us with it. During an inventory of your husband's office effects, a bill was found in the amount of five hundred dollars, submitted by a certain Martin Reape. It is marked simply: 'For services rendered.' We haven't been able to contact this Mr. Reape or determine the nature of the services he rendered. We hoped you might be able to assist us."

I was watching her closely. At my first mention of Martin Reape, her eyes lowered suddenly. She stretched out a hand for her coffee cup and raised it steadily to her lips. She did not look at me while I concluded my question, but set the cup slowly and carefully back into the center of the saucer with nary a clatter.

It was a remarkable performance, but a calculated one. She

should not have taken a sip of coffee in the midst of my question, and she should have, at least, glanced at me as I spoke. Roscoe Dillworth had told me: "They'll take a drink, light a cigarette, bend over to retie their shoelace—anything to stall, to give themselves time to think, time to lie believably."

"Reape?" Mrs. Kipper said finally, meeting my eyes directly. "Martin Reape? How do you spell that?"

"R-e-a-p-e."

She thought a moment.

"Nooo," she said. "The name means nothing to me. Have you found it anywhere else in his records?"

"No, ma'am."

Did I see relief in her eyes or did I just want to see it there as evidence of guilt?

"I'm afraid I can't help you," she said, shaking her head. "My husband was involved in so many things and knew so many people with whom I was not acquainted."

I loved that ". . . people with whom I was not acquainted." So much more aristocratic than ". . . people I didn't know." I was horribly tempted to ask her how Las Vegas was the last time she saw it. Instead, I said . . .

"I understand your husband was very active in charitable work, Mrs. Kipper."

"Oh yes," she said sadly. "He gave generously."

"So Mr. Knurr told me," I said.

There was no doubt at all that this was news to her, and came as something of a shock. She took another sip of coffee. This time the cup clattered back into the saucer.

"Oh?" she said tonelessly. "I didn't know that you and Godfrey had discussed my husband's charities."

"Oh my yes," I said cheerfully. "The Reverend was kind enough to invite me down to Greenwich Village to witness his activities there. He's a remarkable man."

"He certainly is," she said grimly. She took up her cigarette case, extracted and tapped a cigarette with short, angry movements. I was ready with a match. She smacked the cigarette into her mouth, took quick, sharp puffs. Now she was Bette Davis.

"What else did you and Godfrey talk about?" she asked.

"Mostly about the boys he was working with and how he

was trying to turn their physical energy and violence into socially acceptable channels."

"Did he say anything about me?" she demanded. The mask had dropped away. I saw the woman clearly.

I hesitated sufficiently long so that she would know I was lying.

"Why no, ma'am," I said mildly, my eyes as wide as I could make them. "The Reverend Knurr said nothing about you other than that you and your husband had made generous contributions to his program."

Something very thin, mean, and vitriolic came into that wrinkle-free face. It became harder and somehow menacing. All I could think of was the face of Glynis Stonehouse when I told her I knew of her father's poisoning.

"Oh yes," she said stonily. "We contributed. Take a look at Sol's canceled checks. You'll see."

I could not account for her anger. It did not seem justified simply by the fact that I had had a private conversation with the Reverend Knurr. I decided to flick again that raw nerve ending.

"He did say how difficult it had been for you," I said earnestly. "I mean your husband's death."

"So you did talk about me," she accused.

"Briefly," I said. "Only in passing. I hope some day, Mrs. Kipper, you'll tell me about your experiences in the theatre. I'm sure they must have been fascinating."

She hissed.

"He told you that?" she said. "That I was in the theatre?"

"Oh no," I said. "But surely it's a matter of common knowledge?"

"Well . . . maybe," she said grudgingly.

"As a matter of fact," I said innocently, "I think I heard it first from Herschel and Bernard Kipper."

"You've been talking to *them?*" she said, aghast.

"Only in the line of duty," I said hastily. "To make a preliminary inventory of your late husband's personal effects in his office. Mrs. Kipper, I'm sorry if I've offended you. But the fact of your having been in the theatre doesn't seem to me to be degrading at all. Quite the contrary."

"Yes," she said tightly. "You're right."

"Also," I said, "as an employee of a legal firm representing your interest, you can depend upon my rectitude."

"Your *what?*"

"I don't gossip, Mrs. Kipper. Whatever I hear in connection with a client goes no farther than me."

She looked at me, eyes narrowing to cracks.

"Yeah," she said, and I wondered what had happened to "Yes." Then she asked: "What a client tells a lawyer, that's confidential, right?"

"Correct, Mrs. Kipper. It's called privileged information. The attorney cannot be forced to divulge it."

Those eyes widened, stared at the ceiling.

"Privileged information," she repeated softly. "That's what I thought."

Knowing she believed me to be an attorney, I awaited some startling confession. But she was finished with me. Perhaps Knurr had told her I was not a member of the bar. In any event, she stood suddenly and I hastened to rise and move her chair back.

"Well, I'm sure you want to get on with your work, Mr. Bigg," she said, extending her hand, the lady again.

"Yes, thank you," I said, shaking her hand warmly. "And for the coffee. I've enjoyed our talk."

She sailed from the room without answering, her filmy robes floating out behind her.

"Have a good day," I called after her, but I don't think she heard me.

I felt I had to spend *some* time in the townhouse to give credence to my cover story, so I took the elevator up to the sixth floor. I went into the empty, echoing party room and wandered about, heels clacking on the bare floor. I was drawn to those locked French doors. I stood there, looking out onto the terrace from which Sol Kipper had made his fatal plunge.

Small, soiled drifts of snow still lurked in the shadows. There were melting patches of snow on tables and chairs. The outdoor plants were brown and twisted. It was a mournful scene, a dead, winter scene.

He came up here, or was brought up here, and he leaped, or was thrown, into space. Limbs flailing. A boneless dummy flopping down. Suicide or murder, no man deserved that death. It sent a bitter, shocking charge through my mouth, as when you bite down on a bit of tinfoil.

I felt, I *knew*, it had been done to him, but I could not see how. Four people in the house, all on the ground floor. Four apparently honest people. And even if they were all lying, which of them was strong enough and resolute enough? And how was it done? Then, too, there was that suicide note...

Depressed, I descended to the first floor. I stuck my head into the kitchen and saw Chester Heavens and Mrs. Bertha Neckin seated at the pantry table. They were drinking coffee from the same silver service that had just graced the dining room table.

Chester noticed me, rose immediately, and followed me out into the entrance hall where I reclaimed my hat and coat.

"Thank you, Chester," I said. "I hope I won't be bothering you much longer."

"No bother, sah," he said. He looked at me gravely. "You are coming to the end of your work?"

His look was so inscrutable that for a moment I wondered if he knew, or guessed, what I was up to.

"Soon," I said. "It's going well. I should be finished with another visit or two."

He nodded without speaking and showed me out, carefully trying the lock on the outer gate after I left.

I hailed a cab on Fifth and told the driver to drop me at the corner of Madison Avenue and 34th Street. From there I walked the couple of blocks to the ladies' wear shop to buy the green sweater for Yetta Apatoff. I described Yetta's physique as best I could, without gestures, and the kind saleslady selected the size she thought best, assuring me that with a sweater of that type, too small was better than too large, and if the fit wasn't acceptable, it could be exchanged. I had it gift-wrapped and then put into a shopping bag that effectively concealed the contents.

When I got back to my office, Mrs. Gertrude Kletz was seated at her new desk in the corridor. She was on the phone, making notes. I thought, gratified, that she looked very efficient indeed. I went to my own desk, sat down in my coat and hat, and made rapid, scribbled notes of my conversation with Mrs. Tippi Kipper. My jottings could not convey the *flavor* of our exchange, but I wanted to make certain I had a record of her denial of knowing Martin Reape, her admission of heavy contributions to the Reverend Godfrey Knurr, and the anger she had exhibited when she learned of my meeting with Knurr.

I was just finishing up when my new assistant came into the office, carrying a spiral-bound stenographer's pad.

"Good morning, Mrs. Kletz," I said.

"Good morning, Mr. Bigg."

We beamed at each other. She was wearing a tentlike flannel jumper over a man-tailored shirt. I asked her if her desk, chair, telephone, and supplies were satisfactory, and she said they were.

"Did you get all my notes?" I asked her. "Did they make sense to you?"

"Oh yes," she said. "No problems. I found the lab that did business with Professor Stonehouse."

"You didn't?" I said, surprised and delighted. "How many calls did it take?"

"Fourteen," she said casually, as if it was a trifle. A treasure, that woman! "They did two chemical analyses for Professor Stonehouse." She handed me a note. "Here's all the information: date and cost and so forth. They didn't tell me what the analyses were."

"That's all right," I said. "I know what they were. I think. Thank you, Mrs. Kletz."

"On the other research requests—I'm working on those now."

"Good," I said. "Stick with it. If you have any questions, don't be afraid to ask me."

"Oh, I won't be afraid," she said.

I didn't think she would be—of anything. I made a sudden decision. From instinct, not reason.

"Mrs. Kletz," I said, "I'm going out to lunch at one and will probably be back in an hour or so. If you get some time, take a look at the Kipper and Stonehouse files. They're in the top drawer of the cabinet. I'd like your reaction."

"All right," she said placidly. "This is interesting work, isn't it?"

"Oh yes," I agreed enthusiastically. "Interesting."

I took off my coat and hat long enough to wash up in the men's room. Then I put them on again, took up my shopping bag, and sallied forth to take Yetta Apatoff to lunch.

Fifteen minutes later we were seated at a table for two in

the Chinese restaurant on Third Avenue. I ordered eggrolls, wonton soup, shrimp with lobster sauce, and fried rice. After all, it *was* a birthday celebration. Before the eggrolls were served, I withdrew the gift-wrapped package from the shopping bag and presented it to Yetta.

"Many happy returns," I said.

"Oh, Josh," she said, her eyes moons, "you *shouldn't* have. I had no idea . . . !" She tore at the gift-wrapped package with frantic fingers. When she saw the contents, her mouth made an O of delighted surprise.

"Josh," she breathed, "how did you *know?*" Understandably triumphant due to the lead I'd just taken over Hooter in the Apatoff Stakes, I nonetheless managed to smile modestly and flirt sheepishly for the rest of the meal. The warmth of Yetta's grasp as we parted definitely promised an escalation of our relationship in the very near future.

As I approached my office, I noticed Mrs. Kletz was poring over a file on her corridor desk. She was so engrossed that she didn't look up until I was standing next to her.

"Which one is that?" I asked, gesturing toward the folder.

"The Kipper case. I'm almost finished with it. People," she intoned with a sweetly sad half-smile. She wasn't saying, "The horror of them," she was saying, "The wonder of them."

"Yes," I said. "Come into my office, please, when you're finished with it."

I hung away my coat and hat and called Ada Mondora and asked for a meeting with Mr. Teitelbaum. She said she'd get back to me.

Mrs. Kletz had left on my desk the research inquiries she had answered, using the sources I had supplied. She'd done a thorough job and I was satisfied. I typed up first-draft memos to the junior partners and associates who had requested the information and left them for Mrs. Kletz to do the final copies. She came into my office as I was finishing, carrying the Kipper file.

"Sit down, Mrs. Kletz," I said, motioning toward my visitor's chair. "I have just one more rough to do and I'll be through. You did a good job on these, by the way."

"Thank you, sir," she said.

It was one of the few times in my life I had been called

"Sir." I found it an agreeable experience.

I finished the final draft and pushed the stack across the desk to my assistant.

"I'll need two finished copies on these," I said. "Do what you can today and the rest can go over to Monday." I drew the Kipper file toward me and rapped it with my knuckles. "Strictly confidential," I said, staring at her.

"Oh yes. I understand."

"What do you think of it all?"

"Mr. Bigg," she said, "is it always the one you least suspect?"

I laughed. "Don't try to convince the New York Police Department of that. They believe it's always the one you *most* suspect. And they're usually right. Who do you suspect?"

"I think the widow and the preacher are in cahoots," she said seriously. "I think they were playing around before the husband died. He suspected and hired that private detective to make sure. When he had the evidence, he decided to change his will. So they killed him."

I looked at her admiringly.

"Yes," I said, nodding, "that's my theory, and it's a—it's an elegant theory that explains most of the known facts. After Sol Kipper died, Marty Reape tried blackmail. But he underestimated their determination, or their desperation. So he was killed. His widow inherited his files, including his copies of the Kipper evidence. She sold the evidence, or part of it, or perhaps she made copies, realizing what a gold mine she had. She got greedy, so she had to be eliminated, too. Does that make sense?"

"Oh yes. Tippi and Knurr, they were only interested in Mr. Kipper's money. But with the evidence he had, he could get a divorce, and her settlement would have been a lot less than she'll inherit now. So they murdered the poor man."

"It's an elegant theory," I repeated. "There's just one thing wrong with it: they couldn't have done it."

"I've been puzzling that out," she said frowning. "Is it positive there was no one else in the house?"

"A hired killer? The servants say that no one came in and they saw no one leave. The police were there soon after Sol died, and they searched the house thoroughly and found no one."

"Could they be lying? The servants? For money?"

"I don't believe they're lying, and the detective who did the police investigation doesn't think they are either. If they were in on it, they would all have to be in on it. That means five people engaged in a murder conspiracy. I can't see it. The more people involved, the weaker the chain. Too many opportunities for continuing blackmail. Tippi and Knurr are too smart for that. I think it happened the way they told it: four people on the ground floor when Sol Kipper went to his death."

She sighed. "Leaving a suicide note," she said.

"Yes, there's that, too."

"What will you do now?"

"Well, I—" I stopped suddenly. What would I do now? "I don't know," I confessed to Mrs. Kletz. "I don't know what more I can do. I can follow Tippi or the Reverend Knurr. I can definitely establish that they are having an affair. But what good will that do? It won't bring me any closer to learning how the murder of Sol Kipper was engineered. And I'm just as convinced as you are that it *was* murder."

"Chicago," she said.

"What?"

"In your notes, Mr. Bigg. The Reverend told you he was from the Chicago area. Then the Kipper sons told you that they thought Tippi came from Chicago."

I took a deep breath. "Thank you, Mrs. Kletz," I said fervently. "That's exactly the sort of thing I hoped you might spot. I've been too close to this thing, but you came to it fresh. All right, maybe they're both from the Chicago area. What does that prove? Probably nothing. Unless they knew each other before they ended up in New York. Even that might not mean anything unless . . ."

"Unless," she said, "they had been involved together in something similar."

"Back in Chicago?"

"Yes."

"Yes," I agreed. "It's not much, but it might be sufficient to convince the NYPD to reopen their investigation. They've got resources and techniques to unravel this thing a lot faster than I could hope to. Meanwhile, I'll try to dig up what I can on the Chicago background of Tippi and Knurr. It may prove to be nothing, but I've got to—"

The phone rang. Mr. Teitelbaum was free now.

Ada Mondora clinked her gypsy jewelry at me and smiled pertly as I stood before her desk.

"I hear someone had a nice lunch today," she said archly.

"News does get around, doesn't it?" I said.

"What should we talk about?" she demanded. "Torts? Yetta just loves her sweater."

I groaned.

"I think my bet is safe," Ada said complacently. "I'm betting on you. Thelma will just die when she hears about the sweater."

"Thelma Potts? She's betting on Hooter?"

"Didn't you know?" Ada asked innocently, widening those flashing eyes and showing her brilliant white teeth. "As a matter of fact, Thelma and I have a private bet. Lunch at the Four Seasons. I know exactly what I'm going to order."

When I entered Mr. Teitelbaum's office, he was seated, as usual, behind his enormous desk, his pickled hands clasped on top. He motioned me to an armchair, asked for a report on the Stonehouse investigation.

Consulting my notes, I capsuled the results of my inquiries as briefly and succinctly as I could. I told him that I first suspected the nightly cup of cocoa was the means by which Professor Stonehouse was poisoned, but I now realized it was the brandy in the Professor's study. I reported that Stonehouse had submitted two substances for analysis at a chemical laboratory.

"I will try to obtain copies of those analyses, sir," I said. "I'd be willing to bet the arsenic was put into the Professor's cognac."

"By whom?"

I told him about my interviews with Powell Stonehouse and Wanda Chard, and my last meeting with Glynis Stonehouse. I said that Powell seemed to have easiest access to the poison, via Wanda Chard, but since he was banished from his father's home during the period of the poisoning, it seemed unlikely that he was the culprit, unless he was working in collusion with one or more of the other members of the household.

"You think that likely?" Mr. Teitelbaum asked in his surprisingly vigorous voice.

"No, sir."

"Surely not the wife then? On her own?"

"No, sir."

"The servants?"

"No, sir," I said sighing. "The daughter. But I must tell you, I have absolutely no proof to support that suspicion. I don't know where she could have obtained the arsenic. I don't know what her motive might possibly have been."

"Do you think her mentally unbalanced?"

"No, sir, I do not. Mr. Teitelbaum, it might help if you could explain to me what happens legally in this case. I mean, what happens to the assets of the missing man?"

It was his turn to sigh. He entwined his leathery fingers, looked down on his clasped hands on the desktop as if they were a ten-legged animal, a kind of lizard perhaps, that had nothing to do with him.

"Mr. Bumble said that the law is an ass," he said. "I might amend that to say that the law is usually half-ass."

A lawyer's joke. I laughed dutifully.

"The laws concerning the estate of a missing person are somewhat involved," he continued sharply. "Common law, as approved by the Supreme Court in 1878 in the case of Davie versus Briggs, establishes a presumption of death after seven years. However, the Stonehouse case must be adjudicated under the statutes of New York State, of which there are two applying to this particular situation."

I stifled a groan and settled a little deeper into my armchair. I was in for a lecture, when all I had wanted was a one-sentence answer.

"The Estates, Powers and Trusts Law allows a presumption of death after five years of continuous absence, providing—and this is one of the reasons I requested you make a thorough investigation—providing that the missing person was exposed to a specific peril of death and that a diligent search was made prior to application that a declaration of presumed death be issued by the court. At that point, after five years, assuming the two conditions I have just stated have been observed, the missing person may be presumed dead and his will submitted to probate. But if, subsequent to those five years, he suddenly appears, he may legally claim his estate. Thus, 'diligent search' is of paramount importance in the presumption of his death. Are you following me, Mr. Bigg?"

"Yes, sir," I said. "I think so."

"On the other hand," Mr. Teitelbaum said with great satisfaction, and I realized that, to a lawyer, "On the other hand" contains as much emotional impact as "I love you" would to a layman.

"On the other hand," he continued, "the Surrogate's Court Procedure Act, dealing with the administration of the estates of missing persons, provides that not until ten years after the date of disappearance does the missing person lose all interest in his property. The estate is then distributed to his heirs by will or the laws of intestacy. This is simply a statute of limitations on the time in which a missing person may claim his estate. After those ten years, he is, to all intents and purposes, legally dead, although he may still be alive. If he shows up in person after those ten years, he owns nothing."

"And during those ten years, sir? Can his dependents draw on his assets?"

"A temporary administrator, appointed by the court, preserves the assets of the estate, pays the required taxes, supports the missing person's family, and so forth. But once again, a diligent search must be made to locate the missing person."

"Now I am confused, sir," I said. "Apparently, under the first law you mentioned, a missing person can be declared dead after five years. Under the second law, it requires ten years before the estate can be divided amongst his heirs."

"A nice point," Mr. Teitelbaum said. "And one that has occasioned some heated debate amongst our younger attorneys and clerks to whom I assigned the problem. My personal opinion is that the two statutes are not necessarily contradictory. For instance, in the second case, under the Surrogate's Court Procedure Act, during the ten-year administration of the estate, the administrator or any interested person may petition for probate of the will by presenting sufficient proof of death. I would judge," he added dryly, "that the finding of the body would constitute sufficient proof."

"Uh, well, sir," I said, trying to digest all this, "what is going to happen to the Stonehouse family, exactly?"

"I would say," he intoned in his most judicial tones, "after reviewing the options available, that they would be wise to file for relief under the SCPA and accept in good spirit the appointment of a temporary administrator of Professor Stonehouse's estate. That is the course I intend to urge upon Mrs.

Stonehouse. However, in all honesty, Mr. Bigg, I must confess that I have not been moving expeditiously in this matter. Mrs. Stonehouse and the children, while hardly individually wealthy, have sufficient assets of their own to carry them awhile without fear of serious privation. Their apartment, for instance, is a cooperative, fully paid for, with a relatively modest maintenance charge. I have, in a sense, been dragging my feet on an application for appointment of a temporary administrator until we can prove to the court that a diligent search for Professor Stonehouse has indeed been made. Also, I am quite disturbed by what you have told me of the attempted poisoning. I would like to see that matter cleared up before a court application is made. I would not care to see an allowance paid to a family member who might have been, ah, criminally involved in the Professor's disappearance."

"No, sir," I said. "I wouldn't either. Another point: supposing that an administrator is appointed for a period of ten years and nothing is heard from Professor Stonehouse during that time. Then his will goes to probate?"

"That is correct."

"And if no will can be found?"

"Then the division of his estate would be governed by the laws of intestacy."

"Could he disinherit his wife? If he left a will, I mean?"

"Doubtful. Disinheriting one's spouse is not considered in the public interest. However, he might disinherit his wife with a clear reason provable in a court of law."

"Like trying to poison him?"

"That might be sufficient reason for disinheritance," he acknowledged cautiously. "Providing incontrovertible proof was furnished."

"The same holds true for his son and daughter, I presume?"

Mr. Ignatz Teitelbaum took a deep breath.

"Mr. Bigg," he said, "the laws of inheritance are not inviolable. Even an expertly drawn will is not a sacred document. Anyone can sue, and usually does. Ask any attorney. These matters are usually settled by compromise, give-and-take. Litigation frequently results. When it does, out-of-court settlements are common."

"May I pose a hypothetical question, sir?"

"You may," he said magisterially.

"Suppose a spouse or child attempts to inflict grievous bodily harm upon the head of the family. The head of the family has proof of the attempt and disinherits the spouse or child in a holographic will that includes proof of the attempt upon his life. The head of the family disappears. But the will is never found. At the end of ten years, or earlier if the body is discovered, the estate is then divided under the laws of intestacy. The guilty person would then inherit his or her share?"

"Of course," he said promptly. "If the will was never found, and proof of the wrongdoing was never found."

"If the body was discovered tomorrow, sir, how long would it take to probate the will?"

"Perhaps a year," he said. "Perhaps longer if no will existed."

Then he was silent. He unlatched his fingers, spread his brown hands out on the desktop. His head was lowered, but his bright eyes looked up at me sharply.

"You think the body will be discovered tomorrow, Mr. Bigg?" he asked.

"I think it will be discovered soon, sir," I said. "I don't believe whoever did this has the patience to wait ten years."

"You're assuming a second will was drawn," he said. "Perhaps the head of the family never got around to it. Perhaps his original will is in existence and still valid."

I hadn't considered that possibility. It stunned me. But after pondering it a moment, it seemed unlikely to me. After getting the results of those chemical analyses, Professor Yale Stonehouse would surely write a new will or amend the original. It was in character for him to do that. He was an ill-natured, vindictive man; he would not take lightly an attempt to poison him.

"One final request, Mr. Teitelbaum," I said. "I am convinced that when Professor Stonehouse left his home on the night of January 10th, he went somewhere by cab or in a car that was waiting for him. It was a raw, sleety night; I don't think he'd wait for a bus or walk over to the subway. I can't do anything about a car waiting for him, but I can attempt to locate the cab he might have taken. All taxi drivers are required to keep trip sheets, but it would be an enormous task checking all the trip sheets for that night, even if the taxi fleet owners allowed me to, which they probably wouldn't. What I'd like to do is have posters printed up, bearing the photograph of Professor Stonehouse and offering a modest reward for any cabdriver who remembers picking him up at or near his home on the night of January 10th. I admit it's a very long shot. The posters could only go in the garages of fleet owners, and there are many independent cabowners who'd never see them. Still, there is a chance we might come up with a driver who remembers taking the Professor somewhere on that particular night."

"Do it," he said immediately. "I approve. It will be part of that 'diligent search' the law requires."

He started to say more, then stopped. He brought two wrinkled forefingers to his thin lips and pressed them, thinking.

"Mr. Bigg," he said finally, "I think you have conducted this investigation in a professional manner, and I wish to compliment you."

"Thank you, sir."

"However," he said sonorously, "it cannot be openended. The responsibility of this office is, of course, first and foremost to our clients. In this case we are representing the missing Professor Stonehouse and his family. I cannot hold off indefinitely the filing of an application for the appointment of a temporary administrator of the Professor's estate. It would not be fair to the family. Can you estimate how much more time you will require to complete your investigation?"

"No, sir," I said miserably. "I can't even guarantee that I will ever complete it."

He nodded regretfully.

"I understand," he said. "But I cannot shirk our basic responsibility. Another week, Mr. Bigg. I'm afraid that's all I can allow you. Then I must ask you to drop your inquiries into this, uh, puzzling and rather distasteful affair."

I wanted to argue. I wanted to tell him to go ahead with his legal procedures, but to let me continue digging. But in all honesty I didn't know what more I could do in the Stonehouse case after I placed those reward posters in taxi garages. Where did I go from there? I didn't know.

Mrs. Gertrude Kletz had left a memo in the roller of my typewriter. It read:

Mr. Bigg, your notes on the Kipper case question why Tippi was so upset when you told her you had a private meeting with Rev. Knurr. Well, if the two of them are in on this together, as you and I think, it would be natural for her to be upset because they are both guilty, and so must depend on each other. But they would be suspicious as neither of them are dumb, as you said, and so would be very suspicious of each other, fearing the other might reveal something or even connive to turn in the other, like when thieves fall out. I should think that if two people are partners in a horrible crime, they would begin to look at each other with new eyes and wonder. Because they both depend on each other so much, and they begin to doubt and wonder. I hope you know what I mean as I do not express myself very well. G.K.

I knew what she meant, and I thought she might be right. If Tippi and Knurr were beginning to look at each other with "new eyes," it might be the chink I could widen, an opportunity I could exploit.

I called Percy Stilton. The officer who answered said formally, "Detective Stilton is not available." I gave my name and requested that he ask Detective Stilton to call me as soon as possible.

My second call was to Mrs. Effie Dark. I chatted awhile with that pleasant, comfortable lady, and she volunteered the information I sought.

"Mr. Bigg," she said, "I checked my liquor store bills, and Professor Stonehouse didn't order any Rémy Martin for almost two months before he disappeared. I don't know why, but he didn't."

"Thank you, Effie," I said gratefully. "Just another brick in the wall, but an important one."

We exchanged farewells and hung up. It was then late Friday afternoon, the business world slowing, running down. There is a late Friday afternoon mood in winter in New York. Early twilight. Early quiet. Everything fades. Melancholy sweeps in. One remembers lost chances.

I sat there in my broom-closet office, the files of the Kipper and Stonehouse cases on my desk, and stared at them with sad, glazed eyes. So much passion and turbulence. I could not encompass it. Worse, I seemed to have been leached dry of inspiration and vigor. All those people involved in those desperate plots. What were they to me, or I to them? It was a nonesuch with which I could not cope, something foreign to my nature.

Me, a small, quiet, indwelling, nonviolent man. Suddenly, by the luck and accident that govern life, plunged into this foreign land, this *terra incognita*. What troubled me most, I think, was that I had no compass for this terrain. I was blundering about, lurching, and more than discovering the truth, I wanted most to know what drove me and would not let me put all this nastiness aside.

Finally, forcing myself up from the despair toward which I was fast plummeting, I packed the Kipper and Stonehouse folders into my briefcase, dressed in coat, scarf, hat, turned off the lights, and plodded away from the TORT building, the darkness outside seeming not half as black as that inside, not as forbidding, foreboding.

I did arrive home safely. I changed to casual clothes, then built a small blaze in the fireplace. After that luncheon, I was not hungry, but I had a cup of coffee and a wedge of pecan coffee ring. I sat there, staring into the flames. The file folders on the Kipper and Stonehouse cases were piled on the floor at my feet. My depression was again beginning to overwhelm me. I was nowhere with my first big investigation. I was a mild, out-of-place midget in a world of pushers and shovers. And I was alone.

I was alone, late on a Friday evening, wondering as we all must, who I was and what I was, when there came a hesitant tapping at my door. I rose, still frowning with my melancholic reverie, and opened the door to find Cleo Hufnagel, her features as sorrowful as mine. I think it would not, at that moment, have taken much for us to fall into each other's arms, weeping.

"Here," she said stiffly, and thrust into my hands a sealed manila envelope.

"What is this?" I said bewilderedly.

"The information you wanted on arsenic."

I felt the thickness of the envelope.

"Oh, Cleo," I said, "I didn't want *you* to do the research. I just wanted the sources: where to look."

"Well, I did it," she said, lifting her chin. "I thought it might—might help you. Good night."

She turned to go. I reached out hastily, put a hand on her arm. She stopped, but she wouldn't look at me.

"Cleo, what is it?" I asked her. "You seem to be angry with me."

"Disappointed," she said in a low voice.

"All right—disappointed. Have I offended you in any way? If I have, I apologize most sincerely. But I am not aware of—"

I stopped suddenly. Adolph Finkel!

"Cleo," I started again, "we said we wanted to be friends. I know I meant it and I think you did, too. There must be honesty and openness between friends. Please, come inside, sit down, and let me tell you what happened. Give me that chance. If, after I have explained, you still wish to leave and never speak to me again, that will be your decision. But at least it will be based on facts."

I concluded that lawyer's argument and drew her gently into my apartment, closing and locking the door behind us. I got her into the armchair where she sat upright, spine straight, hands clasped in her lap. She stared pensively into the dying flames.

"Could we have a drink?" I asked. "Please? I think it might help."

She gave the barest nod and I hastened to pour us two small glasses of brandy. I pulled a straight-back chair up close to her and leaned forward earnestly, drink clasped at my knees.

"Now," I said, "I presume you are disappointed in me because of something Adolph Finkel may have alleged about my, uh, visitor this morning. Is that correct?"

Again, that brief, cold nod.

"Cleo, that young woman is an important witness in a case I am currently investigating, and I needed information from her. Here is exactly what happened..."

I think I may say, without fear of self-glorification, that I was at my most convincing best. I spoke slowly in a grave, intense voice, and I told Cleo nothing but the truth. I described my bus ride uptown in the storm, the atmosphere at Mother Tucker's, my meeting with Perdita Schug and Colonel Clyde Manila.

"It sounds like a fun place," Cleo said faintly, almost enviously.

"Oh yes," I said, encouraged, "we must go there sometime."

Then I went on to explain my failure to elicit any meaningful intelligence from Perdita during dinner, and how I had decided the evening was wasted and that I should return home alone by any means possible. I described how Perdita and the Colonel insisted on driving me in the chocolate-colored Rolls-Royce, and how we all drank, and they smoked joints en route. I held nothing back.

"I've never tried it," Cleo Hufnagel said reflectively. "I'd like to."

I tried to conceal my amazement at *that*. I described how Perdita Schug had forced her way into my apartment and how, after a drink, she had revealed information of inestimable value in the case under investigation.

"And then . . ." I said.

"And then?" Cleo asked sharply.

As delicately as I could, I explained what happened then.

During this part of my confession, Cleo had begun to smile, and when I described my makeshift bed and how I awoke a mass of aches and pains, she threw back her head and laughed outright. And my telling of the tender conversation in the morning, just prior to Perdita's departure, sent her into a prolonged fit of hearty guffaws and she bent over, shaking her head and wiping her streaming eyes with a knuckle.

"Then we came out into the hallway," I said, "and there was Adolph Finkel. I swear to you, Cleo, on our friendship, that's exactly what happened."

"I believe you, Josh," she said, still wiping her eyes. "No one could have made up a story like that. How did you get her home?"

I told her how we had discovered Colonel Manila still waiting in the snowdrift, and how they had driven me to work and then gone off together.

"Will you see her again?" she asked, suddenly serious.

I thought about that.

"Cleo, I cannot promise you I will not. Things may develop in the investigation that will necessitate additional conversations with her. But I assure you, my only motive in seeking her company will be in the line of business. I have no personal interest in Perdita whatsoever. Would you like another brandy?"

"Please," she said, and I went gratefully to replenish our glasses, fearing she might detect guilt in my face. I had told her the truth—but not the whole truth.

I came back with our drinks, pulled my chair closer, took her free hand in mine.

"Am I forgiven?" I asked.

She was looking uncommonly handsome that night. But each time I saw her I discerned new beauty. The long hair I had once thought of as only gleaming chestnut now seemed to me to have the tossing fascination of flame. The smile I had defined as pleasant but distant now appeared to me mysterious and full of promise. The thin nose was now aristocratic, the high, clear, brow bespoke intelligence, and the wide mouth, instead of being merely curvy, was now sensuous and madly desirable.

As for her figure, I could not believe I once thought her skinny. I saw now that she was elegant, supple as a willow wand, and her long arms and legs, slender hands and feet, were all of a piece, pliant and flowing. There was a fluency to her body, and I no longer thought of her as being a head taller than I. We were equals: that's what I thought.

"Of course I forgive you," she said in that marvelously low and gentle voice. "But there is nothing to forgive. The fault was mine. I have no claims on you. You can live as you please. I was just being stupid."

"No, no," I said hotly. "You were not stupid. Are not stupid."

"It was just that . . ." she said hesitantly. "Well, I was—I was hurt. I don't know why, but I was."

"I would never do anything to hurt you," I vowed. "Never! And I haven't forgotten about the kite either. I really am going to buy a red kite for us. With string."

She laughed. "I'm glad you haven't forgotten, Josh," she said, gently taking her hand from mine. "Now do you want to talk about what I found out? About the arsenic?"

I nodded, even though at that moment I most wanted to talk about us.

She took the envelope from the floor at my feet and opened the flap. I moved the table lamp closer.

"I'll leave all of this for you to read," she said. "Most of it is photocopies, and photostats from medical journals and drug company manuals. Josh, it's awfully technical. Maybe I better go over the main points, and that will be enough for you, and you won't have to read it all. That man you said was poisoned by arsenic—was he killed? I mean, was he fed a large quantity of arsenic at one time and died? Or small amounts over a period of time?"

"Small amounts," I said. "I think. And I don't believe he died. At least not from the arsenic."

"Well, arsenic comes in a lot of different chemical compounds. Powders, crystals, and liquids. There's even one type that fumes in air. Pope Clement the Seventh and Leopold the First of Austria were supposed to have been assassinated by arsenic mixed in wax candles. The fumes from the candles were poisonous, and whoever breathed them died."

"That's incredible," I murmured, and before I could help myself I had flopped to my knees alongside her chair and taken up one of her long, slender hands again. She let me.

"I think what you're looking for, Josh, is arsenic trioxide. It's the common form and the primary material of all the arsenic compounds."

"Yes," I said, putting my lips to the tips of her fingers. "Arsenic trioxide."

"It is white or transparent glassy lumps or a crystalline powder. It is soluble if mixed slowly and used extremely sparingly. It is odorless and tasteless. A poisonous dose would be only a small pinch. There might be a very slight aftertaste."

"Aftertaste," I repeated, kissing her knuckles, the back of her hand, then turning it over to kiss that pearly wrist with the blue veins pulsing faintly.

"Only two- or three-tenths of a gram of arsenic trioxide can kill an adult within forty-eight hours, so you can see how a tiny amount could cause illness." She obviously intended to finish her lecture despite the distractions. "Arsenic affects the red blood cells and kidneys, if I read these medical papers correctly. The symptoms vary greatly, but a victim of fatal arsenic poisoning might have headaches, vertigo, muscle spasm, delirium, and stupor. Death comes from circulatory collapse. In smaller doses, over a period of time, there would probably be a low-grade fever, loss of appetite, pallor, weakness, inflammation of the nose and throat. You notice that those symptoms are quite similar to the flu or a virus, and that's why arsenic poisoning is sometimes misdiagnosed. In tiny doses over a long period of time, there is usually no delirium or stupor."

"Stupor," I said, touching the tip of my tongue to the palm of her hand. Her entire arm quivered, but her voice was steady as she continued.

"After repeated poisonings, loss of hair and nails may result, accompanied by hoarseness and a hacking cough. Arsenic collects in the hair, nails, and skin. There is some evidence that Napoleon may have been poisoned with arsenic on St. Helena. It was found in a lock of his hair years later."

"Poor Napoleon," I whispered. I craned upward to sniff the perfume of her hair, to bury my face in the sweet juncture where neck met shoulder, to breathe her in. She, who would not brook diversion.

"An alert physician may sometimes spot a garlicky odor of breath and feces." She showed no evidence of slowing down. "Also, urine analysis and gastric washings usually reveal the presence of arsenic. But the symptoms are sometimes so similar to stomach flu that a lot of doctors don't suspect arsenic poisoning until it's too late."

"Too late," I groaned, pushing her hair aside gently to kiss her divine ear tenderly. She trembled, a bit, but continued to read from her notes.

"Arsenic is no longer generally used in medicine, having been replaced by more efficient compounds. It was formerly used in the treatment of infections, joint disease, skin lesions, including syphilis, chronic bronchitis, anemia, psoriasis, and so forth. It's still used by veterinarians, but much less frequently than it once was. Most uses of arsenic today are in manufacturing. It is used for hardening copper, lead, and alloys, to make paint and glass, in tanning hides, in printing and dyeing fabrics. It's also used as a pigment in painting, in weed control, for killing rodents and insects, and in fireworks."

"Fireworks," I breathed, touching the fine silkiness of her hair. It was as soft and evanescent as cobwebs.

"Now, as to the availability . . . It's prohibited in food and drugs, and is being phased out as a weed killer. You might find it in rat poison and wood preservatives, but they'd be poisonous for their other ingredients, too. Arsenic is available commercially in large wholesale quantities. It is used in manufacturing parts of car batteries, for instance. But for uses like that, it's bought by the ton, and the government requires disclosure of the end-use. So what is a poor poisoner to do? It would be difficult to purchase an arsenic-containing product in a garden nursery or hardware store or pharmacy. It would probably be impossible."

"Impossible," I moaned. I was kneeling, an arm about her shoulders. The fingers of that hand touched her neck, ear, the loose strands of hair cascading down her back. My other hand stroked the arm closest to me, touched her timorously. I felt her shiver, but too soon she recovered her self-control.

"Still, arsenic trioxide is frequently used in medical and chemical laboratories for research. It is obtained from chemical supply houses by written order, and they must know with whom they are dealing. I mean, a stranger can't just write in and order a pound of arsenic. The usual order from a lab will be for 100 to 500 grams at a time. In its crudest form, it costs about ten dollars for 250 grams. High-purity arsenic trioxide costs about a dollar a gram. It seems to me that the easiest thing for a poisoner to do would be to steal a small amount of arsenic trioxide from the stock room of a research laboratory or a chemical lab at a university. Such a tiny bit is needed to kill someone that the amount stolen would probably never be noticed and— Oh, Josh!" she cried.

She dropped her research papers to the floor, slipped from the chair, fell onto her knees, twisted and flung herself into my arms. In that position, both of us kneeling, we were nearly of a height, and embraced eagerly. We kissed. Our teeth clinked. We kissed. We murmured such things as "I never"— and "I didn't—" and "I can't—" and "I wouldn't—" All of which soon became "I wanted—" and "I hoped—" and "I wished—" and, finally, "I love—"

Not a sentence was finished, nor was there need for it. After a while, weak with our osculatory explorations, we simply toppled over, fell to the floor with a thump, and lay close together, nose to nose in fact, staring into each other's eyes and smiling, smiling, smiling.

"I don't care," Cleo Hufnagel said in her low, hesitant voice. "I just don't care."

"I don't either," I said. "About anything but us."

"Us," she said, wonder in her voice.

"Us," I repeated. I smoothed the hair away from her temples, touched the smooth skin of her brow. When I pressed her yielding back, she moved closer to me, and we clove. I began to scratch her spine gently through the flannel of her jumper. She closed her eyes and purred with contentment.

"Don't stop," she said. "Please."

"I do not intend to," I said, and scratched away assiduously, widening the base of my operations to include shoulder blades and ribs.

"Oh," she sighed. "Oh, oh, oh. Are you a virgin, Josh?"

"No."

"I am."

"Ah?"

"But I don't want to be," she said. Then her eyes flicked open and she looked at me with alarm. "But not tonight," she added hastily.

"I understand," I assured her gravely. "This is grand. Just being with you."

"And having you scratch my back is grand," she sighed. "That's beautiful. Thank you."

"Thank *you*," I said. "Another brandy?"

"I don't think so," she said thoughtfully. "I feel just right. How old are you, Josh?"

"Thirty-two."

"I'm thirty-four," she said sadly.

"So?"

"I'm older than you are."

"But I'm shorter than you are."

She wriggled around so she could hold my face between her palms. She stared intently into my eyes.

"But that doesn't make any difference," she said. "Does it? My being older or your being shorter? That's not important, is it?"

"No," I said, astonished, "it's not."

"I've got to tell you something awful," she said.

"What?"

"I must get up and use your bathroom."

When we kissed goodnight I had to lift onto my toes as she bent down. But I didn't mind that, and neither of us laughed.

"Thank you for a lovely evening," I said.

She didn't answer, but drew her fingertips gently down my cheek. Then she was gone.

6

I REMEMBER THE next day very well, since it had such an impress on what was to follow. It was the first Saturday of March, a gruff, blustery day with steely light coming from a phlegmy sky. The air had the sharp smell of snow, and I hurried through my round of weekend chores, laying in enough food so that I could enjoy a quiet, relaxed couple of days at home even if the city was snowed in.

I took care of laundry, drycleaning, and shopping. I bought wine and liquor. I cleaned the apartment. Then I showered and shaved, dressed in slacks, sweater, sports jacket, and carpet slippers. A little after noon, I settled down with the morning *Times* and my third cup of coffee of the day.

I think I was annoyed when the phone rang. I was enjoying my warm solitude, and the jangle of the bell was an unwelcome reminder of the raw world outside my windows.

"Hello?" I said cautiously.

"Josh!" Detective Percy Stilton cried. "My main man! I'm sitting here in my drawers, my old lady's in the kitchen doing something to a chicken, and I'm puffing away on a joint big as a see-gar and meanwhile investigating this fine jug of Almaden Mountain White Chablis, vintage of last Tuesday, and God's in His Heaven, all's right with the world, and what can I do for you, m'man? I got a message you called."

"You sound in fine fettle, Perce," I said.

"Fine fettle?" he said. "I got a fettle on me you wouldn't believe—a tough fettle, a boss fettle. I got me a sweet forty-eighter, and nothing and nobody is going to pry me loose from hearth and home until Monday morning. You want to know about that crazy elevator—right? Okay, it was on the sixth floor when the first blues got to the Kipper townhouse. They both swear to it. So? What does that prove? Sol could have taken it up to his big jump."

"Could have," I said. "Yes. It's hard to believe an emotionally disturbed man intent on suicide would wait for an elevator to take him up one floor when he could have walked it in less than a minute. But I agree, yes, he could have done it."

"Let's figure he did," Stilton said. "Let's not try jamming facts into a theory. I've known a lot of good men who messed themselves up doing that. The trick is to fit the theory to the facts. How you doing? Any great detecting to report?"

"Two things," I said.

I told him about those bills from Martin Reape I had found at Kipmar Textiles. The bills that had been approved for payment by Sol Kipper. And the canceled checks endorsed by Reape.

I awaited his reaction. But there was only silence.

"Perce?" I said. "You there?"

He started speaking again, and suddenly he was sober . . .

"Josh," he said, "do you realize what you've got?"

"Well, yes, certainly. I've established a definite connection between Sol Kipper and Marty Reape."

"You goddamned Boy Scout!" he screamed at me. "You've got hard evidence. You've got paper. Something we can take to court. Up to now it's all been smoke. But now we've got *paper*. God, that's wonderful!"

It didn't seem so wonderful to me, but I supposed police officers had legal priorities of which I was not aware. I went ahead and told Detective Stilton what I had learned about Tippi Kipper and the Reverend Godfrey Knurr, that they were having an affair and it had existed prior to Sol Kipper's death.

"Where did you get that?" he asked curiously.

I hesitated a moment.

"From the maid," I said finally.

He laughed. "Miss Horizontal herself?" he said. "I'm not going to ask you how you got her to talk; I can imagine. Well, it could be true."

"It would explain the Kipper-Reape connection," I argued. "Sol got suspicious and hired Marty to find out the truth. Reape got evidence that Knurr and Tippi were, ah, intimate. That's when Sol called Mr. Tabatchnick and wanted to change his will."

"Uh-huh. I follow. Sol gets dumped before he can change the will. Maybe the lovers find and destroy the evidence. Photographs? Could be. Tape recordings. Whatever. But street-smart Reape has made copies and tries blackmail. Goom-bye, Marty."

"And then after he gets bumped, his grieving widow tries the same thing."

"It listens," Stilton admitted. "I'd be more excited if we could figure out how they managed to waste Sol. And come up with the suicide note. But at least we've got more than we had before. When I get in on Monday, I'll run a trace on Knurr."

"And on Tippi," I said. "Please."

"Why her?"

I told him what the Kipper sons had said about her Las Vegas background and how she had originally come from Chicago, which had also been Knurr's home.

"May be nothing," Stilton said, "may be something. All right, I'll run Tippi through the grinder, too, and we shall see what we shall see. Hang in there, Josh; you're doing okay."

"I am?" I said, surprised. "I thought I was doing badly. As a matter of fact, one of the reasons I called you was to ask if you could suggest a new approach. Something I haven't tried yet."

There was silence for a brief moment.

"It's your baby," he said at last. "But if I was on the case, I'd tail Tippi Kipper and the Reverend Knurr for a while."

"What for?" I asked.

"Just for the fun of it," he said. "Josh, my old lady is yelling and I better hang up. I think she wants to put me to work.

Keep in touch. I'll let you know what the machine says about Knurr and Tippi."

"Thank you for calling," I said.

"You're perfectly welcome," he responded with mock formality, then laughed. "So long, Josh," he said as he rang off. "Have a good weekend."

I finished the *Times* and my cold coffee about the same time, then mixed a weak Scotch-and-water, turned the radio down low, and started rereading my notes on the Stonehouse case. I went back to the very beginning, to my first meeting with Mr. Teitelbaum. Then I read the record of my initial interviews with Mrs. Ula Stonehouse, Glynis, and Mrs. Effie Dark. I found something interesting. I had been in the kitchen with Mrs. Dark, and the interrogation went something like this:

Q: What about Glynis? Does she work?

A: Not anymore. She did for a year or two but she quit.

Q: Where did she work?

A: I think she was a secretary in a medical laboratory.

Q: But now she does nothing?

A: She does volunteer work three days a week in a free clinic down on the Lower East Side.

I closed the file folder softly and stared into the cold fireplace. Secretary in a medical laboratory. Now working in a clinic.

It was possible.

But Mr. Teitelbaum had given me only another week.

I put in some additional hours reading over the files and planning moves. After a solitary dinner I went out to get early editions of the *Times* and *News*. It was around 8:30, not snowing, sleeting, or raining, but the air was so damp, I could feel icy moisture on my face. I walked rapidly, head down. The streets were deserted. Very little traffic. I saw no pedestrians until I rounded the corner onto Tenth Avenue.

The Sunday *News* was in and I bought a copy of that. But the Sunday *Times* hadn't yet been delivered. There were a dozen people warming themselves in the store, waiting for the truck. I decided not to wait, but to pick up the *Times* in the morning. I started back to my apartment.

My brownstone was almost in the middle of the block. There was a streetlamp on the opposite side of the street. It

was shedding a ghastly orange glow. The lamp itself was haloed
with a wavering nimbus.

I was about halfway home when two men stepped out of
an areaway a few houses beyond my brownstone and started
walking toward me. They were widely separated on the sidewalk. They appeared to be carrying baseball bats.

I remember thinking, as my steps slowed, that what was
going to happen was going to happen to me. Almost at the
same time I thought it was an odd sort of mugging; attackers
usually come up on a victim from behind. I halted and glanced
back. There was a third assailant behind me, advancing as
steadily and purposefully as the two in front.

I looked about wildly. The street was empty. Perhaps I
should have started screaming and continued screaming until
windows opened, heads popped out, and someone had the
compassion to call the police. But I didn't think of screaming.
While it was happening, I thought only of escape.

The two men to my front were now close enough for me
to see they were wearing knitted ski masks with holes at the
eyes and mouth. Now they were swinging their weapons menacingly, and I knew, knew, this was not to be a conventional
mugging and robbery. Their intent was to inflict grievous bodily injury, if not death.

I took another quick look back. The single attacker was still
approaching, but at a slower pace than the two ahead. His
function appeared to be as a blocker, to prevent me from re-
treating from a frontal assault. He was waving the baseball bat
in both hands, like a player at the plate awaiting the first pitch.
He, too, was wearing a ski mask, but though I saw him only
briefly, I did note that one of the eyeholes in the mask appeared
opaque. He was wearing a black eyepatch beneath the mask.

Parked cars, bumper to bumper, prevented my fleeing into
the street. I didn't dare dash up the nearest steps and frantically
ring strange bells, hoping for succor before those assassins fell
upon me. I did what I thought best; I turned and ran back,
directly at the single ruffian. I thought my chances would be
better against one than two. And each accelerating stride I took
toward him brought me closer to the brightly lighted and
crowded safety of Tenth Avenue. I think he was startled by
my abrupt turn and the speed of my approach. He stopped,

shifted uneasily on his feet, gripped the bat horizontally, a hand on each end.

I think he expected me to try to duck or dodge around him, and he was wary and off-balance when I simply ran into him full tilt. There was nothing clever or skilled in my attack; I just ran into him as hard as I could, feeling the hard bat strike across my chest, but keeping my legs moving, knees pumping.

He bounced away, staggered back, and I continued my frontal assault, hearing the pounding feet of the two other assailants coming up behind me. Then my opponent stumbled. As he went down flat on his back with a *whoof* sound as the breath went out of him, I seized the moment and ran like hell.

I ran over him, literally ran over him. I didn't care where my boots landed: kneecaps, groin, stomach, chest, face. I just used him as turf to get a good foothold, and like a sprinter starting from blocks, I pushed off and went flying toward Tenth Avenue, knowing that I was in the clear and not even the devil could catch me now.

I whizzed around the corner, banking, and there was the New York *Times* truck, unloading bundles of the Sunday edition, with vendors, merchants, customers crowding around: a pushing, shoving mob. It was lovely, noisy confusion, and I plunged right into the middle of it, sobbing to catch my breath. I was startled to find that not only was my body intact, but I was still clutching my copy of the Sunday *News* under my arm.

I waited until complete copies of the *Times* had been made up. I bought one, then waited a little longer until two other customers started down my street, carrying their papers. I followed them closely, looking about warily. But there was no sign of my attackers.

When I came to my brownstone, I had my keys ready. I darted up the steps, unlocked the door, ran up the stairs, fumbled my way into my apartment, locked and bolted the door. I put on all the lights and searched the apartment. I knew it was silly, but I did it. I even looked in the closet. I was shivering.

I poured myself a heavy brandy, but I didn't even taste it. I just sat there in my parka and watch cap, staring into the fireplace where there were now only a few pinpoints of red, winking like fireflies.

That black eyepatch I'd spotted under my assailant's ski mask haunted me.

A lot of men in New York wore black eyepatches, I supposed, and were of the same height and build as the young man I had seen at the Tentmakers Club on Carmine Street. Still...

Tippi Kipper had obviously reported to Knurr the details of our conversation. Perhaps she'd told him I'd mentioned the name of Martin Reape to her. Perhaps she'd said that I had asked prying questions, doubly suspicious coming from an attorneys' clerk supposedly engaged only in making an inventory of her husband's estate.

So the two of them must have decided I had to be removed from the scene. Or, at least, warned off.

Was that the way of it?

I had to admit that I wasn't comfortable with that theory. If I knew the name of Martin Reape, then presumably my employers did too, and putting me in the hospital wouldn't stop an inquiry into the alleged bills of the private detective. And as for my "prying questions," I had asked nothing that could not be accounted for by sympathetic interest.

I didn't know why Godfrey Knurr had set up the attack on me. But I was convinced he had. It made me sad. I admired the man.

I looked at my watch. It was a little after ten o'clock. Perhaps if I went to Knurr's place on Carmine Street I could observe the three guttersnipes entering or leaving the club and thus confirm my suspicions.

Disregarding the dozen reasons why this was a foolish course of conduct, I turned off the lights, pulled my parka hood over my watch cap, made certain I had my warm gloves, and went out again into the darkness. It was not the easiest thing I have ever done in my life.

When a cab dropped me off on Carmine Street and Seventh Avenue, I found to my dismay that I had neglected to replenish my wallet. I had enough to pay and tip the driver but that would leave me with only about ten dollars in bills and change, just about enough to get me home again.

I walked east on Carmine Street, hooded head lowered, gloved hands thrust into capacious parka pockets. I walked on the opposite side of the street from the Reverend Knurr's club and inspected it as I passed.

At first I thought it was completely dark. But then, through the painted-over window, I saw a dull glow of light. That could have been nothing more than a nightlight, of course. The club might be empty, the Pastor out somewhere, and I could be wasting my time.

But remembering Roscoe Dollworth's instructions on the need for everlasting patience on a stakeout, I continued down the block, then turned and retraced my steps. I must have paraded down that block a dozen times, up and down.

At that point, already wearying of my patrol, I took up a station in the shadowed doorway of a Chinese laundry, not exactly opposite the Tentmakers Club, but in a position where I could observe the entrance without being easily seen.

I continued this vigil for approximately an hour, huddling in the doorway, then walking up and down the street and back, always keeping Knurr's club in view. The street was not crowded, but it wasn't deserted either. None of the other pedestrians seemed interested in my activities, but I took advantage of passing groups by falling in closely behind them, giving the impression, or so I hoped, that I was part of a late dinner party.

I was back in the doorway, stamping my feet softly, when the light brightened behind the painted window of the Tentmakers Club. I drew farther back into the shadows. I waited. Finally the front door opened. A shaft of yellowish light beamed out onto the sidewalk.

Godfrey Knurr came out. There was no doubt it was he; I saw his features clearly, particularly the slaty beard, as he turned to close and lock the door. He was hatless but wearing a dark overcoat with the collar turned up.

He tried the door, put the keys in his trouser pocket, and then started walking east, toward Sixth Avenue. He strode at a brisk clip, and I moved along with him on the other side of the street, keeping well back and close to the deep shadows of the storefronts and buildings.

He crossed Sixth and stopped at the curb, looking southward. He would raise his hand when a cab approached, then let it fall when he saw it was occupied. I hurried south on Sixth, ending up a block below Knurr. Then I ran across the avenue and took up my station at the curb.

I got the first empty cab to come along.

"Where to?" the driver said.

"Start your meter and stay right here," I said. "I've got about ten dollars. When I owe you eight, tell me and I'll give you ten and get out of your cab. All right?"

"Why not?" he said agreeably. "Beats using gas. You got wife trouble?"

"Something like that," I said.

"Don't we all?" he offered mournfully, then was silent.

The name of the registration card said he was Abraham Pincus. He was a grizzle-haired, middle-aged man with a furrowed brow under his greasy cap and deep lines from the corners of his mouth slanting down to his chin, like a ventriloquist's dummy.

"Mind if I smoke?" he asked.

The passenger's compartment was plastered with signs: PLEASE DO NOT SMOKE and DRIVER ALLERGIC TO SMOKING and the like.

"What about these signs?" I said.

"That's the *day* driver," he said. "I'm the *night* driver."

I had been sitting forward on the rear seat, trying to peer through the bleared windshield to keep Reverend Knurr in sight. He had still not caught a cab. Finally, after about three minutes, one passed us with its roof lights on and began to pull into the curb where Knurr stood and signaled.

"All right," I said. "We're going to move now. Just drive north."

"Why not?" Mr. Pincus said equably, finishing lighting his cigar. "You're the boss. For eight dollars' worth."

I saw Knurr get into the taxi and start north on Sixth Avenue. Then my driver started up and we traveled north, keeping about a block behind Knurr's cab. At 14th Street, Knurr turned left.

"Turn left," I said to my driver.

"We following that cab ahead?" he asked.

"Yes."

"Why didn't you say so? All my life I been waiting for someone to get in my cab and say, 'Follow that car!' Like in the movies and TV—you know? This was my big chance and you blew it. He the guy that's fooling around with your tootsie?"

"That's the one," I said.

"I won't lose him," he promised. "Up to eight dollars, I won't lose him."

Knurr's cab zigzagged northward and westward, with us a block behind but sometimes closing up tighter when my driver feared he might be stopped by a traffic light. Finally we were on Eleventh Avenue, heading directly northward.

"You from New Jersey?" A. Pincus asked.

"No," I said. "Why?"

"I thought maybe he's heading for the George Washington Bridge and Jersey. You can't go there for eight bucks."

"No," I said, "I don't think he's going to New Jersey."

"Maybe you and your creampuff can get back together again," Mr. Pincus said. "As the old song goes, 'Try a little tenderness.'"

"Good advice," I said, hunching forward on my seat, watching the taillights of the cab ahead.

Then we were on West End Avenue, still speeding north.

"He's slowing," Pincus reported, then, "he's stopping."

I glanced at a street sign. We were at 66th Street.

"Go a block past him, please," I said. "Then let me out."

"Why not?" he said.

While I huddled down in my seat, we passed Knurr's halted cab and stopped a block farther north.

"You got about six bucks on the clock," my driver said. "Give or take. You want me to wait?"

"No," I said, "thank you. I'll get out here."

I gave him nine dollars, figuring I could take the bus or subway home.

"Lots of luck," Pincus said.

"Thank you," I said. "You've been very kind."

"Why not?" he said. His cab roared away.

I was on the east side of West End Avenue, on a tree-lined block bordering an enormous apartment development. There were towering buildings and wide stretches of lawn, shrubbery, and trees everywhere. It must have been pleasant in daylight. At that time of night, it was shadowed, deserted, and vaguely sinister.

I had been watching Knurr through the rear window of my cab as he waited for a break in the traffic to dash across the avenue. Now I walked rapidly back to where his cab had stopped.

As I scurried southward, I spotted him on the west side of West End. He was heading for the brightly lighted entrance of a public underground garage in the basement of one of the tall apartment houses bordering the river. There were large signs in front stating the parking rates by the hour, day, week, and month.

I positioned myself across the street from the garage, standing in the deep shadow of a thick-trunked plane tree. I watched Knurr walk rapidly into the bright entrance. As he approached the attendant's booth, a woman stepped out of the shadows, and she and the Reverend embraced briefly. Then an attendant appeared. He and Knurr spoke for a moment. The Pastor handed him something. The attendant turned and disappeared. Knurr and the woman remained where they were, close together, conversing, his arm about her shoulders.

She was wearing what I guessed to be a mink coat that came a little lower than calf-length. It was very full and had a hood that now covered her head, shadowing her features.

Finally, a long, heavy car came rolling into the lighted area of the garage entrance. It was a black Mercedes-Benz sedan, gleaming, solid, and very elegant. The garage attendant got out of the driver's side and handed something to Godfrey Knurr. The Reverend then gave something to the attendant.

Knurr opened the door on the passenger's side. He assisted the lady into her seat, then went around to the driver's side, got in, slammed the door—I heard it *chunk* from where I stood—and slowly, carefully, pulled out into West End Avenue. He turned north. I watched the taillights fade away.

I wasn't thinking about where he might be heading. I couldn't care less. I was too shocked.

For when he had helped the woman into the car, she had flung back the hood of her fur coat. Her features, for a brief moment, were revealed in the bright light. I saw her clearly.

It wasn't Tippi Kipper.

It was Glynis Stonehouse.

Part III

1

THAT NIGHT I awoke frequently, dozed off as often, and finally lost all ability to determine if I was fully conscious or dreaming. I vividly remember wondering if I had actually seen Glynis Stonehouse and Godfrey Knurr together.

My brain continued churning all night, and things were no better when I arose early Sunday morning, showered, dressed, and poked disconsolately at a bowl of sodden corn flakes. I simply didn't know what to do. It seemed to me I was in over my head and badly in need of wise counsel.

I hated to bother Percy Stilton, but what I had learned was of such moment that I wanted him to know at once. I dialed the only number I had for him and learned that he wouldn't be in the precinct until Monday morning.

"Couldn't you call him at home and ask him to contact me?" I tried to convey the urgency of the situation to the officer on the other end of the phone.

"Can't anyone else help you?" he asked, still reticent.

"No," I said firmly. "It's got to be Stilton. It's really very important, honest, to me and to him."

Silence.

"A case he's on?" he said finally.

"Yes," I said, lying valiantly. "Just call and ask him to call Joshua Bigg. As soon as possible."

A short silence again, then: "What was that name—Pigg?"

"Bigg. B-i-g-g. Joshua Bigg. Tell him it's a matter of life and death."

"I'll tell him that," the officer said.

I tried to read the Sunday papers. I watched TV for a while, but didn't see it. My phone finally rang shortly before noon.

"Hello?" I said breathlessly.

The voice was low, husky, soothing. "Mr. Bigg?"

"Yes."

"This is Maybelle Hawks," she said pleasantly. "I am Percy Stilton's consenting adult."

"Yes, ma'am."

"Mr. Bigg, Perce received your message, but he's really in no, ah, condition to speak intelligibly to you at the moment."

"Is he ill?" I asked anxiously.

"You might say that," she replied thoughtfully. "Nothing fatal. I would judge that he will recover, in time. But right now he's somewhat unhinged. It being Sunday morning. I do hope you understand."

"Yes, ma'am," I said miserably. "He's hung over."

"Oh, Mr. Bigg," she laughed gaily, "that *is* the understatement of the year. He's comatose, Mr. Bigg. *Com-a-tose*. He asked that I return your call and explain why it might be best if you call him at the precinct tomorrow."

"Miss Hawks," I said, "is—"

"Call me Belle," she said.

"Thank you. Belle, is there no chance of my seeing him today? It really is urgent. I wouldn't be bothering you if it wasn't. Surely Perce, and you too, of course, have to eat sometime today. It would give me great pleasure if you would both join me for dinner some place. Any place."

"Mr. Bigg, you sound to me like a sober, reasonable man."

"Yes, ma'am," I said, "I mean to be."

"Then you must realize that right now, this second, if I mention food to Percy Stilton, he's like to give me a shot in the chops."

"Oh no, ma'am," I said hastily. "Not right this minute.

What I was thinking was that later this evening, say around six o'clock, he might be recovered sufficiently, and the both of you might be hungry enough to join me for dinner."

"Hmm," she said. "You're getting through to me, Mr. Bigg. All right, I'll see what I can do with the Incredible Hulk here. Where do you want to eat?"

We settled on Woody's at about 6:00 P.M.

I spent the rest of the afternoon leafing through the Sunday papers and then the Stonehouse file once again. I left my apartment at 5:30 and walked to Woody's. It wasn't dark yet, but still I scanned the street before I left the vestibule, and my head was on a swivel during my rapid walk to 23rd Street.

Nitchy greeted me after I had hung my hat and coat on the front rack.

"No princess tonight, Josh?" she said.

"Not tonight, Nitchy," I said.

"It'll happen," she said confidently. "One of these nights you'll waltz through that door with a princess on your arm. You'll see."

As usual she was looped with bangles, hoops, and amulets. Her black helmet of hair gleamed wickedly, and the heavy eye shadow and precisely painted lips accented her sorceress look. She gave me a table where I could watch the front door.

They weren't very late—not more than fifteen minutes. The moment Maybelle Hawks entered the restaurant, and the heads of everyone in the front room began to turn, I realized who she was.

She was one of the most famous high-fashion models in Manhattan. Her classic features had adorned dozens of haute couture magazines, she had posed in the nude for many artists and photographers, and a scholarly art critic had written a much quoted monograph on her "Nefertiti-like beauty" and "ethereal sensuality." She towered over Stilton, who lurked behind her. I guessed her to be 6-4 or 6-5. She was wearing a supple black leather trenchcoat, mink-lined. It hung open, revealing a loose chemise-styled shift in soft, plum-colored wool. There was a fine gold chain about the strong stalk of her neck.

I could see why that art critic had thought of Nefertiti. Her head seemed elongated, drawn out in back so that it had the shape of a tilted egg. Her hair was a cap of tight black curls.

Oriental eyes, Semitic lips, a thin scimitar of a nose. All of her features seemed carved, polished, oiled. Her teeth were unbelievably white.

They made it to my table and sat down. From close range, Percy wasn't looking so good. He was as elegantly clad as the first time I had seen him, but the eyes were sunk deeply and bagged. The whites were reddish and he blinked frequently. There was a sallow tinge to his cordovan skin.

Nitchy asked if we'd like a drink. Belle saw my glass of white wine and said that's what she'd have. Percy raised his bloodshot eyes to Maybelle Hawks.

"Please, babe," he croaked piteously.

"Nitchy," Belle said in tones that were more song than speech, "please bring this basket case a shot of cognac with about a quart of ice water for a chaser."

"Coming up," Nitchy said. She looked sympathetically at Perce. "Got the whim-whams?" she asked.

"Whim-whams?" Belle said with a scoffing laugh. "This is the guy who swore he could mix grass, martinis, wine, bourbon, and brandy stingers. 'I can handle it,' he said."

"Belle," Stilton implored. "Don't shout."

When our drinks were served, Perce sat there staring at his brandy. He took a deep breath. Then he bent forward so he had to lift the glass only a few inches to his lips. He took half of it in one gulp. Then he closed his eyes and clenched his teeth.

"Jesus!" he said finally. "Did you hear that hit?"

He took another deep breath, sat back in his chair, drained off his glass of ice water. Nitchy was there with a pitcher to fill it up again.

"Well now," Percy Stilton said, looking at us with a weak grin. "This is what I should have done eight hours ago."

"I wanted you to suffer," Maybelle Hawks said.

Stilton finished his cognac and handed the empty glass to Nitchy. "Another plasma, please, nurse," he said.

By the time Belle and I had finished our wine, the detective seemed recovered, lighting a cigarette with steady fingers, laughing and joking, surveying his surroundings with interest.

"Nice, comfy place," he said, nodding. "How's the food?"

Nitchy was still hovering, proud at having Maybelle Hawks in her establishment. I had seen her boasting at other tables.

"For you," she said to Stilton, "I suggest a rare sirloin, a mixed green salad, and nothing else."

"Marry me," he said.

"I'll have the same, please," Belle said. "Oil and vinegar on the greens."

I ordered a hamburger and another round of drinks.

"All right, Josh," Percy said, "what's all this about?"

I glanced quickly toward Maybelle Hawks. Stilton caught it. "She knows everything. She thinks it's interesting."

"Fascinating," she said.

"You know all the people involved?" I asked her. "Tippi Kipper? Godfrey Knurr? Marty Reape?"

She nodded.

"Good," I said. "But what I have to say will be new to both of you. I've got a lot to tell."

"Talk away," Percy Stilton said. "We're listening."

I told them about the Stonehouse case: the arsenic poisoning, how I thought it had been done, the personalities of the people involved, how I was attempting to locate a cabdriver who might have picked up Professor Stonehouse on the night he disappeared. They listened intently.

When I told them about the attempted assault on me the previous evening, Detective Stilton paused, his last forkful of steak halfway to his mouth, and stared at me. Then he devoured the final bite, pushed his plate away, and reached for his cigarette case.

I told them how I had shadowed Godfrey Knurr, how he had traveled up to that West Side garage, met a woman, and how the two of them drove northward in a black Mercedes-Benz.

"But it wasn't Tippi Kipper," I said. "It was Glynis Stonehouse."

I finished my hamburger and looked up. Detective Percy Stilton had lighted his cigarette. He was puffing calmly, looking into the space over my head. Maybelle Hawks had also finished her dinner despite my earthshaking news. She was patting her lips delicately with her napkin.

"Good steak," was all she said.

Stilton's eyes came down slowly until he was staring at me.

"Roll me over," he sang softly, "in the clover. Roll me over, lay me down, and do it again."

"Coffee?" the waitress asked.

We agreed and added brandy to the order. Nothing was said until the waitress moved away. Then Detective Stilton struck the top of the table with his palm. Cutlery jumped.

"That fucker," Stilton cried. "That fucker!"

"Easy, babe," Maybelle Hawks said. "Don't get physical."

"You think . . . ?" I said.

"Sheet," the detective said disgustedly. "It's him. It's got to be him. I don't know how he managed the Kipper snuff or what he did with Stonehouse, but it's him, it's got to be him. And he thinks he's going to stroll, chuckling."

"He's doing all right so far," Belle said dryly.

"Yes," I said, nodding. "But it's all guesswork."

Stilton ground out his cigarette, half-smoked, and immediately lighted another.

"Uh-huh," he said. "Guesswork. No hard evidence. Right. Well, I'll tell you, Josh, sometimes it goes like that. You got the guy cold but you can't prove."

"What do you do then?"

He put his head far back, blew smoke at the ceiling.

"Well . . ." he said slowly, "I know a couple of guys who owe me. Not cops," he added hurriedly. "Just friends from my old neighborhood. They like to go hunting."

I looked at him, puzzled.

"They could take this Knurr hunting with them," he said. "In the forest. Lots of trees upstate. Accidents happen all the time. Hunting accidents."

"No," I said.

"Why not?" Stilton demanded harshly.

"Perce," I said, "I don't believe in brute force and brute morality. I don't believe they rule the world. I don't believe they're what make history and form the future. I just don't believe that. I *can't* believe that, Perce. Look at me. I'm a shrimp. If brute force is what it's all about, then I haven't got a chance, I'm dead already. Also, I don't *want* to believe it. If brute morality is the law of survival, then I want to be dead. I don't want to live in a world like that because it would just be nothing, without hope and without joy."

Stilton stared at me, his eyes wide.

"You're a pisser," he said finally.

"That's the way I feel," I said.

Maybelle Hawks reached across the table and put a hand on my arm.

"I'm with you, babe," she said softly.

The detective leaned back and lighted another cigarette.

"And the meek shall inherit the earth," he said tonelessly.

"I didn't say that," I told him angrily. "I want to nail Godfrey Knurr as much as you do. More maybe. He played me for a fool. I'm not meek about it at all. I'm not going to let him escape."

"And just how do you figure to nail him?"

"I've got a good brain—I know I have. Knurr isn't going to stroll away. Right now I can't tell you exactly how I'm going to nail him, but I know I will. Guile and cunning. That's what I'm going to use against him. Those are the only weapons of a persecuted minority. And that is how I consider myself: a member of the minority of shorts."

"All right, Josh," Stilton said. "We'll play it your way—for the time being. Tomorrow I'll see what the machine's got on the Reverend Godfrey Knurr."

"And Tippi Kipper," I reminded him.

"Right. You're going ahead with those posters?"

"First thing tomorrow."

"Take my advice: don't describe Stonehouse on the posters. If you do, you'll get a million calls from smart-asses. Just run his picture and give the address of his apartment house. Then, if you get any calls, you can check how legit they are by asking the caller to describe Stonehouse."

"That makes sense."

"Also," Stilton went on, "check out those chemical analyses Stonehouse had made. Go to the lab, blow some smoke. Get copies of the analyses. You think the arsenic was in the brandy, and you're probably right. But you need paper. Find that clinic where Glynis does volunteer work. See if they have any arsenic."

I was scrawling rapid memoranda in my little notebook. "Anything else?" I asked him.

"If the clinic doesn't work out, try to discover where she worked previously. Maybe they had arsenic."

"I don't even know how long ago she worked there," I said. "Maybe a year or two, or longer."

"So?" Percy Stilton said. "It's possible."

"Do you know when Glynis met Godfrey Knurr?" Maybelle Hawks asked.

"No, I don't," I confessed. "I'll try to find out."

"Uh-huh," Stilton said. "And while you're at it, try to get us a recent photograph of Glynis."

"What for?"

"Oh, I don't rightly know," he said lazily.

I made a note: *Gly foto.*

"Anything else?" I asked.

"I don't know how much time you can put in on this thing," Perce said, "but it would help if you could keep tabs on Knurr. Just to get some idea of the guy's schedule. Where he goes, who he sees. Especially where he goes when he and Glynis take off in that black Mercedes from the West Side garage. That's another thing: try to find out if it's his car."

"It's not. Knurr owns a battered VW," I said.

"Sure," Stilton said genially. "He would. Fits right in with his image of a poor-but-honest man of the cloth. He's probably got a portfolio of blue-chip stocks that would knock your eye out. Well, that's about all I can think of, Josh." He looked at Maybelle Hawks. "You think of anything else, babe?"

"Not at the moment," she said. "I'd feel a lot surer about this whole thing if we could figure out how Knurr and Tippi put Sol Kipper over that railing. Also the suicide note."

"You're a wise old fox," he told her. "Give it some thought. I'll bet you'll come up with something."

"I wish I could say the same about you," she murmured. "Tonight."

"Try me," he said.

"I intend to," she said. "Josh, many thanks for the dinner. And you just keep right on. You're going to crash this; I know you are."

"Thank you," I said. "Perce, would you be willing to give me your home telephone number?"

"Sure," he said immediately, and did.

I waited with them until they got a cab. Maybelle swooped to kiss my cheek.

"I want to see more of you, Josh," she said. "Promise?"

"Of course," I said.

"You'll come up and have dinner with us? I'm really a very good cook. Right, Perce?"

He flipped a palm back and forth.

"So-so," he said.

"Bastard," she said.

I walked home slowly, ashamed. I was embarrassed at confessing how I saw myself as a member of the persecuted minority of the short.

Still, it was true. You may believe I was obsessed by my size. Let me tell how I felt. I have already commented on the rewards society offers to men of physical stature. The tall are treated with respect; the short earn contempt or amusement. This is true only of men. "Five-foot-two, eyes of blue" is still an encomium for a female. Our language reflects this prejudice. A worthy person is said to be "A man you can look up to." An impecunious man is suffering from "the shorts." To be short-tempered is reprehensible. To short-circuit is to frustrate or impede. A shortfall is a deficiency.

Thus does our language reflect our prejudice. And the philosophy that I had in a moment of weakness divulged to Belle and Perce reflected my deepest feelings about being a midget. From my size, or lack of it, came my beliefs, dreams, ideas, emotions, fantasies, reactions. All of which would be put to the test whether I liked it or not, in the rocky week ahead.

2

I ARRIVED AT TORT the next morning before 9:00 A.M. My In basket was piled high with requests for investigations and research, but after shuffling through them, I decided that most could be handled by Mrs. Kletz and the rest could wait.

Shortly before ten, I phoned Gardner & Weiss, who did all the job printing for Tabatchnick, Orsini, Reilly, and Teitelbaum. I spoke directly to Mr. Weiss and explained what I wanted on the Stonehouse reward posters.

"No problem," he said. "I'll send a messenger for the photograph and copy. How many do you want?"

I had no idea. "A hundred," I said.

"Wednesday," he said.

"This afternoon," I said.

"Oh," he said sadly. "Oh, oh, oh."

"It's a rush job. We'll pay."

"Without saying," he told me. "You want to see a proof first?"

"No. I trust you."

"You do?" he said.

"By one o'clock this afternoon?"

"I'll try. Only because you said you trust me. The messenger's on his way."

I dug out the photograph of Professor Stonehouse and typed the copy for the poster: *REWARD! A generous cash award will be paid to any cabdriver who can prove he picked up this man in the vicinity of Central Park West and 70th Street on the night of January 10th, this year.* Then I added the TORT telephone number and my extension.

As usual, Thelma Potts was seated primly outside the office of Mr. Leopold Tabatchnick.

"Miss Potts!" I cried, "you're looking uncommonly lovely this morning."

"Oh-oh," she said. "You want something."

"Well, yes. I have a friend who needs legal advice. I wondered if I could have one of Mr. Tabatchnick's cards to give him."

"Liar," she said. "You want to pretend you're Mr. Tabatchnick."

I was astonished. "How did you know?" I asked her.

"How many do you need?" she asked, ignoring my question.

As I was leaving she dunned me for a dollar for the sick kit. I handed it over.

"Still betting on Hamish Hooter?" I asked her.

"I only bet on sure things," she said loftily.

When Gertrude Kletz came in I called her into my office and showed her the photograph of Professor Stonehouse and the reward copy. I explained that she should expect the posters to be delivered by Gardner & Weiss in the early afternoon. Meanwhile, she could begin compiling a list of taxi garages, which she could get from the Yellow Pages.

"Or from the Hack Bureau," she said.

I looked at her with admiration.

"Right," I said. I told her the posters would have to be hand-carried to the garages and, with the permission of the manager, displayed on walls or bulletin boards.

"I'll need sticky tape and thumbtacks," she said cheerfully. The Kipper file had hooked her; now the Stonehouse case had done the same. I could see it in her bright eyes. Her face was burning with eagerness.

I told her I was off to the lab to check into Stonehouse's tests, and that by the time I got back, she'd probably be out distributing the posters. I put on hat and coat, grabbed up my briefcase, and rushed out, waving at Yetta as I sailed past.

She was wearing the green sweater I had given her, but curiously this failed to stir me.

The chemical laboratory was on Eleventh Avenue near 55th Street. I took a cab over. Bommer & Son, Inc., was on the fourth floor of an unpretentious building set between a sailors' bar (BIG BOY DRINKS 75 CENTS DURING HAPPY HOUR, 9 TO 2 A.M.) and a gypsy fortune teller (READINGS, PAST, PRESENT, FUTURE. SICKNESS). The elevator was labeled FREIGHT ONLY, so I climbed worn stairs to the fourth floor, the nose-crimping smell of chemicals becoming more intense as I ascended.

The receptionist in the outer office was typing away at Underwood's first model. She stopped.

"I'd like to speak to Mr. Bommer, please."

In a few moments a stoutish man wearing a stained white laboratory coat flung himself into the office.

"Yes?" he demanded in a reedy voice.

The receptionist pointed me out. He came close to me, peering suspiciously at my face. I thought him to be in the sixties—possibly the 1860s.

"Yes?"

"Mr. Waldo Bommer?"

"Yes."

I proffered Mr. Tabatchnick's card. He held it a few inches from his eyes and read it aloud: "Leopold H. Tabatchnick. Attorney-at-Law." He lowered the card. "Who's suing?" he asked me.

"No one," I said. "I just want a moment of your time. I represent the estate of Professor Yale Stonehouse. Among his papers is a canceled check made out to Bommer & Son, with no accompanying voucher. The government is running a tax audit on the estate, and it would help if you could provide copies of the bill."

"Come with me," he said abruptly.

I followed him through a rear door into an enormous loft laboratory where five people, three men, two women, all elderly and all wearing stained laboratory coats, were seated on high stools before stone-topped workbenches. They seemed intent on what they were doing; none looked up as we passed through.

Mr. Waldo Bommer led the way to a private office tucked into one corner. He closed the door behind us.

"How do you stand it?" I asked him.

"Stand what?"

"The smell."

"What smell?" he said. He took in a deep breath through his nostrils. "Hydrogen sulfide, hypochlorous acid, sulfur dioxide, a little bit of this, a little bit of that. A smell? I love it. Smells are my bread and butter, mister. How do you think I do a chemical analysis? First, I smell. You see before you an educated nose."

He tapped the bridge of his nose. A small pugnose with trumpeting nostrils.

"An educated nose," he repeated proudly. "First, I smell. Sometimes that tells me all I have to know."

Suddenly he grabbed me by the shoulders and pulled me close. I thought he meant to kiss me. But he merely sniffed at my mouth and cheeks.

"You don't smoke," he said. "Right?"

"Right," I said, pulling back from his grasp.

"And this morning, for breakfast, you had coffee and a pastry. Something with fruit in it. Figs maybe."

"Prune Danish," I said.

"You see!" he said. "An educated nose. My father had the best nose in the business. He could tell you when you had changed your socks. Sit down."

Waldo Bommer shuffled through a drawer in a battered oak file.

"Stacy, Stone, Stonehouse," he intoned. "Here it is. Professor Yale Stonehouse. Two chemical analyses of unknown liquids. December 14th of last year."

"May I take a look?" I asked.

"Why not?"

I scanned the two carbon-copy reports. There were a lot of chemical terms; one of them included arsenic trioxide.

"Could you tell me what these liquids were, please?"

He snatched the papers from my hands and scanned them. "Simple. This one, plain cocoa. This one was brandy."

"The brandy has the arsenic trioxide in it?"

"Yes."

"Didn't you think that unusual?"

He shrugged.

"Mister, I just do the analysis. What's in it is none of my business. A week ago a woman brought in a tube of toothpaste loaded with strychnine."

"Toothpaste?" I cried. "How did they get it in?"

Again he shrugged. "Who knows? A hypo through the opening maybe. I couldn't care less. I just do the analysis."

"Could I get copies of these reports, Mr. Bommer? For the government. The tax thing..."

He thought a moment.

"I don't see why not," he said finally. "You say this Professor Stonehouse is dead?"

"Yes, sir. Deceased early this year."

"Then he can't sue me for giving out copies of his property."

Ten minutes later I was bouncing down the splintering stairs with photocopies in my briefcase. I had offered to pay for the copies, and Bommer had taken me up on it. I inhaled several deep breaths of fresh air, then went flying up Eleventh Avenue. There is no feeling on earth to match a hunch proved correct. I decided to press my luck. I stopped at the first unvandalized phone booth I came to.

"Yah?" Olga Eklund answered.

"Olga, this is Joshua Bigg."

"Yah?"

"Is Miss Glynis in?"

"No. She's at her clinic."

That was what I hoped to hear.

"But Mrs. Stonehouse is at home?"

"Yah."

"Well, maybe I'll drop by for a few moments. She's recovered from her, uh, indisposition?"

"Yah."

"Able to receive visitors?"

"Yah."

"I'll come right over. You might mention to her that I'll be stopping by for a minute or two."

I waited for her "Yah," but there was no answer; she had hung up. Shortly afterward Olga in the flesh was taking my coat in the Stonehouse hallway.

"I'm sorry Miss Glynis isn't at home," I said to Olga. "You think I might be able to call her at the clinic?"

"Oh yah," she said. "It's the Children's Eye, Ear, Nose and Throat Clinic. It's downtown, on the East Side."

"Thank you," I said gratefully. "I'll call her there."

Ula Stonehouse was half-reclining on the crushed velvet couch. She was beaming, holding a hand out to me. As usual, there was a wineglass and a bottle of sherry on the glass-topped table.

"How nice!" she warbled. "I was hoping for company and here you are!"

"Here I am, indeed, ma'am," I said, taking her limp hand. "I was sorry to hear you have been indisposed, but you look marvelously well now."

"Oh, I feel so *good*," she said, patting the couch next to her. I sat down obediently. "My signs changed and now I feel like a new woman."

"I'm delighted to hear it."

I watched her reach forward to fill her glass with a tremulous hand. She straightened back slowly, took a sip, looking at me over the rim with those milkglass eyes flickering. The mop of blonde curls seemed frizzier than ever. She touched the tip of her nose as one might gently explore a bruise.

"Would you care for anything, Mr. Bigger?" she asked. "A drink? Coffee? Whatever?"

"Bigg, ma'am," I said. "Joshua Bigg. No, thank you. Nothing for me. Just a few minutes of your time if you're not busy."

"All the time in the world," she said, laughing gaily.

She was wearing a brightly printed shirtwaist dress with a wide, ribbon belt. The gown, the pumps, the makeup, the costume jewelry: all too young for her. And the flickering eyes, warbling voice, fluttery gestures gave a feverish impression: a woman under stress. I felt sure she was aware of what was going on.

"Mrs. Stonehouse," I said, "I wish I had good news to report about your husband, but I'm afraid I do not."

"Oh, let's not talk about that," she said. "What's done is done. Now tell me all about yourself."

She looked at me brightly, eyes widened. If she wasn't going to talk about her vanished husband, I was stymied. Still, for the moment, it seemed best to play along.

"What would you like to know about me, ma'am?"

"You're a Virgo, aren't you?"

"Pisces," I told her.

"Of course," she said, as if confirming her guess. "Are you married?"

"No, Mrs. Stonehouse, I am not."

"Oh, you must be," she said earnestly. "You *must* listen to me. And you must because I have been so happy in my own marriage, you see. A family is a little world. I have my husband and my son and my daughter. We are a very close, loving family, as you know."

I looked at her helplessly. She had deteriorated since I first met her; now she was almost totally out of it. I thought desperately how I might use her present mood to get what I wanted. "I'm an orphan, Mrs. Stonehouse," I said humbly. "My parents were killed in an accident when I was an infant."

Surprisingly, shockingly, tears welled up in those milky eyes. She stifled a sob, reached to grip my forearm. Her clutch was frantic.

"Poor tyke," she groaned, then lunged for her glass of sherry.

"I was raised by relatives," I went on. "Good people. I wasn't mistreated. But still...So when you speak of a close, loving family, a little world—I know nothing of all that. The memories."

"The memories," she said, nodding like a broken doll. "Oh yes, the memories..."

"Do you have a family album, Mrs. Stonehouse?" I asked softly, and, to my surprise, she responded by producing the album with unexpected rapidity.

What followed was a truly awful hour. We pored over those old photographs one by one while Ula Stonehouse provided running commentary, rife with pointless anecdotes. I murmured constant appreciation and made frequent noises of wonder and enjoyment.

Wedding Pictures: the tall, gaunt groom towering over the frilly doll-bride. An old home in Boston. Glynis, just born, naked on a bearskin rug. Childhood snapshots. Powell Stonehouse at ten, frowning seriously at the camera. Picnics. Outings. Friends. Then, gradually, the family groups, friends, picnics, outings—all disappearing. Formal photographs. Single portraits. Yale, Ula, Glynis, Powell. Lifeless eyes. A family moving toward dissolution.

When Mrs. Stonehouse leaned forward to refill her glass, I rapidly removed a recent snapshot of Glynis from the album and slipped it into my briefcase before she sat back again. "Remarkable," I said, as if I were riveted to the book. "Really remarkable. Happy times."

She looked at me, not seeing me.

"Oh yes," she said. "Happy times. Such good babies. Glynis never cried. Never. Powell did, but not Glynis. It's over."

I didn't dare ask what she meant by that.

"Emanations," she went on. "And visits beyond. I know it's over."

"Mrs. Stonehouse," I asked anxiously, "are you feeling well?"

"What?" she said. "Well," she said, passing a faltering hand across her brow, "perhaps I should lie down for a few moments. So many memories."

"Of course," I said, rising. "I'll call Olga."

I found her seated at the long dining room table, leafing through *Popular Mechanics*.

"Olga," I said, "I think Mrs. Stonehouse needs you. I think she'd like to rest for a while."

"Yah?" she said. She rose, yawned, and stretched. "I go."

In the kitchen Effie was at the enormous stove, stirring something with a long wooden spoon. Her porky face creased into a grin.

"Mr. Bigg!" she said. "How nice!"

She put the spoon aside, clapped a lid on the pot, and wiped her hands on her apron. She gestured toward the white enameled table and we both drew up chairs.

"Effie," I said, "how are you? It's good to see you again."

That was true, and it was a comfort to be honest again. She was such a jolly tub of a woman.

"Getting along," she said. "You look a little puffy around the gills. Not sick, are you?"

"No," I said, "I'm okay. But I've been talking to Mrs. Stonehouse. I'm a little shook."

"Yes," she said, wagging her head dolefully. "I know what you mean. Worse every day."

"Why?" I asked. "What's happening to her?"

She frowned. "I don't rightly know. Her husband disappearing, I guess. Powell moving out. And the way Glynis has been acting. I suppose it's just too much for her."

"How has Glynis been acting?"

"Strange," Effie said. "Snappish. Cold. Goes to her room and stays there. Never a smile."

"Is this recent?" I asked.

"Oh yes. Just since your last visit."

She looked at me shrewdly. I decided to plunge ahead. If she repeated what I was saying to Glynis, so much the better. So I told Effie what I knew about the arsenic. She listened closely, then nodded when I had finished.

"Are you a detective?" she asked.

"Sort of," I said. "Chief Investigator for the legal firm representing Professor Stonehouse."

"You don't suspect me of poisoning him, do you?"

"Never," I lied. "Not for a minute."

"Glynis?"

We stared at each other. I wondered if her silence was meant to imply consent, and decided to act as if it did.

"I must establish that Glynis had the means," I said. "You just can't go out and buy arsenic at Rexall's. And to do that, I need the name of the medical laboratory where she worked as a secretary."

"I'd rather not," she said quickly.

"I was going to ask Mrs. Stonehouse, but she's in no condition to answer questions. Effie, I need the name."

Once again we stared at each other.

"It's got to be done," I said.

"Yes," she agreed sadly.

After a while she got up and lumbered from the kitchen. She came back in a few minutes with a slip of paper. I glanced at it briefly. Atlantic Medical Research, with the address and phone number.

"I had it in my book," Effie explained, "in case we had to reach her at work."

"When did she stop working there?"

She thought a moment.

"Maybe June or July of last year."

About the time Professor Stonehouse became ill.

"Did she just quit or was she fired?"

"She quit, she told us. Said it was very boring work."

"Effie, did you ever hear her mention a man named Godfrey Knurr? He's a minister."

"Godfrey Knurr? No."

"Is Glynis a religious woman?"

"Not particularly. They're Episcopalian. But I never thought she was especially religious. But she's deep."

"Oh yes," I agreed, "she's deep all right. Before her father's disappearance, was she in a good mood?"

Mrs. Dark pondered that.

"I'd say so," she said finally. "She started changing after the Professor disappeared and in the last week she's gotten much worse."

"Me," I said. "I'm troubling her. I told her I knew her father had been poisoned."

"You didn't!"

"I did. Of course I didn't tell her I thought she had done it."

"What are you going to do now?"

"Dig deeper. Try to find out what happened to the Professor. Effie, what kind of a car do the Stonehouses own?"

"A Mercedes."

"Do they keep it in a garage over on 66th Street and West End?"

"Why, yes. The garage people bring it over when we need it. How did you know?"

"I've been looking around."

"You surely have," she said. "Have you found the will yet?"

"Not yet. But I think I know where it is."

"I don't see why it's so important," she said. "If he's dead and didn't leave a will, the money goes to his wife and children anyway, doesn't it?"

"Yes," I said, "but if he left a will, he might have disinherited one of them."

"Could he do that?"

"Probably. With good cause. Like attempted murder."

"Oh," she said softly, "I hadn't thought of that."

"Effie, can I count on your discretion about all this?"

She put a fat forefinger alongside a fatter nose.

"Mum's the word," she said.

I rose, then bent swiftly to kiss her apple cheek.

"Thank you," I said. "I know it's not pleasant. But we agreed, it's got to be done. One last question: will Miss Glynis be in tonight? Did she say?"

"She said she's going to the theatre. She asked for an early dinner."

"Uh-huh. So she'll be leaving about when?"

"Seven-thirty," Mrs. Dark said. "At the latest."

"Thank you very much," I said. "You've been very kind."

I had a Big Mac and a Coke before I returned to the office. Yetta Apatoff was on the phone when I entered the TORT building. She blew me a kiss. I'm afraid I responded with a feeble gesture. Her scarf had come awry and the diving neckline of the green sweater now revealed a succulent cleavage. I wondered nervously when Mr. Teitelbaum or Mr. Tabatchnick would instruct their respective secretaries to order Yetta to cover up.

Mrs. Kletz had left a note on my desk; she was indeed out distributing the reward posters to the taxi garages and had left me a copy of the poster. It looked perfect.

I spent the remainder of the afternoon typing out reports of my morning's activities and adding them to the Stonehouse file, along with the photocopies of the chemical analyses. Then I hacked away at routine inquiries until about 4:00 P.M., when I dialed the number of the Children's Eye, Ear, Nose and Throat Clinic in the Manhattan phone book and asked to speak to the director.

"Who is calling, please?" the receptionist asked.

"This is the Metropolitan Poison Control Board," I said solemnly. "It concerns your drug inventory."

A hearty voice came on the line almost instantly.

"Yes, sir!" he said. "How may I be of service?"

"This is Inspector Waldo Bommer of the Metropolitan Poison Control Board. In view of the recent rash of burglaries of doctors' offices, clinics, hospitals, laboratories, and so forth, we are attempting to make an inventory of the establishments that keep poisonous substances in stock."

"Narcotics?" he said. "We have nothing like that. This is a clinic for underprivileged youngsters."

"What we're interested in is poisons," I said. "Arsenic, strychnine, cyanide: things of that sort."

"Oh, heavens no!" he said, enormously relieved. "We have nothing like that in stock."

"Sorry to bother you," I said. "Thank you for your time."

My second call, to Atlantic Medical Research, was less successful. I went through my Poison Control Board routine, but the man said, "Surely you don't expect me to reveal that information on the phone to a complete stranger? If you care to come around with your identification, we'll be happy to cooperate."

He hung up.

It wasn't 5:00 P.M. yet, but I packed my briefcase with the Kipper and Stonehouse files, yanked on my hat and coat, and sallied forth. Yetta was not on the phone. She held out a hand to stop me.

"Josh," she said, pouting, "you didn't even *notice*."

"I certainly did notice," I said. "The sweater looks lovely, Yetta."

"You like?" she said, arching her chest.

"Fine," I said, swallowing. "And the scarf is just right."

"Oh, this old thing," she giggled, swinging it farther aside. "It just gets in my way when I type. I think I'll take it off."

Which she did. I looked about furtively. There were people in the corridor. Was I a prude? I may very well have been.

"Josh," she said eagerly, "you said we might, you know, go out some night together."

"Well, uh, we certainly shall," I said with more confidence than I felt. "Dinner, maybe the theatre or ballet." The image of Yetta Apatoff at a performance of *Swan Lake* shriveled my soul. "But I've been so busy, Yetta. Not only during the day, but working at home in the evening as well."

"Uh-huh," she said speculatively. She was silent a moment as I stood there awkwardly, not knowing how to break away. It was clear she was summing me up and coming to a decision.

"Lunch maybe?" she said.

"Oh absolutely," I said. "I can manage lunch."

"Tomorrow," she said firmly.

"Tomorrow?" I said, thinking desperately of how I might get out of it. "Well, uh, yes. I'll have to check my schedule. I mean, let's figure on lunch, and if I have to postpone you'll understand, right?"

"Oh sure," she said.

Coolness there. Definite coolness.

I waved goodbye and stumbled out. I felt guilt. I had led her astray. And then I was angry at my own feeling of culpability. What, actually, had I done? Bought her a few lunches. Given her a birthday present. I assured myself that I had never given her any reason to believe I was...It was true that I frequently stared at her intently, but with her physical attributes and habit of wearing knitted suits a size too small, that was understandable.

Such were my roiling thoughts as I departed the office that Monday evening, picking up a barbecued chicken, potato salad, and a quart of Scotch on the way home. Back in Chelsea, I ate and drank with an eye on the clock. I had to be across the street from the Stonehouse apartment at 7:15 at the latest, and I intended to proceed to the Upper West Side at a less-frenzied pace than my recent forays.

Clad in my fleece-lined anorak, I made it there in plenty of time and assumed my station. It was a crisp night, crackling, the air filled with electricity. You get nights like that in New York, usually between winter and spring, or between summer and fall, when suddenly the city seems bursting with promise, the skyline a-sparkle with crystalline clarity.

As I walked up and down the block, always keeping the doorway of the Stonehouse apartment house in view, I could glimpse the twinkling towers of the East Side across the park, and the rosy glow of midtown. Rush of traffic, blare of horns, drone of airliners overhead. Everything seemed so *alive*. I kept reminding myself I was investigating what was fast emerging as a violent death, but it was difficult.

I had been waiting exactly twenty-three minutes when she came out, wearing the long, hooded mink coat I'd seen in the garage.

When she paused outside the lighted apartment lobby for a moment, I was able to see her clearly as she raised and adjusted her hood. Then she started off, walking briskly. I thought I knew where she was going; despite Mrs. Dark's information, it was not the theatre. I went after her. Not too close, not too far. Just as Roscoe Dollworth had taught me, keeping to the other side of the street when possible, even moving ahead of her. It was an easy tail because as we walked west and south a few blocks, I became more and more certain that she was taking me back to that garage on West 66th Street.

Crossing Broadway, she went west on 69th Street, keeping to the shadowed paths of a housing development. A man coming toward her paused and said something, but she didn't give him a glance, or slow down her pace. When she crossed West End Avenue, heading toward the lighted garage, I hurried to catch up, staying on the other side of the street and moving about a half-block southward. I could see her waiting in the entrance of the garage. I stopped the first empty cab that came along.

"Where to?" the driver asked, picking up his trip sheet clamped to a clipboard. He was a middle-aged black.

"Nowhere," I said. "Please start your clock and we'll just wait."

He put the clipboard aside and turned to stare at me through the metal grille.

"What is this?" he said.

"See that woman over there? Across the street, ahead of us? In the fur coat?"

He peered.

"I see her," he said.

I had learned from my previous experience.

"My wife," I said. "I want to see where she's going. I think someone's going to pick her up."

"Uh-huh," he said. "There's not going to be any trouble, is there?"

"No," I said, "no trouble."

"Good," he said. "I got all I can handle right now."

We sat there, both of us staring at the figure of Glynis Stonehouse across the street. The meter ticked away.

Within three or four minutes Knurr arrived. I had expected him to pull up in a cab, then switch to the Mercedes, but instead he raced into the garage entrance, near where Glynis waited, and opened the passenger door of his old VW. As soon as she got in, he backed out fast, swung around, and headed northward again, shoving his way into traffic.

"Follow?" my driver said.

"Please," I said.

"That guy is some cowboy. He drives like he don't give a damn."

"I don't think he does," I said.

We tailed them north. Knurr made a left onto 79th Street, then began to circle the block.

"Looking for a place to park," the cabdriver commented knowledgeably. "If he pulls in, what do you want me to do?"

"Go down to the next corner and wait."

That's what happened. Knurr found a place to park on West 77th Street near Riverside Drive. We went past and pulled in close to the corner. Through the rear window, I watched them both get out and walk past. They passed by my parked cab, talking much too intently to notice me.

I let them turn north on the Drive before I paid and got out of the taxi.

"Thank you," I said to the driver.

"Don't do anything foolish," he said.

As I followed Glynis Stonehouse and Godfrey Knurr into Riverside Park, I noted with relief that a few joggers and groups of raucous teenagers still braved the darkened expanse. And yet my nervousness increased as we penetrated deeper along lonely, descending paths, heading westward. I lurked as best I could in the shadows of leafless trees, trying to tread lightly. But I was being overcautious, for the couple ahead of me walking arm-in-arm were so intent on their talk that they seemed innocent of the secret sharer padding along behind them.

They walked around the rotunda, a large circular fountain girdled by a walk that was in turn enclosed by a ring of archways vaguely Roman in feeling. The fountain had long since ceased to operate; the basin was dried and cracked. All the white light globes were now shattered and dark. The archways were sprayed with graffiti. Splintered glass and broken bits of masonry grated underfoot. The ground was crumbling.

I paused briefly, not wanting to follow Glynis and Godfrey into one of those echoing passages lest they hear my footfall. I waited until they were clear on the other side of the fountain before hurrying through.

Ahead was the molten river, a band of gently heaving mercury in the nightlight. Across were the flickering lights of the Jersey shore. Closer, the swell of black water. I searched frantically about until I spotted them again, approaching the boat basin at 79th Street. I kept well back in the shadows as Glynis and Knurr walked onto the planked pier. They stopped briefly to speak to someone who appeared to be a watchman. Then they continued along one of the slips until they stepped down carefully onto the foredeck of what looked like a houseboat.

Lights came on inside the craft. When I saw curtains drawn across the wide windows, I turned and hurried back the way I had come.

3

I ARRIVED AT the TORT building before 9:00 A.M. on Tuesday morning. The night security guard was still on duty, sitting at Yetta Apatoff's desk.

"There was a telephone call for you about fifteen minutes ago, Mr. Bigg," he said. "The guy wouldn't leave a name or message, but said he'd call back."

"Thank you," I said, and went back to my office. My phone rang before I had a chance to take off my coat. I picked it up and said, "Hello?" A man's voice growled, "You the guy who put up the posters?" I said I was. He said, "How much is the reward?"

I hadn't even considered that. Fifty dollars seemed insufficient; a hundred might tempt a lot of fraudulent claims. But rather, I reasoned, too many replies than too few.

"A hundred dollars," I said.

"Shit," he said, and hung up.

The second call came in ten minutes later. Once again the first question asked was: "How much?"

"A hundred dollars," I said firmly.

"Yeah, well, I carried the guy. Picked him up on Central

Park West and 70th Street the night of January 10th."

"What did he look like?"

"Well, you know, an average-sized guy. I didn't get a real good look at him, but I'd say he was average."

"Kind of short, fat, dumpish?"

"Yeah, you could say that."

"Wearing a sweater and jacket?"

"Yeah, that's the guy."

"No, it isn't," I said.

"Fuck you," he said and hung up.

I sighed, finished my strawberry strudel and black coffee, and started mechanically answering some of the routine research and investigation requests. I wondered if I dared bother Percy Stilton with what I had discovered—the houseboat at 79th Street—and what I was beginning to guess about how Godfrey Knurr had murdered Sol Kipper.

Stilton solved the problem by calling me at about 10:00 A.M.

"Listen, Josh," he said, speaking rapidly, "I know you didn't want me to call you at your office, but this is important. I've only got a minute. Can you meet me in the lobby of the Newsweek building? 444 Madison? Between 49th and 50th?"

"Well, yes, sure," I said. "But I wanted—"

"About five minutes before four o'clock this afternoon."

"I'll be there, Perce," I said, making rapid notes on my scratchpad. "But here are a few things I—"

"Got to run," he said. "See you then."

The line went dead. I hung up slowly, bewildered. The phone rang again almost immediately and I plucked it up, hoping Stilton was calling back.

"Josh," Yetta Apatoff said, giggling, "you haven't forgotten our lunch today, have you?"

"Of course not," I lied bravely. "What time?"

"Noon," she said. "I've got a lot to tell you."

"Good," I said, my heart sinking.

Another call:

"Yeah, I picked up the guy on that night. A tall, skinny gink, right?"

"Could be," I said. "And where did you take him—to the Eastern Airlines ticket office on Fifth Avenue?"

"Yeah," he said, "you're right."

"Waited for him and then drove him back to Central Park West and 70th Street?"

"Uh . . . yeah."

"No," I said, "I don't think so."

He suggested an anatomical impossibility.

Inwardly cursing the venality of mankind, I hung up, then phoned the Kipper house. Chester Heavens answered.

We exchanged polite greetings, inquired as to the state of each other's health, and spoke gravely about the weather, which we agreed was both pleasant and bracing for that time of year.

"Chester," I said, "Mr. Kipper died on Wednesday, January 24th. Is that correct?"

"Oh yes, sah," he said somberly. "I shall never forget that date."

"I don't suppose you will. I know Mr. Godfrey Knurr arrived a few moments after the tragedy. Now my question is this: do you recall if he was at the house on Tuesday, January 23rd, the day before Mr. Kipper died?"

Silence. Then . . .

"I can't recall, sah. But if you'll be good enough to hang on a moment, I'll consult the book."

"Wait, wait!" I said hastily. "What book?"

"The house diary, sah," he said. "The first Mrs. Kipper insisted it be kept. It was one of my father's duties. After the first Mrs. Kipper and my father had both passed away, I kept it with the approval of the second Mrs. Kipper. What it is, sah, is a diary or log of visitors, delivery of packages, repairs to the house, appointments, and so forth. Many large homes keep such a daily record, sah. It is invaluable when it becomes necessary to send Christmas cards, thank you notes, invitations, or to question tradesmen about promised deliveries and things of that nature."

"Very efficient," I said, beginning to hope. "Could you consult the log, please, Chester, and see if the Reverend Knurr visited on Tuesday, January 23rd?"

"Just a moment, sah."

He was gone more than a moment. I had crossed all fingers of both hands and was trying to cross my toes within my shoes when the butler came back on the phone.

"Mr. Bigg?" he said. "Are you there?"

"I am here," I told him.

"Yes, sah, the diary shows that the Reverend Knurr visited on Tuesday, January 23rd. He arrived at approximately 3:30 P.M."

"Any record of when he left?"

"No, sah, there is no record of that."

"Thank you, Chester," I said gratefully, uncrossing my digits. "Just out of curiosity, where is this house diary kept?"

"In the kitchen, sah. In the back of one of the cutlery drawers."

"I wonder if you would do me a favor, Chester. I wonder if you would take the house diary to your apartment and conceal it carefully. I realize that is a strange request, but it is very important."

He didn't speak for a while. Then he said softly:

"Very well, Mr. Bigg, I shall do as you request."

"Thank you," I said.

"My pleasure, sah," he said.

My case was looking better and better. I thought I had Knurr cold, and I refused to worry about how I might begin to prove it.

"I'll check in later," I told Chester conspiratorially.

"I'll look forward to it, sah," he said, then rang off.

The high points of my long, dull morning were two more inconclusive calls from cabdrivers. A few minutes before noon I went into the men's room to freshen for lunch with Yetta. At an adjoining basin Hamish Hooter was combing his black, greasy locks sideways in a futile effort to conceal his growing tonsure.

He saw me reflected in the mirror and sucked his teeth noisily.

"See here, Bigg," he said, the voice reedy but not aggrieved; smug, in fact. "I understand you're having lunch with Yetta Apatoff today."

"You understand correctly," I said coldly.

He dried his hands busily on one paper towel. About a year previously, he had circulated a memo about the wasteful practice of using more than a single paper towel.

Hooter examined himself in the mirror with every evidence of approval. He passed a palm over his slicked-down hair. He attempted to straighten his rounded shoulders. He inhaled mightily, which caused his pot belly to disappear until he exhaled.

"Well," he said, turning to face me, "have a good time. Enjoy it while you can." Then he gave me a foxy grin and was gone.

When I walked out to meet Yetta, I saw at once that she was "dolled up" and looked especially glowing and attractive. I thought this was in anticipation of lunch with me, and I swelled with male satisfaction. At the same time I imagined how shattered she would be by the can't-we-be-friends speech I had in mind. Especially when she'd gone to so much trouble.

Instead of the usual knitted suit she was wearing a dress of some shimmering stuff with a metallic gleam.

About her blonde curls was bound a light blue chiffon scarf. The electric combination of blue and green enhanced her creamy complexion, sweetly curved lips, and the look of innocence in those limpid brown eyes. Was I being too hasty in putting our relationship on a purely friendly basis?

We walked over to the Chinese restaurant, Yetta chattering briskly about a movie concerning creatures from outer space who descend to earth and turn everyone into toadstools. She assured me it had been one of the scariest movies she had ever seen.

"Also," she added, "it made you think."

Then she babbled on about a used car her brother was thinking of buying, and about a girl she went to high school with who had recently obtained a job with the telephone company. Even for Yetta it was a manic performance.

All became clear over the wonton soup.

"Josh," she said breathlessly, "I wouldn't hurt you for the world."

I stared at her, perplexed.

"First of all," she started, "I want it definitely understood that you and I can still be friends."

Naturally I resented that. It was *my* line.

"Second of all," Yetta went on, "I have really enjoyed knowing you and these lunches and everything. I will never forget you, Josh."

"What—" I began.

"And third of all," she said in a rush, "Hamish Hooter asked me to marry him and I said yes. I know that must be a real downer for you, Josh, but I want you to know that I think I'm doing the right thing, and I've given it a lot of thought. He's not as cute as you are, Josh, that I freely admit, but he says he loves me and he needs me. Josh, you don't need me. Do you?"

There was no answer to that. I stared down into my soup bowl, saw it whisked away and a Number Three Combination slid into its place.

"Josh, don't take it too hard," Yetta pleaded. "It's best for all of us."

Could I tell her that my heart was leaping upward like a demented stag?

"You have your work," she continued, "and I know how important it is to you. Will you pass the sweet-and-sour sauce, please? So I thought—Hamish and I thought—that this would be the best way to tell you, honestly and straight out. He wanted to be here, but I said it would be best if I told you myself...Josh," Yetta Apatoff continued, staring at me with those guileless eyes, "I hope you don't hate me?"

"Hate you?" I said, keeping any hint of glee out of my voice. "How could I? All I want is what makes you happy. Yetta, I wish you the best of everything. Hooter is a very lucky man."

"Oh, Josh," she said, sighing, "you're so nice and understanding. I knew you would be. I told Hammy—that's what I call him: Hammy—I said, 'Hammy, his heart may be broken, but he'll wish me the best of everything.' That's what I told Hammy. Josh, is your heart broken? Could I have the mustard, please?"

I resisted the urge to suggest to Yetta that we go Dutch, and the lunch hour passed reasonably amicably, all things considered.

My first visitor upon my return to TORT was Hamish Hooter. "See here, Bigg," he said. "I guess Yetta told you the news?"

"She did," I said, "and I want to wish the two of you the best of everything."

"Yes?" he said, surprised. "Well, uh, thanks."

"I hope you'll be very happy together," I went on enthusiastically. "I'm sure you will be. Congratulations."

"Uh, thanks," he said again. "Listen, Bigg, you're being very decent about this."

I made an "it's nothing" gesture.

"If there's anything I can do..." he went on lamely.

"Well, there is something. You know I've got an assistant now. Temporary at the moment, but my workload seems to increase every day. If a larger office becomes available, I'd appreciate it if you'd keep me in mind."

"Well, uh, sure," he said. "I'll certainly do that."

"Thank you," I said humbly. "And once again, I wish you every happiness."

Next I did what most TORT employees did when they had an intraoffice problem: I went to Thelma Potts.

The news had already spread; she greeted me with a sympathetic smile. "I'm sorry, Mr. Bigg," she said.

"The better man won," I said.

Then she said something so completely out of character that she left me open-mouthed.

"Bullshit," Thelma Potts said. "You're well out of it. The girl is a moron. Not for you."

"Well..." I said, "at least you won."

"You did, too," she assured me with some asperity. "Did you come up here for sympathy?"

"Not exactly," I said. "I've got a problem. Nothing to do with Yetta," I added hastily.

"What's the problem?"

"I want to get together with Mr. Teitelbaum and Mr. Tabatchnick in a kind of conference. I have a lot to tell them, and it's very important, but I don't want to tell them separately. I was hoping you would speak to Ada Mondora and maybe the two of you might arrange something."

"It's that important?"

"It really is, Miss Potts. I wouldn't ask if it wasn't. It concerns a case each of them is handling, and the two cases have come together in a very peculiar fashion."

"Kipper and Stonehouse?" she asked.

"Miss Potts," I said, "is there anything you don't know?"

"Ada and I have lunch together almost every day," she said. "When do you want to meet with the two Mr. T's?"

"As soon as possible." I thought of my appointment with Detective Percy Stilton. "Not today, but tomorrow. If you can set it up."

"I'll talk to Ada," she said, "and we'll see what we can do. I'll let you know."

"Thank you," I said gratefully. "I don't know what we'd all do without you."

She sniffed.

I bent swiftly to kiss her soft cheek.

"Now that I've been jilted," I said, "I'm available."

"Oh *you*!" she said.

I returned to my office and took calls from two more cab-drivers, one of them drunk, then did routine stuff until it was time to leave for my meeting with Stilton. I packed my scruffy briefcase, put on hat and coat, and peeked cautiously out into the corridor.

Yetta Apatoff was seated at her receptionist's post, hands clasped primly on the desk. I ducked back into my office and waited a few moments. When I peeked out again, she was in the same position, still as a statue. I ducked back inside again. But the third time I peered out, she was busy on the phone, and I immediately sailed forth and gave her a sad smile and a resigned wave of my hand as I passed.

Cowardly conduct, I know.

I arrived early at the Newsweek building. A few minutes before 4:00 P.M., Percy Stilton came up behind me and stuck a hard forefinger in my ribs.

"Perce," I said, "I've got to tell you. I was—"

"Sure," he said, "but later. We've got a four o'clock appointment with Bishop Harley Oxman. He's in charge of personnel for the church the Reverend Godfrey Knurr belongs to. You just do as little talking as possible and follow my lead. In this scam, you play a lawyer."

"I've got Mr. Tabatchnick's business card," I offered.

"Beautiful," he said. "Flash it."

The church's personnel headquarters was a brightly lighted, brisk, efficient-appearing office in a five- or six-story commercial building on Forty-ninth between Madison and Park. The walls were painted a no-nonsense beige, the floors covered with practical vinyl tile; partitions between individual offices were steel. I saw no paintings of a religious nature on view. Typewriters clacked away merrily. Men and women moving along the corridors were all in mufti. Percy and I approached the matronly receptionist, and Perce identified himself. She didn't seem surprised that the Bishop would be meeting with a detective of the New York Police Department. She spoke briefly into an intercom, then gave us a wintry smile.

"You may go right in," she said. "Turn left outside, go to the end, and turn right. Last office."

We found the Bishop's office with no difficulty. The door was opened before we had a chance to knock. The man greeting us was tall and broad, though somewhat stooped and corpulent. He was wearing an old-fashioned suit of rusty cheviot and a gray doeskin waistcoat with white piping. His polka-dot bowtie was negligently knotted.

He had a very full, almost bloated face, ranging in hue from livid pink to deep purple. The full, moist, bright rose lips parted to reveal teeth of such startling whiteness, size, and regularity that they could only have been "store-bought." Set into this blood pudding of a face were sharp eyes of ice blue, the whites clear. And he had a great shock of steel-gray hair, combed sideways in rich billows.

"I am Bishop Oxman," he intoned in a deep resonant voice. "Won't you gentlemen come in?"

He ushered us into his office and seated us in leather armchairs in front of his glass-topped desk. Perce Stilton slid his identification across the desk without being asked, and I hastily dug in my wallet and did the same with Mr. Tabatchnick's business card.

While the Bishop was examining our bona fides slowly and with interest, I studied the bare office, its single bookcase, artificial rubber plant, and a framed photograph behind the Bishop. It appeared to be Bishop Oxman's seminary graduating class.

He returned our identification to us, sat back in his swivel chair, squirmed slightly to make himself more comfortable, then laced his pudgy fingers across his paunch. He wasted no time on pleasantries.

"Detective Stilton," he said in his rumbling bass-baritone, "when we spoke on the phone, you stated that a situation had arisen concerning one of our pastors that might best be handled by discussing it with me personally." He glanced briefly at me. "And privately."

"Yes, sir," Percy said firmly but with deference. "Before any official action is taken."

"Dear me," Bishop Oxman said with a cold smile, "that does sound ominous." But he didn't seem at all disturbed.

"It's something I think you should be aware of," Stilton went on, speaking with no hesitation. "Mr. Tabatchnick here represents a young woman who claims she was swindled out of her savings and an inheritance—slightly over ten thousand dollars—by the one of your clergymen who promised her he could double her money in six months."

"Oh my," Bishop Oxman murmured.

"This young lady further alleges that she was persuaded to hand over her money by the promise of the pastor that he would marry her as soon as her money increased."

"What is the young lady's name?" the Bishop asked.

"I don't believe that is germane to this discussion at the present time," Percy Stilton said.

"How old is the young lady? Surely you can tell me that?" Stilton turned to me.

"Mr. Tabatchnick," he said, "how old is your client?"

"Twenty-three," I said promptly.

Oxman turned those piercing eyes on me.

"Has she been married before?"

"No, sir. Not to my knowledge."

The Bishop raised his two hands, pressed them together in an attitude of prayer, then put the two forefingers against his full lips. He appeared to be ruminating. Finally:

"Is your client pregnant, Mr. Tabatchnick?"

Stilton looked at me.

"Yes, sir," I said softly, "she is. I have seen the doctor's report. My client attempted to contact the clergyman to tell him, but was unsuccessful."

"She called the phone number he had given her," Stilton broke in, "a number she had previously used, but it had been disconnected. Both she and Mr. Tabatchnick went to his apartment, in the Murray Hill section of Manhattan, but apparently he had moved and left no forwarding address. Mr. Tabatchnick then reported the matter to the police, and I was assigned to the investigation. I have been unable to locate or contact the man. I felt—and Mr. Tabatchnick agreed—that it would be best to apprise you of the situation before more drastic steps were taken."

"And what is this clergyman's name?"

"The Reverend Godfrey Knurr," Percy said. "That's K-n-u-r-r."

The Bishop nodded and pulled his phone toward him. He dialed a three-digit number and waited. Then:

"Timmy? Would you see if you can find a file on Godfrey Knurr? That's K-n-u-r-r," he rumbled, then hung up. Speaking to us again, he announced with solemnity, "Unfortunately this is not a unique situation. But I must tell you that frequently the minister involved is entirely innocent. A young woman misinterprets sympathy and understanding. When the pastor tries to convince her that his interest is spiritual she becomes hysterical. In her disturbed state, she makes all kinds of wild accusations."

"Yes, sir," Stilton said, "I can imagine. But a complaint has been made and I've got to check it out."

"Dear me, of course! In any event I'm glad you came to me before pursuing the matter further. It's possible the clergyman in question is not a clergyman at all, but a con man acting the role and preying on lonely women."

But such was not to be the case. The Bishop had hardly ceased speaking when there was a light tap on the office door, it was opened, and a young man entered with a manila folder. He placed it carefully on Oxman's desk and turned to leave.

"Thank you, Timmy," the Bishop called. Then he picked up the folder and read the label on the tab. Then he looked at us. "Oh dear," he said dolefully, "I'm afraid he's one of ours. Godfrey Mark Knurr. Well, let's see what we've got . . ."

He began to scan the documents in the folder. We sat in silence, watching him. One of the things he looked at was a glossy photograph.

"Handsome man," he said.

We waited patiently while the Bishop went through all the papers. Then he shut the folder. "Oh dear, oh dear," he said with a thin smile, "it appears that Mr. Knurr has been a naughty boy again."

"Again?" Stilton said.

Bishop Oxman sighed. "Sometimes," he said, "I feel there should be limits to Christian charity. The Reverend Knurr came to us from Chicago where he served as assistant pastor. He seems to have been very popular with the congregation. It appears that he became, ah, intimate with the twenty-two-year-old daughter of one of the vestrymen. When her pregnancy could no longer be concealed, she named Mr. Knurr, claiming he had promised to marry her. In addition, she said, she had made several substantial loans to him. Loans which were never repaid, needless to say. The affair seems to have been hushed up. Knurr, who continued to protest his innocence despite some rather damning evidence against him, was banished from Chicago and sent here."

"Can they do that, sir?" I asked curiously. "Can the church of another city stick New York with one of their problems?"

"Well," the Bishop said, "Knurr may have been part of, ah, an exchange program, so to speak. One of their bad apples for one of ours. Of course there was no possibility of Knurr getting a church here. We are already burdened with a worrisome oversupply of clergymen, and their numbers are increasing every year. But I assure you that the great majority of our pastors are honorable, God-fearing men, deeply conscious of their duties and responsibilities."

"So what did you do with Knurr?" Stilton asked.

"He retained his collar," Oxman said, "and was allowed to make his own way, with the understanding that because of his record, assignment to a parish was out of the question. According to these records, our last communication from the Reverend Godfrey Knurr was a letter from him requesting permission to open a sort of social club for underprivileged youngsters in Greenwich Village. He felt he could raise the required funds on his own. Permission was granted. But there is nothing in his file to indicate if he actually followed through on his proposal. And, I am sorry to say, there is no current address or telephone number listed."

"Where was the letter sent from?" Detective Stilton asked. "The one that asked permission to open the social club?"

"Oh dear," he said. "No address given."

"How about next-of-kin?" Stilton asked. "Have you got that?"

"Yes, that I know we have," the Bishop said, digging

through the papers. "Here it is. A sister, Goldie Knurr, living in Athens, Indiana. Would you like the address?"

"Please," the detective said.

Percy and I were the only ones in the elevator going down. "You did fine," Stilton said.

"Thank you."

"But I knew you would," he went on, "or I'd have made you rehearse. The scam was necessary, Josh, because if I had just waltzed in there and asked to see the file on Knurr, without a warrant or anything, the Bishop would have told me to go peddle my fish. He looks sleepy, but he's no dummy."

In the lobby, Stilton paused to light a cigarette.

"Perce," I said, "how did you get on to this office? I didn't even know which sect Knurr belongs to."

"I looked him up in the telephone book and got the address of that boys' club of his in Greenwich Village. Then I called Municipal Records downtown and got the name of the owner of the building. Then I went to see him and got a look at Knurr's lease for that storefront. Like I figured, when he signed the lease he had to give a permanent or former address. It was the headquarters of his church. I called them and they referred me to Bishop Oxman's personnel offices. So I called him."

I shook my head in wonderment.

"It's a lot easier," the detective assured me, "when you can flash your potsy." He looked at his watch. "I've got maybe a half-hour. You have something to tell me? There's a bar around the corner. Let's have a beer and I'll listen."

In the corner of a small bar on East 48th Street I asked, "Perce, that story you dreamed up about Knurr swindling a girl in New York was almost word for word what he actually pulled out in Chicago. How did you know?"

He shrugged. "I didn't," he said. "Josh, the bad guys don't have *all* the luck. Sometimes we get lucky, too. I figured if we were right about him, that con about your client would be right in character. Now I'm wondering if we got enough on the guy for me to go to my lieutenant and ask that the Kipper case be reopened." He pondered a moment. "No, I guess not," he said finally. "What happened in Chicago a couple of years ago is just background. It's got fuck-all to do with how Sol Kipper died. You got things to tell me?"

I told him about the reward posters and the calls that had

come in, and how I had obtained copies of the chemical analyses of Professor Stonehouse's brandy.

"Mmm," Stilton grunted. "Good. More paper."

I told him I had obtained a photograph of Glynis Stonehouse and the name of the clinic where she presently did volunteer work and the medical laboratory where she had been employed a year ago.

"I checked out the clinic on the phone," I said, "and they claim they don't stock poisons. It sounds logical; it's an eye, ear, nose and throat clinic for children. I got nowhere with the medical lab."

"Give me the name and address," the detective said. "I'll pay them a call."

He copied the information into his elegant little notebook.

Finally I told him about following Glynis Stonehouse to her rendezvous with Godfrey Knurr, and then tailing the two of them to the 79th Street boat basin.

"That's interesting," Stilton said thoughtfully. "You're doing fine, Josh."

"Thank you," I said. "I've saved the best till last. I think I know how he killed Sol Kipper."

The detective stared at me for a moment.

"Let's have another beer," he said.

"There's an old gentleman who lives in the apartment across the hall from me," I said. "He's confined in a wheelchair and he's been rather lonely. Sometimes when I come home from work, he's waiting for me in his chair on the landing. Just to talk, you know. Well, a few times in the past month I've gotten home early, and he didn't know I was already in my apartment, and when I came out later, there he was on the landing, waiting for me."

Stilton looked at me, puzzled.

"So?" he asked.

"That's what gave me the idea of how Knurr killed Sol Kipper. I was already inside the apartment."

He had started to take a gulp of beer, but suddenly put his full glass back on the bar and sat there, staring straight ahead.

"Yeah," he breathed. "That sucker! That's how he did it. Let me tell you: He was in the house all the time. Probably hiding in one of those empty rooms. Only Tippi knew he was there. She leaves her husband, comes downstairs. Knurr goes up to the master bedroom on the fifth floor and wastes Sol Kipper. Maybe with one of those karate chops of his or with the famous blunt instrument—who knows? Then he carries—"

"No," I said, "that's no good. Sol Kipper wasn't a heavy man, but it would be a difficult task to carry him up that narrow rear staircase to the sixth floor. I think Knurr rang for the elevator and took Kipper's body up that way."

"Right," Stilton said decisively. "The first blues on the scene found the elevator on the sixth floor. All right, he gets Sol up on the terrace and throws him over. I mean literally *throws* him. That's why the body was so far from the base of the wall."

"Then Knurr goes down— How does he go down?"

"He takes the stairs. Because the elevator door on the main floor can be seen from the kitchen. And also, the elevator was found on the sixth floor by the first officers to arrive."

"Tippi fainted," I reminded him, "or pretended to."

"Sure. To give Knurr time to get downstairs. Then he goes out the front door, turns right around, rings the bell, and waits for the butler to let him in."

"Yes," I said, nodding, "I think so. You can't see the front door from the kitchen, so even if they were inside when he exited, he was safe. Perce, I think he stayed in the house overnight. The butler keeps a house diary of visitors, deliveries, and so forth. He has a record of the Reverend Godfrey Knurr arriving on Tuesday the 23rd, the day before Kipper died."

"Oh wow," Percy said, "that's beautiful. I hate to admit it, but I got to admire him for that. The balls!"

"Then you think that's how it was done?" I said eagerly.

"Got to be," Perce said. "*Got* to! Everything fits. It was just a matter of planning and timing. That guy is one cool cat. When we take him, I'm bringing along a regiment of marines. But what about the suicide note?"

"I can't explain it," I confessed. "Right now I can't. But I'm going to give it some thought."

"You do that," he said, patting my arm. "Give it some thought. I'm beginning to think Roscoe Dollworth knew exactly what he was doing when he got you the job. Chief Investigator? You better believe it! Josh, I think now I got enough to ask my loot to reopen the Kipper case. I'll lay out the whole shmeer for him, how it ties into the Stonehouse disappearance, and how—"

"Perce," I said, "could you hold off for just a day or two?"

"Well . . . sure, but why?"

"I'm trying to set up a conference with Mr. Tabatchnick and Mr. Teitelbaum. Teitelbaum's the senior partner who represents the Stonehouse family. I want to tell the two of them everything we've discovered and suggest how the two cases are connected. I want them to let me devote all my time to the investigation and stick to it no matter how long it takes. I'd like you to be there at the conference. They have some clout, don't they? Political clout?"

"I guess they do."

"Well, if we get them on our side first, won't it help you to get the Kipper case reopened and maybe be assigned to it full time?"

"Maybe it would," he said slowly. "Maybe it would at that." He ruffled my hair with his fingertips. "You're a brainy little runt," he said.

I didn't resent it at all.

We were back on the sidewalk, about ready to part, when Stilton snapped his fingers.

"Oh Jesus!" he said. "I forgot to tell you. There was nothing in Records on Knurr, which was why I pulled that scam at the church office. Just to get some background on the guy. But Tippi Kipper—she's another story. She's got a sheet. It goes back almost twenty years—but it's there."

"She's done time?" I said unbelievingly.

"Oh no," the detective said. "Just charged. No record of trial or disposition."

"Charged?" I said. "With what?"

"Loitering," he said, "for the purpose of prostitution."

4

BEFORE I LEFT for work early Wednesday morning, I slid a note under Cleo's door: "Mr. Joshua Bigg respectfully requests the pleasure of Miss Cleo Hufnagel's company at dinner in Mr. Bigg's apartment tonight, Wednesday, at 8:00 P.M. Dress optional. RSVP."

I went off to work planning the menu.

I found a memo on my desk from Ada Mondora stating that Mr. Teitelbaum and Mr. Tabatchnick would meet with me in the library at 2:00 P.M. I called Percy, but he wasn't in. I left a message asking him to call back as soon as possible. I then started to type notes on our meeting with Bishop Harley Oxman for the Kipper file.

I was interrupted by a nervous call from Mrs. Gertrude Kletz. She had broken a tooth and the dentist could only take her at eleven o'clock. Would it be acceptable if she came in from twelve to four? I told her that would be fine. A cabdriver called who claimed to have picked up Professor Stonehouse on the night of January 10th. He described his passenger as being short, in his middle 40s, with a noticeable limp.

"Sorry," I said, "that's not the man."

"No harm in trying," he said cheerfully and hung up.

The next call was from Percy Stilton. I told him about the meeting with Teitelbaum and Tabatchnick at 2:00 P.M., and he said he'd do his best to make it. Then he told me that he had visited Glynis Stonehouse's former employer, Atlantic Medical Research, that morning.

"They stock enough poison to waste half of Manhattan," Stilton reported. "And they've got a very lax control system. The poison cabinet has a dimestore lock that could be opened with a heavy breath. The supervisor is the only one with a key, but he keeps it in plain view, hanging on a board on his wall, labeled. He's in and out of his office a hundred times a day. Anyone who works in the place could lift the key, use it, and replace it without being noticed. Every time a researcher takes some poison he's supposed to sign a register kept in the poison locker stating how much he took, the date, and his name. So I had the supervisor run a total on the arsenic trioxide withdrawn and check it against the amount they started with and how much was there this morning. Over two ounces is unaccounted for. He couldn't understand how that could happen."

"I can," I said. "Two ounces! She took enough to kill the old man ten times."

"Sounds like," Stilton agreed, "but no way to prove it. *Now* they're going to tighten up their poison control procedure. By the way, Glynis Stonehouse wasn't fired; she left voluntarily. Cleaned out her desk one Friday and called on Monday to say she wasn't coming in. Didn't even give them a reason or excuse; just quit cold. Well, I've got to run, Josh. I'm going to try to get over to the 79th Street boat basin around noon. And if possible, I'll see you at two o'clock."

I finished typing up my notes on the Bishop Oxman interview and began trying to compose a rough agenda for the meeting that afternoon with the two senior partners. I knew I would make a better impression if my presentation was organized, brief, succinct.

I was scribbling notes when the phone rang again. It was another cabdriver and the conversation followed the usual pattern:

"How much is the reward?" he asked in a gargling voice.

"A hundred dollars," I said automatically, continuing to make notes as I spoke.

"Well," he said, "it isn't much, but it's better than a stick up the nose. I think I picked up the guy. About January 10th. It *could* have been then. On Central Park West and maybe 70th or 71st. Around there."

"What time?"

"Oh, maybe nine o'clock at night. Like that. I was working nights then. I'm on day now."

"Do you remember what the weather was like?"

"That night? A bitch. Lousy driving. Sleety. I was ready to pack it in when this guy practically threw himself under my wheels, waving his arms."

"Do you remember what he looked like?"

"The only reason I remember, he gave me such a hard time. I wasn't driving fast enough. I was taking the long way. The back of the cab was littered and smelled. And so forth and so on. A real ball-breaker, if you know what I mean."

I put my pen aside and took a deep breath. It was beginning to sound encouraging.

"Can you describe him physically?"

"Hat, scarf, and overcoat," the cabdriver said. "An old geezer. Tall and skinny. Stooped over. Ordinarily I don't take a lot of notice of who rides my cab, but this guy was such a fucking asshole I remember him."

He was sounding better and better.

"And where did you take him?" I asked, closing my eyes and hoping.

"The 79th Street boat basin," the cabdriver said. "And he gives me a quarter tip. In weather like that! Can you beat it?"

I opened my eyes and let my breath out in a long sigh.

"Would you tell me your name, please?" I said.

"Bernie Baum."

"And where are you calling from now, Mr. Baum?"

"Gas station on Eleventh Avenue."

"We're on East 38th Street. If you'd be willing to come over and sign a short statement attesting to what you've just told me, you can pick up your hundred dollars."

"You mean that was the guy?" he said.

"That was the guy," I said.

"Well, yeah, sure," he said, "I'll sign a statement. It's the truth, ain't it? But listen, I wouldn't have to go to court or nothing like that, will I?"

"Oh no, no," I said hurriedly. "Nothing like that. It's just for our files."

Maybe someday he would have to repeat his statement in court, but I wasn't about to tell him that.

"Well, I want to grab some lunch first," he said, "but I'll be over right after."

"Fine," I said heartily. "Try to make it before one o'clock."

I gave him our address and told him to ask for Joshua Bigg. I hung up, grinning. Percy Stilton had been right; the bad guys didn't have *all* the luck.

I typed out a brief statement to be signed by Bernie Baum that said only that he had picked up a man he later identified from a photograph as Professor Yale Stonehouse at approximately 9:00 P.M. on the evening of January 10th in the vicinity of Central Park West and 70th Street and had delivered him to the 79th Street boat basin. I kept it as short and factual as possible.

Mrs. Kletz arrived while I was finishing up. She said her tooth was feeling better and she felt well enough to put in her four hours.

I told her about Bernie Baum and she was as pleased as I was.

"A lot has happened since you read the Kipper and Stonehouse files," I said. "Sit down for a moment and I'll bring you up to date."

She listened intently, sucking her breath in sharply when I told her about Glynis and Knurr.

"And that's where the cabdriver took Professor Stonehouse the night he disappeared," I finished triumphantly.

But she was thinking of something else. Those young eyes seemed to have taken on a thousand-yard stare.

"Do you suppose, Mr. Bigg," she said in her light, lilting voice, "do you suppose that either of the two women, Tippi Kipper or Glynis Stonehouse, knows of the other?"

I blinked at her. The question had never occurred to me, and I was angry with myself because it should have.

"I don't know, Mrs. Kletz," I confessed. "I'd say no, neither is aware of the other's existence. If there's anything Knurr doesn't need right now it's a jealous and vindictive woman."

She nodded thoughtfully. "I expect you're right, Mr. Bigg." She went back to her desk and began answering some of the routine requests. As for me, I ordered a pastrami on rye, kosher dill pickle, and tea from a Madison Avenue deli. Bernie Baum arrived and turned out to be a squat, middle-aged man with two days' growth of grizzled beard and a wet cigar. He was wearing a soiled plaid mackinaw and a black leather cap.

I handed him the statement I had prepared, and he took a pair of spectacles from his inside shirt pocket. One of the bows was missing and he had to hold the ramshackle glasses to his eyes to read.

Then he looked up at me.

"What'd this guy do?" he asked in his raspy, gargling voice. "Rob a bank?"

"Something like that," I said.

"It figures," he said, nodding. "Since I talked to you on the phone, I been trying to remember the guy better. I figure now he was nervous—you know? Something was bugging him and that's why he was bugging me."

"Could be," I said.

"Well," said Bernie Baum judiciously, "if he had a yacht stashed in that boat basin, he's probably in Hong Kong by now."

"That could be, too," I said. "Now if you'll just sign the statement, Mr. Baum, I'll get you your money."

He signed Bernard J. Baum, with his address, and I made out a petty cash voucher for $100. We shook hands and I sent him up to the business office with Mrs. Kletz. She was back in five minutes and told me Bernie Baum had received his cash reward and departed happily. She also told me that Hamish Hooter had okayed the request with no demur. In victory, magnanimous . . .

Percy Stilton showed up right on time, dressed, I was happy to see, very conservatively in navy blue suit, white shirt, black tie. No jewelry. No flash. He had judged his audience to a tee. I showed him the statement the cabdriver had signed.

Percy sat there a moment, knees crossed, pulling gently at his lower lip.

"Uh-huh," he said finally. "We're filling in the gaps—slowly. Know what I think? Professor Stonehouse is down in the mud at the bottom of the Hudson River at 79th Street with an anchor tied to his tootsies. That's what I think. I checked out the boat basin about an hour ago. There's a houseboat registered to a *Mister* Godfrey Knurr. Not reverend, but mister. It's a fifty-foot fiberglass Gibson, and the guy I talked to told me it's a floating palace. All the comforts of home and then some."

I sighed.

"It makes sense," I said. "It doesn't make sense to think a man like Knurr would be content to live in the back room of a dingy store down on Carmine Street."

Perce was silent, and I glanced nervously at my watch. We only had a few more minutes.

"Something bothering you?" I asked.

"Do you really think Knurr burned Kipper and Stonehouse?" he asked tonelessly.

"Kipper certainly," I said. "Probably Stonehouse."

"That's how I see it," he said, nodding somberly. "What's bothering me is this: we know of two. How many more are there we don't know about?"

I gathered up my notes and files and we took the elevator up to the library. Neither of us spoke during the ascent.

There was a note Scotch-taped to the library door: "Closed from 2:00 to 3:00 P.M." An effective notice to me that I would be allotted one hour, no more. Stilton and I went in and took adjoining leather-padded captain's chairs at the center of one of the table's long sides.

"Perce, can you get through this without smoking?" I asked him.

"Sure."

"Try," I said.

I arranged my files and papers in front of me. I went over my presentation notes. Then we sat in silence.

When Ignatz Teitelbaum and Leopold Tabatchnick entered together, at precisely 2:00 P.M., Stilton and I rose to our feet. I thought wildly that there should have been a fanfare of trumpets.

Both senior partners were wearing earth-colored vested suits, with shirts and ties of no particular style or distinction. But there the resemblance ended. Tabatchnick, with his brooding simian posture, towered over Teitelbaum, who appeared especially frail and shrunken in comparison.

I realized with a shock that these two men had lived a total of almost a century and a half, and shared a century of legal experience. It was a daunting perception, and it took me a few seconds to gather my courage and plunge ahead.

"Mr. Tabatchnick," I said, "I believe you've already met Detective Percy Stilton of the New York Police Department. Detective Stilton was involved in the initial inquiry into the death of Solomon Kipper."

Tabatchnick gave Percy a cold nod and me an angry glare as he realized I had disobeyed his injunction against sharing the results of my investigation with the police.

I introduced Percy to Mr. Teitelbaum. Again, there was an exchange of frosty nods. Neither of the partners had made any effort to sit down. My longed-for conference was getting off to a rocky start.

"Detective Stilton," Mr. Tabatchnick said in his most orotund voice, "are we to understand that you are present in an official capacity?"

"No, sir, I am not," the detective said steadily. "I am here as an interested observer, and perhaps to contribute what I can to the solution of a dilemma confronting you gentlemen."

I could have kissed him. Their eyebrows went up; they glanced at each other. Obviously they hadn't been aware they were confronted by a dilemma, and just as obviously wanted to hear more about it. They drew up chairs opposite us. I waited until everyone was seated and still.

"Gentlemen," I started, "it would save us all a great deal of time if you could tell me if each of you is aware of my investigation into the other's case. That is, Mr. Teitelbaum, have you been informed of the circumstances surrounding the death of Sol Kipper? And, Mr. Tabatchnick, are you—"

"Get on with it," Tabatchnick interrupted testily. "We're both aware of what's been going on."

"As of your last reports," Mr. Teitelbaum added, his leathery hands lying motionless on the table before him. "I presume you have something to add?"

"A great deal, sir," I said, and I began, using short declarative sentences and speaking as briskly as possible without garbling my words.

I was gratified to discover that I could speak extemporaneously and forcefully without consulting my notes. So I was able to meet the eyes of both men as I spoke, shifting my gaze from one to the other; depending on whether I was discussing matters relating to Kipper or Stonehouse.

It was like addressing two stone monoliths, as brooding and inexplicable as the Easter Island heads. Never once did they stir or change expression. Mr. Teitelbaum sat back in his chair, seemingly propped erect with stiff, spindly arms thrust out, splayed hands flat on the tabletop. Mr. Tabatchnick leaned forward, looming, his hunched shoulders over the table, heavy head half-lowered, the usual fierce scowl on his rubbery lips.

Up through my account of recognizing one of Knurr's street Arabs among my attackers, neither of the attorneys had asked any questions or indeed shown any great interest in my recital. But my telling of the meeting I had seen at the 66th Street garage changed all that.

First of all, both men switched positions suddenly: Tabatchnick leaned back, almost fell back into his chair as if with disbelief, and Teitelbaum suddenly jerked forward, leaning over the table.

"You're certain of that, Mr. Bigg?" he barked sharply. "The Reverend Godfrey Knurr met Glynis Stonehouse? No doubt about it at all?"

"None whatsoever, sir," I said decisively.

I explained that I had then requested a meeting with Detective Percy Stilton and told him everything that had occurred.

"It was necessary, gentlemen," I said earnestly, "because I needed Detective Stilton's cooperation to determine if anyone involved had prior criminal records. Detective Stilton will tell you the results of that investigation. To get back to your question, Mr. Teitelbaum—was I certain that Knurr met Glynis Stonehouse? Yes, I am certain, because I saw them together again two nights ago."

I then told them how I had shadowed Glynis Stonehouse to a rendezvous with Knurr and had tailed both of them to a houseboat at the 79th Street boat basin.

"Perce," I said, "will you take it from here?"

His recital was much shorter than mine, and delivered in toneless police officialese: "the alleged perpetrator" and "the suspect" and so forth. It was courtroom testimony, and both lawyers seemed completely familiar with the phrases and impressed by them.

He told them that he had never been completely satisfied with the suicide verdict in the Kipper case, and gave his reasons why. So, he explained, he had welcomed my independent inquiry and cooperated every way he could, especially since he was impressed by the thoroughness and imaginative skill of my investigation.

I ducked my head to stare at the table as he continued.

He said his hope was that I would uncover enough evidence so that the NYPD would be justified in reopening the Kipper case. To that end, he had run the names of Godfrey Knurr and Tippi Kipper through the computer and discovered Tippi's arrest record. He told them about our interview with Bishop Harley Oxman and the revelation of Knurr's prior offense in Chicago.

He had also, he said, after I had furnished the lead, determined what was probably the source of the arsenic used to poison Professor Stonehouse: a medical research laboratory where Glynis Stonehouse had been employed less than a year ago.

Finally, he had discovered that Godfrey Knurr owned a houseboat moored at the 79th Street boat basin.

Then Stilton turned to me and I told them that a cabdriver had come forward that morning who remembered driving Professor Stonehouse to the boat basin on the night he disappeared.

I slid Baum's statement across the table to the senior partners, but neither reached for it. Both men were staring at Percy.

"Detective Stilton," Mr. Tabatchnick boomed in his magisterial voice, "as a police officer with many years' experience, do you believe that Godfrey Knurr murdered Solomon Kipper?"

"Yes, sir, I do. With premeditation."

"But how?" Mr. Teitelbaum asked in a mild, dreamy tone.

"I'll let Josh tell you that," Percy said.

So I told them.

Mr. Tabatchnick was the first to turn back to me.

"And the suicide note?" he asked.

"No, sir," I said regretfully. "I haven't yet accounted for that. But I'm sure you'll admit, sir, that the wording of the note is subject to several interpretations. It is not necessarily a *suicide* note."

"And assuming the homicide occurred in the manner you suggest, you further assume that Tippi Kipper and the Reverend Godfrey Knurr were joined in criminal conspiracy? You assume that they planned and carried out the murder of Solomon Kipper because he had discovered, through the employment of Martin Reape, that his wife had been unfaithful to him with Godfrey Knurr and had decided to change his will to disinherit her to the extent allowed by law? You assume all that?"

"Yes, sir," I said finally.

But now it was Mr. Teitelbaum's turn.

"Do you further assume," he said in a silky voice, "that Professor Stonehouse, having discovered that his daughter had attempted to poison him, furthermore discovered that she was having an affair with Godfrey Knurr. And you assume that Stonehouse learned of the existence of Knurr's houseboat, by what means we know not, and resolved to confront his daughter and her paramour on the night he disappeared. And you suspect, with no evidence, that he may very well have been killed on that night. Is that your assumption?"

"Yes, sir," I said, fainter than before. "It is."

We all sat in silence. The quiet seemed to go on forever, although I suppose it was only a minute or two before Mr. Teitelbaum pushed himself from the table and leaned back in his chair.

"And what, precisely," he said in an unexpectedly strong voice, "do you suggest be done next in this unpleasant matter?"

"As far as I'm concerned," Percy Stilton said, "I'm going to tell my lieutenant the whole story and see if I can get the Kipper case reopened. You gentlemen might help me there— if you have any influence that can be brought to bear."

"What would be the advantage of reopening the case?" Leopold Tabatchnick asked.

"I would hope to get assigned to it full time," the detective said. "With more personnel assigned as needed. To keep a stakeout on that houseboat so Knurr doesn't take off. To dig deeper into the backgrounds and relationships of the people involved. To check Knurr's bank account, and so forth. All the things that would be done in a homicide investigation."

The two senior partners looked at each other again, and again I had the sense of communication between them.

"We are not totally without *some* influence," Ignatz Teitelbaum said cautiously. "We will do what we can to assist you in getting the Kipper case reopened. But I must tell you in all honesty that I am not optimistic about bringing this whole affair to a successful solution, even with the most rigorous homicide investigation."

"I concur," Mr. Tabatchnick rumbled.

Mr. Teitelbaum scraped his chair farther back from the table and, not without some difficulty, crossed his knees. He sat there a moment, staring into space between Percy and me, not really seeing us. He was, I thought, composing his summation to the jury.

"First of all," he said finally, "I would like to compliment you gentlemen—and especially you, Mr. Bigg—on your intelligence and persistence in this investigation."

"Imaginative," Mr. Tabatchnick said, nodding. "Creative."

"Exactly," Teitelbaum said. "You have offered a hypothesis that accounts for all known important facts."

"It may be accurate," Tabatchnick admitted almost grudgingly.

"It may very well be. Frankly, I believe it is. I believe your assumptions are correct," Teitelbaum concurred.

"But they are still assumptions," Tabatchnick persisted.

"You have little that is provable in a court of law," Teitelbaum persevered.

"Certainly nothing that might justify legal action." Tabatchnick was firm.

"No eyewitness, obviously. No weapons. In fact, no hard evidence of legal value." Teitelbaum was firmer.

"Merely thin circumstantial evidence in support of what is, essentially, a theory." Tabatchnick.

"We don't wish to be unduly pessimistic, but you have told us nothing to indicate that continued investigation would uncover evidence to justify a criminal indictment." Teitelbaum.

"You are dealing here with a criminal conspiracy." The judgment was from Tabatchnick, but the coup de grace was delivered by Teitelbaum as follows:

"Really two criminal conspiracies with one individual, Knurr, common to both."

Perce looked at them dazedly. I was shattered. I thought their rapid dialogue was a prelude to ordering me to drop the investigation. I glanced at Percy Stilton. He was staring intently at the two attorneys. He seemed entranced, as if he were hearing something I couldn't hear, as if he enjoyed being a tennis ball in the Jurisprudential Open.

"It is an unusual problem," Mr. Tabatchnick intoned, inspecting the spotted backs of his clumpy hands. "Sometimes unusual problems require unusual remedies."

"When more than one person is involved in a major criminal enterprise," Mr. Teitelbaum said, uncrossing his knees and carefully pinching the crease back into his trousers, "it is sometimes possible..."

His voice trailed away.

"You have shown such initiative thus far," Mr. Tabatchnick said, "surely the possibility exists that..."

His voice, too, faded into silence.

Then, to my astonishment, the lawyers glanced at each other, a signal was apparently passed, and they rose simultaneously to their feet. Percy and I stood up. They reached across the table and the two of us shook hands with both of them.

"I shall look forward to your progress," Tabatchnick said sternly.

"I have every confidence," Teitelbaum said in a more kindly tone.

Still stunned, I watched them move to the door. I was bewildered because I was sure they had told us something. What it was I did not know.

Mr. Teitelbaum had already opened the door to the corridor when he turned back to address me.

"Mr. Bigg," he said softly, "is Tippi Kipper older than Glynis Stonehouse?"

"What?" I croaked. "Oh yes, sir," I said, nodding madly. "By at least ten years. Probably more."

"That might be a possibility," he said pleasantly.

Then they were gone.

We sank back into our chairs. I waited as Percy lighted a cigarette, took two deep drags, and slumped down in his armchair. Clerks and paralegal assistants began to straggle into the library, heading for the stacks of law books.

I leaned toward Stilton. I spoke in a low voice.

"What," I asked him, still puzzled, "was that all about? Those last things they said? I didn't understand that at all. I'm lost."

Percy put his head far back and blew a perfect smoke ring toward the ceiling. Then, to demonstrate his expertise, he blew a large ring and puffed a smaller one within it.

"They're not lawyers," he said, almost dreamily, "they're pirates. *Pi-rates*!"

"What are you talking about?" I said.

"Incredible," he said, shaking his head. "Infuckingcredible. Teitelbaum and Tabatchnick. T and T. T'n'T. TNT. They're TNT all right. If I ever get racked up, I want those pirates on my side."

"Perce, will you please tell me what's going on?"

He straightened up in his chair, then hunched over toward me so our heads were close together.

"Josh, I think they're right. That's a hell of a plot you came up with about how Knurr offed Sol Kipper. Probably right on. But how are we going to prove it? Never. Unless we break Knurr or Tippi Kipper. Get one to spill on the other. And what have we got on Glynis Stonehouse? We can't even *prove* she tried to poison her father. She shacks up with Knurr on a houseboat. So what? It's not an indictable offense. Your bosses saw right away that the only way we're going to snap this thing is to get one of the main characters to sing."

"And how are we going to do that?"

"Oh, T and T were so *cute*!" he said, grinning and lighting another cigarette. "You notice that not once did either of them say anything that could be construed as an order or instructions to do anything illegal. All they did was pass out a few vague hints."

"But what *did* they say?" I cried desperately.

"Shh. Keep your voice down. They want us to run a game on Knurr. A scam. A con."

I looked at him, startled.

"How are we going to do that?"

"Spook him. Him and the ladies. Stir them up. Let them know they're suspects and are being watched. Play one against the other. Work on their nerves. Wear them down. Push them into making some stupid move. Guerrilla warfare. Mousetrap them. You think Knurr and Tippi and Glynis are smarter than we are? I don't. They got some nice games running, and so far they've worked. Well, we can run plots just as clever. More. That's what T and T were telling us. Run a game on these people and split them. They were right; it's the only way."

"I get it," I said. "Take the offensive."

"Right!"

"And that last thing Teitelbaum said about Tippi Kipper being older than Glynis Stonehouse?"

"He was suggesting that we let Tippi know about Glynis."

Before Perce and I took our leave of each other, we had decided on at least the first play of our revised game plan. I set about implementing it as soon as I got back to my office.

Mrs. Kletz and I sat down to compose a letter which Mrs. Kletz would then copy in her handwriting on plain paper. The finished missive reads as follows:

Dear Mrs. Kipper,

We have met casually several times, but I believe I know more about your private life than you are aware. You'll see that I am not signing this letter. Names are not important, and I don't wish to become further involved. I am writing only with the best of intentions, because I don't want you to know the pain I suffered in a comparable situation.

Mrs. Kipper, I happen to know how close your relationship is with the Reverend Godfrey Knurr. I hope you will forgive me when I tell you that your "affair" is common knowledge and a subject of sometimes malicious gossip in the circles in which we both move.

I regret to inform you that the Reverend is also currently carrying on a clandestine "affair" with a beautiful young woman, Glynis Stonehouse. Believe me when I tell you that I have irrefutable proof of their liaison which has existed for several months.

They have been seen together by witnesses whose word cannot be doubted. Their frequent trysts, always late at night, are held aboard his houseboat moored at the 79th Street boat basin. Were you aware that the Reverend Knurr owned a lavishly furnished houseboat and uses it for midnight meetings with this young beautiful woman? And possibly others?

As I said, Mrs. Kipper, I am writing only to spare you the agony I recently endured in a similar situation. I wish now that a concerned friend had written to me as I am writing to you, in time to prevent me from acting foolishly and deserting a loving husband and family for the sake of an unfaithful philanderer.

I have been able to obtain a photograph of the other

woman, Glynis Stonehouse, which I am enclosing with this letter.

Forgive me for writing of matters which, I am sure, must prove painful to you. But I could not endure seeing a woman of your taste and refinement suffer as I suffered, and am suffering.

A FRIEND

When Mrs. Kletz finished copying the letter, we sealed it with the snapshot of Glynis Stonehouse in a plain manila envelope. Mrs. Kletz addressed it in her hand.

"Just ring the bell at the front gate," I instructed her, as I prepared to send her out on this important assignment. "The butler, a big man, will come out. Tell him you have a letter for Mrs. Kipper, give it to him, and walk away as quickly as you can."

"Don't worry, Mr. Bigg," she said. "I'll get out of there fast."

She put on her Tam O'Shanter and a loden coat as billowy as a tent and set out. A half-hour later I locked the Kipper and Stonehouse files securely away and left the office. Uncharacteristically I took a cab home, so anxious was I to find a message from Cleo. I found it slipped under my door: "Miss Cleo Hufnagel accepts with pleasure Mr. Joshua Bigg's kind invitation to dinner tonight in his apartment at 8:00 P.M."

Smiling, I changed into parka and watch cap, and then checked my larder, refrigerator, and liquor supply. I made out a careful list of things I needed and then set forth with my two-wheeled shopping cart. It was a cold, misty evening, and I didn't dawdle. I bought two handsome club steaks; baking potatoes; sour cream already mixed with chives; butter (should she prefer it to the sour cream); a head of iceberg lettuce; a perfectly shaped, plasma-colored tomato; a cucumber the size of a tough, small U-boat, and just as slippery; a bottle of creamy garlic dressing; and a frozen blueberry cheesecake. I also purchased two small shrimp cocktails that came complete with sauce in small jars that could later be used as juice glasses. A paper tablecloth. Paper napkins. An onion.

I also bought a cold six-pack of Ballantine ale, two bottles of Chianti in raffia baskets, and a quart of California brandy.

And two long red candles. On impulse I stopped at a florist's shop and bought a long-stemmed yellow rose.

She tapped on my door a few minutes after 8:00 and came in smiling. She bent swiftly to kiss my cheek. She had brought me a loaf of crusty sour rye from our local Jewish bakery. It was a perfect gift; I had forgotten all about bread. Fortunately I had butter.

I gave her the yellow rose, which came close to bringing tears to her eyes and earned me another cheek-kiss, warmer this time. I led her to my favorite armchair and asked her if she'd like a fire.

"Maybe later," she said.

I poured a glass of red wine for her and one for myself.

"Here's to you," I toasted.

"To us," she said.

I told her what we were having for dinner.

"Sounds marvelous," she said in her low, whispery voice. "I like everything."

Suddenly, due to her words or her voice or her smile, something struck me.

"What's wrong?" Cleo asked anxiously.

I sighed. "I bought a kite. And a ball of string and a winder. But I left them all at the office. I forgot to bring them home."

She laughed. "We weren't going to fly it tonight. But I'm glad you remembered."

"It's a red kite," I told her. "Listen, I have to go into the kitchen and get things ready. You help yourself to the wine."

"Can't I come in with you?" she said softly. "I promise I won't get in the way."

I couldn't remember ever having been so content in my life. I think my feeling—in addition to the beamy effects of the food and wine—came from a realization of the sense of home. I had never known a real home. Not my own. And there we were in a tiny, messy kitchen, fragrant with cooking odors and the smoke of candles, quiet with our comfort, walled around and shielded.

It was a new experience for me, being with a woman I liked. Liked? Well . . . wanted to be with. I didn't have to make conversation. She didn't have to. We could be happily silent together. That was something, wasn't it?

After dinner, she murmured that she'd help me clean up.

"Oh, let's just leave everything," I said, which was out of character for me, a very tidy man.

"You'll get roaches," she warned.

"I already have them," I said mournfully, and we both smiled. Her large, prominent teeth didn't offend me. I thought them charming.

We doused the candles and straggled back to the living room. We decided a blaze in the fireplace would be superfluous; the apartment was warm enough. She sat in the armchair. I sat on the floor at her feet. Her fingers stroked my hair idly. I stroked her long, prehensile toes. Her bare toes. She groaned with pleasure.

"Do you like me, Cleo?" I asked.

"Of course I like you."

"Then, if you like me, will you rise from your comfortable chair, find the bottle of brandy in the bar, open it, and pour us each a small glass of brandy? The glasses are in the kitchen cupboard."

"Your wish is my command, master," she said humbly.

She was back in a few moments with glasses of brandy, handed me one and, while she was bent over, kissed the top of my head. Then she resumed her sprawling position in the armchair, and I resumed stroking her toes.

"It was a wonderful dinner," she said sighing.

"Thank you."

"I'm a virgin," she said in exactly the same tone of voice she had said, "It was a wonderful dinner."

What could I answer with but an equally casual, "Yes, you mentioned it last time."

"Did I also mention I don't want to be?" she added thoughtfully.

"Ah," I said, hoping desperately that I could eventually contribute something better than monosyllables. When it occurred to me almost at once that a lunge qualified as something better, the ice broke.

I have told you that she was tall. Very tall. And slender. Very slender. But I was not prepared for the sinuous elegance of her body, its lithe vigor. And the sweetness of her skin. She was a rope dipped in honey.

Initially, I think, there was a certain embarrassment, a reticence, on my part as well as hers. But this reserve soon vanished, to be replaced by a vigorous tumbling. She was experiencing new sensations, entering a new world, and wanted to know it all.

"What's this?" she asked eagerly. "And this?"

She was amazed that men had nipples capable of erection. She was delighted to learn that many of the things that aroused her, aroused me; that there could be as much (or more) pleasure in the giving as in the taking. She wanted to know everything at once, to explore, probe, understand.

"Am I doing this correctly?" she asked anxiously. And, "Is it all right if I do this?" and, "What must I do now?"

"Shut up," I replied.

We may have roared. We certainly cried out, both of us, and I dimly recall looking into a face transformed, ecstatic, and primitive. When it was over, we lay shuddering with bliss, so closely entwined that my arms ached with the strain of pulling her closer, as if to engulf her, and I felt the muscular tremor in those long, flexible legs locked about me.

"I love you," she said later.

"I love you," I said.

I buried my face in the soft hollow of neck and shoulder. My toes caressed her ivory shins.

I interrupted our idyll for business reasons only once that evening. Feeling I had to be honest, I informed Cleo that I had to call the floozie spotted earlier leaving my apartment by the evil Finkel. Further, I would seemingly be arranging a rendezvous, really an interrogation. Should Cleo mistakenly conclude I was growing bored with her, I would be glad to prove her wrong as soon as I completed the call. She laughed and kissed me merrily.

The phone rang three times before Perdita Schug answered.

"Yes?"

"Perdita?"

"Yes. Who's this?"

"Joshua Bigg."

"Josh!"

"I apologize for calling so late, Perdita. I hope I didn't wake you."

"Don't be silly. I just came up. We had a dinner for seven tonight. A lot of work."

"Oh? Was Mr. Knurr there?"

"No. Which was odd. First we were told there'd be eight. But he didn't show up. Usually he's here all the time. Are you going to come by Mother Tucker's tomorrow night?"

"I'm certainly going to try," I lied. "Listen, Perdita, I have an unusual question to ask you. When Sol Kipper was alive, did he ever write notes to his wife? You know, little short notes he'd leave where she'd find them?"

"Oh sure," she said promptly. "He was always writing her notes. She was running around so much, and then he'd go out and leave a note for her. I read a few of them. Love notes, some, or just messages."

"Did she keep them, do you think?"

"Tippi? I think she kept some of them. Yes, I know she did. I remember coming across a pile of them in a box of undies in her dressing room. Some of them were hilarious. The poor old man was really in love with her. She had him hooked. And you know how."

"Yes," I said. "Thank you very much, Perdita. Sorry to bother you."

"And I'll see you tomorrow night?"

"I'm certainly going to try." It was getting easier all the time.

5

THURSDAY MORNING: ALIVE, bubbling, laughing aloud. Cleo hadn't wanted to upset her mother by staying the night, but I'd awakened steeped in her recent presence. I sang in the shower ("O Sole Mio"), looked out the window, and nodded approvingly at the pencil lines of rain slanting down steadily. Nothing could daunt my mood. I wore raincoat and rubbers to work, and carried my umbrella. It was the type of bumbershoot that extends with the press of a button in the handle. Very efficient, except that when a stiff wind was blowing, it cracked open and seemed to lift me a few inches off my feet.

However, I arrived at the TORT building without misadventure and set to work planning my day's activities.

My first call was to Glynis Stonehouse. She came to the phone, finally, and didn't sound too delighted to hear from me. I acted the young, innocent, optimistic, bouncy investigator, and I told her I had uncovered new information about her father's disappearance that I'd like to share with her. Grudgingly, she said that she could spare me an hour if I came immediately.

I thanked her effusively, ran out of TORT and, miraculously, given the weather, hailed a cab right in front of the building.

In the Stonehouse hallway the formidable Olga Eklund relieved me of hat, coat, rubbers, and umbrella, and herded me into that beige living room where Glynis Stonehouse reclined in one corner of the velvet sofa, idly leafing through a magazine. Nothing about her posture or manner suggested worry.

If she made an error, it was in her greeting.

"Oh," she said, "Mr. Bigg. Do sit down."

Too casual.

I sat down, opened my briefcase, and began to rummage through it.

"Miss Stonehouse," I said enthusiastically, "I think I'm making real progress. You'll recall that I told you I had discovered your father had been suffering from arsenic poisoning prior to his disappearance? Well, I've definitely established how he was being poisoned. The arsenic was being added to his brandy!"

I handed her the copies of the chemical analyses. She looked at them. I don't believe she read them. I plucked them from her fingers and replaced them in my briefcase.

"Isn't that wonderful?" I burbled on. "What a break!"

"I suppose so," she said in her husky, low-pitched voice. "But what does it mean?"

"Well, it means we now know how the poison was administered."

"And what will you do next?"

"That's obvious, isn't it?" I said, laughing lightly. "Find the source of the poison. You can't buy arsenic at your local drugstore, you know. So I must check out everyone involved to see who had access to arsenic trioxide."

I stared at her. I thought there would be a reaction. There wasn't.

She sighed deeply.

"Yes," she said, "I suppose you will have to keep digging and digging until you discover the ... what do the police call it? ... the perpetrator? You'll never give up, will you, Mr. Bigg?"

"Oh no!" I said heartily. "I'm going to stick to it. Miss Stonehouse, may I speak to Effie Dark for a few moments? I'd like to find out who had access to your father's brandy."

She looked at me.

"Yes," she said dully, "talk to Mrs. Dark. That's all right."

I smiled my thanks, bent to reclasp my briefcase. Before I could stand, she said:

"Mr. Bigg, why are you doing this?"

I shook my head, pretending puzzlement.

"Doing what, Miss Stonehouse?"

"All these questions. This—this investigation."

"I'm trying to find your father."

Her body went slack. She melted. That's the only way I can describe it. Suddenly there was no complete outline around her. Not only in her face, which sagged, but in her limbs, her flesh. All of her became loose and without form. It was a frightening thing to see. A dissolution.

"He was a dreadful man," she said in a low voice.

I think I was angered then. I tried to hide it, but I'm not certain I succeeded.

"Yes," I said, "I'm sure he was. Everyone says so. An awful person. But that's not important, is it?"

She made a gesture. A wave of the hand. A small, graceful flip of dismissal. Of defeat.

Effie Dark was seated at the white enameled table, an emptied coffee cup before her. There was a redolence, and it took me a few seconds to identify it: the air smelled faintly of brandy.

She looked up listlessly as I entered, then smiled wanly.

"Mr. Bigg," she said, and pulled out a chair for me. "It's nice to see a cheerful face."

"What's wrong, Effie?" I asked, sitting down. "Problems?"

"Oh..." she said, sighing, "there's no light in this house anymore. The missus, she's taken to her bed and won't get out of it."

"She's ill?"

"Sherry-itis. And Miss Glynis is as down as I've ever seen her. I even called Powell, thinking a visit from him might help things. But he says he must avoid negative vibrations. That means he's scared misery might be catching. Well..." she said, sighing again, "I was figuring on retiring in a year or two. Maybe I'll do it sooner."

"What will you do, Effie?" I asked softly.

"Oh, I'll make do," she said, drawing a deep breath. "I

have enough. It's not the money that worries me, it's the loneliness."

"Move somewhere pleasant," I suggested. "Warm, sunny weather. Maybe Florida or California. You'll make new friends."

Suddenly she perked up. Those little blueberry eyes twinkled in her muffin face. She lifted one plump arm and poked fingers into the wig of marcelled yellow-white hair. I could have sworn I heard her dentures clacking.

"I might even find myself a husband," she said, looking at me archly. "What do you think of *that*, Mr. Bigg. Think I'm too fat?"

"'Pleasingly plump' is the expression, Effie. There are many men who appreciate well-endowed women."

"Well-endowed?" she spluttered. "How you do go on! You're medicine for me, Mr. Bigg, you truly are. See? I'm laughing for the first time in days. But I don't suppose you stopped by just to make a silly old woman happy. You need some help?"

"Thank you," I said gratefully. I lowered my voice. "Effie, is the door locked to Professor Stonehouse's study?"

She nodded, staring at me with bright eyes.

"You have a key?"

Again the nod.

I thought a moment. "What I'd like you to do is this: I'll wait here while you go out and unlock the door to the study and then come back. I'll go into the study. You'll be here, so you won't see me enter. I'll only be a few minutes. No more than five. I swear to you I will not remove anything from the study. Then I will come back here to say goodbye, and you can relock the study door. That way, if you're ever asked any questions, you can say truthfully that you never saw me in the study, didn't see me go in or come out."

She considered that for a while.

"Glynis is here," she said. "In the living room, I think. And the Sexy Swede is wandering around someplace. Either of them could catch you in there."

"I know," I said.

"I hope I'm doing the right thing," she said.

When I was inside the study, I closed the door softly behind me. I went directly to the wall where the model ship hulls were displayed. I moved along the bottom row, rapping on the hulls gently with a knuckle. Some sounded solid, some hollow. I found the *Prince Royal* in the middle of the third row. I stood on tiptoe to lift the *Prince Royal* plaque off picture hooks nailed into the wall.

I carried the model hull to the desk and set it on top of the littered papers and maps. I switched on the desk lamp. I picked up a pencil and tapped the hull form twice. It sounded hollow. So far so good.

I grasped the hull and lifted gently. It came away. As easily as that. Just came right off. I was astonished, and looked to see what had been holding it to the plaque. Eight small magnets, inch-long bars, four inset into the hull and four in the plaque. They gripped firmly enough to hold the hull when the tablet was on the wall, but released with a slight tug.

Of course I was more interested in the papers folded inside. Most were thin, flimsy sheets, of the weight used for carbon copies. I unfolded them carefully, handling them by the corners. The top four sheets were not typed, but handwritten. It took me awhile to read it through. The writing was as crabbed, mean, and twisted as the man himself.

I, Yale Emerson Stonehouse, being of sound mind and body . . .

It was all there: the holographic last will and testament of the missing Professor Stonehouse. He started by making specific cash bequests. Fifty thousand to his alma mater, and twenty thousand to Mrs. Effie Dark, which I was happy to see. Then there were a dozen cash bequests to cousins and distant relatives, none of whom was to receive more than a thousand dollars, and one of whom was to inherit five bucks. Olga Eklund got one hundred.

The bulk of his estate was to be divided equally between his wife, Ula Stonehouse, and his son, Powell Stonehouse. The will specifically forbade his daughter, Glynis Stonehouse, from sharing in his estate because she had "deliberately and with malice aforethought" attempted to cause his death by adding arsenic trioxide to his brandy. In proof of which, he was attaching to this will copies of chemical analyses made by Bommer & Son and a statement by Dr. Morris Stolowitz that Professor Stonehouse had indeed been suffering from arsenic poisoning.

In addition, the will continued, if the testator was found dead by violence or by what appeared to be an accident, he demanded the police conduct a thorough investigation into the circumstances of his demise, with the knowledge that his daughter had tried to murder him once and would quite possibly try again, with more success.

The will had been witnessed by Olga Eklund and Wanda Chard. I could understand the loopy maid signing anything the Professor handed her and promptly forgetting it. But Wanda Chard?

I carefully folded up the papers on their original creases, tucked them back into the hull of the *Prince Royal*, reattached hull to plaque, and wiped both with my handkerchief. Then, holding the tablet by the edges with my fingertips, I rehung it on the wall, adjusted it so it was level, and returned to the kitchen.

"Thank you, Effie," I said, bending to kiss her cheek.

She looked up at me. I thought I saw tears welling.

"It's the end of everything, isn't it?" she asked.

I couldn't lie to her.

"Close to it," I said.

I went back into the living room. Glynis Stonehouse was standing at one of the high windows, staring down at the rain-lashed street. She turned when she heard me come into the room.

"Finished?" she asked.

"Finished," I said. "Mrs. Dark tells me your mother isn't feeling well. I'm sorry to hear that, Miss Stonehouse. Please convey to her my best wishes and hope for her quick recovery."

"Thank you," she said.

She stood tall and erect. She had recovered her composure. She looked at me steadily, and there was nothing in her appearance to suggest that she knew how close she was to disaster.

"I'll keep you informed of the progress of my investigation, Miss Stonehouse."

"Yes," she said levelly, "you do that."

She was so strong. Oh, but she was strong! If she had weakened, briefly, that weakness was gone now; she was resolute, determined to see it through. I admired her. She was a woman of intelligence and must have known she was in danger, walking the edge. I bade her a dignified good day, then high-tailed it across town to the Kipper manse.

Chester Heavens greeted me with his usual aplomb, but I sensed a certain reticence, almost a nervousness in his replies to my chatter about his health, the weather, etc. We were standing in the echoing entrance hall when I became aware of raised voices coming from behind the closed doors of the sitting room.

"Mom is at home, sah," the butler informed me gravely, looking over my head.

"So I hear," I said. "And Mr. Knurr?"

He nodded slowly.

I hid my pleasure.

"Chester," I said, "I won't stay long. This may be my last visit."

"Oh?" he said. "I am sorry to hear that, sah."

"Just a few little things to check out," I told him.

He bowed slightly and moved away toward the kitchen. I stood at the front door and looked toward the rear of the house. The doorway could not be seen from the kitchen. Then I moved to the elevator. That was in plain view of anyone in the kitchen or pantry.

I saw Mrs. Bertha Neckin standing at the sink. She glanced up and I waved to her, but she didn't respond.

I took the elevator up to the fifth floor and went swiftly into Tippi Kipper's dressing room. I set down my briefcase and began searching. It wasn't hard to find: a cedar-smelling box of filigreed wood with brass corners. It appeared to be of Indian handicraft. It was tucked under a stack of filmy lingerie in a bottom dresser drawer. I may have blushed when I handled those gossamer garments.

The box was unlocked and filled with a carelessly tossed pile of notes. There were jottings on his personal stationery, on sheets from notepads, on raggedly torn scrap paper, and one on a personal check of Solomon A. Kipper, made out to Tippi Kipper in the amount of "Ten zillion dollars and all my love" and signed "Your Sol."

I scanned the notes quickly. My heart cringed. Most were love letters from an old man obviously obsessed to the point of dementia by a much younger woman whose seductive skills those notes spelled out in explicit detail.

And there were notes of apology.

"I am sorry, babe, if I upset you." Wasn't so bad for starters, but then I came across "Please forgive me for the way I acted last night. I realize you had a headache, but I couldn't help myself, you looked so beautiful." As I read on, a pattern of increasing desperation, dependence, and humiliation emerged.

"Can you ever forgive me?" Then, "Here is a little something for you to make up for what I said last night. Am I forgiven?"

It was punishment, reading those revelations of a dead man. I stole two of them:

"Tippi, I hope you will pardon me for the pain I caused you." And, "My loving wife, please forgive me for all the trouble I made. I promise you that you'll never again have any reason to doubt my everlasting love for you."

Those two, I thought, would serve as suicide notes as well as the one found prominently displayed in the master bedroom after Sol Kipper's plunge.

I tucked the two notes into my briefcase, closed and replaced the box, and then went up the rear staircase to the sixth floor. I entered the party room, went over and stood with my back against the locked French doors leading to the terrace.

I looked at my watch. I allowed fifteen seconds for the act of throwing Kipper over the wall. Then I started running. I went down the rear staircase as fast as I could. I dashed along the fifth-floor corridor to the main staircase. I went bounding down rapidly, swinging wildly around the turns. I came down to the entrance hall, rushed over to the front door. I looked at my watch, gasping. About ninety seconds. He could have made it. Easily.

There was no one about, and no sounds from the sitting room. I found my outer garments and donned them and went out into the chill rain without saying goodbye to Chester. I walked toward Fifth Avenue, intending to catch a cab. I was almost there when who should fall into step alongside but the Reverend Godfrey Knurr.

"Joshua!" he said, moving under the shelter of my umbrella. "This *is* nice. Chester told us you were about. If you say this is good weather for ducks, I may kick you!"

He was bright again, his manner jaunty.

I didn't panic. I knew he had been waiting for me, but in a way I couldn't understand, I welcomed the confrontation. Maybe I thought of it as a challenge.

"Pastor," I said, "good to see you again. I didn't want to interrupt you and Mrs. Kipper."

He rolled his eyes in burlesque dismay.

"What an argument that was," he said carefully, taking my arm. "Want to hear about it?"

"Sure."

He looked about.

"Around the corner," he said. "Down a block or so. Posh hotel. Nice cocktail lounge. Quiet. We can talk—and keep dry. On the outside, at least."

A few minutes later we were standing at the black vinyl, padded bar in the cozy lounge of the Stanhope, the room dimmed by rain-streaked windows in which the Metropolitan Museum shimmered like a Monet. We were the only customers, and the place was infused with that secret ambience of a Manhattan bar on a rainy day, comfortably closed in and begging for quiet confessions.

Knurr ordered a dry Beefeater martini up, with lemon peel. I asked for a bottle of domestic beer. When our drinks were served, he glanced around the empty room. "Let's take a table," he said.

He picked up his drink and led the way to a small table in a far corner. I followed with my bottle of beer and a glass.

That was the difference between us: I would have asked the bartender, "Is it all right if we take a table?"

I must admit it was more comfortable sitting in the soft chairs, walls at our backs. We sat at right angles to each other, but we turned slightly so we were facing each other more casually.

Knurr rattled on for a while, gabbing mostly about inconsequential things like the weather, a cold he was trying to shake, how every year at this time he began to yearn for warmer climes, a hot sun, a sandy beach, etc.

I looked into his eyes as he spoke. I nodded occasionally. Smiled. It was the oddest feeling in the world—sitting drinking, exchanging idle talk, with a murderer.

How had I thought a killer would be different—disfigured with a mark perhaps? That would be too easy. As it was, I had to keep reminding myself of who Knurr was and what he had done. But all I was conscious of was the normality of our conversation, its banality. "A miserable day." "Oh yes, but they say it may clear tonight."

Finally he stopped chattering. He put both elbows on the table, scrubbed his face with his palms. He sighed and looked off into the emptiness of the room.

"I counsel a great many people," he said, talking to the air. "As I told you, mostly women. Occasionally they come to feel that my interest in them is not purely in their immortal souls. They assume I have, uh, a more personal interest. You understand?"

"Of course," I said. "It must lead to difficulties."

"It does indeed," he said, sighing. "All kinds of difficulties. For instance, they demand more of my time than I am willing to give, or *can* give, for that matter."

I made sympathetic noises.

"Would you believe," he went on, "that some of my—well, I was about to say patrons, but not all of them are that. For want of a better word, let's call them clients."

"How about dependents?" I suggested.

He looked at me sharply to see if I was being sarcastic. I was not. He punched my upper arm lightly.

"*Very* good, Joshua," he said. "Dependents. I like that. Much better than clients. Well, as I was saying, occasionally some of my dependents become jealous of others, believing I am devoting too much time to them. I don't mean to imply selfishness on their part, but I have found that most unhappy people, women *and* men, are inclined to be self-centered, and when sympathetic interest is expressed, they want more and more. Sympathy becomes an addiction, and they resent it when others share. That's what my disagreement with Mrs. Kipper was about. I am currently counseling other women, of course, and she felt I was not devoting enough time to her and her problems."

It wasn't a clumsy lie, but it seemed to me unnecessarily complex. There was no need for him to explain at all. But having started, he should have kept it simple.

I looked at him as he signaled the bartender for another round of drinks. He did have an imperious way about him, lifting a hand and gesturing curtly.

"How is your social club coming along?" I asked.

"What?" he said vaguely. "Oh, fine, fine. The barkeep put a shade too much vermouth in that last martini. I hope this one will be drier."

The bartender himself brought the drinks over to our table, but did not hover. Knurr sipped eagerly.

"*Much* better," he smiled with satisfaction, relaxing and sliding down a bit in his chair. "Dry as dust."

He was certainly a craggily handsome man, brooding and intense. I could understand why women were attracted to him; he radiated vigor and surety. The slightly bent nose and steady brown eyes gave the appearance of what is known as "a man's man." But the slaty beard framed rosy, almost tender lips that hinted of a soft vulnerability.

"I hope you and Mrs. Kipper parted friends," I said.

He gave a short bark of hard laughter. "Oh, I think I persuaded the lady," he said with a smile.

I didn't like that smile; it was almost a smirk. Did it mean that the photo of Glynis Stonehouse and the Mrs. Kletz letter had gone for naught?

I considered what he knew about me—or guessed. I thought my cover in the Kipper case was still intact, that he accepted my role of law clerk making a preliminary inventory of the estate. In the Stonehouse matter, Glynis would have told him of my investigation into her father's disappearance. He knew that I had uncovered the arsenic poisoning. What he did not know, I felt sure, was that I was aware of his intimate relationship with Glynis.

"That was my last visit to the Kipper home," I offered. "The expert appraisers will take over now."

"Oh?" he said in a tone of great disinterest. "Well, I suppose you have plenty of other things to keep you busy."

"I certainly do," I said enthusiastically. "I've been ordered to devote all my time to a case involving a man who disappeared without leaving a will."

"That sounds interesting," he said casually, taking a sip of his martini. "Tell me about it."

I imagined that was what fencing must be like: lunge, parry, thrust.

"There's not much to tell," I said. "Just what I've said: a man disappeared—it's been two months now—and no will has been found. The legal ramifications are what make the case so fascinating. All the assets are in his name alone. So it will require a petition to the court to free living expenses for his family."

"And if he never shows up again?"

"That's the rub," I said, laughing ruefully as I tried to recall what Mr. Teitelbaum had told me about applicable law. "I think that five years must elapse before a missing person's estate can go to probate."

"Five years!" he exclaimed.

"Minimum," I said. I laughed merrily. "It would be a lot simpler if the missing man's body turned up. If he is, indeed, dead, as everyone is beginning to suspect. But I'm boring you with all this."

"Not at all," he said genially. "Good talk for a rainy afternoon. So if the missing man turned up dead, his estate could be distributed to his legal heirs at once?"

Got him, I thought with some satisfaction.

"That's right," I said airily. "Once proof of death is definitely established, the man's will goes to probate."

"And if no will exists—or can be found?"

"Then the estate is divided under the laws of intestacy. In this case, it would go to his wife, daughter, and son."

"Is it a sizable estate?" he asked slowly.

Greedy bugger.

"I believe it is," I said, nodding. "I have no idea of the exact dollar amount involved, but I understand it's quite sizable."

He pulled pipe and tobacco pouch from his jacket pocket. He held them up to me.

"You don't mind?"

"Not at all," I said. "Go right ahead."

I watched and waited while he went through the deliberate ceremony of filling his pipe, tamping the tobacco down with a blunt forefinger, lighting up, tilting back his head and blowing a long plume of smoke at the ceiling.

"The law is a wonderful thing," he said with a tight smile. "A lot of money there. I mean in the practice of law."

"Yes, sir, there certainly is."

"Sometimes I think justice is an impossible concept," he went on, puffing away. "For instance, in the case you were describing, I would think the very fact of the man's disappearance for two months would be enough to allow his family to share in his estate. He left voluntarily?"

"As far as we know."

"No letter or message to his lawyer?"

"No, nothing like that. And no evidence of foul play. No evidence at all. He may still be alive for all we know. That's why the law requires a diligent search and a five-year grace period. Still, it's murder on the family." I couldn't resist, but, then, neither could he.

"It surely is," he murmured, a wee bit too fervently.

"However," I said, sinking the hook as deeply as I could, "if the body is discovered, regardless of whether he died a natural death or was a victim of accident or foul play, the estate goes to probate." I thought I had said enough and changed the subject abruptly. "Pastor, did you tell me you were from Chicago originally?"

"Not the city itself," he said, meeting my gaze. "A suburb. Why do you ask?"

"I have a cousin who lives there, and he's invited me out for a visit. I've never been in Chicago and wondered if I'd like it."

"You'll find a lot to do there," he said tonelessly.

"Did you like it?" I persisted.

"For a while," he said. "I must confess, Joshua, I get bored easily. So I came on to New York."

"New worlds to conquer?" I asked.

"Exactly," he said with a wry grin.

"And you haven't regretted it?"

"Once or twice," he said, still grinning, "at three in the morning."

I found it difficult to resist the man's charm. For one brief instant I doubted all I had learned about him, all I had imagined.

I tried to analyze why this should be so, why I was fighting an admiration for the man. Most of it, I thought, was due to his physical presence. He was big, strong, stalwart: everything I was not. And he was decisive, daring, resolute.

More than that, he really did possess an elemental power. Behind the bright laugh, the bonhomie, the intelligence and wit, there was naked force, brute force. I realized then how much I wanted him to like me.

Which meant that I feared him. It was not a comforting realization.

We finished our drinks without again alluding to either the Kipper or Stonehouse matters. Knurr insisted on paying for the drinks. He left a niggardly tip.

He said he had an appointment uptown, and since I was returning to the TORT building, we parted company under the hotel marquee. We shook hands and said we'd be in touch.

I watched him stride away up Fifth Avenue, erect in the rain. He seemed indomitable. I tried to get a cab, then gave up and took a downtown bus. It was crowded, damp, and smelled of mothballs. I got back to my office a little after one o'clock and stripped off wet hat, coat, and rubbers. I stuck my dripping umbrella in the wastebasket.

I called Stilton's office and was told he couldn't come to the phone at the moment. I left my number, asking that he call back. Then I sat staring at the blank wall and ignoring the investigation requests filling my In basket.

I was still thinking about the Reverend Godfrey Knurr. I acknowledged that the resentment I felt toward him could be traced to my feeling that he took me lightly, that he patronized me. The glib lies and little arm punches, the genial pats on shoulder and knee, and that bright, insolent laugh. That he considered me a lightweight, a nuisance perhaps, but of no consequence bore out my worst fears about myself. I strove to keep in mind that by attacking my self-esteem, he was attempting to gain control over me.

I opened the Kipper and Stonehouse files and reread only those notes pertaining to Godfrey Knurr. He seemed to move through both affairs like a wraith. I suspected him to be the prime mover, the source, the instigator of all the desperate events that had occurred. I had enough notes *about* the man: his strength, determination, charm, etc. I even had a few tidbits on his background.

But I knew almost nothing about the man himself, who he *was*, what drove him, what gave him pleasure, what gave him pain. He was a shadow. I had no handle on him. I could not explain what he had done yesterday or predict what he might do tomorrow.

I was looking for a label for him and could not find it. And realizing that, I was increasingly doubtful of ensnaring him with our cute tricks and sly games. He was neither a cheap crook nor a cynical confidence man. What he was, I simply did not know. Yet.

My reverie was broken by Percy Stilton returning my call. He was speaking rapidly, almost angrily.

"The Kipper case hasn't been reopened," he said. "Not yet it hasn't. The loot didn't think I had enough, and bucked it to the Captain. God only knows who he'll take it to, but I don't expect any decision until tomorrow at the earliest. I hope your bosses are using their juice. I had my partner call Knurr last night and pretend he was the cabdriver who drove Stonehouse to the boat basin. Knurr wouldn't bite. Hung up, as a matter of fact. He's toughing it out."

"Yes," I said, "I'm beginning to think we're not going to panic him."

I told Stilton about my unearthing the Stonehouse will, then detailed the contents.

"Nice," he said. "That wraps up Glynis. But Jesus, you didn't lift the will, did you? That would ruin it as evidence."

"No," I assured him, "I left it where it was. But I did steal something else."

I described the notes Sol Kipper had written to his wife, and how the two I had purloined could perfectly well have served as suicide notes.

"Good work, Josh," Percy said. "You're really doing a professional job on this—tying up all the loose ends."

I was pleased by his praise.

"Something else," I said. "I had a long talk with Knurr. We had a couple of drinks together."

I reported the substance of our conversation.

"I don't think that photo of Glynis Stonehouse and the poison-pen letter did a bit of good."

"No," Stilton said, "I don't think so either. He got Tippi calmed down and he's going his merry way."

"Another thing . . ." I said, and told the detective how I had fed Knurr information about laws regarding the disposition of the estate of a missing man.

"Uh-huh," Percy said. "You figure that will get him to dump the body? If he's got it?"

"That's what I hoped," I said. "Now I'm not so sure he's going to react the way we want him to. Perce, Knurr is a mystery man. I'm not certain we can manipulate him."

"Yeah," he said, sighing. "If he doesn't spook, and if he can keep his women in line, we're dead."

"There's one possibility," I said. "A long shot."

"What's that?"

"I've been going through all my notes on Knurr. Remember that interview we had with Bishop Oxman? He gave us the name of Knurr's next-of-kin. Goldie Knurr. A sister."

"And?"

"What if she's not his sister? What if she's his wife?"

Silence for a moment.

"You're right," Stilton said finally. "A long shot."

"We've got to try it," I insisted. "You've got the address? I think it was in Athens, Indiana."

He found it in his notebook and I carefully copied it down as he read it to me.

"You going to give her a call?" Percy asked.

"That wouldn't do any good," I said. "If he listed her as a sister, she probably has orders to back him up if anyone inquires."

"So?"

"So," I said, making up my mind at that precise instant, "I think I better go out there and talk to the lady."

That was what I had to do. I knew it on the spur of the moment. I booked a seat on American to Chicago through the office agency. I had no time to ask permission of Teitelbaum or Tabatchnick. I had no time to listen to Orsini as I tore out of the building.

As luck had it, he was coming in as I left, surrounded by his entourage. I attempted to sneak by, but Orsini's glittering eyes saw everything. A hand shot out and clamped my arm. I looked at the diamond flashing on his pinkie. I looked at the glossy manicured fingernails. My eyes rose to note the miniature orchid in his lapel: an exquisite flower of speckled lavender.

"Josh!" he cried gaily. "Just the man I wanted to see! I've got a joke you're going to love."

He glanced smilingly around his circle of sycophants, and they drew closer, already composing their features into expressions of unendurable mirth.

"There's this little guy," Romeo Orsini said, "and he goes

up to this tall, beautiful, statuesque blonde. And he says to her, 'I'm going to screw you.' And she says—"

"Heard it," I snapped. "It's an old joke and not very good."

I jerked my arm from his grip, pushed my way through the circle of aides, and stalked from the building. I didn't look back, but I was conscious of the thunderous silence I had left behind.

I wasted no time in wondering why I had dealt so rudely with Orsini or how it would affect my career at TORT. I was too intent on reaching my bank before it closed, on trying to estimate the balance in my account and how much cash would be required for my trip to Chicago. Luckily, I was covered, and soon was in a cab heading through the Midtown Tunnel toward Kennedy after a hurried trip home to pack.

The flight to Chicago was the only chance to relax in much too long, and I decided to enjoy it. I even laughed at the terrible movie and wolfed down the mystery meat. We touched down in Chicago without incident and, as I walked into the terminal, I found O'Hare Airport to be crowded, noisy, and frantic as Mother Tucker's on East 69th Street in Manhattan. Where, I thought with rueful longing, even at that moment Perdita Schug and Colonel Clyde Manila were probably well along on their Walpurgisnacht.

I wandered about the terminal for a while, continually touching my newly fattened wallet and feeling for my return ticket at irregular intervals. I finally found my way to where cabs, limousines, and buses were available. Obviously a cab to Athens would cost too much. I approached a uniformed chauffeur leaning against the fender of a black behemoth which seemed to have twice as many windows as any gas-driven vehicle deserved.

The driver looked at me without interest, his sleepy eyes taking in my wrinkled overcoat, shapeless hat, and the sodden suitcase pressed under my arm. His only reaction was to switch a toothpick from the right corner of his mouth to the left.

"Do you go to Athens?" I asked.

"Where?"

"Athens. It's in Indiana." I had looked it up in the office atlas.

"Never heard of it," he said.

"It's between Gary and Hammond."

"*Where* between Gary and Hammond?"

"I don't know," I confessed.

"Then I don't go there," he said.

The toothpick switched back again. I know when I've been dismissed. I wandered over to the bus area. There was a uniformed driver leaning against a bus marked Gary-Hammond, gazing about with total disinterest. I decided I'd like to have the toothpick concession at O'Hare Airport, but at least he didn't shift it when I addressed him:

"Could you tell me if I can take this bus to Athens?"

"Where?"

"Athens, Indiana."

"Where is that?"

"Between Gary and Hammond. It's an incorporated village."

He looked at me doubtfully.

"Population 3,079 in 1939," I added helpfully.

"No shit?" he said. "Between Gary and Hammond?"

I nodded.

"You stand right there," he told me. "Don't move. Someone's liable to steal you. I'll be right back."

He went over to the dispatcher's desk and talked to a man chewing a toothpick. The bus driver gestured. Both men turned to stare at me. Then the dispatcher unfolded a map. They both bent over it. Another uniformed bus driver came along, then another, and another. Finally there were five men consulting the map, waving their arms, arguing in loud voices, their toothpicks waggling like mad.

The driver came back to me.

"Yeah," he said, "I go to Athens."

"You learn something every day," I said cheerfully.

"Nothing important," he said.

An hour later I was trying to peer through a misted window as the bus hurtled southeastward. I saw mostly darkness, a few clumps of lights, flickering neon signs. And then, as we crossed the state line into Indiana, there were rosy glows in the sky, sudden flares, views of lighted factories and mills, and one stretch of highway seemingly lined with nothing but taverns, junkyards, and adult book stores.

About ninety minutes after leaving O'Hare Airport, with frequent stops to discharge passengers, we pulled off the road at a street that seemed devoid of lighting or habitation.

"Athens," the driver called.

I struggled from my seat, lifted my suitcase from the over-head rack, and staggered down the aisle to the door.

I bent to look out.

"This is Athens?" I asked the driver.

"This is it," he said. "Guaranteed."

"Thank you," I said.

"You're welcome," he said.

I stood on a dark corner and watched the bus pull away, splashing me from the knees downward. All I could feel was regret at not staying aboard that bus to the end of the line, riding it back to O'Hare, and returning to Manhattan by the earliest available flight. Cold, wet, miserable.

After a long despairing wander I came to what might be called, with mercy, a business district. Most of the stores were closed, with steel shutters in place. But I passed a drugstore that was open, a mom-and-pop grocery store, and at last—O Lord, I gave thanks!—a liquor store.

"A pint of brandy, please," I said to the black clerk.

He inspected me.

"Domestic?" he said.

"Anything," I said. "Anything at all."

He was counting out my change when I asked if there were any hotels in the immediate area.

"One block down," he said, pointing. "Then two blocks to the right. The New Frontier Bar and Grill."

"It's a hotel?"

"Sure," he said. "Up above. You want to sleep there to-night?"

"Of course."

"Crazy," he said, shaking his head.

I followed his directions to the New Frontier Bar and Grill. It was a frowsy beer joint with a dirty front window, a few customers at the bar with blue faces from the TV set, and a small back room with tables.

The bartender came right over; it was downhill. The whole floor seemed to slope toward the street.

"Scotch and water, please," I said.

"Bar Scotch?"

"All right."

He poured me what I thought was an enormous portion until I realized the bottom of the shot glass was solid and at least a half-inch thick.

"I understand you have a hotel here," I said.

He looked at me, then bent over the bar to inspect me closely, paying particular attention to my shoes.

"A hotel?" he said. "You might call it that."

"Could you tell me your rates?"

He looked off into the middle distance.

"Five bucks," he said.

"That seems reasonable," I said.

"It's right next door. Up one flight. The owner's on the desk. Tell him Lou sent you."

I quaffed my Scotch in one meager gulp, paid, walked outside, and climbed the narrow flight of stairs next door. The owner-clerk, also black, was seated behind a desk inclosed in wire mesh. There was a small hinged judas window in front.

He was a husky man in his fifties, I judged, wearing a T-shirt with a portrait of Beethoven printed on the front. He was working a crossword puzzle in a folded newspaper. He didn't look up. "Five bucks an hour," he said. "Clean sheets and running water. Payable in advance."

"I'd like to stay the night," I said. "To sleep. Lou sent me."

He wouldn't look up. "What's an ox with three letters?" he said. "With a long tail and short mane."

"Gnu," I said. "G-n-u."

Then he looked up at me.

"Yeah," he said, "that fits. Thanks. Twenty for the night. Payable in advance."

He opened the window to take the bill and slide a key on a brass medallion across to me.

"Two-oh-nine," he said. "Right down the hall. You're not going to do the dutch, are you?"

"Do the dutch?"

"Commit suicide?"

"Oh no," I protested. "Nothing like that."

"Good," he said. "What's a four letter word meaning a small child?"

"Tyke," I suggested.

Oh, what a dreadful room that was! So bleak, so tawdry.

It was about ten feet square with an iron bed that had once been painted white. It appeared to have the promised clean sheets—threadbare but clean—but on the lower third of the bed, the sheet and a sleazy cotton blanket had been covered with a strip of black oilcloth. It took me awhile to puzzle that out. It was for customers too drunk or too frantic to remove their shoes.

I immediately ascertained that the door could be double-locked from the inside and that there was a bolt, albeit a cheap one. There was a stained sink in one corner, one straight-backed kitchen chair and a small maple table, the top scarred with cigarette burns. There was no closet, but hooks had been screwed into the walls to compensate, and a few wire coat-hangers depended from them.

I went into the corridor to prowl. I found a bathroom smell-ing achingly of disinfectant. There was a toilet, sink, bathtub with shower. I used the toilet after latching the door with the dimestore hook-and-eye provided, but I resolved to shun the sink and tub.

I went back to my room and hung up my hat and overcoat on a couple of the hooks. After a great deal of struggling, I opened the single window. A chill, moist breeze came billow-ing in, still tainted with sulfur. It didn't take long to realize that there was no point in sitting around in such squalor, and soon I had reclaimed my hat and coat and headed back down-stairs.

"Going to get something to eat," I said to the owner-clerk, trying to be hearty and cool simultaneously.

"A monkey-type creature," he said. "Five letters."

"Lemur," I said.

The New Frontier Bar and Grill had gained patrons during my absence; most of the barstools were occupied, and there were several couples, including a few whites, at tables in the back room. All the men were big, wide, powerfully built, with rough hands, raucous laughs, and thundering angers that seemed to subside as soon as they flared.

I was pleased to note the bartender remembered what I drank.

"Scotch?" he asked as if it were a statement of fact.

"Please. With water on the side."

When he brought my drink, I asked him about the possibility of getting sandwiches and a bag of potato chips.

"I'm a little fandangoed at the moment," he said. "When I get a chance, I'll make them up for you—okay?"

"Fine," I said. "No rush."

I looked around, sipping my shot glass of whiskey. The monsters on both sides of me were drinking boilermakers, silently and intently, staring into the streaked mirror behind the bar. I did not attempt conversation; they looked like men with grievances.

I turned back to my own drink and in a moment felt a heavy arm slide across my shoulders.

"Hi, sonny," a woman's voice said breezily.

"Good evening," I said, standing. "Would you care to sit down?"

"Sit here, Sal," the man next to me offered. "I got it all warmed up for you. I'm going home."

"You do that, Joe," said the woman, and a lot of woman she was, too, "for a change."

They both laughed. Joe winked at me and departed.

"Buy a girl a drink?" Ms. Sal asked, swinging a weighty haunch expertly atop the barstool.

"A pleasure," I said.

"Can I have a shot?" she asked.

"Whatever you like."

"A shot. Beer makes me fart."

I nodded sympathetically.

"Lou!" she screamed, so loudly and so suddenly that I leaped. "The usual. I've got a live one here."

She dug a crumpled pack of cigarettes from a stuffed purse. I struck a match for her.

"Thanks, sonny," she said. She took a deep inhalation and the smoke just disappeared. I mean, I didn't see it come out *anywhere*.

She was a swollen, bloated woman in her middle forties. She looked like the kind of girl who could never be surprised, shocked, or hurt; she had seen it all—twice at least.

The bartender brought her drink: a whiskey with a small beer chaser.

Sal looked me up and down.

"You work in the steel mills, sonny?"

"That Sal," the bartender said to me, "she's a card."

"Oh no," I said to her. "I'm not from around here. I'm from New York."

"You could have fooled me," she said. "I would have sworn you were a puddler."

"Come on, Sal," the bartender said.

"That's all right," I told him. "I know the lady is pulling my leg. I don't mind."

She smacked me on the back, almost knocking me off the stool.

"You're okay, sonny," she said in a growly voice. "I like you."

"Thank you," I said.

"What the hell you doing in Gary?"

"Gary?" I said, fear soaring. "I thought this was Athens. Isn't this Athens, Indiana?"

"Athens?" she said. She laughed uproariously, rocking back and forth on her barstool so violently that I put out an arm to assist her in case she should topple backward.

"Jesus Christ, sonny," she said, wiping her eyes with the back of her hand, "this place hasn't been called Athens in years. It was absorbed by Gary a long time ago."

"But it *was* Athens?" I insisted.

"Oh sure. It was Athens when I was a kid, more years ago than I want to remember. What the hell you doing in Athens?"

"I work for a law firm in New York," I said. "It's a matter of a will. I'm trying to locate a beneficiary whose last address was given as Athens, Indiana."

"No shit?" she said, interested. "An inheritance?"

"Oh yes."

"A lot of money?"

"It depends on what you mean by a lot of money," I said cautiously.

"To me," she said, "anything over twenty bucks is a lot of money."

"It's more than twenty bucks."

"What's the name?"

"Knurr," I said. "K-n-u-r-r. A woman. Goldie Knurr."

"Goldie Knurr?" she repeated. "No," she said, shaking her

head, "never heard of her. Lou!" she screamed. When the bartender came over, she asked, "Ever hear of a woman named Goldie Knurr?"

He pondered a moment, frowning.

"Can't say as I have," he said.

"Buy me a double," Sal said to me, "and I'll ask around for you."

When she returned she slid onto the barstool again, spanked her empty glass on the bar.

"What the hell's your name?" she demanded.

"Josh."

"My name's Sal."

"I know. May I buy you another drink, Sal?"

She pretended to consider the offer.

"Well . . . all right, if you insist." She signaled the bartender, holding up two fingers. "Bingo," she said. "I found a guy who knows Goldie Knurr. Or says he does. See that old swart in the back room? The gray-hair, frizzy-haired guy sitting by himself?"

I turned. "I see him," I said.

"That's Ulysses Tecumseh Jones," she said. "Esquire. One year younger than God. He's been around here since there was a here. He says he knew the Knurr family."

"You think he'll talk to me?" I asked.

"Why not?" she said. "He's drinking beer."

"Mr. Jones?" I said, standing alongside his table with my drink in one hand, a stein of beer in the other.

He looked up at me slowly. Sal had been right: he had to be ninety, at least. A mummy without wrappings. Skin of wrinkled tar paper, rheumy eyes, hands that looked like something tossed up by the sea and dried on hot sands.

"Suh?" he said dimly.

"Mr. Jones," I said, "my name is Joshua Bigg and I—"

"Joshua," he said. "Fit the battle of Jericho."

"Yes, sir," I said, "and I would appreciate it if we could share a drink and I might speak to you for a few moments."

I proffered the stein of beer.

"I take that kindly," he said, reaching. "Set. Sal says you asking about the Knurrs?"

"Yes, sir," I said, sliding onto the banquette next to him.

The ancient sipped his beer. He told me a story about his old army sergeant. He cackled.

"What war was that, sir?" I asked.

"Oh..." he said vaguely. "This or that."

"About the Knurrs?" I prompted him.

"It was about '58," he said, not bothering to tell me which century. "On Sherman Street that was. Am I right? Sherman Street?"

"You're exactly right, sir," I said. "That's the address I have. One-thirteen Sherman Street."

"If nominated, I will not run," he recited. "If elected, I will not serve."

"That's wonderful," I marveled. "That you remember."

"I still got all my nuts," he said, nodding with satisfaction. He suddenly grinned. No teeth. No dentures. Just pink gums.

"This was in 1958?"

"Nineteen and fifty-eight," he said. "Maybe long before. I tell you something funny about that family, suh. They was all G's. Everybody in that family had a name with a G."

"Goldie Knurr," I said. "Godfrey Knurr."

"Zactly," he said. "The father, George Knurr. The mother, Gertrude Knurr. Three other tads. Two sons: Gaylord Knurr and Gordon Knurr. Another daughter: Grace Knurr."

"You've got an incredible memory, sir."

"I sure do," he said. "Ain't nothing wrong with my nuts."

"What happened to them?" I asked. "The Knurr family?"

"Oh..." he said, "the old folks, George and Gertrude, they died, as might be expected. The kids, they all went away, also as might be expected. Goldie, I hear tell, is the only one around still."

It was not good news. If this old man's memory was accurate, Goldie Knurr was indeed the sister of my target.

"Mr. Jones," I said, "how is it you know so much about the Knurr family?"

"Oh," he said slowly, "I used to do this and that around their house. Little jobs, you know. And my third wife, Emily that was—no, Wanda; yes, the third was Wanda—she was like a mother to the kids."

"You don't recall anything about Godfrey Knurr, do you, Mr. Jones?" I asked. "One of the sons?"

"Godfrey Knurr?" he repeated, his eyes clouding. "That would be the middle boy. Became a preacher man, he did. Left town. Can't blame him for that."

"No indeed," I said fervently, "I really can't. You don't remember anything else about Godfrey? Anything special?"

"Smart young one," he said. "Big and strong. Liked the girls. Played football. Something . . ."

He stopped suddenly.

"Something?" I prompted.

"I don't rightly recall."

"Something good or something bad?"

He stared at me with eyes suddenly clear and piercing and steady.

"I don't rightly recall," he repeated.

6

I OPENED MY eyes Friday morning, bewildered for an instant before I recalled where I was. I rose, did a few halfhearted stretching exercises. I looked in vain for soap, washcloth, towel. I made do by sponging myself with a handkerchief dipped in water from my corner sink. As promised, it was running water. Cold. But invigorating.

I then dressed. My suit, of course, was badly wrinkled, but that seemed a minor consideration.

The owner-clerk was still in his wire mesh cage, drinking coffee from a cardboard container and reading a copy of *Architectural Digest*.

"When is checkout time, please?" I asked.

"Every hour on the hour," he said. "Oh, it's you. Checkout time for you will be around eight or nine tonight."

I stepped outside to find the rain had ceased, but the sun was hidden behind an oysterish sky. It put a dull tarnish on the world. I walked a few blocks. It took all my optimism to keep my spirits from drooping: block after block of mean row houses, a few scrubby trees.

I finally found a luncheonette that seemed to be doing a

thriving business, went in, and had a reasonably edible breakfast. When I paid my bill, I got directions to Sherman Street.

Sherman Street was absolutely no different from any other in Athens: a solid culvert of row houses, jammed together, all of the same uninspired design, all three stories high, either clapboard or covered with counterfeit brick siding.

I found 113 Sherman Street. I climbed the three steps to the stoop, pushed the bell, heard it ring inside the house, and waited.

The door opened a cautious crack.

"Miss Goldie Knurr?" I asked, taking off my hat.

"I'm not buying anything," she said sharply.

"I don't blame you, ma'am," I said, smiling so widely that my face ached. "Prices being the way they are. But I'm not selling anything. It's about your brother, Godfrey Knurr."

The door was flung open.

"He's dead!" the woman wailed.

"Oh no," I said hastily. "No, no, no. Nothing like that. I saw him, uh, yesterday, and he's healthy and, uh, in fine shape."

"Law," she said, pressing a fist into her soft bosom, "you gave me such a start. Come in, sir."

She let me into a hallway, paused to lock, chain, and bolt the door, then turned to face me.

"You saw Godfrey yesterday?" she said in a voice of marvel: Robert Browning asking, "Ah, did you once see Shelley plain . . . ?"

"I did indeed, ma'am."

"And he's all right?"

"As far as I could tell, he's in excellent health. He has a beard now. Did you know?"

"A beard?" she cried. "Think of that! Did he give you a message for me?"

"Ah . . . no," I said softly. "But only because I didn't tell him I was coming to see you. May I tell you about it?"

"Of course you may!" she said loudly, recalling her duties as a hostess with a guest in the house. "Here, let me take your coat and hat, and you come into the parlor and we'll have a nice chat. A cup of tea? Would you like a nice cup of tea?"

"Thank you, ma'am, but no. I just finished my breakfast."

I waited while she hung my hat and coat on brass hooks

projecting from an oak Victorian rack with a long, silvered
mirror, lidded bench, and places for umbrellas with shallow
pans to catch the dripping. Then I proffered my business card.

"Leopold Tabatchnick, ma'am," I said, "of New York.
Attorney-at-law."

"He's not in any trouble, is he?" she asked anxiously,
scarcely glancing at the card.

"None whatsoever," I assured her, reclaiming my card.
"Please let me tell you what this is all about."

"Oh, law," she said, pressing a fist into her bosom again,
"I'm just so discombobulated. It's been so long since I've heard
from Godfrey. Do come in and sit down, Mr.—what was that
name?"

"Tabatchnick. Leopold Tabatchnick."

"Well, you just come in and sit down, Mr. Leopold," she
said, "and tell me what brings you to Gary."

She led the way into the parlor. There were the bright colors
missing from outdoor Gary. Red, green, blue, yellow, purple,
pink, orange, violet: all in chintz run wild. The sofa, chairs,
pillows, even the tablecloths were flowers and birds, butterflies
and sunrises. Parrots on the rug and peonies in the wallpaper.
Everything blazing and crashing. Overstuffed and overwhelming. The room stunned the eye, shocked the senses: a funhouse
of snapping hues in prints, stripes, checks, plaids. It was hard
to breathe.

Goldie Knurr was just as overstuffed and overwhelming.
Not fat, but a big, solid-soft woman, as tall as Godfrey and
just as husky. She was dressed for a garden party in a flowing
gown of pleats and flounces, all in a print of cherry clumps
that made her seem twice as large and twice as imposing.

Sixty-five at least, I guessed, with that rosy, downy complexion some matrons are blessed with: the glow that never
disappears until the lid is nailed down. I saw the family resemblance; she had Godfrey's full, tender lips, his steady, no-
nonsense brown eyes, even the masculine cragginess of his
features.

Her figure was almost as broad-shouldered as her brother's,
but softened, plumpish. Her hands were chubby. The hair,
which might have been a wig—although I suspected she might
call it a "transformation"—was bluish-white, elaborately set,
and covered with a scarcely discernible net.

She sat me down in an armchair so soft that I felt swallowed. When she came close, I smelled lavender sachet, sweetly cloying. I hoped she wouldn't take a chair too near, but she did. She sat upright, spine straight, ankles crossed, hands clasped in her lap.

"Yes, Mr. Leopold?" she said, beaming.

"Tabatchnick, ma'am," I murmured. "Leopold Tabatchnick. Miss Knurr, I represent a legal firm on retainer to the Stilton Foundation of New York. You've heard of the Stilton Foundation, of course?"

"Of course," she said, still beaming. Her voice was warm, burbling, full of aspirates. A very young, hopeful voice.

"Well, as you probably know, the Stilton Foundation makes frequent grants of large sums of money to qualified applicants in the social sciences for projects we feel will benefit humanity. Your brother, the Reverend Godfrey Knurr, has applied for such a grant. He desires to investigate the causes of and cures for juvenile delinquency. He seems well qualified to conduct such a research project, but because the amount of money involved is considerable, we naturally must make every effort to investigate the background, competence, and character of the applicant. And that is why I am here today."

She was dazzled. I was not sure she had quite understood everything I had thrown at her, but she did grasp the fact that her brother might be granted a great deal of money if this funny little man in the wrinkled suit lost in her best armchair gave him a good report.

"Of course," she gasped. "Any way I can help..."

"I understand yours was a large family, Miss Knurr. Five children, and—"

"Five *happy* children," she interrupted. "And five *successful* children. Not one of us on welfare!"

"Most commendable," I murmured. "About Godfrey, could you tell me if—"

"The best," she said firmly. "Absolutely the best! We all knew it. There was no jealousy, you understand. We were all so proud of him. He was the tallest and strongest and most handsome of the boys. Star of the football team, president of his high school class, captain of the debating team, good marks in every subject. Everyone loved him—and not just the family. *Everyone!* You'll find that no one has a bad word to say about

Godfrey Knurr. We all knew that he was destined for great things, and that's just the way it turned out."

She sat back, smiling, nodding, panting slightly, pleased with the panegyric she had just delivered.

But I couldn't let it go at that. This was the woman who instinctively suspected sudden death when her brother's name was first mentioned, who asked if he was in trouble when she learned I was a lawyer, who apparently hadn't seen or heard from the favored brother in years. It didn't jibe with the dream she had recalled.

"Then he was never in any, ah, trouble as a boy?"

"Absolutely not!" she said definitely, then decided to amend that. "Oh, there were a few little things you might expect from a high-spirited youngster. But nothing serious, I do assure you."

"He had friends?"

"Many! Many! Godfrey was very popular."

"With his teachers as well as his peers?"

"Oh, law, yes," she said enthusiastically. "He was such a good student, you see. So quick to learn. The other boys, they talked about going into the mills and things like that. But Godfrey would never be satisfied with that. He aimed for higher things. That boy had ambition."

It was the unreserved love of a sister for a handsome, talented younger brother. I found it hard to break through that worship.

"Miss Knurr," I said, "about Godfrey's choice of the ministry as a career—was he very religious as a boy?"

Lucky shot. Up to that point her answers had been prompt and glib. Now she paused before answering. She was obviously giving some thought to framing her reply, and when she spoke the timbre of her voice had changed. I thought her uncertain, if not fearful.

"Well..." she said finally, "ours was a God-fearing family. Church every Sunday morning without fail, I can tell you! I can't say that Godfrey was any different from the rest of us children as far as religion was concerned. But when he announced he was going to study for the ministry, we were all very happy. Naturally."

"Naturally," I said. "And the other boys, Godfrey's brothers, did they really go into the mills?"

"No," she said shortly, "they never did. They were both drafted, of course, and Gaylord decided to stay in the army. Gordon owns a gas station in Kentucky."

"And Godfrey became a minister," I said encouragingly. "Your church is in the neighborhood?"

"Two blocks south on Versailles Street," she said, pronouncing it "Ver-sales." "It's St. Paul's. The pastor then was the Reverend Stokes. He's retired now."

"And who took his place?" I asked.

"Reverend Dix," she said stonily. "A black." Then she brightened. "Would you like to see our family album? Pictures of all of us?" She rose briefly, left the room, and returned with the album. Then she sat down on a posy-covered sofa and motioned me to sit beside her.

What is it about old snapshots that is so sad? Those moments in sunshine caught forever should inspire happiness and fond memories. But they don't. There is a dread about them. The snapshots of the Knurr family weren't photographs so much as memento mori.

We finished the album and I turned back to the section devoted to photographs of Godfrey.

"Who is this he's with?" I pointed at a snapshot of two stalwart youths in football uniforms standing side by side, legs spread, hands on hips. The boy alongside Godfrey Knurr was a black.

"Oh, that's Jesse Karp," she said, and I thought she sniffed. "He's principal of our high school now—would you believe it?"

"They were close friends?"

"Well . . . they were friends, I guess."

"And this priest with Godfrey—is he the Reverend Stokes?"

"That's right. He helped Godfrey get into the seminary. He helped Godfrey in so many ways. The poor man . . ."

I looked up.

"I thought you said he's retired?"

"Oh, he is. But doing, ah, poorly."

"I'm sorry to hear it."

"You're not planning to talk to him, are you?"

"I wasn't planning to, no, ma'am."

"Well, he's not all there—if you know what I mean."

"Ah. Too bad. Senile?"

"Not exactly," she said, examining the pink nails on her plump fingers. "I'm afraid the Reverend Stokes drinks a little more than is good for him."

"What a shame," I said.

"Isn't it?" she said earnestly. "And he was such a *fine* man. To end his days like that . . . So if you *do* talk to him, Mr. Leopold, please keep that in mind."

"Tabatchnick," I murmured. "I certainly shall."

I turned to a page of six snapshots, each showing a young, confident Godfrey with a muscular arm about the shoulders of a different and pretty girl. The posture was possessive.

"He seems to have been popular with girls," I observed.

"Oh law!" she cried. "You have no idea! Calling him at all hours. Hanging around outside the house. Sending him notes and all. Popular? I should say! No flies on Godfrey Knurr."

One of the six photos showed Godfrey with a girl shorter and younger than the others. Long, long flaxen hair fell to her waist. Even in the slightly out-of-focus snapshot she looked terribly vulnerable, unbearably fragile. I looked closer. One of her legs was encased in a heavy iron brace.

"Who is this girl?" I asked casually, pointing.

"Her?" Goldie Knurr said too quickly. "Just one of Godfrey's friends. I don't recall her name."

It was the first time she had actually lied to me. She was not a woman experienced in lying, and something happened to her voice; it weakened, became just a bit tremulous.

I closed the album.

"Well!" I said heartily. "That was certainly interesting, and I thank you very much, Miss Knurr, for your kind cooperation. I think I've learned what I need."

"And Godfrey will get the money?" she asked anxiously.

"Oh, that isn't my decision to make, Miss Knurr. But I've certainly discovered nothing today that will rule against it. Thank you for your time and hospitality."

She helped me on with my coat, handed me my hat, went through the rigmarole of unlocking the door. Just before I left, she said . . .

"If you see Godfrey again, Mr. Leopold . . ."

"Yes?"

"Tell him that he owes me a letter," she said, laughing gaily.

I went next to McKinley High School. It occupied an entire block with its playgrounds and basketball courts. As I marched up the front steps, the plate glass door opened and a black security guard, uniformed and armed with a nightstick, came out to confront me.

"Yes?" he said.

"Could you tell me if Mr. Jesse Karp is principal of this school?" I asked.

"That's right."

"I'd like to talk to him if I could."

"You have an appointment?"

"No, I don't," I admitted.

"Better call or write for an appointment," he advised. "Then they know you're coming—see? And you go right in."

"This is about the record of a former student of McKinley High," I said desperately. "Couldn't you ask?"

He stared at me. Sometimes it's an advantage to be diminutive; I obviously represented no threat to him.

"I'll call up," he said. "You stay here."

He went back inside, used a small telephone fixed to the wall. He was out again in a moment.

"They say to write a letter," he reported. "Records of former students will be forwarded—if you have a good reason for wanting them. Please enclose a stamped, self-addressed envelope."

I sighed.

"Look," I said, "I know this is an imposition and I apologize for it. But could you make another call? Please? Try to talk to Mr. Karp or his assistant or his secretary. The student I want to ask about is Godfrey Knurr. That's K-n-u-r-r. I'd like to talk to Mr. Karp personally about Godfrey Knurr. Please try just one more time."

"Oh man," he said, "you're pushing it."

"If they say no, then I'll go away and write a letter. I promise."

He took a deep breath, then made up his mind and went back to the inside telephone. This time the conversation took longer and I could see him waiting as he was switched from phone to phone. Finally he hung up and came out to me.

"Looks like you clicked," he said.

A few moments later, through the glass door, I saw a tall

skinny lady striding toward us. The guard opened the door to let me enter just as she came up.

"To see Mr. Karp?" she snapped.

"Yes, ma'am," I said, taking off my hat. "I'd like to—"

"Follow me," she commanded.

The guard winked and I trailed after that erect spine down a waxed linoleum corridor and up two flights of stairs. Not a word was spoken. From somewhere I heard a ragged chorus of young voices singing "Frère Jacques."

We entered a large room with a frosted glass door bearing the legend: PRINCIPAL'S OFFICE. My conductress led the way past three secretaries, typing away like mad, and ushered me to the doorway of an inner office. The man inside, standing behind a desk piled high with ledgers and papers, looked up slowly.

"Mr. Karp?" I said.

"That's right," he said. "And you?"

I had my business card ready.

"Leopold Tabatchnick, sir," I sang out. "Attorney-at-law. New York City."

He took the proffered card, inspected it closely. "And you want information about Godfrey Knurr?"

"That's correct, sir."

I launched into the Stilton Foundation spiel. Through it all he stared at me steadily. Then he said:

"He's in trouble, isn't he?"

I almost collapsed. But I should have known it had to happen eventually. "Yes," I said, nodding dumbly, "he's in trouble."

"Bad?"

"Bad enough," I said.

"Had to happen," he said.

He went to the door of his office and closed it. He took my hat and coat, hung them on an old-fashioned bentwood coat tree. He gestured me to the worn oak armchair, then sat down in a creaking swivel chair behind his jumbled desk. He leaned back, hands clasped behind his head, and regarded me gravely.

"What's your real name?" he asked.

I decided to stop playing games.

"Joshua Bigg," I said. "I'm not a lawyer, but I really do work for that legal firm on the card. I'm the Chief Investigator."

"Chief Investigator," he repeated, nodding. "Must be important to send you all the way out from New York. What's the problem with Godfrey Knurr?"

"Uh, it involves women."

"It would," he said. "And money?"

"Yes," I said, "and money. Mr. Karp, if you insist, I will tell you in detail what the Reverend Godfrey Knurr is implicated in, and what he is suspected of having done. But, because of the laws of slander, I'd rather not. He has not been charged with any crimes. As yet."

"Crimes?" he echoed. "It's come to that, has it? No, Mr. Bigg, I really don't want to know. You wouldn't be here if it wasn't serious. Well . . . what can I tell you?"

"Anything about the man that will help me understand him."

"Understand Godfrey Knurr?" he said, with a hard grin that had no mirth to it. "No way! Besides, I can't tell you about the *man*. We lost touch when he went away to the seminary."

"And you haven't seen him since?"

"Once," he said. "When he came back to visit his sister years and years ago. He looked me up and we had a few drinks together. It was not what you'd call a joyous reunion."

"Well, can you tell me about the boy? Maybe it would help me understand what he's become."

"Maybe," he said doubtfully. "Mr. Bigg, when my family came up here from Mississippi, we were one of the first colored families in the neighborhood. It wasn't easy, I do assure you. But my daddy and older brothers got jobs in the mills, so we were eating. That was something. They put me in grade school here. Mostly Irish, Polish, and Ukrainian kids. I was the only black in my class. It would have been worse if it hadn't been for Godfrey Knurr."

I must have looked surprised.

"Oh yes," he said. "He saved my ass more than once, I do assure you. This was in the eighth grade, and he was the biggest, strongest, smartest, best-looking boy in school. The teachers loved him. Girls followed him down the street, passed him notes, gave him the cookies they baked in home economics class. I guess you could say he was the school hero."

"Is that how you saw him?"

"Oh yes," he said seriously, "I do assure you. He was my hero, too. Protected me. Showed me around. Took me under his wing, you might say. I thought I was the luckiest kid in the world to have a friend like Godfrey Knurr. I worshiped him."

"And then . . . ?" I asked.

"Then we went to high school together—right here in dear old McKinley—and Godfrey began to call in my markers. Do you know what that means?"

"I know."

"It started gradually. Like we'd have to turn in a theme, and he'd ask me to write one for him because he had put it off to the last minute and he wanted to take a girl to the movies. He was something with the girls. Or maybe we'd be taking a math test, and he'd make sure to sit next to me so that I could slip him the answers if he got stuck."

"I thought you said he was smart?"

"He was. The smartest. If he had applied himself, and studied, he could have sailed through high school, just *sailed*, and ended up first in his class. But he had no discipline. There were always a dozen things he'd rather be doing than home-work—mooning around with girls, playing a game of stickball in a vacant lot, going into Chicago to see a parade—whatever. So he began to lean on me more and more until I was practically carrying him."

"You didn't object to this?"

Jesse Karp swung his creaking swivel chair around until he was looking out a window. I saw him in profile. A great brown bald dome. A hard, brooding expression.

"I didn't object," he said in a rumbling, ponderous voice. "At first. But then I began to grow up. Physically, I mean. I really sprouted. In the tenth grade alone I put on four inches and almost thirty pounds. After a while I was as tall as Godfrey, as strong, and I was faster. Also, I was getting wiser. I realized how he was using me. I still went along with him, but it bothered me. I didn't want to get caught helping him cheat. I didn't want to lie for him anymore. I didn't want to do his homework or lend him my notes or write his themes. I began to resent his demands."

"Do you think . . ." I said hesitantly, "do you think that when you first came up here from the south, and he took you under his wing, as you said, do you think that right from the start, the both of you just kids, that he saw someone he could use? Maybe not right then, but in the future?"

Jesse Karp swung around to face me, to stare at me somberly.

"You weren't raised to be an idiot, were you?" he said. "I gave that question a lot of thought, and yes, I think he did exactly that. He had a gift—if you can call it that—of selecting friends he could use. If not immediately, then in the future. He *banked* people. Just like a savings account that he could draw on when he was in need. It hurt me when I realized it. Now, after all these years, it still hurts. I thought he liked me. For myself, I mean."

"He probably did," I assured him. "Probably in his own mind he doesn't know the difference. He only likes people he can use. The two are inseparable."

"What you're saying is that he's not doing it deliberately? That he's not consciously plotting?"

"I think it's more like an instinct."

"Maybe," he said. "Anyway, after I realized what he was doing, I decided against a sudden break. I didn't want to confront him or fight him or anything like that. But I gradually cooled it, gradually got out from under."

"How did he take that?"

"Just fine. We stayed friends, I do assure you. But he got the message. Stopped asking me to do his themes and slip him the answers on exams. It didn't make any difference. By that time he had a dozen other close friends, some boys but mostly girls, who were delighted to help him. He had so much *charm*. Even as a boy, he had so damned much charm, you wouldn't believe."

"I'd believe," I said. "He's still got it."

"Yes? Well, in our senior year, a couple of things happened that made me realize he was really bad news. He had a job for an hour after school every day working in a local drugstore. Jerking sodas and making deliveries—like that. He worked for maybe a month and then he was canned. There were rumors that he had been caught dipping into the till. That may or may not have been true. Knowing Godfrey, I'd say it was probably true. Then, we were both on the high school football team. Competitors, you might say, because we both wanted to play quarterback, although sometimes the coach played us both at the same time with one of us at halfback. But still, we both wanted to call the plays. Anyway, in our last season, three days before the big game with Edison High, someone pushed me down the cement steps to the locker room. I never saw who did it, so I can't swear to it, but I'll go to my grave believing it was Godfrey Knurr. All I got out of it, thank God, was a broken ankle."

"But he played quarterback in the big game?"

"That's right."

"Did McKinley High win?"

"No," Jesse Karp said with grim satisfaction, "we lost."

"And who ended up first in the class? Scholastically?"

"I did," he said. "But I do assure you, if Godfrey Knurr had applied himself, had shown some discipline, there is no way I could have topped him. He was brilliant. No other word for it; he was just brilliant."

"What does he *want*?" I cried desperately. "Why does he do these things? What's his motive?"

The principal fiddled with an ebony letter opener on his desk, looking down at it, turning it this way and that.

"What does he want?" he said ruminatively. "He wants money and beautiful women and the good things of this world. You and I probably want exactly the same, but Godfrey wants them the easy way. For him, that means a kind of animal force. Rob a drugstore cash register. Push a competitor down a flight of cement steps. Make love to innocent women so they'll do what you want. What you *need*. He goes bulling his way through life, all shoulders and elbows. And God help you if you get in his way. He has a short fuse—did you know that? A really violent temper. He learned to keep it under control, but I once saw what he did to a kid in scrimmage. This kid had made Godfrey look bad on a pass play. The next time we had a pileup, I saw Godfrey go after him. It was just naked violence; that's the only way I can describe it. Really vicious stuff. That kid was lucky to come out alive."

I was silent, thinking of Solomon Kipper and Professor Yale Stonehouse. They hadn't come out of the pileup.

"What does he want?" Jesse Karp repeated reflectively. "I'll tell you something odd. When Godfrey and I were kids, almost everyone collected baseball cards. You know—those pictures of players you got in a package of bubblegum. Godfrey never collected them. You know what he saved? He showed me his collection once. Models and movie stars. Yachts and mansions. Jewelry and antiques. Paintings and sculpture. He wanted to own it all."

"The American dream?" I asked.

"Well . . ." he said, "maybe. But skewed. Gone bad. He wanted it all *right now*."

"Why did he go into the ministry?" I asked.

He lifted his eyes to stare at me. "Why do you think?"

"To avoid the draft?"

"That's my guess," Jesse Karp said, shrugging. "I could be wrong."

"Was Knurr ever married?"

"Not to my knowledge," he said too quickly.

"I understand there is a Reverend Stokes who helped him?"

"That's right. The Reverend Ludwig Stokes. He's retired now."

"Goldie Knurr hinted that he's fuddled, that he drinks too much."

"He's an old, old man," Jesse Karp said stonily. "He's entitled."

"Could you tell me where I might find him?"

"The last I heard he was living in a white frame house two doors south of St. Paul's on Versailles."

He glanced obviously at his wristwatch and I rose immediately to my feet. I thanked him for his kind cooperation. He helped me on with my coat and walked me to the door.

"I'll let you know how it all comes out," I told him.

"Don't bother," he said coldly. "I really don't want to know."

I was saddened by the bitterness in his voice. It had all happened so many years ago, but he still carried the scars. He had been duped and made a fool of. He had thought he had a friend who liked him for what he was. The friend had turned out to be just another white exploiter. I wondered how that discovery had changed Jesse Karp's life.

At the doorway, I thought of something else and turned to him.

"Do you remember a girl Knurr dated, probably in high school—a short, lovely girl with long blonde hair? She had a heavy metal brace on one leg. Maybe polio."

He stared at me, through me, his high brow rippling.

"Yes," he said slowly, "I do remember. She limped badly. Very slender."

"Fragile looking," I said. "Wistful."

"Yes, I remember. But I can't recall her name. Wait a minute."

He went back to the glass-enclosed bookcase set against the far wall. He opened one of the shelf doors, searched, withdrew a volume bound in maroon. Plastic stamped to look like leather.

"Our yearbook," he said, smiling shyly. "The year Godfrey and I graduated. I still keep it."

I liked him very much then.

I stood at his side as he balanced the wide volume atop the mess at his desk and flipped through the pages rapidly. He found the section with small, individual photographs of graduating seniors, head-and-shoulder shots. Then Jesse Karp turned the pages slowly, a broad forefinger running down the columns of pictures, names, school biographies.

"Here I am," he said laughing. "God, what a beast!"

I leaned to look: Jesse Karp, not a beast, but an earnest, self-conscious kid in a stiff white collar and a tie in a horrendous pattern. Most of the other boys were wearing suit jackets, but Karp wasn't. I didn't remark on it.

"Not so bad," I said, looking at the features not yet pulled with age. "You look like it was the most solemn moment of your life."

"It was," he said, staring down at the book. "I was the first of my family to be graduated from high school. It was *something*. And here's Godfrey."

Directly below Karp's photograph was that of Knurr, wearing a sharply patterned sport jacket. He was smiling at the camera, his chin lifted. Handsome, strong, arrogant. A Golden Boy. He had written an inscription in the yearbook directly below Karp's biography: "To Jesse, my very best friend ever. Godfrey Knurr." I guessed he had written that same sentiment in many McKinley High yearbooks.

Each student had a pithy motto or prediction printed in italic type below his biography. Jesse Karp's said: *A slow but sure winner*.

Godfrey Knurr's was: *We'll be hearing of him for many years to come*.

The principal continued flipping through the pages of stamp-sized portraits. Finally his finger stopped.

"This one?" he said, looking at me.

I glanced down. It was the same girl I had seen in Goldie

Knurr's photo album. The same pale gold beauty, the same
soft vulnerability.

"Yes," I said, reading her name. "Sylvia Wiesenfeld. Do
you know anything about her?"

He closed the yearbook with his two hands, slapping the
volume with what I thought was unusual vehemence. He went
back to the bookcase to restore the book to its place and close
the glass door.

"Why are you asking about her?" he demanded, his back
to me. I thought something new had come into his voice: a
note of hostility.

"Just curious," I said. "She's so beautiful."

"Her father owned a drugstore," he said grudgingly. "He's
dead now—the father. I don't know what happened to her."

"Was this the drugstore where Godfrey Knurr worked after
school?"

"Yes," he said shortly.

He insisted on personally accompanying me through the
outer offices, down the hallways and staircases to the front
entrance of McKinley High School. I didn't know if he was
being polite or wanted to make certain I didn't loiter about the
premises.

I thanked him again for his kindness and he sent me on my
way. He didn't exactly push me out the door, but he made
certain I exited. I didn't think he regretted what he had told
me about Godfrey Knurr. I thought he was ashamed and angry
at what he had revealed about himself. I had set the old wounds
throbbing.

On the sidewalk, I turned and looked back at the high
school, a pile of red brick so ugly it was impressive. I had
brief and sententious thoughts of the thousands—maybe millions!—of young students who had walked those gloomy corridors, sat at those worn desks, who had laughed, wept, frol-
icked, and discovered despair.

I found the white frame house two doors south of St. Paul's
on Versailles Street. Perhaps it had once been white, but now
it was a powdery gray, lashed by rain and wind, scoured by
the sun. It looked at the world with blind eyes: uncurtained
windows with torn green shades drawn at various levels. The
cast-iron fence was rusted, the tiny front yard scabby with
refuse. It was a sad, sad habitation for a retired preacher, and

I could only wonder how his parishioners could allow their former pastor's home to fall into such decrepitude.

I went cautiously up the front steps and searched for a bell. There was none, although I discovered four stained screwholes in the doorjamb, a larger drilled hole in the middle, and the faint scarred mark of a square enclosing them all. Apparently a bell had once existed but had been removed.

I rapped sharply on the peeling door and waited. No answer. I knocked again. Still no reply.

"Keep trying," someone called in a cackling voice. "He's in there all right."

I turned. On the sidewalk was an ancient black man wearing a holey wool cap and fingerless gloves. He seemed inordinately swollen until I realized he was wearing at least three coats and what appeared to be several sweaters and pairs of trousers. He was pushing a splintered baby carriage filled with newspapers and bottles, cans, an old coffee percolator, tattered magazines, two bent umbrellas, and other things.

"Is this the home of the Reverend Stokes?" I asked him.

"Yeah, yeah, that's it," he said, nodding vigorously and showing a mouthful of yellow stumps. "What you do is you keep pounding. He's in there all right. He don't never go out now. Just keep pounding and pounding. He'll come to the door by and by."

"Thank you," I called, but he was already shuffling down the street, a strange apparition.

So I pounded and pounded on that weathered door. It seemed at least five minutes before I heard a quavery voice from inside: "Who is there?"

"Reverend Stokes?" I shouted. "Could I speak to you for a moment, sir? Please?"

There was a long pause and I thought I had lost him. But then I heard the sounds of a bolt being drawn, the door unlocked. It swung open.

I was confronted by a wild bird of a man. In his late seventies, I guessed. He was actually a few inches taller than I, but his clothes seemed too big for him so he appeared to have shrunk, in weight and height, to a frail diminutiveness.

His hair was an uncombed mess of gray feathers, and on his hollow cheeks was at least three days' growth of beard: a whitish plush. His temples were sunken, the skin on his brow so thin and transparent that I could see the course of blood vessels. Rheumy eyes tried to stare at me, but the focus wavered. The nose was a bone.

He was wearing what had once been a stylish velvet smoking jacket, but now the nap was worn down to the backing, and the elbows shone greasily. Beneath the unbuttoned jacket was a soiled blue workman's shirt, tieless, the collar open to reveal a scrawny chicken neck. His creaseless trousers were some black, glistening stuff, with darker stains and a tear in one knee. His fly was open. He was wearing threadbare carpet slippers, the heels broken and folded under. His bare ankles were not clean.

I was standing outside on the porch, he inside the house. Yet even at that distance I caught the odor: of him, his home, or both. It was the sour smell of unwashed age, of mustiness, spilled liquor, unmade beds and unaired linen, and a whiff of incense as rancid as all the rest.

"Reverend Stokes?" I asked.

The bird head nodded, pecking forward.

"My name is Joshua Bigg," I said briskly. "I'm not trying to sell you anything. I'd just like to talk to you for a few minutes, sir."

"About what?" he asked. The voice was a creak.

"About a former parishioner of yours, now an ordained minister himself. Godfrey Knurr."

What occurred next was totally unexpected and unnerving. *"Nothing happened!"* he screamed at me and reached to slam the door in my face. But a greenish pallor suffused his face, his hand slipped down the edge of the door, and he began to fall, to sag slowly downward, his bony knees buckling, shoulders slumping, the old body folding like a melted candle.

I sprang forward and caught him under the arms. He weighed no more than a child, and I was able to support him while I kicked the door shut with my heel. Then I half-carried, half-dragged him back into that dim, malodorous house.

I pulled him into a room that had obviously once been an attractive parlor. I put him down on a worn chesterfield, the brown leather now crackled and split. I propped his head on one of the armrests and lifted his legs and feet so he lay flat.

I straightened up, breathing through my mouth so I didn't have to smell him or the house. I stared down at him, hands on my hips, puzzling frantically what to do.

His eyes were closed, his respiration shallow but steady. I thought his face was losing some of that greenish hue that had frightened me. I decided not to call the police or para-medics. I took off my hat and coat and placed them gingerly on a club chair with a brown corduroy slipcover discolored with an enormous red stain on the seat cushion. Wine or blood.

I wandered back into the house. I found a small kitchen from which most of the odors seemed to be emanating. And no wonder; it was a swamp. I picked a soiled dishtowel off the floor and held it under the cold water tap in the scummed sink. Pipes knocked, the water ran rusty, then cleared, and I soaked the towel, wrung it out, soaked it again, wrung it out again.

I carried it back to the parlor. I pulled a straight chair alongside the chesterfield. I sat down and bent over the Rev-erend Stokes. I wiped his face gently with the dampened towel. His eyes opened suddenly. He stared at me dazedly. His eyes were spoiled milk, curdled and cloudy.

A clawed hand came up and pushed the towel aside. I folded it and laid it across his parchment brow. He let me do that and let the towel remain.

"I fainted?" he said in a wispy voice.

"Something like that," I said, nodding. "You started to go down. I caught you and brought you in here."

"In the study," he whispered, "across the hall, a bottle of whiskey, a half-filled glass. Bring them in here."

I looked at him, troubled.

"Please," he breathed.

I went into the study, a shadowed chamber littered with books, journals, magazines: none of them new. The room was dominated by a large walnut desk topped with scarred and ripped maroon leather. The whiskey and glass were on the desk. I took them and started out.

On a small marble-topped smoking stand near the door was a white plaster replica of Michelangelo's "David." It was the only clean, shining, lovely object I had seen in that decaying house. I had seen nothing of a religious nature—no pictures, paintings, icons, statuary, crucifixes, etc.

I brought him the whiskey. He raised a trembly hand and I held the glass to his lips. He gulped greedily and closed his eyes. After a moment he opened his eyes again, flung the towel from his brow onto the floor. He took the glass from my hand. Our fingers touched. His skin had the chill of death.

"There's another glass," he said. "In the kitchen."

His voice was stronger but it still creaked. It had an unused sound: harsh and croaky.

"Thank you, no," I said. "It's a little early for me."

"Is it?" he said without interest.

I sat down in the straight chair again and watched him finish the tumbler of whiskey. He filled it again from the bottle on the floor. I didn't recognize the label. It looked like a cheap blend.

"You told me your name?" he asked.

"Yes, sir. Joshua Bigg."

"Now I remember. Joshua Bigg. I don't recognize you, Mr. Bigg. Where are you from?"

"New York City, sir."

"New York," he repeated, and then with a pathetic attempt at gaiety, he said, "East Side, West Side, all around the town."

He tried to smile at me. When his thin, whitish lips parted, I could see his stained dentures. His gums seemed to have shrunk, for the false teeth fitted loosely and he had to clench his jaws frequently to jam them back into place. It was like a pained grimace.

"I was in New York once," he said dreamily. "Years and years ago. I went to the theatre. A musical play. What could it have been? I'll remember in a moment."

"Yes, sir."

"And what brings you to our fair city, Mr. Bigg?"

I was afraid of saying the name again. I feared he might have the same reaction. But I had to try it.

"I wanted to talk to you about the Reverend Godfrey Knurr, Pastor," I said softly.

His eyes closed again. "Godfrey Knurr?" Stokes repeated. "No, I can't recall the name. My memory..."

I wasn't going to let him get away with that.

"It's odd you shouldn't remember," I said. "I spoke to his sister, Miss Goldie Knurr, and she told me you helped him get into the seminary, that you helped him in so many ways. And I saw a photograph of you with young Godfrey."

Suddenly he was crying. It was awful. Cloudy tears slid

from those milky eyes. They slipped sideways into his sunken temples, then into his feathered hair.

"Is he dead?" he gasped.

First Goldie Knurr and now the Reverend Stokes. Was the question asked hopefully? Did they wish him dead?

I turned my eyes away, not wanting to sit there and watch this shattered man weep. After a while I heard him snuffle a few times and take a gulp from the glass he held on his thin chest. Then I looked at him again.

"No, sir," I said, "he is not dead. But he's in trouble, deep trouble. I represent a legal firm. A client intends to bring very serious charges against the Reverend Knurr. I am here to make a preliminary investigation..."

My voice trailed away; he wasn't listening to me. His lips were moving and I leaned close to hear what he was saying.

"Evil," the Reverend Ludwig Stokes was breathing. "Evil, evil, evil, evil..."

I sat back. It seemed a hopeless task to attempt to elicit information from this old man. Goldie Knurr had been right; he was fuddled.

But then he spoke clearly and intelligibly.

"Do you know him?" he asked. "Have you seen him?"

"Yes, sir," I said. "I spoke to him yesterday. He seems to be in good health. He has a beard now. He runs a kind of social club in Greenwich Village for poor boys and he also counsels individual, uh, dependents. Mostly wealthy women."

His face twisted and he clenched his jaw to press his dentures back into place. A thin rivulet of whiskey ran from the corner of his mouth and he wiped it away slowly with the back of one hand.

"Wealthy women," he repeated, his voice dull. "Yes, yes, that would be Godfrey."

"Reverend Stokes," I said, "I'm curious as to why Knurr selected the ministry as his career. I can find nothing in his boyhood that indicates any great religiosity." I paused, stared at him. "Was it to avoid the draft?" I asked bluntly.

"Partly that," he said in a low voice. "If his family had had the money, he would have wished to go to a fashionable eastern college. That was his preference, but it was impossible. Even I didn't have that kind of money."

"He asked for it? From you?"

He didn't answer.

"I understand he had good marks in high school," I went on. "Perhaps he could have obtained a scholarship, worked to help support himself?"

"It wasn't his way," he said.

"Then he could have gone to a low-tuition, state-supported college. Why the ministry?"

"Opportunity," the Reverend Stokes said without expression.

"Opportunity?" I echoed. "To save souls? I can't believe that of Godfrey Knurr. And surely not the monetary rewards of being an ordained minister."

"Opportunity," he repeated stubbornly. "That's how he saw it."

I thought about that, trying to see it as a young ambitious Godfrey Knurr had.

"Wealthy parishioners?" I guessed. "Particularly wealthy female parishioners? Maybe widows and divorcées? Was that how his mind worked?"

Again he didn't answer. He emptied the bottle into his tumbler and drained it in two gulps.

"There's another in the kitchen," he told me. "In the cupboard under the sink."

I found the bottle. I also found a reasonably clean glass for myself and rinsed it several times, scrubbing the inside with my fingers. I brought bottle and glass back to the parlor, sat down again, and poured him half a tumbler and myself a small dollop.

"Your health, sir," I said, raising my glass. I barely wet my lips.

"He was a handsome boy?" I asked, coughing. "Godfrey Knurr?"

He made a sound.

"Yes," he said in his creaky voice, "very handsome. And strong. A beautiful boy. Physically."

I caught him up on that.

"Physically?" I said. "But what of his personality, his character?"

Another of his maddening silences.

"Charm," he said, then buried his nose in his glass. After he swallowed he repeated, "Charm. A very special charm.

There was a golden glow about him."

"He must have been very popular," I said, hoping to keep his reminiscences flowing.

"You had to love him," he said, sighing. "In his presence you felt happy. More alive. He promised everything."

"Promised?" I said, not understanding.

"I felt younger," he said, voice low. "More hopeful. Life seemed brighter. Just having him near."

"Did he ever visit you here, in your home?"

Again he began to weep, and I despaired of learning anything of significance from this riven man.

I waited until his eyes stopped leaking. This time he didn't bother wiping the tears away. The wet glistened like oil on his withered face. He drank deeply, finished his whiskey. His trembling hand pawed feebly for the full bottle on the floor. I served him. I had never before seen a man drink with such maniacal determination, as if unconsciousness could not come soon enough.

He lay there, wax fingers clamped around the glass on his bony chest. He stared unblinking at the ceiling. I felt I was sitting up with a corpse, waiting for the undertaker's men to come and take their burden away.

"I understand he was in trouble as a boy," I continued determinedly. "In a drugstore where he worked. He was accused of stealing."

"He made restitution," the old man said, his thin lips hardly moving. "Paid it all back."

"You gave him the money for that?" I guessed.

I hardly heard his faint, "Yes." Then . . .

"I gave him so much!" he howled in a voice so loud it startled me. "Not only money, but myself. I gave him *myself!* I taught him about poetry and beauty. Love. He said he understood, but he didn't. He was playing with me. He teased me. All the time he was teasing me, and it gave him pleasure."

I felt suddenly ill as I began to glimpse the proportions of this tragedy. Now I could understand that screeched, *"Nothing happened!"* And the statue of David. And the whispered, "Evil, evil, evil . . ."

"You loved him?" I asked gently.

"So much," he said in a harrowed voice. "So much . . ."

He lifted his head to drain his tumbler, then held it out to me in a quavery hand. I filled it without compunction.

"You never married, Reverend?" I asked.

"No. Never." He was staring at the ceiling again, seeing things that weren't there.

"Did you tell Godfrey how you felt about him?"

"He knew."

"And?"

"He used me. *Used* me! Laughing. The devil incarnate. All I saw was the golden glow. And then the darkness beneath."

"Knowing that, Pastor, why did you help him become a man of God?"

"Weakness. I did not have the strength of soul to withstand him. He threatened me."

"Threatened you? How? You said that nothing happened."

"Nothing did. But I had written him. Notes. Poems. They would have ruined me. The church . . ."

Notes again. I was engulfed in notes, false and true . . .

I took a deep breath, trying to comprehend the extent of such perfidy. The pattern of Godfrey Knurr's life was becoming plainer. An ambition too large for his discipline to contain was the motive for trading on his charm. He moved grinning from treachery to treachery, leaving behind him a trail of scars, wounds, broken lives.

And finally, I was convinced, two murders that meant no more to him than a rifled cash register or this betrayed wreck of a man.

"So you did whatever he demanded?" I said, nailing it down. "Got him out of scrapes, got him into the seminary? Gave him money?"

"All," he said. "All. I gave him everything. My soul. My poor little shriveled soul."

His words "shriveled soul" came out slurred and garbled, almost lost between his whiskey-loosened tongue and those ill-fitting dentures. I did not think he was far from the temporary oblivion he sought.

"Sylvia Wiesenfeld," I said. "You knew her?"

He didn't answer.

"You did," I told him. "Her father owned the drugstore where Godfrey stole the money. A lovely girl. So vulnerable. So willing. I saw her picture. Did she love Godfrey, too?"

His eyes were closed again. But his lips were moving

faintly, fluttering. I rose, bent over him, put my ear close to his mouth, as if trying to determine if a dying man still breathed.

"What?" I said sharply. "I didn't hear that. Please repeat it."

This time I heard.

"I married them," he said.

I straightened up, took a deep breath. I looked down at the shrunken, defenseless hulk. All I could think of was: Godfrey Knurr did that.

I took the whiskey glass from his strengthless fingers and set it on the floor alongside the couch. He seemed to be breathing slowly but regularly. The tears had dried on his face, but whitish matter had collected in the corners of his eyes and mouth. Occasionally his body twitched, little moans escaped his lips like gas released from something corrupt.

I wandered about the lower floor of the house. I found a knitted afghan in the hall closet, brought it back to the parlor, and covered the Reverend Ludwig Stokes, a bright shroud for a gray man.

Then I went back into his study and poked about. I finally found a telephone directory in the lowest drawer of the old walnut desk. There was an S. Wiesenfeld on Sherman Street, not too far from the home of Goldie Knurr. It seemed strange that such tumultuous events had occurred in such a small neighborhood.

The woman who answered my ring was certainly not Sylvia Wiesenfeld; she was a gargantuan black woman, not so tall but remarkable in girth. Her features, I thought, might be pleasant in repose, but when she opened the door, she was scowling and banging an iron frying pan against one redwood thigh. She looked down at me.

"We ain't buying," she said.

"Oh, I'm not selling anything," I hurriedly assured her. "My name is Joshua Bigg. I represent a legal firm in New York City. I've been sent out to make inquiries into the background of Godfrey Knurr. I was hoping to have a few minutes' conversation with Miss Wiesenfeld."

She looked at me suspiciously.

"You *who*?" she said. "You New York folks talk so fast."

"Joshua Bigg," I answered slowly. "That's my name. I'm

trying to obtain information about Godfrey Knurr. I'd like to talk to Sylvia Wiesenfeld for a few moments."

"You the law?" she demanded.

"No," I said, "not exactly. I represent attorneys who, in turn, represent a client who is bringing suit against the Reverend Godfrey Knurr. I'm just making a preliminary investigation, that's all."

"You going to hang him?" she demanded. "I hope."

I tried to smile.

"Well . . . ah . . ." I said, "I'm sure our client would like to. May I speak to Miss Wiesenfeld for a few moments?"

She glared at me, making up her mind. That heavy cast-iron frying pan kept banging against her bulging thigh. I was very conscious of it.

"Well . . ." she said finally, "all right." Then she added fiercely, "You get my honey upset, I break yo' ass!"

"No, no," I said hastily, "I won't upset her, I promise."

She stared down at me again.

"You and me," she said menacingly, "we come to it, I figure I come out on top."

"Absolutely," I assured her. "No doubt about it. I'll behave; I really will."

Suddenly she grinned: a marvelous *human* grin of warmth and understanding.

"I do believe," she said. "Come on in, lawyer-man."

She led me into a neat entrance hall, hung my coat and hat on an oak hall rack exactly like the one in Miss Goldie Knurr's home.

"May I know your name, please, ma'am?" I asked her.

"Mrs. Harriet Lee Livingston," she said in a rich contralto voice. "I makes do for Miz Sylvia."

"How long have you been with her?"

"Longer than you been breathin'," she said.

The enormous bulk of the woman was awesome. That had to be the largest behind I had ever seen on a human being, and the other parts of her were in proportion: arms and legs like waists, and a neck that seemed as big around as her head.

But her features were surprisingly clear and delicate, with slanty eyes, a nice mouth, and a firm chin that had a deep cleft precisely in the center. You could have inserted a dime in that cleft. Her hands and feet were unexpectedly dainty, and she moved lightly, with grace.

Her color was a briar brown. She wore a voluminous shift, a shapeless tent with pockets. It was a kaleidoscope of hues: splashes of red, yellow, purple, blue, green—all in a jangling pattern that dazzled the eye.

"You stand right here," she said sternly. "Right on this spot. I'll tell Miz Sylvia she's got a visitor. I takes you in without warning, she's liable to get upset."

"I won't move," I promised.

She opened sliding wooden doors, squeezed through, closed the two doors behind her. I hadn't seen doors like that since I left my uncle's home in Iowa. They were paneled, waxed to a high gloss, fitted with brass hardware: amenities of a bygone era.

The doors slid open again and Mrs. Livingston beckoned me forward.

"Speak nice," she whispered.

"I will," I vowed.

"I be right here to make sure you do," she said grimly.

The woman facing me from across the living room was small, slight, with long silvered blonde hair giving her a girlish appearance, although I knew she had to be at least forty. I could not see a leg brace; she wore a collarless gown of bottle-green velvet, a lounging or hostess gown, that fell to her ankles.

She was a thin little thing, still with that look of tremulous vulnerability that had caught my eye in the photos in the Knurr family album and Jesse Karp's yearbook. She seemed physically frail, or at least fragile, with narrow wrists, a white stalk of a neck, a head that appeared to be pulled backward, chin uptilted, by the weight of her hair.

She had a luminous quality: pale complexion, big eyes of bluish-green (they looked like agates), and lips sweetly bowed. I saw no wrinkles, no crow's feet, no furrows—nothing in her face to mark the passage of years. If she had been wounded, it did not show. The smooth brow was serene, the dim smile placid.

But there was a dissonance about her that disturbed. She seemed removed. The lovely eyes were vacant, or focused on something no one else could see. That half-smile was, I soon realized, her normal expression; it meant nothing.

I recognized Ophelia, looking for her stream.

"Mr. Bigg?" she said. Her voice was young, utterly without timbre. A child's voice.

"Miss Wiesenfeld," I said, bowing, "I know this is an intrusion, and I appreciate your willingness to grant me a few moments of your time."

"Oh la!" she said with a giggling laugh. "How pretty you do talk. Doesn't he talk pretty, Harriet?"

"Yeah," Mrs. Livingston said heavily. "Pretty. Mr. Bigg, you sit in that armchair there. I sits on the couch here. Honey, you want to rest yourself?"

"No," the lady said, "I prefer to remain standing."

I seated myself nervously. My armchair was close to the corner of the big davenport where Mrs. Livingston perched, not leaning back but balancing her bulk on the edge. She was ready, I was certain, to lunge for my throat if I dared upset her honey.

"Miss Wiesenfeld," I started, "I have no desire to rake up old memories that may cause you pain. If I pose a question you don't wish to answer, please tell me so, and I will not persist. But this is a matter of some importance. It concerns the Reverend Godfrey Knurr. I represent a legal firm in New York City. One of our clients, a young woman, wishes to bring serious charges against Reverend Knurr. I am making a preliminary investigation in an attempt to discover if Knurr has a past history of the type of, ah, activities of which he is accused."

"Pretty," she murmured. "So pretty. It's nice to meet someone who speaks in complete sentences. Subject, verb, object. Do all your sentences parse, Mr. Bigg?"

She said that quite seriously. I laughed.

"I would like to think so," I said. "But I'm afraid I can't make that claim."

She began moving across the room in front of me. I saw then that she limped badly, dragging her left leg. Below the hostess gown I could see the foot bound in the stirrup of a metal brace.

She went close to a bird cage suspended from a brass stand. Within the cage, a yellow canary hopped from perch to perch as she approached.

"Chickie," she said softly. "Dear, sweet Chickie. How are you today, Chickie? Will you chirp for our guest? Will you sing a lovely song? How did you find me, Mr. Bigg?"

The abrupt question startled me.

"I saw your photograph in the Knurr family album, ma'am. With Godfrey. Mr. Jesse Karp supplied your name. The Reverend Ludwig Stokes provided more information."

"You have been busy, Mr. Bigg."

"Yes, ma'am," I said humbly.

"The busy Mr. Bigg," she said with her giggling laugh. "Busy Bigg." She poked a pale finger through the bars of the cage. "Sing for Busy Bigg, Chickie. What is Godfrey accused of?"

I had determined to use Percy Stilton's scam. The one that had worked with Bishop Oxman.

"He is accused of allegedly defrauding a young woman of her life's savings by promising to double her money."

"And promising to marry her?" Sylvia Wiesenfeld asked.

"Yes," I said.

"He is guilty," she said calmly. "He did exactly that."

A low growl came from Mrs. Livingston.

"I'd like to have him right here," she said in her furred contralto. "In my hands."

"Miss Wiesenfeld," I said, "may I ask you this: were you married to Godfrey Knurr?"

"Chickie," she said to the bird, "why aren't you chirping? Aren't you feeling well, Chickie?"

She left the cage, came back to the long davenport. The housekeeper heaved her bulk and assisted Sylvia to sit in the corner, the left leg extended, covered with the skirt of her long gown. Mrs. Livingston reached out, tenderly smoothed back strands of blonde hair that had fallen about her mistress' pale face.

"Oh la!" Miss Wiesenfeld said. "A long time ago. Where are the snows of yesteryear? Reverend Stokes told you that?"

"Yes, ma'am."

"It happened in another world," she said. "In another time."

Her beautiful eyes looked at me, but she was detached, off somewhere.

"But you were married?" I persisted. "Legally?"

"Legally," she said. "A piece of paper. I have it."

"How long were you married, Miss Wiesenfeld?"

She turned those vacant eyes on the enormous black woman. "Harriet?" she said.

"Fourteen months," Mrs. Livingston said. "Give or take."

"And then?" I asked.

"And then?" she repeated my question, perplexed.

"Did you separate? Divorce?"

"Harriet?" she asked again.

"He cleared out," Mrs. Livingston told me furiously. "Just took off. With everything of my honey's he could get his hands on. But her daddy was too smart for him. He left my honey some kind of a fund that cur couldn't touch."

I tried to remember when I had last heard a man called a "cur." I could not recall ever hearing it.

"So you are still married to Godfrey Knurr?" I asked softly.

"Oh no," Sylvia Wiesenfeld said with her disturbingly childish laugh. "No, no, no. I have a paper. Don't I, Harriet? So much paper. Paper, paper, paper."

I looked beseechingly at Mrs. Livingston.

"We got us a letter from a lawyer-man in Mexico," she said disgustedly. "It said Godfrey Knurr had been granted a divorce from his wife Sylvia."

I turned to Miss Wiesenfeld in outrage.

"Surely you went to an attorney, ma'am?" I said. "I don't know divorce law all that well, but the letter may have been fraudulent. Or Mexican divorces without the consent of both parties might not have been recognized in the state in which you were married. I hope you sought legal advice?"

She looked at me, eyes rounding.

"Whatever for?" she asked in astonishment. "I wanted him gone. I wanted him dead. He hurt me."

I swallowed.

"Physically, ma'am?" I said gently.

"Once," Mrs. Livingston said in a deadly voice. "I told him he puts hands to her again, I kill him. I told him that. But that's not what she means when she says he hurt her. He broke my honey's heart."

She was speaking of her mistress as if she was not present. But Miss Wiesenfeld did not object. She just kept smiling emptily, face untroubled, eyes staring into the middle distance.

"Oh la!" she said. "Broke poor Sylvia's heart."

I was not certain of the depth of her dementia. She seemed to flick in and out, sometimes in the same sentence. She was lucid in speech and controlled in manner, and then suddenly she was gone, flying.

"Ma'am," I said, hating myself, "what did Godfrey Knurr do with your money? When you were married?"

"Ohh," she said, "bought things. Pretty things."

Mrs. Livingston leaned toward me.

"Women," she said throatily. "High living. He just pissed it away."

That "pissed" shocked me. It was hissed with such venom that I thought Godfrey Knurr fortunate to have escaped the vengeance of Mrs. Harriet Lee Livingston. She would have massacred him.

"Harriet," Sylvia said in a petulant, spoiled child's voice, "I want to get up again."

"Sure, honey," the housekeeper said equably, lurching to her feet. She helped her mistress stand. Miss Wiesenfeld dragged her leg back to the bird cage.

"Chickie?" she said. "Chirp for me?"

There were other questions I wanted to ask. I wanted to probe deeper, explore the relationship between Sylvia and Knurr, discover how the marriage had come about, when, and why it had dissolved. But I simply didn't have the stomach for it.

It seemed to me that all day I had been poking through the human detritus Godfrey Knurr had left in his wake. I was certain Roscoe Dollworth would have persevered in this investigation, but I lacked the ruthlessness. He had told me never to let my personal feelings interfere with the job, but I couldn't help it. I *liked* all these victims, shared their misery, their sad memories, and I had heard just about all I could endure. Probing old wounds was not, really, a noble calling.

When I departed from the living room, Sylvia Wiesenfeld was still at the bird cage. Her forefinger was reaching through the bars. "Chickie?" she was saying. "Dear, sweet Chickie, sing me a song."

I didn't even thank her or say goodbye.

Out in the hallway, Mrs. Livingston helped me on with my coat.

"You going to mash him?" she demanded.

I stared at her a moment.

"Will you help?" I asked.

"Any way I can."

"I need that marriage license," I said. "And the letter from the Mexican lawyer, if you can find it. But the marriage license is most important. I'll try to get copies made this afternoon and bring the originals back to you. If I can't get copies made, I want to take the originals to New York with me. I'll return them; I swear it."

"How do I know?" she said mistrustfully.

"I'll give you money," I said. "I'll leave fifty dollars with you. When I return the license, you return the money."

"Money don't mean nothing," she said. "You got a pawn that means something to you?"

I looked down at myself.

"My wristwatch!" I said. "My aunt and uncle gave it to me when I was graduated from school. It means a lot to me. But it's a cheap watch. Not worth even fifty dollars."

"I'll take it," she said. "You bring the marriage license back, or mail it back, and you gets your watch back."

I agreed eagerly and slipped the expansion band off my wrist. She dropped the watch into one of her capacious pockets.

"You wait right here," she commanded. "Don't move a step."

"I won't," I said, and I didn't as I watched her climb the carpeted steps to the second floor. That was really a leviathan behind.

She came stepping down in a few minutes, carrying two folded documents. I took a quick look at them. A marriage license issued to Sylvia Wiesenfeld and Godfrey Knurr by the State of Indiana, dated February 6, 1959, and a letter from a Mexican attorney dated fourteen months later, informing Sylvia that a divorce had been granted to Knurr. I refolded both documents, slid them into my inside jacket pocket.

"You'll get them back," I promised once more.

"I got your watch," she said, and then grinned again at me: that marvelous, warm, human smile of complicity.

"Thank you for all your help," I said.

"I don't know why," she said, "but I trusts you. You play me false, don't never come back here again—I tear you apart."

On the early evening New York-bound airliner, a Scotch-and-water in my hand, I relaxed gratefully. The seats on both sides of me were empty, and I could sprawl in comfort. I emulated the passenger across the aisle and removed my shoes.

I wiggled my stockinged toes, a pleasurable sensation at 33,000 feet, and planned the defeat of Godfrey Knurr.

It seemed to me that our original assessment of the situation had been correct; in the absence of adequate physical evidence the only hope of bringing the Kipper and Stonehouse cases to satisfactory solutions was to take advantage of the individual weaknesses of the guilty participants. If we had failed so far in trying to "run a game" on them, it was because we did not have sufficient leverage to stir them, set one against the other, find the weakest link and twist that until it snapped.

By the time we started our descent for LaGuardia Airport in New York, I thought I had worked out a way in which it might be done. It would be a gamble, but not as dangerous as the risks Godfrey Knurr had run.

Also, it would require that I mislead several people, including Detective Percy Stilton.

I was sorry for that, but consoled myself by recalling that at our first meeting he had given me valuable tips on how to be a successful liar. Surely he could not object if I followed his advice.

I arrived home at my apartment in Chelsea shortly after 11:00 P.M. It looked good to me. I was desperately hungry, and longing for a hot shower. But first I wanted to contact Percy Stilton while my resolve was still hot. I had rehearsed my role shamelessly, and knew I must be definite, optimistic, enthusiastic. I must convince him, since as an officer of the law he could add the weight of his position to trickery that would surely flounder if I tried it by myself.

I called his office, but they told me he was not on duty. I then called his home. No answer. Finally I dialed the number of Maybelle Hawks' apartment. She answered:

"Hello?"

"Miss Hawks?"

"Yes. Who is this?"

"Joshua Bigg."

A short pause, then:

"Josh! So good to hear from you. How are you, babe?"

"Very well, thank you. And you?"

"Full of beans," she said. "Literally. We just finished a pot of chili. Perce said you went to Chicago. You calling from there?"

"No, I'm back in New York. Miss Hawks, I—"

"Belle," she said.

"Belle, I apologize for calling at this hour, but I'm trying to locate Percy. Is he—"

"Sure," she said breezily, "his majesty is here. You got something to tell him about those cases?"

"I certainly do," I said heartily.

"I'll put him on," she said. "Mind if I listen on the extension?"

"Not at all," I said. "It's good news."

"Great," she said. "Just a minute . . ."

There was a banging of phones, voices in the background, then Stilton came on the line.

"Josh?" he said. "How you doing?"

"Just fine. Sorry to disturb you."

"I'm glad you did. Lousy dinner. Dull broad."

"Up yours," Maybelle Hawks said on the extension.

"Got some good news for you, Josh. They reopened the Kipper case. Your bosses swung some heavy clout."

"Good," I said happily. "Glad to hear it. Now listen to what I've got . . ."

I kept my report as short and succinct as I could. I told him Goldie Knurr really was Godfrey's sister. I gave a brief account of my meeting with Jesse Karp and what he had told me of the boyhood of Godfrey Knurr. I went into more detail in describing the interviews with the Reverend Ludwig Stokes and Sylvia Wiesenfeld. I told Stilton I had returned with the original marriage license. I did not mention the letter from the Mexican attorney.

They didn't interrupt my report, except once when I was describing Knurr's physical abuse of Sylvia Wiesenfeld, which I exaggerated. Maybelle Hawks broke in with a furious "That bastard!"

When I finished, I waited for Stilton's questions. They came rapidly.

"Let's take it from the top," he said. "This priest—he's how old?"

"About seventy-five. Around there."

"And Knurr has been blackmailing him for twenty-five years?"

"About."

"Why didn't he blow the whistle before this?"

"Personal shame. And what it would do to his church."

"What did Knurr take him for?"

"I don't know the exact dollar amount. A lot of money. Plus getting Knurr into the seminary. And performing the marriage ceremony, probably without the bride's father's knowledge."

"And you say this Stokes is willing to bring charges now?"

"He says so. He says he's an old man and wants to make his peace with God."

"Uh-huh. What kind of a guy is he? Got all his marbles?"

"Oh yes," I said, and found myself crossing my fingers, a childish gesture. "He's a dignified old gentleman, very scholarly, who lives alone and has plenty of time to think about his past life. He says he wants to atone for his sins."

"He may get a chance. All right, now about the wife . . . The marriage license is legit?"

"Absolutely."

"No record of a divorce, legal separation—nothing like that?"

"She says no. She's living on a trust fund her father left her. After the way Knurr treated her, she was glad to get rid of him and assume her maiden name."

"He deserted her?"

"Right," I said definitely. "She was happy to find out where he is. I don't think it would take much to convince her to bring charges. The reasons are economic. That trust fund that seemed like a lot of money twenty years ago doesn't amount to much now. She's hurting."

"And what kind of a woman is she? A whacko?"

"Oh no," I protested. "A very mature, intelligent woman."

There was silence awhile. Then Detective Stilton said: "What we've got are two out-of-state possibles. Charges would have to be brought in Indiana, then we have extradition. If that goes through, we've lost him on the homicides."

"Correct," I agreed. "The blackmail and desertion charges are just small ammunition. But the big guns are that marriage license—and his affair with Glynis Stonehouse."

He knew at once what I meant.

"You want to brace Tippi Kipper?" he said.

"That's right, Perce. Be absolutely honest with her. Lay out all we've got. Show her the marriage license. I think she'll make a deal."

"Mmm," he said. "Maybe. Belle, what do you think? Will it work?"

"A good chance," she said on the extension. "I'll bet my left tit he never told her he was married. A guy like him wouldn't be that stupid. And when you tell her about Glynis Stonehouse, it'll just confirm what she read in that poison-pen letter Josh sent her. She'll be burning. He played her for a sucker. She's a woman who's been around the block twice. Her ego's not going to let him make her a patsy. I'm betting she'll pull the rug on him."

"Yeah," Stilton said slowly. "And we can always try the publicity angle on her, just happen to mention we know about her prostitution arrest. She's a grand lady now; she'd die if that got in the papers."

"Let's go after her," I urged. "Really twist."

He made up his mind.

"Right," he said, "we'll do it. Go in early before she's had a chance to put herself together. Josh, I'll meet you outside the Kipper place at nine o'clock tomorrow morning. Got that? Bring all the paper, especially that marriage license."

"I'll be there," I promised.

"We'll break her," he said, beginning to get excited by the prospect. "No rough stuff. Kid gloves. Very sincere and low-key. Treat a whore like a lady and a lady like a whore. Who said that, Josh?"

"I'm not sure. It sounds like Lord Chesterfield."

"Whoever," he said.

"If you believe that, Perce," Maybelle Hawks said, "it makes me a lady."

We all laughed, talked for a moment of how we should dress for our confrontation with Tippi Kipper, and then said goodnight.

I went immediately to my kitchen and began to eat raven-ously. I cleaned out the refrigerator. I had three fried eggs, a sardine and onion sandwich, almost a quart of milk, a pint of chocolate ice cream. Then, still hungry, I heated up a can of noodle soup and had that with two vanilla cupcakes and half a cucumber.

Belching, I undressed and went into the shower. The water

was blessedly hot. I soaped and rinsed three times, washed my hair, shaved, and doused myself with cologne.

Groaning with contentment, I rolled into bed about 1:00 A.M. It may have been my excitement, or perhaps that sardine and onion sandwich, but I did not fall asleep immediately. I lay on my back, thinking of what we would do in the morning, what we would say to Tippi Kipper, how important it was that we should break her.

I did not pray to God because, although I am a religious man, I did not much believe in prayer. What was the point—since God must know what is in our hearts? But I felt my lies and low cunning would be pardoned if they succeeded in bringing down Godfrey Knurr.

He was an abomination. As Jesse Karp had said, Knurr went bulling his way through life, all shoulders and elbows. He just didn't *care;* that was what I could not forgive. He exemplified brute force and brute morality. I felt no guilt for what I was trying to do to him.

Just before I fell asleep, I remembered Cleo Hufnagel. I realized, groaning, that she had been out of my thoughts for days. I felt guilt about *that*.

7

ON SATURDAY, THE March sky was hard, an icy blue whitened by a blurry sun, and in the west a faded wedge of morning moon. Not a cloud. But an angry wind came steadily and swirled the streets.

I took a cab uptown and marveled at how sharp the city looked, chopped out, everything standing clear. The air was washed clean, and pierced.

I was wearing my good pinstripe suit, vested, with a white shirt and dull tie. Stilton and I had agreed to dress like undertakers: conservative, solemn, but sympathetic. Men to be trusted.

A dusty-blue Plymouth was parked in front of the Kipper townhouse. Behind the wheel was a carelessly dressed giant of a man with a scraggly blond mustache that covered his mouth. Percy sat beside him, looking like a judge. He motioned me into the back seat. I climbed in, closed the door. I held my scruffy briefcase on my lap.

"Josh," Perce said, "this slob is Lou, my partner."

"Good morning, Lou," I said.

"Got all the paper?" Stilton asked.

"Everything," I said, feeling slightly ill.

"Good," he said. "When we get inside, let me do the spiel. You follow my lead. Just nod. You're the shill. Got that?"

"I understand."

"Act sincere," he said. "You can act sincere, can't you?"

"Of course," I said in a low voice.

"Sure you can," he said. I knew he was trying to encourage me and I appreciated it. "Don't worry, Josh, this is going down. This is going to be the greatest hustle known to living man. A classic."

Lou spoke for the first time.

"The world is composed of five elements," he stated. "Earth, air, fire, water, and bullshit."

"You're singing our song, baby," Percy told him. "Okay, Josh, let's *do* it."

Chester Heavens came to the door.

"Gentlemen?" he said somberly.

"Good morning, Chester," I mumbled.

"Morning," Percy said briskly. "I am Detective Percy Stilton of the New York Police Department. I believe we've met before. Here is my identification."

He flipped open his leather, held it up. Heavens peered at it.

"Yes, sah," he said. "I remember. How may I be of service?"

"It's important we see Mrs. Kipper," Stilton said. "As soon as possible. She's home?"

Chester hesitated a moment, then surrendered.

"Please to step in," he said. "I'll speak with mom."

We waited in that towering entrance hall. Heavens had disappeared into the dining room and closed the door. We waited for what I thought was a long time. I fidgeted, but Stilton stood stolidly. Finally Chester returned.

"Mom will see you now," he said, expressionless. "She is at breakfast. May I take your things?"

He took our coats and hats, hung them away. He opened the door to the dining room, stood aside. Percy entered first. As I was about to go in, Chester put a soft hand on my arm.

"Bad, sah?" he whispered.

I nodded.

He nodded, too. Sorrowfully.

She was seated at the head of that long, shining table. Regal. Wearing a flowing, lettuce-green peignoir. But her hair was down and not too tidy. Moreover, as I drew closer, I saw her face was slightly distorted, puffy. Staring, I saw that the left cheek from eye to chin was swollen, discolored. She had attempted to cover the bruise with pancake makeup, but it was there.

Then I understood Godfrey Knurr's smarmy comment: "I think I persuaded the lady."

Stilton and I stood side by side. She stared at us, unblinking. She did not ask us to sit down.

"Ma'am," Percy said humbly, "I am Detective—"

"I know who you are," she said sharply. "We've met. What do you want?"

"I am engaged in an official investigation of the Reverend Godfrey Knurr," Stilton said, still apologetic. "I hoped you would be willing to cooperate with the New York Police Department and furnish what information you can."

She turned her eyes to me.

"And what are you doing here?" she demanded.

"Mr. Bigg asked to come along, ma'am," Percy said swiftly. "The request for an investigation originated with his legal firm."

She thought about that. She didn't quite believe, but she didn't *not* believe. She wanted to learn more.

"Sit down then," she said coldly. "Both of you. Coffee?"

"Not for me," Perce said, "thank you, Mrs. Kipper. You, Mr. Bigg?"

"Thank you, no," I said.

We drew up chairs, Stilton on her right, me on her left. We had her surrounded, hemmed in. I don't think she expected that.

She shook a cigarette from an almost empty pack. Stilton was there with his lighter before I could make a move. I think his courtesy reassured her. She blew smoke at the ceiling.

"Well," she said, "what's this all about?"

"Ma'am," Stilton said, hunching forward earnestly, "it's a rather involved story, so I hope you'll bear with me. About two weeks ago the NYPD received a request from the police department of Gary, Indiana, asking us to determine if the Reverend Godfrey Knurr was in our area. A warrant had been issued for his arrest. Two warrants, actually."

"Arrest?" she cried. "What for?"

"One was for blackmail, Mrs. Kipper. Allegedly, for a period of many years, Knurr has been blackmailing an elderly clergyman in the neighborhood where he grew up. The other warrant was for desertion."

We were both watching closely. She may have been an actress, but she couldn't conceal her reaction to that. The hand that held the cigarette began to quiver; she put her wrist on the table to steady it. Her face paled; the bruise stood out, a nasty blue. She leaned forward to pour herself more coffee.

Maybelle Hawks had been right; she hadn't known.

"Desertion?" she asked casually, and I noted that the charge of blackmail hadn't stirred her at all.

"Oh yes," Detective Stilton said. "Knurr was married about twenty years ago and has never been divorced or legally separated. Mr. Bigg, do you have the license?"

I plucked it from my briefcase and held it up before Tippi Kipper, making certain it did not leave my hands. She leaned forward to read it.

"Yes," she said dully, "I see."

Percy leaned back in his chair and folded his hands comfortably on the tabletop.

"Well," he said, "the request from the Gary, Indiana, police was circulated, and a copy came across my desk. Ordinarily I would just file it and forget it. I'm sure you appreciate how busy we are, ma'am, and how an out-of-state request gets a very low priority on our schedule. You can understand that, Mrs. Kipper?"

I admired the way he was taking her into his confidence— even confessing a little weakness with a small chuckle.

"Oh sure," she said, still stunned. "I can understand that."

"But the name caught my eye," Detective Stilton went on. "Only because I had interviewed Godfrey Knurr in connection with your husband's unfortunate death. So I knew who he was and where I could find him."

She didn't say anything. She was pulling herself together, sipping her coffee and lighting another cigarette. Fussing. Doing anything to keep from looking at us.

"Then," Stilton continued, speaking gently and almost reflectively, "before we had a chance to reply to the request from the Gary police, Mr. Bigg came to us, representing the attorneys he works for. They wanted us to dig deeper into the case of a missing client of theirs. A Professor Yale Stonehouse. He had disappeared under mysterious circumstances. Well, we looked into it and discovered that prior to his disappearance he had been the victim of arsenic poisoning. Mr. Bigg?"

I whipped out the chemical analyses and held them up before her eyes. I don't think she even read them, but she was impressed. They were official documents. I began to appreciate Detective Stilton's insistence on such evidence. They could be true or false, but printed foolscap carried weight.

"So," Percy went on, sighing, "we dug deeper and discovered that the poison had apparently been administered by Glynis Stonehouse, the daughter of the missing man. In addition, we found out that Glynis has been having an affair, is still having an affair, with the Reverend Godfrey Knurr. We do not know for sure, but we suspect that Professor Stonehouse has been murdered and that Knurr is deeply involved. So we are here, Mrs. Kipper, to ask you to help by telling us what you can about this man. He's already charged with blackmail and wife desertion. It's only a matter of time before we can bring a first-degree homicide charge against him."

For a moment I thought we had her. She stood up, circled her chair, started to sit down again. Then she stalked off to a far corner of the room, twisting her hands. We watched her. She stood, facing a blank wall, then turned and came back. The air vibrated; you could feel it.

I had to admire her. She had been rocked, there was no doubt of that, but she rallied. I thought of the word "spunk."

She sat down again, carelessly this time, sprawled. No longer the queen. She dug a last cigarette from the crumpled pack. Percy Stilton was there with his lighter. She inhaled deeply, let the smoke escape lazily from her nostrils.

The silver-blonde hair was damp and tangled. The profile had lost its crispness; the bruise bulged an entire side of her face. The eyes seemed muddy, the thin lips were tightened and drawn. The chin she once carried so high had come down; there was soil in the wrinkles of her neck. Her body had slackened; the breasts sagged under the peignoir, the thighs had flattened.

Is it possible to suffer from an excess of sympathy? At that moment I felt sorry for her. She was being buffeted cruelly, but was far from surrender.

"This is very, uh, distressing," she said finally.

"I can imagine," Detective Stilton said.

I nodded madly.

We stared at her, silent again.

"All right," she burst out, "the man was a—a—"

"Close friend of yours?" Percy suggested.

"Not exactly," she said quickly, already cutting her losses. "More like a—a—"

"Spiritual adviser?" I said innocently.

She looked at me sharply.

"Yeah," she said, "spiritual adviser. For a few years. All right—bad news. Now he turns out to be a bummer. He's wanted. But what's it got to do with me?"

The use of the slang—the "yeah" and the "bummer" was the first indication I had that she was slipping back to her origins. The grand lady was fading.

Stilton, the gentleman, still treated her with soft politesse, leaning toward her with a manner of great solicitude.

"Let me tell you what we've got, Mrs. Kipper," he said. "Warrants have been issued for Knurr's arrest and the arrest of his paramour, Glynis Stonehouse. In addition, we have search warrants for her home, his home, and his houseboat. Sooner or later we're going to pick him up."

"So?" she said. "Pick him up. It's got nothing to do with me."

Percy sat back, crossed his knees, selected a cigarette from his case and lighted it with slow deliberation.

"I think it does," he said, looking at her steadily. "I think it has a great deal to do with you. In addition to the out-of-state charges and complicity in the disappearance of Professor Stonehouse, the Reverend Godfrey Knurr will also be charged with the murder of Martin Reape."

"Who?" she croaked. "Never heard of him."

"No?" Stilton said. "Your late husband employed him." He motioned toward me. "Mr. Bigg, the canceled checks, please."

I dug into my briefcase, came up with copies of Martin Reape's bills and the canceled checks. I showed them to her. She looked at them with smoky eyes.

"Martin Reape was a private detective," Stilton went on

inexorably. "He was pushed to his death beneath the wheels of a subway train. We have the testimony of two eyewitnesses placing the Reverend Godfrey Knurr at the scene of the homicide at the time it occurred. Reape's widow was also murdered. We have evidence proving Knurr's complicity in that homicide as well."

He lied so skillfully I could hardly believe it. His lies were "throwaway" lines, spoken casually, as unemphasized as if he had mentioned "Chilly out today." They were absolutely believable. He was stating falsehoods and giving them no importance. He was saying, "These things exist; everyone knows it."

Tippi Kipper had gone rigid. She was motionless. Frozen. I think that if I had flicked her flesh, it would have pinged. She was in an almost catatonic state. Every time she had adjusted to a blow, thought she had countered it, Stilton had jolted her again. He kept after her, feeding her confusion.

"So," he said, "on the basis of this and other evidence, the investigation into the circumstances of your husband's death has been reopened, Mrs. Kipper. If you doubt that, I suggest you call the New York Police Department and verify what I am saying. We now believe your husband was murdered."

"Murdered?" she cried. Impossible! He left a suicide note."

Detective Stilton held out a hand. I gave him the notes I had taken from Tippi Kipper's dressing room. Percy held them up before her.

"Like these?" he asked stonily.

She glanced at them. Her face fell apart.

"Where did you get those?" she yelled.

"I, uh, obtained them," I said.

She whirled and glared at me.

"You little prick!" she said.

I bowed my head.

"As I said," Percy went on relentlessly, "the investigation into your husband's murder has been reopened. We know how it was done: Knurr staying in an empty room overnight, going upstairs, killing the victim, running downstairs, going out the door only to turn around and ring the bell, coming right back in again while all of you were at the body in the backyard."

"Ridiculous," she said. "You'll never prove it."

"Oh, I think we will," Stilton said. "We've filed for a search warrant for these premises. On the basis of what we've got, I think it will be granted. We'll come in here and tear the place apart. The lab boys will vacuum every inch. They'll find evidence of Godfrey Knurr spending the night in an upstairs room. Dust from his shoes, a partial fingerprint, a thread or crumbs of his pipe tobacco, maybe the weapon he used. Maybe just a hair or two. It's impossible for a man to sleep somewhere overnight without leaving some evidence of his presence. And we'll confiscate that house diary the butler keeps. It shows Godfrey Knurr arrived the afternoon before the day your husband was killed, with no record of his departure. Oh yes, I think we have enough for an indictment, Mrs. Kipper. Godfrey Knurr for homicide and you as accomplice. Both of you are going down the tube."

She made gulping sounds. Stilton continued lecturing.

"And even if we can't make it stick," he said tonelessly, "there's the publicity. Tabloids, radio, TV. The fashionable Mrs. Tippi Kipper, active in social and charitable affairs, with a prior arrest record for prostitution."

I could barely hear. Her head was down. But she was saying, "Bastard, bastard, bastard . . ."

Percy Stilton looked around. He spotted the handsome, marble-topped sideboard with a display of crystal decanters. He went over, inspected the offerings, selected a captain's decanter bearing a porcelain label: BRANDY. He brought it back to the dining room table, poured a healthy wallop into the dregs of Tippi Kipper's coffee cup.

"Drink up," he ordered.

She drained it, holding the cup with trembling hands. He poured in another shot, set the bottle on the table close to her. She dug, fumbling, into her empty cigarette pack. Percy offered his case, then held his lighter for her again. He didn't look at me. There was no triumph in his manner.

"Mrs. Kipper," he said, "I've been as honest with you as I know how. As of this moment there is no warrant out for *your* arrest. But I think it's time we talked about you, your legal position, and your future."

"Now comes the crunch," she said bitterly.

"Correct," he said equably. "Now comes the crunch. We're going to pick up Godfrey Knurr; you know that. We're going

to lean on him. Do you really think he's going to remain
steadfast and true? Come on, Mrs. Kipper, you know better
than that. He's going to sing his rotten little heart out. Before
he's through, the whole thing will be *your* idea. *You* seduced
him, *you* planned the murder of your husband; he was just the
innocent bystander. You *know* that's how he's going to play
it. That's the kind of man he is."

She rose abruptly, scraping her chair back on the polished
parquet floor. She stood leaning forward, knuckles on the table:
a chairman of the board addressing a meeting of hostile executives. But she was not looking at us. She was staring between us, down the length of that gleaming table, the trans-
lucent china, the silver candelabrum. Wealth. Gentility.
Security.

"The first one in line makes the best deal," Detective Percy
Stilton said softly.

Her eyes came back to him slowly.

"Talk business," she said harshly.

We had her then, I knew, but Perce didn't change expression
or vary his polite, solicitous manner.

"This is how I suggest it be done," he said. "We didn't
come to you; you came to us. You called Mr. Bigg at the law
firm that represented your late husband, and Mr. Bigg then
contacted me. But you made the initial move. You volunteered.
Mr. Bigg and I will so testify."

He looked at me. I nodded violently.

"What was my motive for calling in the cops?" she asked.

"You wanted to see justice done," Stilton said.

She shook her head. "It won't wash," she said.

"Duress," I said. "Physical assault. Knurr threatened you.
So you went along with his plan. But now you're afraid for
your life."

Percy looked at me admiringly.

"Yeah," Tippi Kipper said, "that's just how it was. He said
he'd kill me if I didn't go along. I'll take off my makeup and
you can get a color picture of this." She pointed at the puffy
bruise on her cheek. "He punched me out," she said furiously.
"He has a wicked temper, and that's the truth. I was afraid for
my life."

"Beautiful," Percy said. "It fits."

"You think the DA will believe it?" she asked anxiously.

Stilton leaned back, crossed his knees again, lighted another cigarette.

"Of course not," he said. "he's no dummy. But he'll go along. You're going to be his star witness, clearing up three homicides and probably four. So he'll play ball. We're giving him *something*."

"What do you think I'll draw?" she asked him.

"*Bupkes*," he said. "Time suspended and probation. You'll walk."

"And the prostitution arrest?" she demanded.

"Buried," Stilton said. "Nothing to the press. You have my word on that."

She took a deep breath, looked around that lovely room as if she might never see it again.

"Well . . ." she said, "I guess we better get the show on the road. Can I get dressed?"

"Of course," Percy said, "but I'll have to go upstairs with you. I hope you understand."

We all moved out into the entrance hall. Chester Heavens, Perdita Schug, and Mrs. Neckin were gathered in a tight little group in the corridor to the kitchen. They watched, shocked, as their mistress and the detective entered the elevator. I retrieved my hat and coat and left hurriedly. I didn't want to answer their questions.

Lou, behind the wheel of the blue Plymouth, saw me coming. He leaned across to the passenger's side and rolled down the window.

"How'd it go?" he asked.

"Fine," I said. "They'll be coming out soon."

"Is she going to spill?"

I nodded.

"It figures," he said. "That Perce, he's something. I'm glad we're on the same side. If he was on the wrong, he'd end up owning the city."

Then we waited in silence. I didn't want to get into the car. I wanted to look at that pure sky, breathe deeply in the sharp, tangy air. I didn't want to think about what had just happened. I wanted to savor the wide, wide world.

They came out in about fifteen minutes. Tippi Kipper was wearing a belted mink coat that seemed to go around her three times. She was hatless, carrying an oversized black alligator purse. She had removed her makeup. The bruise was hideous. Percy Stilton was carrying a small overnight case of buttery pigskin.

He opened the back door of the Plymouth for her. She climbed in without looking at me. Perce put the little suitcase in the front seat. Then he took me by the elbow, led me aside.

"End of the line for you, Josh," he said.

"Can't I—" I started, but he shook his head regretfully and interrupted.

"It's all official from now on," he said. "I'll call you as soon as we get something. Where will you be?"

"Either at the office or home. Perce, promise you'll call."

"Absolutely," he vowed. "I'll keep you up on things. You deserve all the credit."

"Thank you," I said faintly.

He looked at me narrowly.

"They were divorced, weren't they?" he said. "Knurr and that Sylvia? And she and the old priest are a couple of whackos. Am I right?"

I nodded miserably.

He laughed and clapped me on the shoulder.

"You're good," he said, "but not *that* good. Never try to scam a scammer."

I watched the Plymouth pull away, Stilton sitting next to Tippi Kipper in the back seat. When the car had turned the corner and disappeared, I walked over to Fifth Avenue and headed south. I decided to walk down to the TORT building.

I should have been exultant but I wasn't. It was the morality of what I had done that was bothering me. All that chicanery and deceit. I would have committed almost any sin to demolish Godfrey Knurr, but conniving in the escape of Tippi Kipper from justice was more than I had bargained for. And I *had* connived. I had worked almost as hard as Percy Stilton to convince her to betray Knurr. It had to be done. But as Perce had said, she was going to walk. An accomplice to murder. Was that fair? Was that justice?

I realized I didn't really know what "justice" meant. It was not an absolute. It was not a color, a mineral, a species. It was a human concept (what do animals know of justice?) and subject to all the vagaries and contradictions of any human hope.

How can you define justice? It seemed to me that it was constant compromise, molded by circumstance.

I would make a terrible judge.

The brisk walk downtown refreshed my spirits. The sharp air and exercise were cleansing. By the time I signed in with the security guard at the TORT building, I had come to terms with what I had done. I was still regretful, but guilt was fading. I reckoned that if all went well, in a few weeks I would be proud of my role in bringing the Reverend Godfrey Knurr to justice—whatever that was.

Mrs. Gertrude Kletz had left me a sheaf of notes and a stack of requests for investigations and research. I set to work with pleasure, resolutely turning my mind from the Kipper and Stonehouse cases and concentrating on my desk work.

I labored all afternoon with no breaks except to rise occasionally to stretch, walk into the corridor to loosen my knees. I accomplished a great deal, clearing my desk of most of the routine matters and making a neat list of those that would require personal investigation.

Shortly before 5:00 P.M., after trying to resist the urge, I called Percy Stilton's office. I was told he was "in conference" and could not come to the phone, so I assumed the interrogation of Tippi Kipper was continuing.

I put away the Kipper and Stonehouse files, emptying my cruddy briefcase. I considered buying a new one. Perhaps an attaché case, slender and smart. But that battered briefcase had been left to me by Roscoe Dollworth and I was superstitious enough to believe it had magical properties: good luck and wisdom.

I left the TORT building at about 5:50, remembering to take with me the wrapped red kite, string, and winder. I signed out, walked over to Broadway and took a bus down to West 23rd Street. I went directly to Woody's Restaurant, trying to recall how long it had been since I had enjoyed a decent dinner.

As usual, Nitchy was on duty, looking especially attractive in her exotic, gypsy way. I told her so and she tapped her fingers against my cheek.

"No princess tonight, Josh?" she asked.

"Not tonight," I said, smiling tiredly.

I think she caught my mood, because she ushered me to a small table in a quiet corner and left me alone. I had two

Scotch-and-waters, a club steak, baked potato, string beans, salad, a bottle of beer, coffee and brandy.

When I left, I was subdued, thoughtful, content. I carried the kite back to my apartment and settled in to wait. I tried to read but ended up with a copy of *Silas Marner* on my lap, staring into the cold fireplace and trying to make sense of everything that had happened in the last month.

I came to no great conclusions, was subject to no great revelations. I tried to understand what motives, what passions, might drive apparently sane men and women to commit the act of murder. I could not comprehend it, and feared the fault was mine: I was not emotional enough, not *feeling* enough to grasp how others of hotter blood, of stronger desires, might be driven to kill.

I was a mild little man, temperate, reflective. Nothing in my life was dramatic except what was contributed by others. It seemed incredible that I could survive in a world of such fiery wants and insatiable appetites.

When the phone rang at about 8:20, I did not leap to answer it, but moved slowly, calmly. I think I may have been dreading what I expected to hear.

"Josh?" Stilton's voice.

"Yes."

"Percy. She spilled. Everything. It went down the way you figured. She doesn't know exactly how he did it—a karate chop or a hunk of pipe. She didn't ask. She didn't want to know. Ditto Martin Reape and his wife. Knurr just told her not to worry, he'd take care of everything."

"And he did," I said.

"Yes," Perce said. "Jesus, I'm tired. Anyway, we're organized now. There's a team up at the Stonehouse apartment, looking for the will. Another at Knurr's place in the Village. And another staked out at his houseboat. We're also going into the Kipper townhouse. I don't think they'll find anything there, but you never can tell."

"No hairs?" I said. "Dust? Crumbs of tobacco?"

"Come on," Stilton said, laughing. "You know that was all bullshit."

"Yes," I said.

"Anyway, we've got a fistful of warrants. Lou and I are going up to the houseboat. Want to drag along?"

I came alive.

"I certainly do," I said.

"Pick you up at your place," Percy said. "Josh, do us a favor?"

"Of course. Anything."

"We're starved. Get us some sandwiches, will you? And maybe a six-pack?"

"That's easy," I said. "What kind of sandwiches?"

"Anything. We'll pay you."

"Nonsense. This will be on Tabatchnick, Orsini, Reilly, and Teitelbaum."

"You're sure?"

"Absolutely."

"We'll be outside your place in half an hour."

I had secured the sandwiches and was waiting on the sidewalk when the dusty-blue Plymouth pulled up, Lou driving. I climbed into the back seat. I handed the brown paper bag to Stilton, up front.

"I got them at a deli on Tenth Avenue," I said. "Roast beef on white with mayonnaise, and bologna on rye with mustard. Two of each. And a cold six-pack of Miller's. Is that all right?"

"Plasma," Lou groaned. "Plasma!"

They dived into the bag and ripped tabs from the beer cans. Percy turned sideways, talking to me as he ate.

"We got the Stonehouse will," he said. "They're going through Glynis's personal stuff now. She wasn't there. Her mother says she went to a matinee this afternoon. She's probably with Knurr. No sign of the two of them yet. If we haven't picked them up by midnight, we'll put out an all-precincts, then gradually expand it if needed."

"They're searching Knurr's social club on Carmine Street?" I asked.

"Oh sure," Stilton said. "Found a lot of official records. He was doing all right. How does half a mil grab you?"

"Incredible," I said.

"Ah well," Lou mumbled, starting another half-sandwich, "he was a hard worker."

"What about Chester Heavens' house diary?"

"Got it," Percy said. "Also Tippi's collection of notes her husband wrote her. Josh, the DA will want all the paper you're holding. Monday morning will be time enough."

"Does Tippi have legal counsel?"

"She does now," he said. "Not from your firm. Some hotshot criminal lawyer. He and the DA's man are kicking it around right now, sewing up the deal. Lots of screaming."

"Do you really think she'll go free?"

"Probably," he said without interest. Then he looked at me closely. "Josh, it happens all the time. You give a little, take a little. That's how the system works."

They finished the sandwiches and four of the beers.

"Dee-licious," Lou said, scrubbing his mustache with a paper napkin. "Now I'm ready for a fight or a frolic. Thanks, pal."

"We're going up to the boat basin," Stilton told me. "We've got a search warrant for the houseboat. There's a car with two men on Riverside Drive at 79th Street and one guy on the dock. The three of us are going into the boat. We'll be in touch with the others by walkie-talkie in case Knurr shows up. If the radios work."

"They won't," Lou said casually. "Let's go."

We drove north on Tenth Avenue, into Amsterdam, and turned west on 79th Street. The two detectives talked baseball for most of the trip. I didn't contribute anything.

We parked in a bus-loading zone near West End Avenue. We got out of the car, Percy and Lou taking their radios in leather cases. They didn't look around for the stakeout car. We walked across the park, down a dirt path. We came to the paved area and the rotunda.

It was a ghostly place, deserted at that hour. I thought again of an archeological dig: chipped columns, dried and cracking foundation, shadowed corridor leading to the murky river. It was all so broken and crumbling. Ancient graffiti. Splits in the stone. A world coming apart.

We walked down the steps to the promenade by the river. A few late-hour joggers, pairs of lovers tightly wrapped, solitary gays on benches, an older man frisking with his fox terrier, several roller skaters doing arabesques, a few cyclists. Not crowded, but not empty either.

Stilton rattled the gate, calling, and when the marina manager came out from his shed to meet us, Percy and Lou showed their identification. Stilton held up the search warrant for the man to read through the fence. He let us in, pointing out

Godfrey Knurr's houseboat south of the entrance.

We paced cautiously down planked walkways floating on pontoons. They pitched gently under our tread.

"You said you've got a man on the dock?" I asked anxiously.

The detectives laughed.

"The guy with the dog," Lou said.

"Al Irving," Stilton said. "He always takes his mutt along on a stakeout. Who's going to figure a guy with a dog is a cop? That hound's got the best assist record in the Department."

We stepped down from the wharf onto the foredeck of Knurr's long fiberglass houseboat. There was a thick cable leading to an electric meter on the dock. The sliding doors to the cabin were locked. Lou bent to examine them.

"Piece of cake," he said.

He took a leather case of picklocks from his jacket pocket. He fiddled a moment, pushed the door open. He stood aside.

"Be my guests," he said.

But I noticed he had unbuttoned his coat and jacket and his hand was on his hip holster. Percy Stilton went in first. His revolver was in his hand, dangling at his side. He found the switch and turned on the lights.

"Beautiful," he said.

And it was. We went prowling through. Chairs, tables, couches. Drapes and upholstery in cheery plaid. Plenty of headroom. Overhead lights. Tub and shower. Hot water heater. Toilet. Lockers and cabinets. Wall-to-wall carpeting. Beds, sinks. Larger than my apartment, and more luxurious. A floating home.

We searched all through the houseboat, stared at the twin engines, bilge pump, climbed to the sundeck, marveled at the forward stateroom and the instrument panel in the pilothouse. We ended up in the galley, looking at an electric range/oven and an upright refrigerator.

And a horizontal chest freezer.

It didn't look like standard equipment. It had been jammed into one corner, tight against a bulkhead and the refrigerator. The lid was secured with a cheap hasp and small padlock.

The two detectives looked at each other.

"Wanna bet?" Lou asked.

"No bet," Percy said.

Lou leaned down to examine the padlock.

"Five-and-dime," he reported. "I saw some tools in the engine room."

We waited, silent. Lou was back in a minute with a small claw bar. He hooked the curved end into the loop of the padlock and yanked upward. It popped with a screech of metal.

"Cheese," Lou said, flipping open the hasp. He gestured toward Percy. "Your treat," he said.

Stilton stepped forward and threw back the lid of the freezer.

We all craned forward. He was in there, wrapped in what appeared to be drycleaner's bags. I could make out the lettering: THIS BAG IS NOT A TOY.

He had been jammed in, arms folded, knees drawn up. Plastic had frozen tightly around his head. I could see the face, dim and frosted. A long, sunken face, boned, gaunt, furious.

"Professor Stonehouse, I presume," Percy Stilton said, tipping his hat.

"Shut the goddamn lid," Lou said, "before he thaws."

I turned away, fighting nausea. Percy was on his walkie-talkie, trying to contact the team on Riverside Drive and the man on the dock. All he got in return was ear-ripping static.

"Shit," he said.

"I told you," Lou said. "They're great until you need them."

We were standing there discussing who would go to the nearest telephone when we heard the thump of feet on the outside deck and the houseboat rocked gently. Before I knew what was happening, the two detectives were crouched by the galley door, guns drawn.

"Josh," Stilton hissed, *"drop!"*

I went down on all fours, huddled near that dreadful freezer. Percy peered cautiously around the door frame. He smiled, rose, motioned us up.

"In here," Stilton shouted to someone outside.

Glynis Stonehouse entered slowly. She was wearing her long fur coat, the hood thrown back to rest on her shoulders. Following her came the Reverend Godfrey Knurr, dressed like a dandy: fitted topcoat, wide-collared shirt with a brocaded cravat tied in a Windsor knot, a black bowler tilted atop his head.

After them came Al Irving, grinning. He was holding his fox terrier on a leash. In his other hand was a snub-nosed revolver. The dog was growling: low, rumbling sounds.

"Look what I got," Detective Irving said. "They walked into my arms, pretty as you please. I tried to contact you. These new radios suck."

"What is the meaning of this?" Godfrey Knurr thundered.

It was such a banal, melodramatic statement that I was ashamed for him.

Percy Stilton gave him a death's-head grin and took two quick steps to the freezer. He threw back the lid.

"What is the meaning of *this*?" he demanded.

Then nobody had anything to say. We were all caught, congealed in a theatrical tableau. Staring at each other.

Only the pallor of her face marked Glynis Stonehouse's agitation. Her hands did not tremble; her glance was steady and cool. Did nothing dent her? She stood erect, aloof and withdrawn. Her father lay there, frozen in plastic, a supermarket package of meat, and she was still complete, looking at all of us with a curious disdain.

Godfrey Knurr was feeling more—or at least displaying more. His eyes flickered about, his mouth worked. Nervous fingers plucked at the buttons of his coat. His body slumped slightly until he seemed to be standing in a half-crouch, almost simian, taut and quivering.

His stare settled on me. So indignant, so furious. He looked me up and down, disbelieving that such a meek, puny creature could be responsible for his downfall. He made a sound. Like a groan. But not quite a groan. A protest. A sound that said, "It isn't fair . . ."

"Listen, Joshua," he said hoarsely, "I want you to know something . . ."

None of us moved, intent on what he was saying, waiting to hear what he wanted me to know.

"I think you—" he said, then suddenly whirled into action. He was so fast, so *fast!*

He pivoted on his left foot, turned, clubbed down with the edge of one hand on Detective Al Irving's gun arm. We all heard the crack of bone. Knurr completed a full turn, a blur, and bulled his way past Glynis and Lou, all shoulders and elbows.

Then he was into the main cabin, running.

Stilton was the first to recover.

"Watch the woman," he yelled at Lou, and took up the chase.

I went rushing along at his heels.

Godfrey Knurr hurtled down the wharf, swerved left onto the pontooned walkway. It tilted and rocked under his pounding feet.

A young couple was approaching, chatting and laughing. He simply ran into them, through them, over them. They were flung wailing into the fetid water.

Stilton and I charged after him. I didn't know what I was doing, except that I didn't want Percy to be alone.

Knurr smashed through the gate and headed for the south staircase leading up to the rotunda. Stilton had his gun in his hand, but there were people on the promenade, strollers and cyclists. They scattered when they saw us coming, but Percy didn't want to risk a shot.

Godfrey Knurr went leaping up the steps, two at a time. I remember that his derby flew off and came bouncing down. By then we were straining up the stairs. I thought I was fast, but Percy was stronger; he was closing on Knurr and I was falling behind.

We all, the three of us, went thundering through the arched corridor, a crypt. Two pedestrians, hearing and seeing us coming, flattened themselves in terror against the stained wall.

We came into the rotunda. Knurr circled to his left, running frantically, hoping to gain the exit. His unbuttoned coat flapped out behind him.

Now Percy Stilton had a clear field of fire. He stopped, flexed his knees, grasped his massive revolver with both hands, arms extended, elbows slightly bent.

"Hold it right there!" he yelled.

Suddenly, unexpectedly, Knurr rounded the fountain basin and came racing back toward us. His hair was flying, the bearded face twisted, bright with rage.

"Hah!" he shouted, raising one hand high in a classic karate position, fingers together, the palm edge a cleaver.

"Oh for God's sake!" Percy Stilton said disgustedly, sighted carefully, and shot the Reverend Godfrey Knurr in the right leg. I saw the heavy slug pucker the trouser a few inches above the knee.

The blow spun Knurr around. He pirouetted as gracefully as a ballet dancer. His momentum and the force of the bullet kept him turning. His arms flung wide. A look of astonishment came to his contorted features.

He whirled, tilting, and fell backward over the rim of the ruined fountain. He went down heavily. I heard the sound of his head smacking cracked cement. His legs and feet remained propped up on the basin rim. His head, shoulders, and torso were flat within.

We walked up to him cautiously, Stilton with his gun extended. Knurr was beginning to bleed, from the wound in his leg and from a head injury. He looked up at us dazedly.

"Idiot!" Stilton screamed at him. "You fucking idiot!"

Godfrey Knurr's vision cleared.

He glared at me.

I turned away, walked away, went over to one of the scarred pillars and pressed my forehead against the cold concrete.

After a moment Percy came over to me, put an arm across my shoulders.

"Josh," he said gently, "he wasn't a nice man."

"I know," I said dully. "Still . . ."

8

THERE WAS A party at the house in Chelsea. The last had been such a success they all wanted another.

It was a marvelous party. All the tenants were there, of course, and a boisterous bunch from the music world, Madame Zora Kadinsky's friends. Captain Bramwell Shank had invited a few cronies from his seafaring days aboard the Staten Island ferry. They were cantankerous old coots who spent most of their time at the two card tables set with food and drink.

The party was well begun, noisy with talk and laughter, when I arrived. At the last minute I had run out and bought a two-pound box of chocolate-covered cherries at the local drugstore. I presented it to Mrs. Hufnagel and got a warm kiss on my cheek in return. Madame Kadinsky insisted on introducing me to all her friends. I didn't remember any of their names, which seemed to be composed solely of consonants.

As we moved about the apartment, my eyes were searching for Cleo. After the introductions were finished, I finally saw her in the kitchen, talking to Adolph Finkel. Or rather, he was talking and she was listening, a bemused expression on her face. They both held paper cups of wine.

I observed her a few moments before I approached. She looked so *clean* to me. Physically clean, of course, but more than that. There was an innocent purity about her. She seemed untouched by violence, or even by evil. I could not conceive of her acting through malice or hate, greed or envy.

She was wearing a loose chemise of challis wool in a sort of forested print. She was without makeup; her face was clear and serene. How could I ever have thought her plain? She was beautiful! That high, noble brow; the lovely hazel eyes; a dream of a nose; lips delicately sculpted. Her teeth were not large and prominent at all; they were jewels, sparkling. The chestnut hair fell free, gleaming. And when I remembered that elegantly slender body, now hidden within the billowing chemise, I felt a surge of blood to my face, my breath caught, my knees turned to water.

I waited a moment longer, until my respiration had returned to normal, then I went toward the kitchen. Cleo looked up, saw me approaching. Her eyes widened, her face became animated, she glowed.

"Josh!" she cried happily, "Where have you *been*?"

"Out of town," I said. "How are you, Cleo? Finkel, good to see you again."

"Bigg," he said.

Cleo, speaking in her soft, shy whisper, began telling me how concerned she had been—all the tenants had been concerned—because no one had seen me or heard me moving about since Thursday morning, and they feared I had met with some misadventure.

I assured her I was in good health, all was well, and I had a great deal to tell her about matters we had previously discussed.

Adolph Finkel had listened to this intimate dialogue with some discomfiture, his pallid features becoming more and more woebegone. I thought tears might flow from those weak eyes. He looked mousier than ever, the dull hair a tangle, a doomed smile revealing the discolored tombstone teeth.

"Well, Bigg," he broke in suddenly, "I guess the best man won."

He drained off his paper cup of wine, gave us a look of such martyrdom that I wanted to kick his shins, and shambled away, shoulders slumping. We looked after him with astonishment. I turned back to Cleo.

"The best man?" I said, remembering Hamish Hooter and Yetta Apatoff.

Then Cleo and I were giggling, leaning toward each other, our heads touching.

"Listen," I said, "can we leave as soon as possible? There's so much I want to tell you."

She looked at me steadily.

"Where do you want to go?" she asked.

I took a deep breath.

"There's a nice restaurant on 23rd Street," I said casually. "Woody's. It's open on Sundays. Good food. I know the woman who runs the place. We can have dinner and drinks in real glasses."

"You're sure you want to go out with me?" she said, still looking into my eyes. She knew I had been afraid of being seen with her. Mutt and Jeff.

"Positive," I said stoutly.

"I'd love to go to Woody's with you," she said smiling.

I eased out the door, took my hat and coat, and waited for Cleo in the entrance hall. She came flying down a few moments later in a coat and tam and we set out.

It was a hard, brilliant day, flooded with sunshine. But the wind was gusting strongly, whipping our coats, tingling our cheeks. Cleo took my arm, and I looked nervously at passersby, watching for signs of amusement when they saw this tall, willowy woman with her runty escort.

But no one gave us a glance, and after a while I stopped caring what people might think.

"I brought the kite home," I told Cleo. "And the string and winder."

"Too windy today," she said. "But we'll fly it another day."

"Sure we will," I said.

We hung coats and hats on the rack just inside the door of Woody's. We waited a moment, and then Nitchy came toward us from the back dining room.

"Cleo," I said, "I'd like you to meet Nitchy, a good friend. Nitchy, meet Cleo."

The two women shook hands. Nitchy looked up searchingly at Cleo's face. Then she turned to me, smiling. She put a soft hand on my arm.

"At last!" she said.

LAWRENCE SANDERS

"America's Mr. Bestseller"

___THE EIGHTH COMMANDMENT   10005-7 — $4.95
___THE DREAM LOVER   09473-1 — $3.95
___THE PASSION OF MOLLY T.   10139-8 — $4.50
___THE FIRST DEADLY SIN   10427-3 — $4.95
___THE MARLOW CHRONICLES   09963-6 — $3.95
___THE PLEASURES OF HELEN   10168-1 — $3.95
___THE SECOND DEADLY SIN   10428-1 — $4.95
___THE SIXTH COMMANDMENT   10001-4 — $4.95
___THE TANGENT FACTOR   10062-6 — $3.95
___THE TANGENT OBJECTIVE   10331-5 — $3.95
___THE TENTH COMMANDMENT   10002-6 — $4.95
___THE TOMORROW FILE   08179-6 — $4.50
___THE THIRD DEADLY SIN   10429-X — $4.95
___THE ANDERSON TAPES   08174-5 — $3.95
___THE CASE OF LUCY BENDING   10086-3 — $4.50
___THE SEDUCTION OF PETER S.   09314-X — $4.50
___THE LOVES OF HARRY DANCER   08472-8 — $4.50
___THE FOURTH DEADLY SIN   09078-7 — $4.50

Available at your local bookstore or return this form to:

THE BERKLEY PUBLISHING GROUP
Berkley • Jove • Charter • Ace
THE BERKLEY PUBLISHING GROUP, Dept. B
390 Murray Hill Parkway, East Rutherford, NJ 07073

Please send me the titles checked above. I enclose _____. Include $1.00 for postage
and handling if one book is ordered; add 25¢ per book for two or more not to exceed
$1.75. CA, NJ, NY and PA residents please add sales tax. Prices subject to change
without notice and may be higher in Canada. Do not send cash.

NAME_____

ADDRESS_____

CITY_____ STATE/ZIP_____

(Allow six weeks for delivery.)   22